I0766912

FAR FOREST SCROLLS

Rise Above the Storm

Bokan
Cappadocia
Castle Goreme
Hala River
Keski River
Sata River
Gulf of Dapur
Lake Maia
Arbre Fonce (Dark Forest)
Hills of Feen
Marskimaa Wetlands
Kay'n'nissa streams
Effeus Woods
Leita Falls
Western Joo
Inukshuk West
Bets Rocks
Polas Fruse
Central
Siochain Pass
Ice Falls
Lake Glosere
Teorainn Hills and Mountains
Storm Field
Vahse Plains
Cavalo Horses
Cruinniu
Eleftheria
Rebelde Plains
Kylo
Giant
Umulig Mountains
Boiste Pass
Atacama Valley
Oasis Vastaus
Desert of Calor
Eada River
Lake Paco
Ragers of Outpost
N. Kaksi River
S. Kaksi River
Creber Forest (Elves of Creber)
Lake Qualitas
Aos Basin
Aard Mountains
River Alta
River Horn
Kiksi
Venio Pass
Kapu Mountains
Chatelaine
Western Elves
Plain of Dunn
Black Tower
Tornol
Torpe
Tundra
Bay of Ritain
Gulf of Lampa
Way of Trepas
Temple Ovest
Citadel Rettengolo Ter
Elevado Mount
Mines of Teras
Southern Tingji Mountains
West Tijil River
Mines of Kavos
Southern Dwarf Kingdom
Kavos Mine
Mines of Kulta
Torf
Ruins of Idor
Mohado Mire
East Mohado Mire

Tebartha Springs
Eastern Jaa
Inukshuk East
Nord
Jaa
Inukshuk Mitte
Pino Mountains
Koori Mountains
Northern Dwarves
Mount Hanoo
Keha Haudella Volcanoes
Shorter Flower Fields
Anen
Ruins of Murbh
Kippe
Cosan Bridge
Territory Origins
Orottite Mountains
Ruins of Jalokivi
Tende Ensel
Eluvies Delta
Cliffs of Karst
Frozen Sea
Isle of Hirmulisko
Haj
Piscium
Ryba
Kala
Isdo
Taiheart
Glan
Piscium
Tasc
Pescore
Haavi
N. Azul River
Temple Paluoa
Miksi River
Pullen Lake
Tall Shaor
Ager
Liberum
River Vita
Azul River
Azul Dela River
Maatila
Tascair
Juopa Canal
Proliate Channel
Proliate Archipelago
Proliate Islands
Dark Sea
Temple Palio
Kovo Cliffs
Kissa Tuikea Mountains
Talican Temple
Pearii

After battling there, the Tournament of Flags held no comfort. The Knights and their allies are targeted as traitors. The Dragon Battle turned disastrous as Finn fell to one of the fiercest dragons in all of Verngaurd. An early blocking spell shielded the dragon, prolonging the battle and ultimately leading to the death of the beloved Knight. Bellae met Eaglian Arend and Elf Kainen, who warned her of an impending disaster and the upcoming, enigmatic quest. As the Tournament of Flags was set to restart, revitalized with new, but flawed, hope, a group of beleaguered Proliate and Magicians blast into the arena.

FAR FOREST SCROLLS

Rise Above the Storm

BOOK THREE

For more information please visit:
www.FarForestScrolls.com

Scrolls from 1000 C.E.
discovered during an archeological dig
in the Far Forest region of England,
the soul of this ancient fantasy tale
is reborn in your mind's eye.

Author: AAAA (Alpha Four) ⚜ Illustrations: AAAA & Paganus
Scroll translation to English: Radek Novotny PhD ⚜ Image Restoration: Altier Restoration

Library of Congress Control Number: 2020903070

ISBN (Hardcover, color edition) 978-1-7321499-7-7
ISBN (Paperback, black & white edition) 978-1-7321499-8-4
ISBN (e-book) 978-1-7321499-9-1

Our excursion through Book Two withers as we tumble upon the stormy fields of Book Three. Uruz denotes strength, courage, and primal power, symbolizing the complexities of the territorial war threatening to tear Verngaurd apart. This woodcarving was on the third wooden chest in the Far Forest of England. For Verngaurd, and those encountered in the first two books, Rune Uruz unleashes the brutally raw and untamed struggle coiled to encase the globe within the ferocious power of a world at war.

Whether living in disdain or ignorance of its existence, those of us encumbered with consciousness are snared in a web of interconnectedness, an intertwined lacework as fragile as dew but as monumental as the air we breathe. A thousand acts of kindness evaporate under the gust of a single wound or wafting cruel word. The humanity that supposedly defines us is afflicted with the same delicate, easily evaporated, temperament.

As individuals and as a society, we constantly, and precariously, balance primal power with intellectual integrity. We all live within our own experiences, and too often our interconnectedness is severed and our diaphanous compassion obliterated by the constraining primal forces of greed, hate, mistrust, and jealousy, which tip the scales of civilization into base and savage violence.

The world is saturated with enough of everything but contentment.

Carved under the lid, Uruz Reversed symbolizes the monumental missed opportunity Verngaurd had to avert disaster and come together. This failure upsets the precariously balanced equilibrium of primal power and intellect/reason.

{Aside: The rune carvings found in the chests from Far Forest are the Elder Futhark (the oldest runic script). The Elder Futhark is divided into three Aettir/families consisting of eight runes. Each Aett of eight runes is named for a god associated with the first rune. Jera (Book One) and Hagalaz (Book Two) are from the second Aett known as Hagal's (or sometimes Heimdall since little is known of the Norse god of weather–Hagal). Uruz is from the first, or Freyr's, Aett.}

Table of Contents

A sincere welcome back to the world of the Far Forest Scrolls. Return to its embrace, increasing (we humbly hope) your Wisdom of how to Live.

End of Book Two

The door to the holding chamber under the coliseum opened the next morning. "Knights and squires, this way," a Proliator guard commanded.

"All of us?" Arquero asked.

"Everyone follow me," Friar said, grinning broadly.

As they left the darkness of the holding area, the crowd erupted in applause. Curious, but unsure of what was going on, the Knights and squires followed Friar towards Veneficus levitating in the center of the arena.

Raising his hands for silence, Veneficus began, "Over this Tournament we have grown closer, learning to stop focusing on differences and to celebrate what we have in common. The Knights agreeing to finish the Tournament despite the devastating loss of one of their own symbolizes the courage and resolve of the inhabitants of Verngaurd.

"We have to, and we will, come together to defeat any and all enemies!" he said to a deafening roar of approval. "Let us turn the tragic death of this Knight into something constructive, something healing, a harmony across our lands.

"There is one last task I must attend to before we open the final day of the Tournament," he said, drifting down to earth.

Black flags and shields magically appeared where each country's own colors had just been as the arena floor became inundated with competitors from all of Verngaurd.

"Welcome, warriors of Verngaurd! We stand together, united in our spirit and resolve!" Veneficus said, smiling. "I would like to bring back an ancient tradition of the Knights one last time. When a Knight died, a charmed pin called a kalma-kunnia was given to the oldest child. Sired deep in the forges of the Northern Dwarves of magic metal supplied by Magicians, it was indestructible.

"When anyone in Verngaurd saw the kalma-kunnia, great honor was bestowed upon the wearer. Their parent was a hero who gave their life for our future. Such a gift has not been given in over a century. But today, that changes," he said as the bandaged Ritari and Sorea parted to open a path. Tears blurred Bellae's vision as Veneficus approached.

"Desino avta," he said, his voice no longer amplified.

He knelt to be eye to eye with her. "As his Inion it is fitting that this gift goes to you."

He pinned the award on her cloak, and the two embraced warmly as the stadium erupted into cheers.

Veneficus released her and chanted something inaudible, immediately flying upwards. "If you are not too tired of applauding, let the third and final day begin!" he said, his voice amplified again.

A great cheer erupted as the Knights circled Bellae to congratulate her. She pulled up her cloak to get a better view of the mysterious silver medallion with a yellowish glow. It consisted of two rhomboid shapes with the one on top slightly askew, making it look like a small box with the lid open.

Bellae felt dizzy at the constant stream of hands, congratulations, and faces of warriors from the different nations passing before her. After what seemed like hours, the crowd began to thin.

Her Knight dies, and she gets all this attention? Jumeaux huffed enviously.

"Let's begin! Competitors in the distance run assemble!" Veneficus said, still levitating above the arena. All the shields and flags turned back into their nations' standard colors.

BOOM! A loud crash from the northern part of the arena rocked the stadium. Magicians had blown apart the northern gate, which now lay in splinters. Several bloodied Proliate Red Guard and a few Magicians stumbled into the arena. As they moved closer, it became apparent they were carrying numerous injured people. Blood was so ubiquitous in the ghastly scene that it was hard to tell whether the blood was theirs or from those they carried.

"STOP! Listen to us!" one of them yelled fiercely. He coughed, sending an eruption of blood from his mouth. Shaking his head, he added, "Everyone stop!"

Figure 52: All previous goodwill quickly evaporates as battered Magicians and bloodied Proliate warriors stream into the arena, carrying countless dead and assisting numerous wounded civilians.

The untamed power of Uruz erupts as we commence Book Three. For Verngaurd it symbolizes the birth of the face of our fragility: pride, our frail fondness to fall for the camaraderie with "our" group, and treacherous ego as the forces of primal power snake their way around reason, choking out compassion and embroiling the world in a storm of discontent.

Chapter One

Wake for Those Asleep

Scroll 1: Joy, Not So Long Lasting

The first three Proliate through the north gate of the coliseum carried lifeless bodies of children. Screams filled the arena as the warriors parted to allow them to pass. The first Proliator held a frail boy, his dead body draped limply over the warrior's powerful arms. His mouth gaped open, caught in an eternal, silent scream. Each step towards Veneficus caused the boy's dangling arm to swing in torpid, powerless arcs. He wore pale blue clothes, covered by a yellow cloak, designating him a Piscinian. The thin, almost wasted, boy had disheveled brown hair and a dark, gaunt complexion.

"It's Sumar!" Bellae screamed, the first to recognize his deceased body. She ran a few steps towards him before stopping at the sight of the scores of arrows piercing his body. Stiff, crusting black highlighted the deadly punctures in outline, while molten red tracked away.

To the left another warrior carried a dead Piscinian boy with a pair of nunchaku wrapped uncivilly around his neck. Dull, gray eyes bulged in frozen horror. His extruded and swollen blue tongue slapped limply against his cheek.

There was an old man wearing the simple tan colors of Ager being carried to the right of Sumar. His fragile old skin was littered with multiple bruises. Blood oozed in gruesome black and red streaks from his eyes, nose, and mouth. They carefully laid the victims down at the feet of Veneficus. Behind them, dozens more followed. Their much-abused armor displayed the brutality of the fight through myriad scrapes and battered dents, with generous dashes of blood as accents.

"The encampment to the north has been ransacked," a Proliate officer declared in a fatigued voice.

"What?" Veneficus asked, astounded.

A shaky female voice cried out from behind the Red Guard. "They killed all the children and most of the elderly. They killed him!" The woman sobbed, bursting between several of the Proliate. "This was my babeee!" she wailed.

The last sound merged into a howl of pain. Stopping, she fell to her knees near the boy with the nunchaku wrapped around his neck. She moved her hands around the boy's face, careful to always keep them a fraction of an inch away, as if an invisible barrier of horror surrounded him.

"You did this! Kill that Elf! You bloody pointy-eared..." the woman shrieked as she suddenly rose and bolted towards Kempe. The large Elf from Creber stared in dumbfounded silence. He remained motionless as the woman began beating on his leather chest protector. Several Proliate restrained her, and she finally collapsed in a heap of misery. A shocked silence settled on the crowd. Ritari glanced at Friar, who returned a wide-eyed look of utter confusion and dread.

It's happening, Friar thought. *This is where Verngaurd fractures.*

Veneficus moved to examine the bodies. "These weapons and arrows are definitely those of the Elves of Creber," he said, looking suspiciously at Kempe.

"We had nothing to do with this," Kempe replied helplessly. Panic and fear etched on his rough, dark brown skin. He looked to Friar and Ritari for some help, but both were too stunned to say anything.

"What happened? What did you see?" Veneficus asked anxiously.

"Those tree bark monsters killed my boy," the sobbing woman

muttered. A man, presumably her husband, fruitlessly attempted to comfort her.

"We were stationed to the north of the encampment," one of the Proliate began, "where the people of Piscium and Ager had congregated. Early this morning, a band of Elves from Creber and Northern Dwarves descended upon them out of nowhere."

Angry murmurs buzzed through the coliseum.

"We were called in, but by the time we got there, they had taken almost everything of value and killed all the children and elderly."

A gasp of horror went up, quickly followed by angry yelling.

"Silence!" Veneficus yelled. "We will hear the entire account."

"When we arrived, only a few dozen attackers were still around. Initially, they fought fiercely, but we quickly put them to flight, injuring most of them."

"They were definitely Elves of Creber and Northern Dwarves?" Veneficus questioned.

"They were trying to kill us, which makes them kind of hard to miss. I did not specifically see Kempe," the guard answered. "But the survivors described him well enough. He's bigger than most Elves, and you saw the response of the poor mother."

Kempe scoffed, anger overtaking him. "I don't kill innocent people or children. Plus, no Elf of Creber was within a mile of that encampment."

"Liar! How do you explain your weapons and arrows?" someone asked.

"They must have been stolen," Kempe answered.

"How did your nunchaku end up on my dead child?" the father asked, his eyes red with tears and swollen with anger. "I *saw* you!"

Kempe reached to his side where his nunchaku normally sat, and his head swiveled in panic, searching for them. "I had them last night…" he stammered.

"Revenge! Kill them!" a voice rang out.

"NO!" thundered Veneficus, levitating again.

"Listen," Kempe pleaded. "We would never do this—the forest provides all that we need. Plus, it makes no sense. We would never just kill the elderly and children, leaving witnesses to easily identify us later."

The crowd burst into angry comments that blurred together.

"That didn't come out right," Ritari whispered.

"You think?" Friar said, his anxiety rising.

"So you're saying you wished you had killed us all?" a villager yelled, further inciting the crowd.

"Justice!" a man from Piscium yelled to the rousing agreement of the crowd. "We know you have been aiding the Dark Warriors, but this? Arboreal miscreants!"

"Wait!" a woman's voice rang out. "I saw the last of the fighting," she said, moving near the dead boy.

"Gleoi Dea!" Bellae whispered excitedly as the Knight continued. "I saw the way those Elves and Dwarves were moving, and it was unnatural. I can tell you, they were not *real* Elves or Dwarves, only made to look like them, by dark magic."

"A likely story, coming from an Elf!" someone shouted.

"I'm a Knight!" she said sharply.

"Those pointy ears tell me you're an Elf, sure enough," a grubby little old man said through a toothless grin. A round of laughter went around the arena as his eyebrows rose in appreciation of the attention. He held his crooked fingers out and waved like a king on parade.

"Kill them! Kill all the Elves and Northern Dwarves!" someone yelled.

"Wait!" King Abernan of the Northern Dwarves yelled. "We had nothing to do with this. Those are weapons of the Elves."

Kempe and Friar looked at him aghast for selling out the Elves.

"It is true enough," Abernan said defensively, their stares boring into him.

"We must stick together and keep our heads. There must be a rational explanation," Friar stated.

"Yeah, the explanation is they did it and need to pay," the twisted old man wheezed. He beamed as a fresh round of laughter and murmurs of agreement greeted his comment.

"Gleoi Dea is right. We are being manipulated," Friar yelled, but few heard him over the angry din.

A loud clanging noise distracted them as a bloody Draak sword rattled to the ground. "This was found near one of the dead," a Proliate guard said somberly.

King Abernan was genuinely confused. "We…had nothing to do with this."

"Yeah, we heard your story. No one believes you, nonhuman scum!" an angry voice howled.

"That sword looks real enough to me," said another.

"It's coated in real blood—the blood of *our* children!"

"Remember we Western Elves had nothing to do with this," Bondi, the ruler of Western Elves said. Herra Isanta, their sleek warrior, stood next to him.

A murmur, half approving, half disapproving, went up through the crowd.

"It's true!" one of the bloodied Proliate yelled. "They had nothing to do with it."

"Please, think about what we are allowing to happen," Friar pleaded. "We are back to infighting, tearing ourselves apart!"

A man from the crowd limped forward. "First, the Dark Warriors ravage our lands while you Knights do nothing. Now, your closest allies are going on racial killing binges, and what do you do? Nothing! You have no authority in these lands anymore. Hail to the Magicians and Proliate, our true defenders!"

Shouts of infamy and hatred filled the arena. The adrenaline-filled admiration and hope for unity that had prevailed during the ceremony for the Knights were obliterated under the violent, herd-mentality loathing.

Veneficus' eyes locked with Friar's. All previous optimism was replaced by sadness and shock.

When Veneficus said nothing, Friar shouted, "This makes no sense!"

The crowd murmured angrily, as one shouted, "Of course, killing innocent children and defenseless elderly makes no sense!"

"I mean it's a set-up. You heard Gleoi Dea—the White Wizard is using dark magic to drive us apart."

Angry yelling bellowed forth.

"Why would the Elves of Creber and Northern Dwarves attack on the last morning of competition?" Friar asked.

Several shouts answered. "They are dimwitted nonhumans who know no better."

"They couldn't wait!"

"I don't think this is helping," Ritari whispered to Friar.

The Knights, Elves of Creber, and Northern Dwarves gravitated together in the center of the arena. The rest of Verngaurd congealed around them.

"This is starting to feel claustrophobic," Luchar growled.

"Enough!" shrieked Veneficus, his eyes filled with rage and uncertainty.

He levitated higher over the crowd as the shields and flags around the arena once again shifted to black for mourning. "I would like everyone to return to their barracks at the Zenia. I am canceling the last day of competition and placing a curfew on the Citadel."

A murmur of disapproval roared from the crowd. "Justice!" someone screamed.

The parents of Sumar limped weakly towards the Knights, their eyes wide with horror and vacant with loss. Sumar's father stopped suddenly as his thoughts turned to the moments before the tragedy struck—getting ready, walking around their tent, Sumar's smile, smelling the spicy tea brewing, talking to his wife about what they would plant next year. The simple series of memories, while unpretentious in nature, were powerfully attractive, serving as a last hold on reality—a refuge, when life was normal. The memories of that morning would become worn thin from repeated use over the coming years until, eventually, growing wide enough to obscure his view of the beauty of present-day life.

Shaking his head to bring his mind back to the present, the level of hatred behind his eyes rose. His thoughts rushed back into the emptiness of his son's death like a flood.

"You cowards are responsible for his death!" Sumar's father said, swinging a bony finger at the Knights. "I would expect this from the nonhuman vermin, but never from you. I see now that your day is truly over. You are weak and pathetic!"

Tragedy, slipping eagerly into the cordial fold of hatred, sparked a craving for raw revenge, spiraling him into the ancient solution of wanting to inflict harm on others under the fraudulent promise of easing his own suffering. His eyes flashed loathing before dulling as he collapsed in a fit of sobbing.

Gimelli reached down to comfort him. Suddenly, his wife slammed into her, sending the squire flying back. "You stay away from him, my family, and Piscium!" she screeched as the crowd cheered. Hatred and tears swam as violent collaborators behind her eyes.

Friar looked at Veneficus and mouthed, "We need to leave, now."

Billowing black clouds suddenly engulfed the blue sky lulling above. The large heavy clouds churned and gyrated as they sped across the sky.

Veneficus thundered, "There will be no more violence! I will personally lead an investigation into this massacre, and those responsible will have justice heaped upon them. No one, and I mean no one, will take justice into their own hands. The Knights, Elves of Creber, and Northern Dwarves will be escorted to the Zenia, and after questioning will be allowed to leave."

The crowd let out a fresh round of boos.

"Strange things are happening in our lands, but I assure you the culprits will pay," Veneficus boomed.

Several divisions of Red Guard appeared and separated the three beleaguered nations from the angry crowd. As their ring was closing around them, Bellae looked one last time on the limp body of Sumar. His dark eyes were open, staring lifelessly ahead. His right arm extended out towards her, as if reaching for help. The Elfin arrows were still upright, standing at silent attention.

A murmur went through the crowd as several Southern Dwarves began to push against the Proliators escorting the Northern Dwarves. Thunder and lightning crashed out of the dark sky as a sheet of rain pounded down on the coliseum.

"I said, no more violence!" Veneficus shouted, raising his crosier ominously. He shot his head back and let out a frustrated howl of outrage. With all traces of the suns gone, the arena was plunged into an uneasy darkness. The black flags ringing the arena fluttered violently in the wind and rain. "Get them out of here!" he yelled.

Figure 1: Veneficus lets his frustration storm out.

Dejected and embarrassed, the Knights, Elves of Creber, and Dwarves of the North departed. Bellae looked at Veneficus floating menacingly above the crowd. He looked fearsome outlined against the raging sky, an epitome of his mood. Occasionally, he would swing one of his arms down and lightning would flash ominously. The good feelings of the morning vanished as quickly as the sunshine. If not for the pin on her cloak, Bellae would have wondered if the ceremony ever happened.

Scroll 2: Of Elves and Men

"Ailante, thank you for seeing me," Friar said to the leader of the Elves of Creber.

"These are troubling times, my friend," Ailante responded, his green eyes sad and disheartened. He wore soft gray robes with a tree emblazoned upon his chest.

"How did the Magician questioning go?" Friar asked.

"Actually, not as bad as I anticipated. After the response of the crowd, I half-expected them to pronounce us guilty."

"If I didn't know you and the Northern Dwarves were innocent, I would have believed it myself. The treachery of the White Wizard is evolving, becoming increasingly complex and sophisticated," Friar stated. "First, they only attack around us. Now the Dark Warriors impersonate you and the Northern Dwarves with black magic to frame you for a massacre. Their deception is driving a wedge between the nations of Verngaurd."

"Their plan is working," Ailante said. Suddenly, he seemed tired and sat down. "The Magicians and Proliate will surely find us guilty and declare war. If they don't, the White Wizard will keep pushing until they do. You were right, Friar. I can't fathom how you knew this day was coming, but you were right about war against the Proliate. Many of my most trusted advisors were against us committing to your complex, and frankly, brutal battle plan, but I trusted you and I am glad for it."

"We should still try for a diplomatic solution, especially with Veneficus," another Archerian said.

"Agreed," Friar stated. "Peace shall be our hope, but if the reality is war, we shall be ready. They underestimate us, and if we shock them with a major defeat, we should be able to bring them to the negotiating table to focus Verngaurd on the Dark Warriors."

"Your plan is elaborate and ferocious," the head Elf commented.

Friar sighed. "I've heard that complaint before. However, with the Proliate's sheer numbers and superb training, I see no alternative. We have to level the battlefield."

"Will Jaa or the Southern Dwarves fight with us?" Ailante asked.

"Uncertain times breed uncertain answers," Friar responded. "After the massacre we were just framed for, I don't know. It might convince them to fight with the Proliate. I trust Princess Hamaza, but Queen Antiopay dislikes the Knights. The Southern Dwarves have clearly shown their intention to side with the Proliate. We can only count on the Knights, Rebelde Plains, the Northern Dwarves, and your Elven warriors."

"The Western Elves allegiance to the Proliate is a foregone conclusion," Ailante sneered. "Anyway, we are leaving the Citadel to make the preparations for Finn's funeral. I regret the circumstances, but it will be nice to see you in Creber," Ailante added, as he and the other Archerians filed out.

The Knights stood in separate groups outside the Citadel. Even its normally sparkling white marble seemed gray and lifeless against the dreary sky. The two Veli and their Knights would head directly to their respective castles. The advance guard of the Liberum Knights would take the siege machines and extra equipment directly home. Heading to the Forest of Creber to bury Finn, with a single supply wagon, included

Friar, the Knights from Liberum: Ritari, Lovag, Sorea, Luchar, and Arquero, the squires from Liberum: Gimelli, Bellae, Scelto, Jumeaux, and Lontas, and Gleoi Dea from Taiheart Castle. Honey would pull a makeshift wooden travois with Finn's body.

"I can carry you and Finn," Crann pleaded with Bellae. *"Send Honey to Liberum."*

"Friar has already made up his mind. Let's just get along."

Crann neighed in protest but said no more as Friar and the two Veli went off to talk.

"I spoke with Veneficus, and things aren't good. He's the only one not convinced of our guilt in both the matter of the massacre, and aiding the Dark Warriors. I think it is safe to say the war we feared is coming," Friar said stoically.

"The bloody Proliate are spreading like wildfire!" Veli Falciss growled. "Their numbers just within the Citadel are enough to overwhelm us."

"You would think they were too busy training and praying to reproduce!" Veli Pingius laughed. When it was clear the others did not think it was funny, he stopped.

"I know you have been against parts of my plan, Falciss. Right now, I need us all to commit," Friar said.

Pingius' jolly face took an earnest tone. "I'm not in favor of provoking a fight."

"We will not move until forced to do so. However, if we have to fight, it will be on our terms," Friar stated. "Work on the drills I gave you. Keep in contact and stay alert. Most of Verngaurd is turning against us—we will need to move soon. Questions?"

When no one spoke, Friar said, "Safe travels."

They recited together, "Wisdom, courage, temperance, and justice," as they gave the Knights' salute to each other. The Knights and squires of Liberum watched the others head east.

"With all the hostility, I don't like the idea of traveling to Creber with so few Knights," Ritari whispered to Friar.

"I agree, but the siege engines and supplies would slow us down and never make it into the woods. I don't want to leave them unattended at the doorstep of the Forest. The Elves already left to make burial preparations, so we didn't have much choice," Friar answered as they headed into the gray, towards the west and the Way of Trepas.

"Quite a sight," Ritari said, after they had been riding for many hours.

Friar remained silent, staring at the massive walls of Temple Ovest towering to their north. In front of them they could see the soaring Tingij Mountains, and to the south were rolling plains.

"I know that look. Coming up with more ideas, are we?" Ritari asked.

Friar laughed. "Yes, you could say that."

"I wouldn't want to try to butt my head against those walls," Lovag quipped. He craned his neck up to look at the gigantic white walls lined with countless fluttering red flags bearing Tallcon's phoenix image. Proliate peered at them from the ramparts with the same respect a horse does a fly—nothing but a nuisance.

Friar's hope for peace was fading, and the dark skies overhead seemed to be following them towards the Way of Trepas.

Scroll 3: Wet Walk–Long Talk

Late the next day, Friar turned one last time to look at the shrinking Way of Trepas as the Knights traveled southwest, towards Creber. The Tingij Mountains loomed claustrophobically high on their left. The jagged tops stared down menacingly like spear tips, daring anyone to cross. The ragged range stretched itself across the middle of Verngaurd from the Ice Falls of Lake Glasere in the north to the Mohado Mire in the south. The Way of Trepas was the only significant break in the monstrous sierra. Their height stood in sharp contrast to the flat Rebelde plains stretching out under waving rows of tall grass in front of them and to their right.

A fine mist pelted Bellae and cast a heavy, dreary smudge across the landscape. The earth itself appeared to be mourning for Finn, and the gloom seemed so weighty that it would never depart, as if magnetically drawn to their melancholy.

The dismal scenery added injury to insult at having to transport her Knight, friend, and surrogate father. Bellae could feel the emotion and hurt bubble up within her, materializing as tears hastening down her cheeks. As her fount of cathartic tears neared the bottom of its well, she began to feel the slightest bit better. Looking up, she could only smile at the sky's response. *Even the rain is broken into pieces*, she thought as the mist lashed against her face in a fine spritz. Absently, she grabbed the medal from Veneficus, the kalma-kunnia.

"Ow!"

As her hand brushed against it, she felt a shock as a disturbing pair of eyes flashed in front of her. They looked familiar, but she could not place them. She seized her Inion Medallion and rubbed it, unsure of what just happened.

"How are you?" a voice startled.

Replacing the medal inside her cloak, she nodded at Friar Pallium and his cautious smile. Despite his thin grin, a layer of sadness rested over his expression.

Letting the tears streaming down her cheeks serve as her answer, she silently stewed, fed up with people asking how she was, sick of trying to answer, and tired of feeling guilty that part of her was mad at Finn for leaving. A rush of tears were drawn up from the deep well of pain within her and splashed onto her face.

Closing her eyes, Bellae willed another image to take the place of Finn's lifeless expression, but none came. "How do I stop seeing his dying face?"

"Pick somewhere that you enjoyed, a special memory. It doesn't have to be complicated." Looking up, he said, "Think of something with Finn and the rain."

Bellae thought for a moment, and then smiled. "I loved how the rain ran over his skin, making the softest of waterfall sounds as it ran through the rough grooves of his skin."

Friar nodded, keeping silent to let her enjoy the memory.

After cantering for a few minutes, Friar spoke, "I have seen too many die and watched different people from all over Verngaurd deal with it. Tears can be cleansing—each one that falls is an offering, reclaimed by the earth, which somehow manages to push up our spirits and bring us back into balance.

"I wish I had a magic answer for your pain, but I don't. Death is all around, every day. Sometimes it's dramatic and painful like the death of our friend, but there are less noticeable examples that we swim through every day. As the seasons change, grass, flowers, insects, and animals die in incredible numbers."

"If this is supposed to cheer me up, it isn't."

Friar Pallium chuckled. "No, I suppose not. The point is, just because something is intimately familiar doesn't mean we understand it."

"I just miss him."

"It is a mistake to think we can hold onto something or someone. What you love, you should love now, in the moment. Nothing is eternal. Not us, not our emotions, none of the wondrous things we see around us.

"To love with passion, to soak up each moment in the present, to enjoy every second with them, that is perfect love. You did that, Bellae. That is not a bad measure of successful living."

Bellae was filled with so much emotion she thought she might explode. An effervescent sensation began to burn deep within her stomach. Burying her face in Crann's upright mane, she let the emotion flow. After a tumultuous cry, she felt tired.

"I'm not doing so well at cheering you up," Friar said, gently patting her back. "The similarities between the words 'morning' and 'mourning' have always amazed me. Both present us the opportunity to be 'reborn' into a new phase of our life, a little wiser and stronger."

Bellae looked puzzled. Friar watched her with a wisdom born of passing years, patiently waiting for her to process and then speak her thoughts.

"Friar, how can death bring wisdom?"

"Any event that prompts us to contemplate life, the future, is a worthy endeavor and often leads to greater wisdom. No one wants death to happen, but there are some things we can't control. The discerning person will use it to broaden their understanding."

Bellae's expression had transformed to frustration that was now mingling affably with confusion. "Friar?" she pleaded in consternation.

"I didn't mean to frustrate you. Few squires have been closer to their Knight than you were to Finn.

"Death is the worst and best thing about our limited time here. It can be a motivator, inspiring people to succeed with the little time we are granted. How we act and our accomplishments stand as our only true legacy. Our actions should serve as gifts to the future, making things better."

"The real question is, where is Finn?"

Friar looked intently at the young squire. "Bellae, the moment you were carried through our gates, I knew you had been born with an old soul. You just asked the million-pound question. The number of answers you get depends on the number of people you ask. The Proliators believe in Tallcon and rebirth. Jaainians believe the northern spirits and lights are a refuge for their dead. The people of Ager consider death as the mother of sleep. They believe we practice every night for the ultimate sleep of death, and our return to the earth. To my mind, no matter how you look at it, standing between the bookends of eternity is a massive, and in my mind, unfair amount of literal and figurative pressure."

Ritari cleared his throat loudly as he galloped up to them.

"Yes, Captain," Friar said.

"We've been advancing a long time. We're exhausted and wet."

"Oh, really?" Friar asked jokingly. "In my day, we used to travel twice as far, uphill both ways, with no horses or supplies."

Bellae and Ritari chuckled. Ritari suddenly laughed hysterically.

"It wasn't that funny," Friar remarked.

"I was thinking of what Finn told me after the dragon burnt my hair, 'When this is over, you have to tell me who does your hair. It looks absolutely fantastic.'" They all laughed so hard tears of joy replaced, and masked, those of sorrow.

"I miss him," Ritari said, becoming solemn. A small commotion erupted behind them. Scelto signaled he had it under control as he held back Jumeaux.

"Jumeaux has been extra sarcastic, cracking exceptionally bad jokes," Ritari said.

"For some, sarcasm is cast out like a shield to avoid pain. His passive aggressive behavior is pushing people away because he is afraid of showing how much he loves you. Letting yourself love is a set-up for potential heartbreak. So, acting tough is a defense mechanism to make it seem as though we don't care," Friar said.

Bellae rotated to see her brother. He was sulking, no doubt reeling from being chastised. Even in the dreary, smoky drizzle, Friar's words made her see him in a new light. Bellae thought of all the people he had lost, including their parents. *Maybe the only thing worse than not knowing what happened to our parents is knowing, and living through, what happened.*

"Still, it's a funny way to show love," Bellae stated.

"By *not* showing affection he is protecting himself against loving too much," Friar answered. "In his mind he is throwing a protective wall up, to not get hurt, when in reality the lost opportunities to love, to risk, weigh down his soul, and such a jaded act, if performed long enough, becomes reality, blunting his heart."

Ritari scoffed, "I don't know. Sometimes people just act like jerks."

Friar nodded. "Understandable. The world, unfortunately, judges us solely on our actions and words, never taking into account the past we endured, our heart, our motivation. It is a reminder to make each deed count, because our actions, not intentions, often define who we are."

"Will we make it to the forest tonight?" Bellae asked after another day of travel.

"No. We don't want to enter the forest at night. The Elves are fiercely protective and, I would imagine, even more so after what happened at the Tournament," Friar explained.

Luck seemed to be with them as Arquero brought down a large buck, and they found a series of large trees to make camp.

Later that night, Bellae sat up, surrounded by the others but feeling infinitely alone. Everyone but the first watch, Friar, and Ritari slept. Bellae had purposefully placed her spot on the outskirts of the camp, closer to Finn. She looked at the pitch-black outline of the Forest of Creber. *That's where you grew up.* Despite abhorring the circumstances, she was anxious to see his home.

It stopped raining, but the ground was still damp and uncomfortable. She slid towards the supply wagon and looked underneath the wheels to study the wrapped body of Finn. A thick canvas was tucked protectively around his linen-shrouded body, which had been so lovingly prepared during the AnFilleadh ritual at the Citadel.

"You keeping time?" Ritari asked Friar. Bellae froze to avoid detection.

"You don't want to stay up all night?"

"Can, just prefer not to," Ritari said, smiling.

"I'm keeping time. Hopefully, the weather will stay dry."

Suddenly, a loud, almost panicked, screech blasted through the air.

"What the…" Ritari asked.

"It's getting closer," Friar replied. "I heard a softer version of that cry several times already."

"What is it? A Watcher?"

"I don't think so…but not sure."

I know. My friend, Arend, Bellae thought, imagining the magnificent Eaglian watching over her. *He's letting me know he's here for me.*

Checking that her mice friends were still asleep, and feeling a little more secure, Bellae reached out and placed her hand on Finn's corpse. With cavernous questions about what she would see tomorrow swimming though her head, she finally drifted under to sleep.

Scroll 4: This is Good

Veneficus stood near the fire, looking back at the prophecy scroll he had finally found as it magically hovered over his desk. Withered streaks of age flashed across its yellowing parchment like lightning strikes of fragility and age. A bored-looking Valo floated nearby, throwing a sleepy, disinterested light onto the scroll.

Frustrated, the Magician shook his head. He had been reading and rereading the tattered scroll all night. Despite his intense effort, the contents of the ancient scroll seemed strangely distant. He had never forgiven himself for letting the animal talkers steal the Macht Power Crystals in the first place. They used a feeble, misguided excuse about "preventing evil" from using the Macht Crystals to destroy the world.

"I know what's good for Verngaurd!" Veneficus thundered.

The startled Valo threw out more light as the golden gargoyle stretched groggily from his ornate pedestal.

"What is it?" the gargoyle asked. Fluttering his spiked wings, he flew over to the desk. His upturned nose sniffed at the scroll while he flashed his sharp teeth.

"Good of you to wake up, Irvikuva. You've been sleeping too much this century. I was just lamenting the Ainmhi Caint."

"Bloody traitors!" the gargoyle huffed, his eyes flashing rage.

"Indeed, only I can keep Verngaurd safe, prevent it from falling into evil."

"Exactly, delusional fools. Then creating this stupid prophecy scroll to 'protect the crystal's location.' What a bunch of malarkey!"

"My spies showed great resolve in acquiring this scroll."

"They also showed a lot of torture and sharp blades," a Valo smirked.

"Actions required for success were executed," Veneficus assured. "When I first obtained the prophecy scroll, there were still plenty of mindre or lesser crystals for our crosiers. Now, not so much."

"Are you saying you got complacent, Big Guy?" a Valo leered.

Veneficus' eyes blazed, but his rage quickly subsided as he remembered his dismay when the Ainmhi Caint managed to steal the prophecy scroll back.

"I can't believe they thieved it from you again," the gargoyle Irvikuva said. "As I remember, it cost them many a life to pilfer it and even more when you retrieved it back."

"Yeah, many of them suckers died a very, very unpleasant death!" a

Valo said cheerfully. "Good times! Good times. Then the Ainmhi Caint disappeared—good riddance."

Rumors flew wildly as everyone speculated on their fate. Most believed the Proliate or even the White Wizard had exterminated them.

"They were gone but replaced by the dreadful League of Truth," Irvikuva said, shuddering in disdain.

"Their self-righteous aim of 'guarding and protecting' the stolen crystals? Absurdity!" Veneficus voiced. "Is this the original scroll, Irvikuva?"

"I honestly don't know."

When Veneficus first examined the recovered scroll, eons ago, it had seemed different, but enough time had passed, doubts lingered. Now, with a desperate shortage of mindre crystals, crisis zoomed forward like a rapidly approaching arrow.

"It's the boy, then? The brother? Not the girl?" Veneficus asked.

"It would certainly make more sense that it is the girl, the animal talker," the gargoyle said. "However, the Ainmhi Caint are just devious enough that they would go with the less obvious choice for the Chosen One, the brother of the last Ainmhi Caint."

A knock startled them.

"Come in," Veneficus called out gruffly as the gargoyle, hating company, flew to his pedestal and instantly froze back into a statue.

Lidenskap and a thin, sickly looking Magician entered. They stood in silence as Veneficus stared at the scroll, his left hand reaching towards the yellowing and cracking parchment before suddenly stopping. He could recite it by heart but still liked scouring the words for hidden clues. His arm stood frozen for a moment before retreating back into his blue robes.

Sitting heavily in his chair, he waved his hand. "Lidenskap, go."

Another Valo light appeared and swished over to the Proliate general.

"Wow, wow, wow. Graced by *THE* general himself! I'm honored to spread light upon your righteousness!"

"More like self-righteous," another Valo whispered. "Pomped-up general, I say."

Lidenskap scowled but ignored the floating lights, "Sir, we just had a griffin fly in from the scouts of the Ragorsaf Outpost. A large force of Dark Warriors is amassing near the northeast corner of the Forest of Creber. It appears that multiple smaller squads, the ones we are used to dealing with, are congealing."

"Interesting," Veneficus said, but his tone was one of distinct indifference. His eyes stayed fixed on the scroll, willing it to speak, recounting the truth. *The boy, or the girl? Which can solve the riddle of the prophecy?*

He wished his magic could entice the scroll to let him know if this was the original scroll or a forgery. However, the Ainmhi Caint had enough magic to block most of his enchantments. "Will they attack the Forest of Creber?"

Lidenskap scoffed, "It's more likely they will be joined by the traitorous Elves!"

"What strength are the Dark Warriors?"

"Their numbers are still growing. However, it appears to be enough to form a large company or even a small battalion," Lidenskap answered.

Veneficus paused. "So, in the hundreds?"

"Thousands."

After another pause, Veneficus finally looked up. "You and Storlax should ride in that direction immediately. A brisk, pious, all-night ride should do your soldiers good. I leave it in your capable hands to determine the number you will need to deal with them. Don't move against them until we know their true strength and target, in case it's a trap."

"Excellent," Lidenskap replied.

The Valo hovering near him mockingly mouthed the word, "Excellent."

Veneficus stared at the general for several moments. "That's all," he said curtly. Lidenskap bowed and left the room. Veneficus rarely dealt directly with Storlax since, years earlier, the two had fallen out when Storlax demanded to attack the Knights.

Turning to the sickly looking Magician, his sunken and pale complexion made haunting by the sallow light of the Valo, Veneficus asked, "Fino?"

"Any decision on the scroll?"

"My gut tells me there's something wrong, it's not the original," Veneficus confided.

"But, sir, it has been in Magicians' hands for centuries."

"Ah, but it is precisely the time when it was *out of our hands* I am worried about. Those egotistical Ainmhi Caint had just enough magic and time to make a forgery to throw us off," Veneficus huffed. "The fools thought they were protecting us but have only made us weak."

"It seems as if time has finally caught up with the prophecy scroll," Fino wheezed.

Veneficus paused, mentally weighing his words before nodding. "If the prophecy is not interpreted quickly and the Power Crystals found, we shall have to fight the looming war with good intentions instead of enchantments! Unless the lesser mindre crystals are reunited with the Macht Crystals soon, our crosiers will be glorified walking sticks."

"Should we inform the other Magicians and the Academy of Magic? They are already inundated with rumors and innuendos."

Veneficus looked down. "I have to admit, I never foresaw the severity of this catastrophe. Many times I have wondered if we shouldn't limit the Magical knowledge to one hundred Magicians—like the old days. In some ways I only agreed to the Academy of Magic being formed in order to find the one who could help us solve the prophecy. The animal talkers have strong, intrinsic magic and would be easily recognized.

"I hope we will find the Power Crystals before disaster strikes. Unfortunately, this war will drain the mindre faster than ever. We have no choice but to trust the scroll. It's the boy, Jumeaux, brother to the animal talker that is the Chosen One."

Fino sighed heavily. "Perhaps we should have moved earlier. The boy was just here for the Tournament."

Veneficus' eyes widened with anger. "What should we have done? Kidnap him? Take him before I was sure?"

"If need be, yes. We must have him, this Jumeaux," Fino said boldly. "We have wasted valuable time debating whether this is the original or a forgery."

Am I that out of touch with my fellow Magicians? Do they think me a fool? Veneficus wondered. Planning and caution, taking nothing for granted, these were the pillars that had kept him in power for so long, longer than any of them could comprehend. He stared with scorching intensity until several beads of sweat oozed out onto Fino's frail brow under the vigor radiating from Veneficus.

"He's gonna blast you!" one of the Valo whispered with wicked delight.

"Nope. He's going to dismember him," another whispered, chuckling quietly. "You will be a 'Fino puzzle' with lots and lots of itty-bitty, tiny little pieces."

Fino's eyes widened, his already pasty complexion completely washing out.

"Quiet, you fools!" Veneficus huffed, his eyes softening. "Fino is correct. Now is the time to move. This recent development with the Dark Warriors might serve our purpose well. Unlike the Proliate, I don't believe the Elves of Creber are helping the Dark Warriors. Assuming they aren't, even thousands of Dark Warriors would be far too few to move against the Elves barricaded within their fortress of trees. Therefore, the White Wizard must have sent them after the Knights traveling with Finn's body."

"Reasonable, but why?" Fino asked.

"It should be obvious. The White Wizard is onto the prophecy and after the Knights and Jumeaux. Imagine if he is the only one with magic." Veneficus rose and began pacing. "The chaos of battle shall provide the perfect cloud to allow us to move in and get him, passing it off as a 'rescue.'"

"Oh, golly, Master V, that sure is an amazing plan!" a Valo sneered sarcastically as the others snickered.

"Shall I inform Storlax of the target, and that we will join them?" Fino asked, ignoring the floating menaces dancing maliciously around his head.

"No," Veneficus thundered. "He can handle himself militarily, but I don't want him blundering into our mission. Let them take care of the Dark Warriors while we get Jumeaux. I will tell Lidenskap. I trust him."

"What of the girl?" Fino asked. "Do we grab the animal talker as well?"

"I think it wise. Bring Bellae here as well to hedge our bets. If the legend is true, it should be pretty easy to tell who the so-called Chosen One is to solve the prophecy. The League of Truth is cunning and relentless and could have altered the prophecy scroll we now possess to throw us off."

"I understand the situation," Fino said, bowing with a slight smile, feeling quite proud of himself for thinking of Bellae. Veneficus' laugh wiped the smile off his face. Fino stared at him with disappointment and confusion.

"You understand? Do you?" Veneficus asked, his laugh turning deeper. "That makes one of us."

"Yeah, dingleberry, now there is one of us who understands!" a Valo laughed.

With a wave of his crosier, Veneficus magically hurled the floating light across the chamber.

"Thank you so much," the light muttered sarcastically after slamming into the wall. "I *totally* deserved that well-justified, completely warranted, entirely suitable, quite equitable punishment. My back, if I had one, I am sure, would feel better after crashing into the hard stone. So thanks."

Changing tone and ignoring the light, Veneficus continued, "Inform the other Magicians I will join you. We ride hard through the night. Once we catch up to the Proliate, we shall speed them along with the prodigiosis volo enchantment. I do not think we will arrive in time without it."

"Ye-yes, Supreme Master," Fino said, nervous about riding with Veneficus.

"Have several reserve forces ride out after us to secure Jumeaux and Bellae in case they get past us. Make sure they have griffins. You may go."

"Hey, Pasty Boy, go eat some red meat," a Valo whispered to the sallow Magician.

"Maybe eat some liver you anemic louse!" another advised.

"After five to six years of that, you might get some color in your pale-arse keister!"

"Oh, do shut up and let Fino hurry off!" Veneficus thundered.

Another Valo sarcastically mouthed, "Oh, do shut up!" repeatedly as Veneficus laid his head on his desk. Reaching out, he rested his hand on the tattered scroll, *Soon. The prophecy will be revealed, and the Chosen One will be on his quest to return the Macht Crystals to me.*

Scroll 5: That Will Wake You Up

"Friar!" Arquero said, shaking him.

"I'm up," Friar said groggily, stiffly moving his blanket back. There was a hint of sunrise off to the east, but the Tingij Mountains created enough of a hurdle for the Mardin sun that it was still fairly dark. The fire's sleepy embers simmered while everyone else still dozed.

A surge of fear flashed into Friar's mind. "Are we under attack?" he demanded, springing up. There was no time for stiffness now.

"No, just something odd."

Friar woke Ritari, and the three men walked up a small hill, peering toward the eastern horizon. A lone figure stood in stark contrast to the brightening morning sky. His weight was shifted to his right leg, and he seemed completely at ease.

"At first, I thought it was just some farmer or villager. However, he has been standing there alone for a full hour, and I saw him brandish a sword at me a minute ago. I can put in arrow into him from this distance," Arquero suggested excitedly.

"It's a Dark Warrior," Friar said.

Surprised by Friar's answer, the other two scrutinized the figure more closely.

"Permission to take him out?" Arquero requested, unslinging his bow.

"No!" Friar said quickly. "For every scout you see, there are several others watching. If we kill him, we are likely to provoke an immediate attack. They want to take control of the situation by getting us to react hastily. Wake everyone and send Gleoi Dea to me."

Ritari returned with her, and the four watched the motionless figure on the skyline.

"We will ride hard for Creber," Friar said. "If the Dark Warriors pop up in front of us, as I suspect, we will stand and fight while you break off and ask the Elves for help."

"But it's just one guy," Gleoi Dea expressed.

"Plus, he's behind us, not blocking our way to the forest," Arquero added.

Friar scoffed. "Some lessons you must learn the hard way. Others you can acquire from an old man who has been in this situation before. The Dark Warriors are trying to bait us into a mistake. Trust me, we are surrounded, and when we are so bloody close to the Forest of Creber."

After a questioning glance at the lone warrior, the Knights quickly readied themselves in somber silence.

A loud screech stung the air. Bellae felt a chill, sensing the panic within the Eaglian watching over her, Arend. She felt foolish. The call last night was not to let her know he was there—it was a warning.

They quickly ate cured meat before heading south towards Creber, away from the lone Dark Warrior. They had traveled at a good pace for several hours when a break in the shiftless clouds could be seen to the east, promising a sunny day.

"There," said Arquero, pointing to a shadowy figure briefly peeking up behind and to their left.

"How can they keep up with our horses?" Ritari cried in frustration.

"They are in absurd condition," Friar responded. "I was half expecting an attack by now."

"That's good, isn't it?" Arquero asked.

"No, I don't think so," Friar replied grimly. "It likely means they're waiting for greater numbers before springing their trap."

"Their scouts are sloppy. They keep showing themselves," Ritari stated.

"No. Never underestimate them," Friar said with surprising vigor, born from painful memories. "They're baiting us into sending some of our Knights to take out their scouts. Then, they would ambush and kill them. Sometimes they torture or mutilate their bodies in plain sight to try to get us to charge in an unorganized and ineffective manner. We learned that the hard way during the Dark War. They are fearless, maniacally intelligent, and patient. Act impulsively and you lose."

"Are they targeting us?" Ritari asked.

"We wouldn't be able to see them if they weren't. Their raiding parties have been platoon strength of twenty to thirty, so I would expect about that number waiting for us." Friar swiveled, "Scelto!"

The large squire pushed his horse forward.

"Do you know where the extra bows and weapons are?"

"Of course."

"When the time comes, you are in charge of arming all squires."

"Yes, sir," Scelto replied.

Without warning, Dark Warriors appeared on the horizon directly in front of the Knights. They stood in ranks on the last hill before the Forest of Creber. The dense forest and the refuge it promised stood tantalizingly close, yet frustratingly out of reach.

Feeling exposed and vulnerable, ineptly shielded by only his cloak, Friar Pallium whispered, "I know you."

"The scouts *have* been herding us all along," Ritari grumbled.

"Should we try to go around them?" Lovag asked. "We could ditch the supply wagon and Honey can move quickly, even with Finn's sled."

"No," Friar stated plainly. "This is certainly not the entire force. They won't show their true strength until it's to their advantage. That hill is concealing their numbers."

"Will the Elves send help?"

"I doubt they can see us. So, unless Gleoi Dea can make it there, no," Friar answered. "I would guess the Dark Warriors have most of their reserve troops to our right. They probably expect us to try and go around them to get to the bulk of the forest. Gleoi Dea, we will drift in that direction while you linger to our left. When I give the signal, we will charge to our right, while Gleoi Dea breaks left, around their flank. I need to see the speed of that kameli of yours."

"Yes, sir."

"Friar!" Lontas shouted. "Behind us!"

To the north of their position a Watcher gracefully hovered thirty feet off the ground. His ice-blue eyes narrowed in their cocoon of red as he shrieked. Arrow after arrow flew towards him. The Watcher easily batted them away with his magic. His four wings beat feverishly as his crackled brown skin flaked with each powerful movement.

Abruptly, another creature streaked through the air towards the Watcher. His majestic head and fierce yellow beak made it to within a few yards of the Watcher before being flung to the ground with magic.

"The Watchers are fighting each other!" Luchar said.

Bellae whispered to Lontas, "It's Arend...I mean, the Eagl...I mean, it's the creature watching over us."

"Who's Arend?" Lontas asked but was distracted as several new Watchers filled the sky surrounding the young Eaglian. His large yellow eyes blazed with determination. His human torso had two massive wings for flight while his legs held brown feathers over sharp yellow talons.

One of the new arrivals grabbed the Eaglian and brutally flung him to the ground as he squawked in pain. With amazing agility, Arend sprung back up and flew headlong into the pack of Watchers. Two grabbed his muscular arms while a third pounded his abdomen and ribcage with powerful blows.

The source of the arrows became evident as a young Elf sprinted forward, yelling fiercely and firing arrows at the Watchers, who merely laughed in disdain, easily blocking the projectiles.

"Floating guy and bladed-bow warrior are approaching from the southeast," Arquero said indifferently. "Again, probably not the weirdest thing we'll see today."

Tacet-Vand levitated by them in a flash. His wizened face and balding head were a blur as he passed, his simple robes fluttering briskly. He raised his wooden crosier, and a bright light shot out, arcing across the sky and scattering the Watchers, who howled in pain.

IleZuri ran effortlessly up to the Knights. "We'll hold off the Watchers as best we can, move towards the safety of the forest. I'm sure you're aware, but there is a massive army of Dark Warriors blocking your way."

His long blonde hair flowed onto a red cape and old, but solid, silver and bronze armor. His fearsome bow held multiple sharp blades on either end. "Bellae, I will do my best to protect your friends Arend and Kainen."

Friar nodded. "We appreciate the help." *How can Veneficus think Tacet-Vand is behind some of these troubles?*

Lontas looked at Bellae, his eyes full of betrayal. "Arend?"

"Sorry," she said sincerely. "The Eaglian and Elf came to me after Finn died. They told me not to tell anyone, plus I still have no idea what's going on," Bellae said, seeing his despondency.

Disappointment clouded his face. "I'm not just 'anyone,'" he said, more than a little hurt at the exclusion and feeling dense at not recognizing an Eaglian.

Bellae embraced him. "I know you're not. Won't happen again."

He nodded, patting her shoulder.

With an occasional nervous glance to the battle raging to the north, the Knights continued to move forward while straying to their right as Gleoi Dea began to wander left. The details of the army in front of them slowly began to crisp. They were at company strength, around sixty or so warriors, and formed a single line, each one maliciously swinging a different weapon with anxious glee. Huge smiles adorned the faces of the Dark Warriors, suggesting an unholy eagerness for battle. Some of them had black chest plates with images of horned creatures and demons. A few wore helmets, but many had their faces painted or lined with tattoos consisting of various patterns and symbols. Almost all had pale hair framing pallid faces.

Suddenly, Friar startled them with a shout, "Go, Gleoi Dea! Ride around their flank, then break towards the forest! Everyone else, move right."

Gleoi Dea urged her kameli forward. With a high-pitched bleat it took off with surprising speed, despite its awkward pacing gait. Its ungulate hooves pounded the grass as its horns and tusks flashed menacingly.

"Arquero, Sorea, and Lovag, be ready to provide cover," Friar ordered. "Don't fire now—that might prompt a charge against us or Gleoi Dea."

"Are these the Dark Warriors?" Jumeaux asked, in utter disbelief. Everyone was taken aback by their pasty complexions.

"Their hearts give their name," Friar stated, his eyes tracking Gleoi Dea. Her kameli's head bobbed forward and backwards as she yanked on the reigns. Its relatively thin legs looked gangly and awkward, but there was no doubting the resultant velocity.

"Go!" Gimelli called in a mix of encouragement and worry.

A band of ten Dark Warriors abruptly sprinted towards Gleoi Dea.

"She didn't go wide enough," Friar lamented. "Hold here, archers, loose!"

"She won't make it," Ritari screamed as they watched helplessly.

A Dark Warrior spear shot out. It was a spectacular throw. A juicy splat and a horrific wail followed as the spear sliced into the kameli's shoulder, narrowly missing Gleoi Dea's leg. The beast collapsed and rolled. Gleoi Dea sprang up, somersaulting over the beast's convulsing body.

"Run!" Friar encouraged, even though she had already started.

The Warrior who brought down the kameli stepped forward with a new spear. Before Friar could give another order, a bolt and two arrows slammed into him. His spear fell fruitlessly a dozen yards in front of his crumpled body. A round of laughter and a few cheers went up from the Dark Warriors as they looked indifferently at their fallen comrade. Several began to shout insults as his collapsed body bled. One approached his corpse, kicking him, "Nice throw! Congratulations, you speared the earth!"

"Yeah, dirt spear, dirt spear!" several chanted.

Gleoi Dea suddenly broadened out her course.

"She must see more of them behind the hill," Friar stated, sucking in his breath as Gleoi Dea disappeared over the ridge, desperately attempting to steer clear of hidden Dark Warriors.

"Will she make it?" Gimelli asked.

"Yes," Friar said with more confidence than he felt.

"Come on, you bloody cowards!" Luchar yelled, dismounting. His breath fluttered, fettered with the weight of guilt and sadness that had entrenched itself upon his shoulders from the time lucidity returned to his battered brain screaming Finn was dead. Loss, regret, guilt, sorrow, all of which he saw as abominable signs of weakness, tormented him.

No longer.

If I hadn't been knocked out, Finn would be alive. The thought was so onerous it took on a physical component.

Now, he would enter his world. The ordinary moments of life: conversations, manners, small talk, these were repugnant. He would show respect to Finn's memory by bludgeoning the enemy, transferring mental pain into their physical agony. The smell of battle felt like coming home.

"That new helmet looks shinny. They'll think you're rookie," Ritari joked.

"Not for much longer," Luchar replied. He hit his helmet several times with his axe, savoring the familiar bell of battle ringing in his ears. However, he was not completely healed from his run-in with the dragon, and his brain protested with a diffuse, aching pain.

Nothing to be done now—no way he was sitting this one out.

"Oh, crap." Sorea sighed as another two platoons materialized on either side of the Dark Warriors already in front of them. Her sore ribs and aching head would make this fight miserable.

"Everyone dismount. Sorea, right, and Lovag, left," Friar ordered. "Watch the flanks, quivers ready. The rest form up a quarter-moon defense. Scelto, get Ritari, all the squires, and myself outfitted with bows. Squires, take the horses to the rear, and then prepare for battle. No one sits this one out."

"Friar," Ritari called wearily as three more rows of Dark Warriors slid over the horizon. Hundreds of savage eyes glared at the Knights. The sheer number of Dark Warriors was enough to pull mercilessly on the spirits of the Pantteri. The most frightening thing they carried was their smiles.

All the Knights except Luchar seemed shaken by their absurd behavior. "Ahhhh, now we're talking!" he roared, swaying side to side with pent-up energy. "More of you fanatics and freaks to kill!"

Luchar's words caused a riot of laughter to erupt from the Warriors' lines. Several pointed and whispered before cackling maniacally. They were maddeningly sincere in their disregard for battle and death. The absurdity of it chilled the Knights to the bone.

"Is that funny, dogs!" Luchar cried, shaking with rage. "Wait until I slam this into your skulls." He finished by brandishing his battle-axe. His anger grew their joviality.

"What are they waiting for?" Ritari asked, given their clear superiority in numbers.

Before Friar Pallium could answer, portals to Ifrean opened on either side of the Dark Warrior lines. The ground shook as more sprinted through. The Knights found themselves staring at a "U" shaped assemblage of warriors blocking off any hope of moving around the army before them.

The savagery in their eyes awoke a seed within Friar, which sprouted into a nightmarish memory of himself as a young squire facing the Dark Warriors. Images and emotions grew rapidly once released from their pitch-black hole: bloody battles, chaos, and death flashed quickly and vividly, culminating with a lump in his throat.

"This isn't a few squads roaming the countryside as a scare tactic. This is a full battalion," Friar said numbly. He felt like a drop of sweat in the ocean, insignificant against the massive numbers arrayed against them. Shaking his head, Friar tried to uproot his memories to focus on the moment.

"Sorea, Arquero, and Lovag," Father Pallium began, "introduce yourselves. Kill shots only. Wounding them does nothing to deter a Dark Warrior's will to fight."

With a nod the three Knights began to issue their greeting. Lovag's chainmail hanging from the back of his helmet chimed lightly with each arrow that left for its mark. Sorea had her crossbow string humming, but at half the rate. The Knights watched as the arrows and bolts found their marks over and over again.

"All arrows to their center!" Friar shouted.

From the ruffle of air as the projectiles left the bows until the moment they squished into their human targets, the Knights watched. In eerie silence the Dark Warriors stared on, almost longingly, as Arquero, Sorea, and Lovag found their marks repeatedly. Soon, the other Knights and squires joined in.

Still no response.

The silence sprouted into a deafening, maddening dread as their minds strained to hear a scream or shout come from the warriors. If not from those hit, surely their comrades should yell, cry out?

No sound came, no effort swelled to get out of the way of the raining arrows—motionless except for loathing smiles.

"What is this insanity?" Ritari questioned, putting into words what they were all thinking. They watched as each wave of arrows struck into the center of the facing line and set into motion the unwavering machine of discipline. They calmly picked up, and then moved the bodies to the rear of their ranks. They watched impassively as the lethal shower of arrows rained down on them, those behind peacefully stepping forward as soon as the dead were removed.

"Ritari and Scelto, hold your fire and come here," Friar said with more desperation than he had hoped. "Bring up the Horn of Kayda." It was one of a dozen enchanted horns from the time when the Knights were ruled by kings. The call for help signaled a force of Knights was under attack.

Scelto retrieved it from Ritari's saddlebag.

"Plug your ears," Ritari stated, taking a long deep breath before blowing out a booming but melodic blast that reverberated down into their bones.

"There's no one…" Lovag started, before rephrasing. "Is there anyone to come?"

Before Friar could answer, Luchar growled, "We don't need any stinking help. Just sound the charge and let me kill them all!"

"We have to hold out hope someone will hear," Friar answered.

The Dark Warriors temporarily stopped passing dead bodies to look at the Knights with a mixture of humor and relief at their call for help. A fresh round of indescribable laughter burned through their ranks, eating at the nerves of the Knights.

"Friar, so help me! Let me at these guys before they drive me crazy," Luchar said.

"For once," Sorea said softly, "I agree with Luchar. We're not getting out of here alive, so we might as well get it on and take as many of them with us as possible."

"That is exactly what they want. Keep your cool. There's always a way to win," Friar stated, as calmly as he could. His words sounded hollow and insincere in the face of odds so preposterous.

Seeing their skeptical faces he added, "Sometimes, the best you can do is fight with all your heart and not worry about the consequences. Squires, fire at will until they charge, then back up to the supply wagons and draw your swords—they will quickly outflank us."

The squires took a deep breath and fired as Friar had instructed. The torrent of arrows seemed to do nothing to thin the Dark Warriors' ranks or determination.

Despite the arrows flying, the Dark Warriors seemed more enthusiastic. Two of them ran out in front of the ranks and made rude and mocking gestures at the Knights. Several actually jumped in front of arrows to make sure they were hit.

At that, even Luchar had a chill run down his spine.

Scroll 6: Plum Pudding

"It has to be an act?" Arquero ventured questioningly.

"They are plum pudding crazy," Lovag mumbled.

"Remember, you are Knights, and you will not falter."

"They want crazy? I can give them crazy," Luchar said menacingly.

Bellae fired her small bow. The arrow landed next to the cluster of her previous failed attempts, well short of their line.

"It's okay. Little more oomph!" Friar encouraged.

Bellae reloaded and fired. It was stronger but still looked as if it would fall well short. Astonishingly, one of the laughing Dark Warriors began running towards the arrow as if attempting to catch it. As her arrow fell, he dove.

Thunk! It squished into his side, splattering blood. He pushed himself to a kneeling position and gave Bellae a thumbs up before mouthing something. At first it was too soft to hear. Louder and louder he began to chant, "Pairrr-aaaaaa-diiiiice."

Finally, he screamed, "Paradise!"

"Paradise!" the other Dark Warriors chanted back. "Paradise! Paradise!"

"They are stark raving mad," Lovag said, panic oozing from his words.

Tears welled in Bellae's eyes.

"On second thought, I need you to guard Finn's body," Friar said with more alarm than he wanted to show.

The smiling Dark Warrior contorted his face into imbecilic scowls as if putting on some frivolous show for the benefit of the young child. Jumeaux remained silent. The bizarre behavior of the Dark Warriors and their gleeful desire to die made his head spin. Friar led Bellae towards Finn's body. Upon returning, he whispered quietly, "End this."

Instantly, three projectiles slammed into the kneeling warrior's face. Two arrows, from Lovag and Arquero, sliced into the right side of his face. A bolt from Sorea stabbed into his left eye. The three instantaneous thuds erased the absurd expression, replacing it with gushing blood as his unrecognizable head thrashed backwards, leaving a trail of splattered gore as his body fell.

"This is our time to do as much damage as we can," Friar said.

Each arrow and bolt that found its mark deposited more blood onto the red-stained ground. The blood flowed so freely it became hard to imagine it could ever be washed away. Several times the Dark Warriors moving in to replace the dead slipped on the thick puddles of slimy blood. The absurdity of the Dark Warriors' behavior continued to eat away equally at the Knights' confidence and sanity. Battle was one thing, but this was a massacre of the insane.

"Why do they chant, 'Paradise?'" Lontas asked.

"No idea, but I remember that from when I was a squire," Friar said.

Jumeaux grabbed his head. The lunacy and horror of the situation cast a hazy net around his brain. Feeling light-headed, he looked longingly to the open land behind them. A shimmering white form waved for him to come. In his mind he could hear the Nishi repeatedly whispering, "Follow me. Follow me to safety."

For once he was glad to see the specter.

"Follow me," the Nishi repeated.

"We need to run," Jumeaux cried as all heads jerked towards him.

Gazing at the psychotic warriors, Jumeaux's knees felt weak. Looking into the eyes of the Pantteri, they seemed no less hostile. *I'm not supposed to be here. My stupid parents die, and I get sent to shithole Liberum?* "We can't win," he muttered as irate looks shot back at him, the ghost's words still hissing in his ears.

"Don't look at me like *I'm* the crazy one!" he wailed defensively. "You are as nuts as those lunatics. We *have to* run. We can't defeat these psychos. They obviously want to die and outnumber us hundreds to one!"

"Come on, Jumeaux. We need to stand together," Lontas said.

"Give it a rest, super-klutz. You're so sad, even your imaginary friends make fun of you!" Jumeaux replied.

"Fire!" Friar said, urgently. The twang of bows had already begun as he approached Jumeaux. "There are different versions of victory. Standing and fighting against all odds in defense of friend and family, that is the greatest of triumphs."

"If by 'victory' you mean death or torture…have fun with that because I'm out," Jumeaux said. His head felt foggy, as if it was spinning and he was floating in an out-of-body experience. *This is madness.*

"If we keep our heart and stand together despite our fear, that is a victory. Perhaps it is the greatest victory one can hope to achieve. It's always easier to stand with the side enjoying the majority. How history will score the outcome is not significant. Sticking together for the right reason is what matters," Friar said.

Jumeaux glanced nervously at his sisters. He struggled to rouse the cords of deep brotherly love he was supposed to feel. He mentally reached and tried to pluck them but felt no resonance of connection. Instead, panic washed over him. The idea of standing to die for some sort of honor code or for this so-called family was absurd.

"Stand and fight, or run. If you flee, you are sure to die. If you stay and fight, we have a chance, however small."

"You're staying to fight," Luchar said matter-of-factly.

"*Stay, J,*" Gimelli encouraged her brother telepathically. "*Think of Bellae.*"

Jumeaux nodded.

The others smiled, convinced his nod affirmed his belief in them. In Jumeaux's heart he knew the reason—his legs felt like jelly and Luchar would club him to death if he tried to run. Doing the right thing for the wrong reason can make one rationalize and then aggressively defend the imperfect reasoning. Animosity towards his sisters soared.

Everyone but Luchar, Bellae, and Jumeaux were now shooting, sending a steady stream of arrows gashing the air. As Friar Pallium predicted, unless the wound was mortal, the Dark Warriors stood their ground and sneered hatred.

Jumeaux ruffled his already unruly hair, his ears started ringing as his mind screamed out a hazy alarm, the panic befuddling his thoughts.

He couldn't help speaking up again, "We can't stand against so many!"

"There's always hope, until there isn't—when we greet our final demise," Friar said stoically, moving to the left flank.

"Jumeaux, if you don't stop sniveling, I will personally filet and deliver you on a platter to those crazy cheese brains," Luchar said as quietly as he had ever spoken. However, the sincerity was clear enough to send a wave of fear through Jumeaux.

Bellae put her hand on Finn. Looking up, she saw Tacet-Vand struggling to keep a flock of Watchers at bay with a blinding burst of light from his wooden crosier when a minotaur exploded from a small grove of trees, heading straight for the wizard.

Running on its three hooves while holding a massive war hammer in its one human hand, the immense creature with the head of a bull dashed for the elderly wizard. The young Elf Kainen quickly put three arrows into the minotaur's left leg, but this did nothing to slow its charge. Tacet-Vand began to back up while struggling to maintain the magic light keeping the Watchers away.

IleZuri sprinted towards the beast, cutting the minotaur's shoulder with the long reach of the blade on the end of his bow. Screeching in pain, the minotaur stood up and faced the warrior. The beast's massive hammer swung with blistering speed. IleZuri arched backwards, ducking just below the colossal thrust as it blurred in an angry whoosh over his head. Trying to stay in between the minotaur and Tacet-Vand,

IleZuri began spinning his bladed bow in a figure-eight pattern, deflecting the repeated blows by the beast.

Frustrated, the minotaur made several thrusting strikes with the spear tip on the end of his war hammer, each one easily deflected by the whirling reinforced bow of IleZuri.

The minotaur, increasingly enraged, swung his mighty war hammer in ferocious arcs. IleZuri stopped spinning his bladed bow and began dodging the massive blows. The blonde warrior began lunging with the sharp blades on the end of his weapon. Several slashes cut deeply into the beast, but due to his thick skin and colossal muscles, none penetrated deep enough to cause a mortal wound.

Bellowing loudly, the minotaur dropped down on three hooves, lurching toward IleZuri. Twice the blades on the end of his bow cut into the beast but could not stop his momentum. The minotaur's shoulder slammed into IleZuri, knocking his bow away. With a satisfied roar, the minotaur punched IleZuri with its hooved hand, sending the warrior toppling backwards into the wizard.

Tacet-Vand's body flipped over before landing hard, the light on his crosier extinguishing as the minotaur pounced. Arend swooped in from the sky, his brutal talons ripping into the neck and shoulder of the beast. Flapping his wings savagely, Arend managed to stop the minotaur inches from the wizard.

With screams of fury, the Watchers soared towards the battle, their deranged expressions foretelling they were hungry for revenge. Shaken, but up and moving, IleZuri staggered forward as Kainen continued to put arrows into the minotaur, its thick skin rendering them little more than a nuisance to the monstrous creature.

A surge of lightning erupted from the closest Watcher, shocking into Arend. The Eaglian shrieked in pain, releasing the minotaur.

The minotaur lunged for the wizard, "Die, you mute old-fool!"

Just as the mighty war hammer hurtled towards Tacet-Vand, IleZuri jumped into the air. Raising his bow above his head with two hands, he used all his weight to slam the lower blade into the minotaur's spine. The outer tissue squished, nuggets of bone chunked off vertebrae before the blade's sharp edge severed the spinal cord.

With a howl of pain, the minotaur dropped his weapon, his legs limp.

"Tacet-Vand," IleZuri called. "The Watchers!"

Instantly the wizard was up, blasting his purifying light, sending a stream of dust, small particles, and screams from the retreating Watchers.

"What did you do?" the minotaur bellowed at his flaccid and unresponsive legs. Rage fueled his still functioning upper body as he clawed his way towards IleZuri.

"I will strangle you with your own intestine!" the beast howled.

With a fearsome squawk, the recovered Eaglian clasped onto the minotaur's horns with his powerful talons.

"Swing now!" Arend squawked.

IleZuri obliged. Twisting his body, he whipped his bladed bow with all his might. At the same time, the young Eaglian ripped the minotaur's head upwards. The razor-sharp edge slashed into the minotaur's exposed neck, which, despite its massive muscles, was flayed open. Bright red blood, detoured from delivering oxygen to the brain, suddenly found itself spurting out in a massive arc of gore. IleZuri closed his eyes and mouth while spinning to avoid the carnage pulsing outwards.

The wide-eyed minotaur scratched and groped forward in a rage-filled surge. Kainen moved with youthful swiftness, his bow shouldered and sword drawn. He sank his blade deep into the back of the beast just before Arend wrenched the horns in a violent jerking motion, a sickening crack, signaling the neck breaking, blistered the air as the minotaur's head twisted into a nauseating angle.

With a final gurgle and a full-body spasm, the minotaur became flaccid. Blood and drool washed over his fangs and jaw, trickling down his protruding tongue from a head barely holding on to its body via a few frail, sinewy muscles.

Bellae could barely hear the shouts of the Watchers, who were now flying a safe distance from Tacet-Vand's light. They suddenly stopped shouting and began laughing.

Abruptly two more minotaurs shot towards the Elf, Eaglian,

warrior, and wizard. Anger welling up, Bellae drew the dagger Friar had given her. "I will defend your body, Finn." *To the death,* she thought. The idea of death so recently thrust upon her was still awkward and unbalanced as it rattled around in her head.

For once, she truly understood Luchar. The anticipation gnawed ravenously at her courage. She shook her head. "I shall stand and fight." *When they come, I will stand my ground.*

Just then, a Nishi fluttered up over Finn's body, its hands grasping and fondling Finn's corpse.

"Get away from him, you fiend!" Bellae howled.

"Guess what, pet?" the spirit wailed. "My master has changed his mind *again*! Now he wants you alive after spies discovered the Blue Wizard changed his mind *once more*!"

The Nishi's eyes widened in lunatic vigor as her head bobbled side to side. "Capture you, kill you, capture you, kill you, capture you, kill you…I mean, just make up your mind! Am I right you scabby, stupid squire?"

Bellae, slightly confused, just stared at the Nishi.

"So, stay here and die," the Nishi said. "Or, come with me, and I promise to get you to the White Wizard alive. Good de…"

The Nishi's words morphed into a howl as Bellae's forearm charm slammed into the specter's body, causing it to disappear.

"I seriously hate those things," Bellae whispered.

Jumeaux looked longingly at the open space behind them. The shimmering form of another Nishi wavered in the breeze. "I can save you. Come here," it called. He considered going to the specter before his gaze settled on his younger sister, who was mumbling.

She mocks me with her fake bravery, he thought. The seeds of enmity with his family were now blossoming into a fully grown tree of loathing.

"Bellae," Honey neighed, tied, along with the other horses, to the supply wagon. *"Let me loose!"* she pleaded.

Crann answered for her, *"She can't. If you show fear, the humans will as well. We must help them stay calm."*

"Too late for that, Cranny," Honey said icily. *"We are fodder, tied up."*

"See to the horses, Bellae," Friar instructed.

"I told you to shut it," Crann said quietly to Honey.

"Soon enough, I will," Honey said ominously.

"Hush, please."

"For Bellae, be quiet," Crann stated.

"For her," Honey replied.

"Keep it down out there," Grym said angrily. He gasped, seeing for the first time the horde before them. *"I have no problem with you humans being brave, but this seems especially foolish."*

"If you leave, Grym, don't come back," Bellae challenged. He scanned the fields behind them. Rolling his eyes, he slunk into her pocket. She smiled and gave him a gentle pat.

A great cheer rose up from the Dark Warriors' ranks. Just to the right of the bloodstained zone, a small gap was made to allow one of them to pass through. The man wore a full set of matching black armor accented with a woven pink and yellow cloth tied around his waist. Instead of a helmet he had several purple and white flags standing straight up across his head. His chest plate had sloppily painted symbols and pictures splattered across it. Most were unrecognizable, but a few could be identified as birds, flowers, and rainbows.

As he danced forward, a fresh round of laughter went up from the army. He was swinging a wooden staff with great flair. His wild gesticulations and random pointing seemed to excite his soldiers. Slopped with splotchy gold paint, his staff was adorned with all manner of odd objects, such as eggs, feathers, meat, wooden cups, and other trinkets, which swung wildly from the staff.

"This crap is seriously giving me a headache!" Luchar grumbled in frustration.

"It's their commander, dressing to mock opposing kings and generals with their ornate armor and grand insignia," Friar said solemnly.

"I don't think they had you in mind," Ritari said, chuckling.

"No, I suppose not." Friar smiled. "When he appears, it means their charge is imminent. Sound the Horn of Kayda one more time. Gleoi Dea, now would be a good time to make an entrance with the Elves."

"Can I shoot him?" Lovag begged.

"No, let him go through his gyrations. It would only make them charge sooner. We can use every second," Friar advised.

"Bring the squire boy to the White Wizard and you will be rewarded!" the Dark Warrior commander screamed. The Knights looked at each questioningly as Friar wheeled around to gaze upon Jumeaux.

Stop staring at me, old man, Jumeaux growled in his head.

The commander shouted something garbled. The Knights could only make out the words, "Reward…death of the girl." He then went right back to his odd gesturing.

"Should we make a break for the woods like Gleoi Dea?" Lontas asked, his arms sore and shaking from firing his bow so often.

"They want us to make that mistake so they can cut us down. We still have a chance if the Elves come," Friar said soberly. *Very slim, but still…*

Ritari took the horn and blew as hard as he could. The sound blasted again, but the Dark Warriors ignored it, too busy watching their commander's odd dance. His back was turned to the Knights as he made wild gestures.

Luchar grabbed Lontas' bow and fired awkwardly. The arrow pierced the commander's right thigh.

"Luchar!" Friar chastised.

"I can't take this crap annn-eeee-more!"

The Dark Warrior commander turned and smiled. "Paradise! You give my family Paradise!" He then repeated it in the language of the East.

His soldiers rumbled a deep chant, "Paradise!" Over and over in an ominously low tone they continued, while the commander changed the intensity of his signals.

"Bring him down! Bring him down, now!" Friar cried. Even as the arrows flew and pierced the backs of his legs and arms, he continued the signals. As the second volley of arrows slammed off the back of his chest plate, he turned, smiling. Blood was flowing freely from his many wounds. He gave them a nod, as if thanking them. His smile grew broader, revealing bloodstained teeth. He began coughing, and blood washed out his mouth, splashing onto the front of his armor and the ground.

Bellae looked up as something caught her eye. Arend, standing over three dead minotaurs, was gesticulating frantically for her to come to him. *I'm not leaving Finn or family!*

"Fire at their center and prepare for the charge! Stay close—do not get divided. They will quickly outflank us," Friar said as the commander dropped first to his knees and then fell on his face in a lifeless heap.

The Dark Warriors raised their weapons and yelled, "White Wizard, see my bravery! To die! To Paradise!" As a solitary mass, they charged towards the small band of Knights.

Arrows continued to slam into the center of their line. They no longer bothered sending the dead back but merely stepped over them.

"Bellae, leave Finn and stand behind me. Quickly, now, we must stay together. When they move around our flanks, draw up into a tight circle. Never surrender. There are things worse than death. Fight to our collective last breath," Friar instructed.

"But…Finn?" Bellae said, reluctant to leave his body.

"Bellae? Do not leave me tied up to be slaughtered," Honey pleaded.

"Can I free the horses?"

Friar did not answer because at that moment, a blood-curdling scream arose from the Dark Warriors. The center section formed a "V" wedge and made straight for the small line of Knights. Even with the arrows raining down upon the advancing triangle, the dead were instantly replaced. Like a breaker capping on the shore, anyone who fell was instantly replaced to keep the cresting wave intact.

"Yeeeeeees!" Luchar yelled, brandishing his massive battle-axe.

"Bellae!" Crann neighed desperately.

Gazing at Friar, Bellae saw his focus was totally on the advancing Dark Warriors.

"Crann, get to the forest and find Gleoi Dea!" she said, sprinting back to cut Crann's rope.

"I am not leaving without you. Get on," he said. Bellae smiled and shook her head as she let Honey loose. *"Stay safe,"* she pleaded. *"Getting the Elves is our only hope."*

"I will see you again," Honey said. Bellae had a tingling pain as she remembered Finn telling her the same thing before the dragon battle.

"Bellae! Back, now!" Friar yelled frantically. Bellae had never heard such alarm in his voice, or in anyone's, before.

The Dark Warriors were closing quickly. The warriors on the sides were already moving around to circle behind them.

With a quick glance towards Crann, she saw the horse cresting the hill towards the Forest of Creber. With a huge burst of speed, Honey was not far behind. The Dark Warriors were uninterested in the rider-less horses.

"Go child, cut the rope," Behalen beseeched.

Without a word, Bellae began cutting the rope of Lovag's horse.

"Bellae!" Gimelli yelled.

"Sorea, switch to your talons! Squires, draw swords. Lovag and Arquero, at your preference, switch."

The Dark Warriors were twenty yards and closing. Their huffing breath could now be heard as Bellae freed Musta-Yo, who joined Behalen near their Knights.

Klaufi, the aged horse of Lontas, was next.

"Back to Bellae, form up in front of the supply wagon," Friar said in a calm, resigned voice. With the supply wagon forming the back side, the Knights and squires formed a half circle in front of it. "Bellae, come, now!" Friar commanded.

Bellae could see the Dark Warriors closing in around them out of the corner of her eye. As she cut Klaufi loose, tears formed in her eyes. She would not leave Finn and the horses. A loud yell made her look. One of the Dark Warriors coming around on the side was sprinting ahead of the others and making a run for Bellae. She brandished her dagger towards him.

His eyes were savage with a lust for blood, and he was closing in fast. He wore tattered black clothes with sporadic silver armor. His pale blond hair was flying wildly as he ran. Trying to remember what Friar taught her, she placed her feet in a good stance and braced herself for the imminent impact.

The tip of the Dark Warriors' centerline was only a few yards away from the Knights. Arquero and Lovag shot one last time before drawing swords. Luchar roared with anger, but it was swallowed by the loud clangs echoing across the field as the mass of Dark Warriors fell against the frail line of Knights.

Luchar hacked furiously at the enemy, rage empowering his bedrock prowess. The fury coursing his veins was laced with enough restraint to make it lethal. He blocked a sword blow with the top of his axe. He then spun it down, slamming it into the attacker's chest. Before the blood splatter had fallen, his blade arced to his right and sliced through the thin chest armor of another attacker. The heavy axe obliterated the man's ribs and sternum on its way to cleaving his heart and chinking part of the spine. Without hesitation, he dislodged it in time to thrust it like a spear into the face of another, whose nose and mid face shattered and collapsed. The dead were quickly piling up in front of the Knights, the impromptu bulwark slowing down the Dark Warriors' assault.

Bellae trembled at the furious sounds of battle behind her. She took a step back as one of the Warriors closed in. Tears blurred her vision. *I will join you soon, Finn.*

"White Wizard reward me for killing the girl!" the man yelled. "Paradise!"

Twisting her body, she raised her dagger to swing at the attacker. Just as she did, an arrow whizzed just over her left shoulder, plowing into the warrior. It struck him right in the heart. His expression went blank as his knees buckled and skidded forward along the ground before his body collapsed backwards.

A hand grabbed Bellae's cloak and pulled her back towards the Knights. "Come with us," a familiar voice yelled as she stumbled backwards.

"I won't leave Finn!" she yelled, but the hands holding her overwhelmed even her intense will.

"Slide under the wagon!" Ritari yelled. With a fleeting glance towards Finn's body, Bellae obliged. For the first time, she realized it was

Lontas who was still holding onto her cloak. Once they squeezed under the supply wagon, she looked up to see a swarm of angry Dark Warriors closing in around them. With a yell, Ritari rammed his sword up into the stomach of a Dark Warrior who had tried to leap on top of him. The momentum of his jump and Ritari's strength sent the man flying up over his head and onto the supply wagon. Ritari slashed his sword across the soldier's chest. With his back to the enemy, a stream of the Dark Warriors cut between Luchar and Ritari, effectively cutting their meager forces in two.

Luchar, Lovag, Gimelli, and Jumeaux were on the right. The rest were on the left of the stream of Dark Warriors.

Jumeaux's head was spinning. *This can't be happening,* he thought as spasms of images squeezed through his eyes. Scenes of the chaotic battle flashed surreally in his mind. If the havoc had not surrounded him, he would have run. For the moment, at least, the enemy seemed to be focusing on Luchar.

"Oh, Bellae," Lontas said, finally releasing her cloak.

"Thanks, Lontas," Bellae said weakly as the horde surged all around them. Both of them realized it was just a matter of time before they would die.

"I got you," Arquero said, blocking a sword thrust meant for the two squires, quickly bringing his sword around he severed the neck of the attacker, only to be hit in the face by a war hammer. Bellae screamed as the sickening crunch of his jaw shattering echoed through her ears. Stunned, Arquero stood frozen, for a moment—fragments of teeth and bone snowed down the rivers of blood like miniature icebergs. His tongue flopped down, uncomfortably exposed with no lower jaw. Time seemed to slow as the squires watched his body convulse as blow after blow from the Dark Warriors landed on his ravaged body.

Luchar was now surrounded and swinging his axe wildly, slashing and hacking any Dark Warrior unwise enough to get close. Their heads could be seen popping backwards, doubling over, or being spun around. Suddenly, a large sword sliced into his right shoulder, sliding up and between his overlapping armor. The pain brought him to his knees, and he screamed loudly. The sword was withdrawn and readied for another strike. Luchar recoiled and then sprang forward, slamming his helmet into the uncovered face of the Dark Warrior just as he had raised his sword to strike again.

The Dark Warrior's head whipped backwards, blood spurting from his nose and forehead. Luchar's head exploded with pain as ringing echoed through his ears. Lights flashed across his eyes before dizziness swirled in his head. A Dark Warrior slammed a war hammer onto Luchar's new helmet. The lights in front of his eyes flared up in blinding brilliance before the world turned black and he fell hard to the ground.

He came to and howled in frustration—his helmet was again dented onto his head. He struggled to remove it as he cursed. Luchar stopped struggling. He could hear the loud clanging of metal desperately crashing into metal as the overwhelmed Knights battled around him. Time seemed to slow. He could hear Ritari yelling and the loud whoosh of his broadsword as it sliced through the air. Arquero groaned weakly, sounding as if he had a cloth jammed in his mouth. A loud thud was followed by Bellae uttering a weak, "Gimelli!"

Gimelli was screaming now. Jumeaux was sniveling.

Enraged, Luchar reached for his axe with his good arm. Trying to raise it with both hands, he howled—his injured arm made it too heavy.

"Looks as if we found a chubby pig stuffed into some dented armor," a cold voice rang. This time laughter resonated all around him.

Surrounded and blind, Luchar realized as his heart pounded with anxiety and anger. *To die like this? Not going to happen.* He forced both of his arms to grab his axe and sprang up.

"This swine has some fight left in him," the voice remarked, laughing.

Screaming, Luchar violently twisted his body to help his damaged arm swing the heavy axe. It whizzed through the air but hit nothing but wind.

"Whoa. Watch out boys," the Dark Warrior said. "This little piggy has spirit."

"He's hungry. Sorry, we have no slop for you!"

Pain seared into Luchar's arm, and he dropped to one knee. His axe fell lifelessly to the ground. Standing, he shook his head as laughter surrounded him.

Somewhere close he heard a horse neighing loudly and stamping.

Not gonna die like this! he thought. Breathing deeply and lowering his head, he charged blindly straight ahead. A surprised Dark Warrior gasped as the air was knocked out of his bewildered body. Ignoring the pain in his right shoulder and head, Luchar began swinging his fists and elbows wildly. He struck the surprised warrior repeatedly. He could feel hands clawing and hitting at his back to separate him from the squealing Dark Warrior. Now he could feel himself being lifted up.

Still swinging wildly, he heard a loud neighing right before a forceful blow slammed into his already distressed head. Once again, the world faded to black. His body went limp and crashed onto the ground.

"Luchar!" Bellae yelled. She had been separated from Lontas and had crawled back under the supply wagon. She pulled back her bow and released. A Dark Warrior fell as the arrow sliced into his neck. Seeing her, a dozen Dark Warriors moved in.

"Is that the brat we need, or the one we kill?" one asked casually.

"Doesn't he want them both now?"

Before anyone could answer, Honey, Crann, Musta-Yo, Behalen, and the other horses formed a ring around Bellae. They neighed loudly and reared up, lashing out violently with their front hooves.

"What are you doing here? I saw you run!" Bellae exclaimed, a small tear of gratitude forming in the corner of her eye.

"We saw no Elves, so decided to come back and fight," Honey neighed.

Bellae was grateful her horses had come back but sad that they would die with her. The warriors around her were brandishing spears.

"Watch out for the spears," Bellae yelled to her friends.

A loud crack of thunder behind them was followed by a darkening of the sky to the north.

After Tacet-Vand made several gestures to IleZuri, the warrior turned to whisper to the young Elf.

"Arend, we have to leave, right now!" Kainen screamed.

Nodding, the tired Eaglian took off and flew in a semi-circle before gently picking up his friend, heading away from the coming tempest. He squawked in rage at the army surrounding the one person he was charged with protecting, Bellae.

"I know, I know!" Kainen yelled. "I see her too, but we have to get out of here!"

"Time for us to depart as well, Tacet-Vand," IleZuri yelled. The wizard nodded. A bright light engulfed both of them just before they disappeared.

The remaining Watcher quickly burned the bodies of the dead minotaurs and Watchers before disappearing himself.

Pausing the combat, the Dark Warriors, Knights, and squires saw colossal black storm clouds rolling and lurching with unnatural fury and speed straight for them.

Scroll 7: Sight for Sore Eyes

A loud horn blasted through the air.

The Horns of Infula! Friar thought gratefully.

Bellae grabbed one of the Knights' spears from the supply wagon behind her. Using all of her diminutive weight, she lunged forward. The tip glided between Crann and Honey, slicing into the mouth of one of the Dark Warriors who had been gazing up at the supernatural clouds. The tip went in deeper than she expected, smashing into the back of his skull. Blood spurted everywhere as he gurgled and fell. The horses took that as an order to attack, instantly rearing up and slamming their hooves into the heads and chests of the distracted Dark Warriors.

Seeing a warrior move towards Crann, Bellae lunged again. Her spear sliced into the man's stomach. She grunted as it severed his descending aorta before crashing into his spine. Unaware of the laceration, his faithfully beating heart blindly pumped his blood into his abdomen and pelvis.

Growing paler by the second, he keeled over quickly. With her spear and the horses' hooves, they slowly began to push the Dark Warriors back.

Surrounded by Dark Warriors, Lovag, Gimelli, Lontas, and Jumeaux stood back to back over Luchar's unconscious body. Lovag's skin was littered with superficial cuts. Wounds oozing blood crisscrossed all over his body as the slashes started to blur together.

Friar, Sorea, Scelto, and Ritari had formed a circle around Arquero's lifeless body as the massive and chaotic bank of storm clouds thundering across the sky moved over them.

"Veneficus!" Friar yelled, laughing.

Tears of joy and relief formed in the corners of his eyes. He looked down to see his cloak stained with blood and coated with fragments of tissue, looking like the bits left over from a great feast. He could feel the aches in his body and the throbbing pain from the cuts and lacerations sporadically answering a roll call from around his body.

The Dark Warriors looked confused for a moment. A cry from the back of their line rang out. "The Proliate and Magicians!"

Instead of fear, they seemed exhilarated, once again shouting their bewildering mantra, "Paradise!"

Storlax and Lidenskap rode on either side of Veneficus. The Proliate commanders seemed to be enjoying the unnatural speed Veneficus' magic offered. The horse's feet barely touched the ground as each stride carried them forward five times farther than without the spell.

Veneficus hunched forward, holding his crosier out like a lance. Its crystal glowed blindingly bright while he chanted repeatedly, "Prodigiosis volo omnes!"

"The Blue Wizard is with them!" a Dark Warrior yelled. "Kill him, and the White Wizard will reward your family!"

"Paradise!" the army screeched. Seeming to forget the Knights, the army of Dark Warriors lustily streamed out to meet the charging Proliate and Magicians.

"Desino avta aon-prodigiosis volo!" Veneficus shouted. The horses of the Proliate and Magicians slammed to the ground, no longer uplifted with magic. With a cloud of dust, they managed to keep running with normal strides as the dark storm above them slowly dissipated.

The Dark Warriors closest to the advancing Proliate formed up lines to prepare for the new attackers. Directly behind Veneficus and General Lidenskap were about twenty Magicians. Spread out on the heels of the Magicians were several divisions of Proliators. The ultra-loyal and fierce Sanctus Divisions with their red shields and helmets took the center.

Figure 2: A large force of Dark Warriors has appeared outside the Forest of Creber, and Supreme Master Magician Veneficus speeds his fellow Magicians and the Proliate Warriors to battle.

On the flanks were the Ultor Divisions with their silver shields and helmets. All the Proliate had their ferocious merja spears pointing forward.

Laughing and pointing, the Dark Warriors seemed more excited to face the approaching army than they had the Knights.

"Take that," Crann neighed fiercely. He shot his hooves out in a series of repeating strikes. Each combination crumpled the back of a Dark Warrior's head in deeper.

About thirty Dark Warriors remained to cordon off the Knights. Their eyes danced furtively in the direction of the Proliate, seemingly discouraged, as if missing the opportunity to partake in the main event.

The dead lay scattered like leaves all around the Knights. In various places, the bodies were piled so high the contorted corpses looked like bloodied piles of logs.

As they approached the charging Proliate, the first row of Dark Warriors yelled, "See me, White Wizard!" They purposefully ran headlong towards the Magicians and glistening tips of the Proliators' merja spears. The second and third rows followed close behind.

The two forces were only twenty yards away from each other. The small row of magicians all chanted, "Faire incendie." Dazzling beams of hot light flew out of their crosiers, slicing through the Dark Warriors. Some Dark Warriors had holes burned clean through their bodies, the cauterizing light blackening the edges. Some beams took off heads, others arms or legs.

As the Magicians were about to crash into the enemy, they pulled their horses' reins and chanted. The horses levitated, letting the Red Guard ride underneath them to take the front line as the Magicians flew to the rear.

A wall of iron spears closed in on the Dark Warriors. Any gaps caused by the Magician's enchantments were quickly filled in with the Warriors' second row, who also screamed, "Paradise!"

The Proliate lowered their merja spears to heart level of the front line of Dark Warriors running towards them.

The Proliate front line yelled a war cry with their spears mere inches from their targets. The tips ripped into the chests and abdomens of the sporadically armored Dark Warriors. The sickening crunch of bones shattering mixed with a wet, fleshy squish that sent blood and bodily fluids flying up like a savage wave. The bodies of the speared warriors were wrenched violently. Some folded like limp leaves as the weight of the rider and horse easily forced the spear clear through their badly gashed bodies.

Others had various parts of their bodies torn or ripped apart. Some had their shoulders blown apart as their bodies spun and flailed wildly before slumping to the ground. A few had their heads whipped back as the relatively weak mid face and orbits of their skulls were obliterated. Almost to a man, the frontline of Dark Warriors were instantly killed.

Most Proliate spears were buried too deeply within the Dark Warriors' dead bodies to be withdrawn, rendering them useless. The sprinting second line of the Dark Warriors took advantage of this, leaping forward to viciously kill the Proliate horses. Some dove underneath the spears and skewered bodies while others wove their way sideways to get access. Slicing wildly at the horses' front legs or underbellies, the second line of the Dark Warriors brought the entire first line of Proliate horses crashing down. Neighing cries of pain spewed out from the dying horses. Bellae gasped and closed her eyes as she felt their searing agony.

The front line of Proliate riders were pitched forward violently, many thrust over the necks of their dying horses. Howls of anguish and pain filled the air as the second line of Dark Warriors mercilessly set upon the fallen Proliate, quickly cutting them down.

The hard charging second line of Proliate quickly closed in on the second line of Dark Warriors, killing their comrades. A sickening thud resonated on the field of battle as their merja spears found their marks. The savage strikes easily slid into the flesh and bones of the Dark Warriors. Several were purposefully hit in the head, whipping their necks backwards as their skulls fragmented, sending chunks of brain spraying. Others had the spear tips slice into their chests or abdomens, exploding flesh and ripping vital organs.

An unusual, high-pitched horn pierced the air. Wordlessly, the Dark Warriors began an orderly retreat to regroup. Those still unscathed began sprinting back behind their lines. Any Dark Warriors too injured to regroup threw themselves wildly at the second line of the Proliate.

Their suicidal stand had created a mass of dead horses, Proliate, and Dark Warriors, forming an almost impenetrable barrier.

Only half the Dark Warriors guarding the Knights stood their ground, watching the battle like spectators while the rest joined the others regrouping to fight the Proliate. Exhausted, bloodied, and still outnumbered, the beleaguered Knights were content to continue their role as observers during the temporary stalemate.

The flanks of the bloody barricade of dead and dying exploded with activity as the speeding Proliate rounded the corners on both ends of the obstruction. "Re-form lines!" Storlax shouted the order as the Proliate pouring around the ends began to converge, some right where the Dark Warriors surrounded the Knights.

Complete chaos ensued. The Proliate began attacking the Dark Warriors around the Knights and squires, not seeming to know what to make of the ring of horses and Bellae.

"Get on!" Crann said desperately.

"No! Get on me. I'm faster," Honey yelled. The two horses collided as a wave of Proliate cavalry descended upon them. Bellae was knocked back on top of Finn and separated from the horses. Pounding hooves and slashing weapons created havoc. She tried to stand up, but a horse's shoulder slammed into her. She struggled to get back to her horses as the mayhem of the advancing army swarmed over her. She barely escaped being trampled several times. Thinking she heard Crann, she dashed under a slow-moving horse and continued to dodge and weave precariously between the charging Proliators and dying Dark Warriors. The other squires were embroiled in similar confusion. Gimelli, Lontas, and Jumeaux were driven towards Lidenskap.

Seeing the three squires, he gasped, "Children!" *It's Jumeaux, the one Veneficus spoke of,* he thought, quickly yelling orders. "Move these children to the rear of the line and then to Ragorsaf outpost. This is your *only* priority!"

"Where are the others?" Lidenskap asked, searching for Bellae.

"Not sure—we were separated," Gimelli gasped.

They felt hands grabbing, yanking, pulling them roughly up and onto the horses next to the armored bodies of the Proliate. The squires found themselves lying uncomfortably on their stomachs as their riders turned and rode for the rear. Lidenskap motioned to several other Red Guard to follow them as he rode into the fighting. The three squires were starting to feel motion sick when they heard a familiar voice.

"Squires!" Veneficus shouted frantically. "Are you injured?" he asked sincerely. His eyes scanned their bodies for damage. "Jumeaux, are you injured?"

"No, sir," Jumeaux stated, awed that such a great man would remember him, or care.

"Wonderful," he said, relieved. "We were on the way when we heard the Horn of Kayda and came as quickly as possible. Thank you for bringing the squires this far, my Proliate brothers. I will take charge of these youngsters," Veneficus stated.

The Red Guard looked at each other, deeply concerned about disobeying Lidenskap's orders, but relented, more terrified of going against the Supreme Master Magician.

Veneficus nodded understandingly. "I, along with the Magical League, will take full responsibility with your commanders," he said, helping get the children down from the Proliate horses.

As the Proliate reluctantly left, Veneficus leaned towards the children. "Where are the rest of the squires?" He signaled to some of the Magicians lingering behind them to move forward to search for Bellae.

"We were separated," Gimelli said. "There were so many Dark Warriors. Arquero is dead, and Luchar is badly injured."

Several Magicians rode up with two extra horses from dead Proliate, and the gangly Klaufi. "Ride these," a thin, pasty looking Magician said. His deep-set brown eyes looked warm and caring.

"Klaufi! I can't believe you made it!" Lontas howled as the squires quickly mounted the horses.

"You know this wretched beast?" a Magician scoffed.

Lontas nodded proudly.

"You are in grave danger here. Go with my companions. I will see you soon," Veneficus said, riding off to search for Bellae.

The three squires and Magicians began to ride around the left flank of the flesh, blood, and gore that was the curtain of dead soldiers and horses littering the battlefield.

"I wonder where Bellae is?" Gimelli asked Jumeaux internally. She was also worried about Scelto but knew Jumeaux would make fun of her if she mentioned him.

"I don't know," he answered coldly. *Can't she just be happy I'm here and alive?*

Several dozen Dark Warriors broke off from their main lines to attack the Knights and Proliate now battling around their supply wagon and Finn's dead body.

Honey appeared in front of Bellae and yelled, *"Grab my mane!"*

"So glad to see you!"

She desperately lunged up and grabbed onto the large horse's mane. With a slight wince the horse shot off, trying to get Bellae away from the battle. A couple of wounded Dark Warriors managed to pull themselves up and brandished spears at the massive horse.

"Get down. I'll fight off these soldiers. Make for the forest," Honey stated while snorting angrily at the warriors in front of her.

I'll come back for you, Finn, Bellae thought, obliging her horse and running for the forest. Her route was too close to the back of the Dark Warriors reforming lines, and several broke off in pursuit.

In the chaos of battle, Scelto was separated from Friar, Sorea, and Ritari while they were fighting above Arquero's body. The squire struggled against three Dark Warriors by himself. After picking up a discarded shield, he was holding his own. Despite his youth he had the size and strength of a man. Seeing him fighting, the Red Guard slammed into action to help. They drew their swords and began hacking at the Dark Warriors. As the horses jockeyed around him, Scelto was knocked to the ground and about to be trampled when Lidenskap rode up and ordered his Proliate to form up around Scelto.

"Come, boy! Get up if you can," Lidenskap commanded.

Just then the Dark Warriors' sickly sounding horn blared out again.

"They have re-formed and are attacking," Storlax shouted over in the center of the Proliate line. "Re-form into lines, now!"

"You three, take this squire to Ragorsaf, where the other squires are going," Lidenskap shouted, still unaware they had been diverted by Veneficus. Even after the news of the massacre at the end of the Tournament, the idea, planted by Tallcon himself, of unifying the Knights under Proliate rule still flickered as a possibility. If nothing else, perhaps he could steal a future Knight.

As Scelto headed off to the west with his Proliate escort, Lontas, Jumeaux, and Gimelli followed the Magicians northeast, riding back towards the Way of Trepas.

"There's Bellae!" Lontas yelled, pulling up on his sickly and lagging horse.

Gimelli looked back to see Bellae being chased by two Dark Warriors towards the Forest of Creber. "Bellae! How in the world did she get way over there? Come on, Lontas! We have to help her," she shouted desperately.

The Magicians riding with them quickly surrounded the squires' horses.

"You *will* come with us to safety. Let the Proliate deal with the Dark Warriors and that squire," the thin Magician said calmly.

"The Proliate are re-forming lines preparing for a counter attack!" Gimelli cried, her voice cracking with desperation. "Do you see anyone going to help my baby sister?"

"We're not a-a-a-sking. We're telling. We r-r-r-*are* going after her," Lontas said coldly. He felt a surge of adrenaline as the memories of all the times Bellae had come to his aid flooded his mind.

The Magicians raised their crosiers ominously. Gimelli swatted the closest one aside. She was about to say something when Jumeaux cried out, "The Dark Warriors are attacking! Let's get out of here."

The thin dark-eyed magician nodded approvingly. "Wise, very wise, young man."

"Jumeaux! How can you leave your sister?" Gimelli demanded, ignoring the Magician. Tears were now glistening in her eyes as she pointed to Bellae, who was getting close to the edge of the Forest of Creber.

"Would you come after me?" he asked her telepathically.

"You better know the answer to that. I always have your back, Jumeaux."

"I guess you mean you 'own my back,' given the daggers you have stabbed into it," he replied maliciously.

"You better not believe that. Now, wake up and fight for your sister," she scolded out loud.

"We are going after our sister, now," Gimelli declared, urging her horse forward. The Magicians shined their bright crosiers in front of the three squires as the thin, gaunt Magician moved forward. "You," he yelled, a sinister look flashing behind his cavernous eyes. Stopping, he took a calm, deep breath. "We appreciate your bravery. However, we have our orders from Veneficus himself. We *will* take you to safety. You can ride with us freely or, if you prefer, you can be paralyzed and levitated there."

"Cool!" Jumeaux cried out in excitement. Gimelli shot him a menacing look. Lontas and Gimelli looked at each other in frustration. They had no choice but to ride with the Magicians and bide their time.

Seeing the children's resignation, the Magician nodded. "That's better."

The pack of Magicians and three squires rode off through the flies that had started to flock to the smells of spilled blood and opened flesh wafting about. Scavenger birds circled above, patiently waiting for the armies to prepare their feast by finishing killing each other. Behind them they could hear the shouts of the Proliate and neighing of horses as they formed up for the Dark Warriors charge.

Leaning towards Lontas, Gimelli whispered, "Stay alert and wait for my signal."

He nodded, but a bead of sweat appeared on his forehead as his heart rate surged anxiously. The two rode off behind Jumeaux and the

Magicians. The hooves of their horses squished, more than galloped, through the blood-soaked ground. The moans of the dying tugged at their hearts as the stench encroached on their nostrils. Gimelli twisted to see Bellae entering the Forest of Creber with Dark Warriors closing in.

From across the battlefield, Friar also looked up to see Bellae devoured by the massive forest. Part of him ached, knowing he would never see her again. *I have taught you all I could in the short time we had. Now, as is each generation's duty, you must learn and live on your own time.*

Scroll 8: Darkness Descends

Keep running and use your size to move quickly, Bellae thought as she crashed into the thick Forest of Creber. Moving deeper, the world quickly became dim, save for rare streaks of light shearing their way through the leafy canopy. She pushed through the lower branches as golden leaves crunched under her feet. Her breathing seemed loud and labored.

Eventually, her eyes adjusted to the dark, allowing her to speed up and put some distance between herself and the attackers. She tried to take slow deep breaths to calm her pounding heart but could feel the weight of their presence pushing down on her back. She had seen enough of them to know she could expect no mercy. She winced as each crunching step seemed a beacon for them to follow.

Finn, guide me! she screamed in her mind.

The Dark Warriors shattered through the forest. Despite her effort, they were closing. A little whimper of terror escaped from her dry lips as she pushed forward.

"IIIIIIIIIII caaaaaaan *SEEEEEEE* youuuuuuu!" one of the Dark Warriors belted out tunefully. Ominous laughter followed.

A shiver of fear ripped through her. Weakness dripped into her knees, and they buckled. Panting, she slid behind a tree.

Where are the Elves? Where's Gleoi Dea? she wondered fearfully.

Looking around she took note of the trees around her. They were different from the arbor breith or birth trees that Finn had described. *These must be the outer ring trees that he talked about.*

"What's going on here?" Grym interrupted.

Bellae motioned for him to be quiet as an evil laugh erupted from behind her. Their loud stomping would help her move without giving away her position. Every inch of her wanted to curl up and hide, but she knew that would lead to certain death.

Get up, keep moving.

Advancing as quickly and carefully as possible, she made her way deeper into the forest, trying to time her steps to flow with theirs.

A dark streak rustled in the trees to her right, causing her to abruptly stop. *What is that?* Her heart raced as the darkness conjured its usual set of otherworldly tricks, placing masks of terror all around her. Simple twigs morphed into claws, branches into swaying foes. Terror gripped her as the black figure shot up between two trees, moving in silhouette against the gloomy upper canopy of the forest. Its back shuddered, and she made out wings.

Arend! she thought hopefully. *Or, is it a Watcher?* She shivered in revulsion at their flaking skin and piercing eyes. A part of her wanted to scream, *"If you're a Watcher, come end this!"*

Finn's smiling face flashed across her mind. *"My spirit will always be by your side."* She rubbed her Inion medal, closing her eyes. *I need that to be true.*

Opening her eyes, she peered into the unforgiving forest, spreading out in all directions like a dark, endless ocean of trees and obstacles. Looking up, she could see hints of cheap light, diluted by sheets of leaves and their supporting branches. The Dark Warriors continued to trudge through the forest like clumsy oxen. She could hear but not see them. A sudden loud rustle came from her right. It was the winged creature. The Dark Warriors, hearing it as well, moved towards the sound.

Bellae sighed deeply. *I have to find Gleoi Dea or the Elves,* she thought, rubbing her Inion medallion. *They have to help. I'm Finn's daughter.*

That thought opened up a deep bed of emotions that percolated up, flooding her with sadness. Death, loss, being alone, tired, hungry, darkness, parched lips, sweaty clothes. Each emotion demanded to be comforted and attended to. The burden pressed down on her soul and undermined her determination.

Closing her eyes, she leaned back against the tree. The tears came. She did not want them, but they did not ask permission or seem to have any interest in her wishes.

Hiding her face in her sleeve, she began to weep. At first, shaking slightly, but with each moment, the sobbing grew until they shook her into audible whimpers.

"Ah, I hear our little prize. We appreciate the sniveling," one of the Dark Warriors said, changing direction. "Don't worry your ugly rat head about crying. After we get to you, you won't have to suffer much longer. Well, you will, when we torture and slice you up, but after that you're home free."

Bellae whipped her head up. Something in the Dark Warrior's toxic words made her emotions snap from despair to fury. Standing up, she could see them now. Drawing her dagger, she pointed it towards the advancing attackers and yelled, "Come on, bloody swine! How about I gut you?"

As their laughter rang in her ears, she knew the words had no impact. She didn't care, suddenly understanding Luchar's anger. *Simple,* he had told her. Combat is simple. *Me against them.*

"What does despair smell like? We just found the stench in the girl's sniveling!" one of the Dark Warriors howled.

Wiping the tears from her eyes, she faced them. The two warriors lumbered noisily through the brush towards her. Evil gusts of laughter echoed off the trees so that the noise seemed to be coming from all around her.

She began kicking leaves and debris away, clearing a small area for good footing. *There's always a way to win. You better be right, Friar. Either way, it ends here and now.* Her left foot hit some loose dirt. Kneeling down, she picked up a handful. She rose just as the two came into full view.

"Oh, that's a cute little dagger," one of them said, laughing cruelly. He was the larger of the two. He had pale blonde hair that seemed to glow in the darkness of the forest. His face was covered with dirt and blood splatter from the fighting. Only his pale blue eyes were spared the exterior grime—their fiendish glow revealing his malicious heart. He held a mace in his right hand and a large axe in his left.

The other warrior was short and stocky. He wore chainmail under a muddy gray surcoat, which displayed a skeleton clutching a heart, and carried a large sword. A skull helmet covered his eyes but gave a perfect view of his grimy, filed teeth. His lips curled back in queasy delight. Smeared blood covered his face and hair.

"The big double-double-u will be most happy with us finding the girl," the tall one said.

"You mean the White Wizard?" the one with the grimy teeth asked.

"Who else in the bloody netherworld would I mean, dimwit?"

"You threw me."

"A leaf would throw you off, pinhead," the tall one yelled. "It's a riddle."

"What?"

"Clean the pile of wax out of your deaf ears, idiot."

"Not wax. When I gutted that Proliate Pig, I thought it would be cool to spread his guts and blood on my face."

"So stupid."

"No—intimidating it is. But I got some in my ears."

"Moron. You know what goes through the intestine? Anyway, did you hear the White Wizard speaking through your brain? The new order is take this putrid girl alive. Apparently, a spy in the Citadel informed him the Blue Wizard wants her as well as the boy."

"We don't get to kill her anymore?"

"That's what I just said! However, he did say injured was acceptable…"

Bellae was sizing them up while they continued arguing. She noted the short stocky one with bad teeth would have trouble moving his large sword in the thick forest. *Throw dirt in the eyes of the tall one, then attack grimy tooth one,* she planned. *Make him miss with that massive sword and strike at his neck.*

The taller one was making his way to her left while the stout one was coming straight for her. They began laughing. This time, Bellae held her tongue and waited for them to get closer. Thoughts of Finn steadied her mind.

Five feet away.

Each step was heavy and loud as it crunched the leaves and twigs. A loud creaking sound and thunderous shaking of leaves and branches shattered the air. The surprise and power of it unsettled Bellae and made her knees buckle. The feeling she had at the cemetery and other times she had seen the winged creature came flooding back. *Arend!*

A dark figure swooped down. The branch he had been perching on curved backwards violently under the force of its takeoff. Looking up, she saw two giant razor-like claws rip into the shorter Dark Warrior. One stabbed into his face before slashing upwards, degloving flesh and ripping the fake skull helmet off to reveal a real one. Each claw had three large talons pointing towards the front with a single claw to the back. The second claw dug into the warrior's right shoulder. Wrenching it up, the Eaglian tore the entire shoulder, chainmail and all, completely off. Bright red arterial blood erupted vigorously while the sapphire venous splashed limply.

With literal blind fury the hemorrhaging warrior began swinging his sword wildly through the air with his one good arm, the weight of the sword temporarily overcome by a burst of adrenaline. Arend tried to spread his wings, but the thick forest limited their movement. He let out a yelp of pain as they scraped across two trees.

After one last desperate slash, the shorter warrior finally succumbed to his injuries and fell, spasming in his death throes. A loud rustling sound drew Bellae's attention. Charging hard at her was the taller warrior. He raised his mace high. When he was three steps away, he leapt forward.

Taking two quick steps back, she raised her dagger to block the mace. With a loud clang, her dagger shot backwards under the force of his strike. Her small body was flung rearward, and she landed hard on her back. Skidding to a stop, she rose immediately. He was over her in a flash, this time swinging his axe. Bellae ducked, and the blade whizzed overhead, biting deeply into a tree.

Muttering, the Dark Warrior pulled, trying to release the embedded axe. Bellae seized the moment and slashed with an overhead strike. Her dagger bit deeply into his arm, bouncing back when it hit bone. His face convulsed in pain. Leaving his axe in the tree, he swung his mace. Bellae leaned backwards as the top of it whizzed right in front of her. He swung again. She dodged his blow while backpedaling. Her back abruptly rammed into a tree, violently halting her movement.

"It took longer than I thought, but now I get to have some fun with you. The Wizard didn't say nothin' about you being in one piece," he said, smiling. Even from this distance Bellae could smell the putrid odor swirling from his filthy mouth.

Twisting back, he wound up to swing his mace. Bellae sank down and whirled around, ducking behind the tree. As the mace crashed into the bark, she was up and running, this time not worrying about silence, just distance. Behind her, a loud rustling sound was followed by a gurgling scream of pain. A louder thud sounded as the second Dark Warrior's body hit the forest floor.

She was not going back to risk an encounter with the creature killing the warriors. She thought it was Arend, but fear had blunted her ability to feel him. *What if I'm wrong?* Instead, she ran, ignoring the biting scrapes of stray branches as they whipped across her body, pulling, scratching.

When her muscles cried out in agony for her to stop, the darkness had come close to complete. Her legs gave out, and she fell, skidding to a stop on the bed of leaves. Tears she had not even known were falling coated her face. Just wanting all of her emotion, fatigue, and loneliness to go away, she closed her eyes.

Her ears strained for noise. *How long have I been running?*

Gently swaying and shifting sounds of the forest, along with the insects it harbored, performed around her in a comforting melody. Exhaustion reared up, and she faded into the refuge of sleep.

Scroll 9: Rescued Rescue

A hooting owl startled her awake. Groggily lifting her head from the cold, hard ground, wet leaves clung aggressively to her face. Urgent messages fired up across her body. Aches, pains, soreness, and tingling sensations from muscles that had fallen asleep during her deep doze all assaulted her brain. Swinging onto her back, she tried to sit up, her stiff muscles protesting but reluctantly obeying. She shook her arms and legs to try to get the pins and needles out of them and restore full feeling.

A shiver of uneasiness shook through her as panic knocked on her heart. The world was, in essence, no more dangerous than it had been the week before. However, Finn's death, the massacre at the Tournament, and the attack by the Dark Warriors had caused a monumental shift in her outlook on the world. Sometimes such mental frames of reference can be just as powerful as physical injuries, shaking the familiar until we feel unsteady and uncertain. Such uninvited reminders of life's frailty are frequently unwelcome, and universally unsettling.

Looking up to the owl, his large eyes opened and closed lazily as the top of its head bobbed gently up and down, completely relaxed.

"About time you woke up," Grym said, his voice agitated.

"Give it a rest," Borb said in Bellae's defense.

"Hey guys," Bellae croaked, her dry tongue bumping over parched lips. Despite Grym's grumpiness, she was happy to see the two familiar faces sitting to her left.

"What?" Grym complained. *"I have a right to gripe. She almost crushed us, we haven't eaten, and that owl up there has been biding his time to devour us."*

"She's had a bit of a rough time as well," Borb replied.

The owl hooted loudly, staring excitedly at the squeaking mice.

"Quick, get in," Bellae said, sitting down and holding open her pocket.

"What about food?" Grym demanded as she shoved them in.

Scooting back against the tree, she searched the area around her. The darkness and wide-awake owl made her realize it was the middle of the night. The only faint light was courtesy of that reflected from Verngaurd's many moons.

Her ears perked at each cracking twig, rustling leaf, and animal call. Her eyes buzzed in shades of black as the shadows danced with life. The sounds of the forest seemed magnified and ominous, swimming in the inky night.

Her eyes scanned the pitch-black woods, mysterious shadows dancing in different gradations of darkness. *Whoever wrote about the stillness of the night was not out in it. They must have been looking out a window,* Bellae thought, bathed in a soup of gloom percolating with life.

"How long till morning?" she asked the owl.

No response.

"Excuse me, owl, how much longer until daylight?"

He puffed himself up and turned his head away.

Perhaps he wants my mice before he will talk? Bellae thought. *"Not going to happen. No more of my friends are dying."*

Loud cracking twigs all around her seized her attention. Shadows of movement whirled everywhere. She tentatively reached out her hand until it seemed to disappear in the soupy darkness. Her heart rate quickened and her chest tightened as fear slithered through her body. Thoughts of Dark Warriors stretching their hands into the darkness and grabbing her fueled her dread.

She placed her hands on top of her head and tried to slow her breaths. The forest seemed to spin, faster and faster. Trees, branches, leaves, and ground blurred into a dizzying backdrop.

Her brain screamed, *There's no way out!* The thick and massive trees whirled closer, forming a prison, as the world started to spin.

This is a cage.

There is no escape.

Gasping for air, the blurring scenery became solid black.

Sometime later, Grym and Borb rustled her awake.

"Get up! Get up!" Borb screamed.

"Oh, did we have a nice little nap?" Grym snapped. *"Perfect time for it—nothing really going on or anything. It's not like we are surrounded by hungry beasts."*

"How long was I out?"

"Way longer than would be prudent," Grym spouted.

Looking up, Bellae saw the owl still perched above but startled at a loud crashing sound extremely close by. Hooting, the owl flew off in a panic.

She reached for the dagger at her waist, but it was gone. *Oh, no!*

It must have fallen. Her heart filled with dread. A high-pitched howl from somewhere near pierced the night, inflating her apprehension.

Grym and Borb hustled into her pocket. *"That's as close as it sounds."*

A series of incredibly near howls confirmed the creatures' proximity.

The snapping of twigs and a multitude of footsteps circling all around the forest reminded her of the need to find her dagger. She searched desperately until her fingers tightened around its hilt. Just then, a series of concave black pupils floating ominously in a sea of bright yellow appeared right in front of her. They temporarily disappeared as their heads tilted backwards to bay at the dark tree canopy. Shivers sparked down Bellae's spine.

When the howling stopped, the terrifying eyes came into view again, and she pressed her back into the tree, wishing she could sink into it and escape.

"It's a baby human, not an Elf, so we can eat it!" a harsh, husky voice vibrated to her left. She turned to see two bright yellow eyes about four feet from hers.

"I-I'm no baby, and my father is an Elf," she stuttered through parched lips.

Her eyes darted around the forest in arcs, catching flashes of yellow eyes and shadows of large animals moving all around her.

"You understand us?" a voice rang out a couple feet in front of her.

She let out a little scream of surprise, not realizing one had moved so close. It was a large wolf with ears standing straight up, panting with anticipation. Bellae could feel its ravenous hunger. Unfortunately, it flashed sizable fangs dripping with slaver. Around the jaw area, a good portion of its gray fur was smattered rose—blood memories from previous kills.

Moving closer, its large mouth curled into a relaxed smile. It obviously saw her as no threat. *"You understand us?"* the wolf asked again, impatiently.

"Yes." The tree suddenly felt cold and rough against her back. She squeezed the hilt of the dagger tightly as four more wolves appeared in a ring around her. The one to her left, who had called her a baby, was closest. He was pitch black, except for glowing eyes. His head was down

with his nose only half an inch off the ground. Even in the darkness, moonlight would occasionally glisten off the saliva dripping methodically, expectantly.

Bellae looked from one to the other. She stopped on the only one that had glowing blue eyes.

"Beautiful eyes," she said. The other wolves chuckled.

"Did you hear that? You have beautiful eyes!" one of them growled.

The blue-eyed wolf snarled menacingly, first at the one who had spoken, and then at Bellae. He moved closer until she could hear his harsh, expectant breathing. Her mind raced for a way out. She took a chance. *"I know you cannot kill Elves, and I am the daughter of an Elf,"* she said, full of false courage. Reaching into her cloak, she brought out her Inion medallion.

The blue-eyed wolf paused. "You don't look or smell like an Elf. You lie."

"Even if you are part Elf, we're too hungry to care, little girl. Plus, the great snows will soon be softly falling in these woods," another growled.

A chorus of snarls ripped through the air as they all displayed their fangs. Bellae raised her dagger and slowly stood up despite the cries of sore muscles.

"She has a little knife—this will be fun," the wolf in front snarled. As he did, his whole nose scrunched backwards and wrinkled under his eyes, baring his sharp fangs. His tongue curled in excitement as clear saliva glistened in the pale moonlight.

A small opening in the forest allowed her to glimpse a moon just as wispy clouds slid around its edges, causing its reflected light to shimmer and dance in the mist as if it were bracing a frigid wind. She felt a chill of fear mingling with rising anger. *What do I do?* Thinking of Friar, she answered herself. Moving with surprising quickness, she slashed with her dagger and cut deeply into the first wolf's neck. He howled in pain as blood gushed onto the forest floor. Two of the other wolves sprang towards her in a rage.

Out of nowhere, two large hooves punched into the sides of the lunging wolves. They howled in agony and as they flew past her, slamming into the two remaining pack members. The four enraged and tangled wolves slid into a tree to her right. Looking up, she saw a massive horse snorting with fury.

"HONEY!" Bellae squealed in pure joy. For the first time in a long while, her body shook with utter happiness. *"Get them!"* she encouraged.

The wolf she had slashed lay writhing in front of her. The blood spurting from the gaping wound in his neck was joined by blood gurgling out of his nose and mouth.

"Nice kill," Honey cheered as she jumped over the writhing wolf and landed hard on two of the entangled wolves. She proceeded to stomp them repeatedly. Over and over her hooves battered into their bodies, sending up a chorus of sickening cracks and crunches, which echoed as their bones fractured. Soon, their lifeless bodies had blood trickling from all barren orifices: eyes, noses, and mouths.

The two remaining wolves skirted away and began circling about six feet away. Honey snorted while rising up on her back hooves, her front legs kicking wildly.

The wolves circled a few times. Howling at the moons in agonal frustration, they left. For several minutes after their departure, Honey paced and sniffed while scanning the woods for any sign of them.

"Honey, we need to go. They may come back, with friends."

"Just relax for a moment," Honey said.

"Where are the others? Where's Gimelli? I need to get to Friar."

Honey walked over to stand directly in front of her. The mare neighed and seemed to smile. Quickly rearing up, she smashed the dagger from Bellae's hand. Stinging pain rang up her arm from the jarring blow as the dagger fluttered into the woods.

"Honey!" Bellae said, hopelessly bewildered.

"You won't be going anywhere except to the White Wizard," Honey said ominously. *"I will take you to a portal and Ifrean."*

Shaking her head, Bellae chuckled.

"This is funny?"

All Bellae's previous joy evaporated, leaving a shell of exhaustion and confusion. She leaned back against the tree and shook her head in disbelief. *"You know what? Yeah, it kind of is. You have GOT to be kidding me. Can this get any worse?"*

"That's a fool's question," Honey snorted in disgust, reveling in Bellae's misery. *"Things can always get worse, much worse. My master would have hated it if those idiots killed you. He wants to savor eliminating you, of course, after he tortures you for information about the crystals you and your putrid kind keep hidden,"* Honey stated coldly. *"Oh, did you think you were the only one who can speak with animals?"*

"What information? What crystals?"

Honey neighed, snorting in her face. *"I would advise you not to play the stupid act. It will prolong your agony. He was afraid you would get past the Nishi, so sent me in."*

"Honey, I honestly have no idea what you're talking about."

Honey snorted in contempt. *"The White Wizard instructed me to infiltrate your castle, knowing your fondness for animals. I can't believe I had to spend all that time with the old fool, Quengeln, just to get to you. That buffoon can't even control his own urine, much less a horse. He was always wetting himself and blaming us for 'spilling water' on his pants. Then I had to listen to you and your stupid mice string along your banal banter day after day. After all that, here you are telling me you know nothing?"*

The horse paused. *"You better remember the prophecy and the location of the Power Crystals before you meet the White Wizard. Or is it your jerk brother, Jumeaux, who knows? The White Wizard was shrewd to change the order and bring you both in."*

Tears formed in Bellae's eyes as her arms dropped heavily to her sides. *"I don't know anything about the ridiculous prophecy and I couldn't care less about it,"* she added, holding her Inion. Her hand brushed against the kalma-kunnia, and a spark ran through her body, and, briefly, two evil eyes flashed before her.

"Ah, I guess I can let you in on a little secret. The White Wizard swapped the original kalma-kunnia with that version so he could keep tabs on you," Honey said impassively. *"That's how I found you."*

Bellae wrenched it off and threw it deep into the forest.

"The master won't like you hurling away his toy. I hope he lets me watch your torture. Maybe he'll even let me help. Half the fun is the screaming," Honey said icily.

The surprise of Honey's betrayal did as much damage as the double-cross itself. "No, no, no, no," Bellae said through thickening tears. Wanting to yell and scream in frustration, she raised her head. No new sound came, only her continued sobs. Bellae shook her head in disgust at how wrong she had been about this horse.

"Who are you?" she sobbed.

"I am the one who fooled the famous animal talker, the Chosen One, or at least the sister to the One. I couldn't fool Crann, the slug. I'm the one who will make you walk and beg the whole trip to the portal, and then on to the White Wizard. Maybe a few bruises to soften you up, huh?" the horse said, rearing up to hit her. Bellae closed her eyes and waited.

A loud neigh pierced the air followed by a booming thud as hoof met flesh. Bellae cringed, her eyes shut so tightly it contorted her face in ghastly anticipation.

Nothing.

She waited longer before cautiously opening her eyes, peering into the gloom.

"YEAH!" she screamed louder than she ever had in her life. There, in front of her was Crann. His upright mane stood at attention, and his eyes blazed with rage. A growling neigh rumbled through him. His thick cord-like tail swayed ominously—it would be the one advantage that he had against the much larger Honey.

"I knew you were an evil jackass," Crann neighed. *"I followed you. Thanks for leading me to Bellae, you second-rate donkey!"*

"Getting to kill you, and take the girl? Fantastic!" Honey replied.

The two horses stood looking at each other. Both had fire and malice in their eyes. Honey moved first, rearing up and baring her teeth. Both front legs kicked wildly. Crann also reared up and started kicking. Honey moved quickly to her right side and bit down deeply on the back of Crann's neck. With her teeth clamped, she shook her head, tearing and ripping at the flesh of Crann's neck.

Bellae's knees wobbled, stunned at the pain radiating from her beloved horse's neck.

Crann shook his head wildly and tried to buck away. Honey let go only to take several more bites, each sending blood gushing. Crann used a break to whip his tail. It smacked loudly against Honey's neck. The blow startled the large mare long enough to allow Crann to turn around and kick both rear legs up. His back right hoof slammed into Honey's chest. The blow startled her, and she briefly put her head down in pain.

Crann circled around and raised his front hooves in hopes of hammering Honey's stunned head. Crann came down on air as Honey quickly raised up before biting down on Crann's already battered neck. Crann neighed in agony at the new gash inflicted. The two horses circled each other like a tornado, both trying to get the upper hand and bite the other's neck. They crashed head to head hard enough to buckle their front knees, and both went down briefly. Honey was the first one up, and she pounded Crann's head with two quick blows before spinning and landing a back kick to his shoulder. In desperation Crann sent his tail limply flying towards Honey. It landed ineffectively as Honey neighed pompously. Bellae screamed and frantically began searching for her dagger.

"Crann will not die!" she shrieked. Frustration ripped at her, wondering why she hadn't looked for her dagger earlier. Honey was talking to Crann in a quiet voice, and she knew she had to hurry. Finally, she saw a faint glint of moonlight on metal a few feet away and quietly picked up her dagger. Morning was just starting to manifest itself as the predawn light whirled together with the still-controlling darkness.

A loud rattling noise from the canopy above made Bellae jump, and she dropped her recently found prize. A black form dropped down from the sky and landed right on Honey. Two gigantic talons ripped into Honey's neck and back. The mare whinnied in pain, and her whole body convulsed in agony. Large wings spread out and blocked out the small amount of light that had been filtering through the canopy above.

Honey reared up high and bared her teeth. She chomped desperately several times before starting to weaken. A feeble whinny gurgled out. The creature's face slammed into Honey's muzzle, and its razor-sharp beak ripped off the entire front half of the horse's face.

Like a torrential rain, blood roared out of the horse's destroyed face, forcibly splattering on the dry fall leaves. Honey collapsed with a resounding thud. Nothing left of her life but the flow of sterile blood to be fed back to the earth.

Bellae turned from the horror to grab her dagger.

"You will not kill Crann!" she screamed. Her hand closed around the hilt in a death grip. It would not fall from her hand again. She swiveled to see the giant creature with its two large talons dug deep into the bloodied back of Honey. The creature raised its head and let out a primordial screech. With several intense flaps of its wings, it lifted the limp horse up and swung it out of the way, spraying blood ubiquitously over all the nearby trees. Honey's body flopped to a heavy landing and then was completely still. A rigid silence settled on the forest.

Crann looked up at the creature with dazed eyes. Bellae rushed to stand between the creature and Crann.

"Don't you recognize me, Bellae?"

"Arend?"

"Of course. Sorry I couldn't get to you sooner. Several groups of Dark Warriors made it into the forest looking for you," the Eaglian said. "After I took care of them, I was disoriented and couldn't find you until you screamed."

His white-feathered head was stained cardinal with blood. Bellae flinched at the blood and strands of flesh dripping freely from his terrifying orange-yellow beak. Human-like hands rose up to pick at rows of teeth, which came into view as he opened his fearsome beak.

As Bellae looked closer, she saw his muscular shoulders, arms, and abdomen were like a human's. Waist down, he was covered in thick brown feathers. His legs dove backwards before doubling back underneath, as if his knees were backwards. They ended in two mammoth claws.

Crann neighed weakly, and Bellae felt his pain.

"Oh, Crann. I'm so sorry," she said thickly, her throat choking with emotion at his bloodied body.

"I told you that horse was evil," Crann said feebly.

"Rub it in. I deserve it. Although, you didn't use your tail enough in the fight."

"Always a critic," Crann neighed. His brain whirled in fatigue and pain. His eyelids fluttered before closing as his body crumpled to the ground.

"Crann!" Bellae cried in desperation, quickly putting her head to his chest. His heart was beating. She moved her cheek to his mouth. Warm air was flowing regularly.

"Oh, Crann, I love you. I shall never ride another horse again."

"Are you okay?" Arend asked, looking over Bellae with concern.

"Yes," she replied in Ainmhi Caint.

"You just talk with me, Bellae," he said. "I don't understand when you use your gift."

"Of course, I'm sorry."

"I never knew someone could get into as much trouble as you. My dad always said girls are trouble—I guess he was right." At this, he started truly laughing. Suddenly, the laughter stopped, and a series of high-pitched noises reverberated out of him, "Yee-weeent-weeent-weeeent... yee-weeeeeent-yee-weeeeent."

Seeming embarrassed at the noise, he stopped laughing and looked down.

"My dad says that sound is primitive and comes from here," he said, pointing at his chest. "Our syrinx is a place where regular birds make their noises, but of course, we Eaglians are part human and have vocal cords as well and..." he paused, and for the first time, Bellae saw him for what he was, a boy.

He moved his two arms as he talked, and his large talons shuffled nervously as he continued. "Dad says we use should use our vocal cords—we are not simple birds."

He stopped abruptly. This time he cocked his head from side to side and twisted his head around.

"What is it?" Bellae asked, peering into the brightening forest.

Chapter Two

The League

Scroll 1: Stop Humming

As Bellae crashed into the forest chased by Dark Warriors, Storlax was yelling to his Proliate. "Reform the bloody lines!"

Suddenly, a strange humming sound arose from the Dark Warriors as the Proliate began to reform.

The gruff High Commander of the Proliate had always hated cavalry, thinking it "cheating." Storlax shook his head, *Enough fighting on horseback.*

"Red Guard, dismount. Get off the cursed horses and form shield wall!" he yelled in anger and frustration. "Silvers, take flanks, bring up the sprak," he said to the newly arrived Ultor Division.

The Proliate Red Guard dismounted and formed up opposite the Dark Warriors. As ordered, the Silver Ultor Divisions formed up on the far flanks with their dreaded lizard creatures, the sprak. The creatures' forked tongues flickered over their razor-sharp, backwards-slanting teeth. Occasionally, one would spit out reddish mucous or spread its menacing, sail-like appendages. They had not yet had their feeding for the day, and the spine-chilling beasts were itching for meat.

"I am pretty sure, other than Bellae, the squires have gone behind the Red Guard lines," Sorea stated to the Knights.

"Good," Friar replied as he anxiously scanned the bloody battle-field for them. "They'll be safe there. What about Arquero, Luchar, and Finn's body?"

"No sign of them," Lovag stated gravely.

The four searched with no luck until several cries went out from the Dark Warriors. "Let's head to the Proliate lines," Friar stated. "We'll finish the search after the battle."

"After what the Proliate and Magicians did? Running us out of the Citadel and blaming our allies for something they didn't do, the swine!" Ritari protested.

"Life offers us few easy, black and white choices. We usually have to choose between two bleak, gray alternatives," Friar stated. "In this case, I choose the Proliate over the crazies over there," he said, gesturing to the Dark Warriors.

"There's Finn's wooden sled, but I don't see his body," Lovag cried.

"If those sleazebags have his body…" Sorea said angrily.

"This is a mess," Friar said, surveying the carnage around them. "Let's get to the Red Guard."

As they approached the line, Lidenskap waved them over. Friar and Lidenskap embraced awkwardly. "Thank you for coming," Friar said humbly.

"Our pleasure," Lidenskap said proudly, purposefully saying nothing of his run-in with the squires.

"May we join your Proliate for this last charge?"

"It would be our honor to fight together," Lidenskap said, nodding.

Standing in formation with the Proliate, the Knights made a comical sight. The dirt, grime, and blood slopped all over the Knights stood in sharp contrast to the well-ordered Proliate. The Knights received more than one look of contempt.

"Some of our squires and injured Knights may be behind your lines," Friar stated.

"Once the Dark Warriors are defeated, we'll look for them," Lidenskap replied.

"Have you ever seen such a large force of Dark Warriors?" Friar asked.

"No," he answered anxiously. "This is very concerning for the future."

"We are grateful you came so quickly," Friar stated.

"You can thank Veneficus. He was the one with the foresight."

Once again, he comes to our aid, Friar thought.

As Storlax walked down the line, he noted the Knights. A malicious smile crept over his face, and he yelled, "If the detestable Elves come out from their hiding spot in the forest, kill them. Kill them all!"

Friar turned to see Storlax glaring back, daring Friar to challenge his order. Knowing it would do no good, Friar held his tongue. The Knights and Proliate spent a few moments bearing an uncomfortable silence.

Gratefully, Sorea broke the quiet. "What is that horrid humming?"

"The Dark Warriors have a death hum for their last charge," Friar answered. "They will attack until victory, or death."

"They hum?" Sorea challenged in disbelief.

"They do," Friar answered.

"Evil humming? I mean…an evil scream or wicked chanting, sure, but humming?"

"Sorea, there are some questions I just can't answer," Friar said with a slight smile.

She scrunched her face in dissatisfaction.

Leaning closer to Friar, Lidenskap whispered, "I hope the events at the end of the Tournament and this blatant attack have convinced you."

"Of what?" Friar asked, fearful of where the conversation was going.

"That you need to come under Proliate control," Lidenskap said.

The general quickly added, "Of course, you would be in command of your Knights, but a garrison of Red Guard would be stationed at each castle to watch over the temple we would build there. All expenses for the construction would be ours, naturally. We could then guarantee your protection."

Friar stared at him in awe. The humiliating idea of having the Red Guard inside their castles was such a blasphemous insult it left him speechless.

Lidenskap returned his gaze with fading hopefulness. "I know you and your squires felt the power and freedom of Tallcon at the ceremony.

Plus, with the atrocities committed by your so-called friends, an alliance with us seems an obvious choice. United we can defeat the insurgents and then face the Dark Warriors."

"I don't see that happening…"

Friar paused as the tattered shreds of optimism fragmented and fell, only to be quickly replaced with fury.

"…ever," Friar finally finished, not mincing words. "At least while one Knight still holds breath, our castles shall be our own. Your definition of 'alliance' is different than ours and sounds more like control."

"That troubles me," Lidenskap replied ominously. "We won't always be around to bail you out, and if your renegade friends keep aiding the Dark Warriors, I can't guarantee we won't end up fighting each other. That last Knight discarding his last breath may be closer than you think."

"No one can be assured of the future," Friar answered. The two men stared at each other, unblinking, for several moments before Lidenskap spoke again.

"You saw only a fraction of the allegations against you and your allies. There are even greater rumors circulating in the East, of terrible tragedies and traitorous deeds by the Elves of Creber and Northern Dwarves."

"That's the problem with ethereal gossip, isn't it?" Friar stated. "You stand these false rumors up against us, but they have no substance to them. They are like invisible ghosts, impossible to bring down with physical weapons or reality. Each sword blow we throw against them only serves to fan the flames of these lies."

"I could say the same thing about your claims. Given the mounting evidence, your denials have no substance either."

"The difference between them, good general, is ours has the wonderful advantage of being true."

"Time will tell," Lidenskap declared menacingly.

"Yes, it will. I assure you, our friends are no more insurgents than we are."

"Victory to the righteous, in Tallcon's good time," Lidenskap replied.

"Is that Luchar?" Sorea asked anxiously, greatly missing his martial comments.

Friar looked, thankful to have his attention diverted from Lidenskap. "That's him," Sorea said, dashing off.

Ritari went sprinting after her. The two arrived just as Luchar tried to sit up. He had the dead bodies of half a dozen Dark Warriors around and partially on him.

Luchar moaned and started to lie back down. The two Knights looked at each other and then back to Luchar. His "new" helmet was plastered onto his head just as the old had been at the Tournament. The rough outline of a hoof was stamped into it.

"Ritari!" Sorea shouted, panic etched on her face as she gazed at Luchar's bloody right shoulder. She ripped fabric from the shirt of a fallen warrior, carefully applying a pressure dressing as Ritari flipped the dead off his body.

Mumbling inaudibly, Luchar let out an occasional groan. Dried blood sat defiantly over every visible inch of his face and helmet. Sorea tried to gently lift it off, but he sat bolt upright, howling in pain. Looking dazed, he peered at Sorea through a small, dented opening. A flicker of recognition showed in his blood-rimmed eyes.

"Can you stand?" Sorea asked gently.

"I need to ask you something, and be honest," Luchar declared.

"All right," Sorea agreed, nervously eyeing the Dark Warriors' line.

"Is this injury to my head going to affect my status as a ladies man?" Both Ritari and Sorea burst out laughing.

"I thought you were going to ask whether you were going to die."

"Ah. These are but superficial scratches," he replied. His voice was steady, but his body wavered. A huge roar went up from the Dark Warriors line just as Friar and Lovag showed up at their side.

"Come on big guy," Lovag stated. "We need to get you moving, now."

"Just give me my axe and point me towards those dogs," Luchar declared. "Although you better stand me up first," he added. The others chuckled as he slowly got to his feet. Lovag got under his left arm, and Sorea stabilized his bloodied right side.

"At least the humming has stopped," Sorea said, hobbling towards the Proliate.

"Idiot helmet!" Luchar bellowed. "Twice in one week? Hephaestus is going to make my next one."

"I am not sure even he could build something to stand up to the punishment you dish out," Friar answered. "Right now, let's just get to the Proliate line."

"Yes, good idea. Give me my axe and get me to the center," Luchar said shakily.

"We better get that helmet off and your wounds looked at first," Friar said.

"You two, please see him to the back of the line, then, when you are able, rejoin us," Friar ordered Lovag and Sorea.

"I can make it. I don't need a stinking healer," Luchar growled.

"Humor me," Friar said, before whispering to Sorea, "Make sure the healer keeps him out of the battle. His head is hard, but even Luchar has limits."

Sorea nodded as they slowly made their way to the Proliate line.

A loud battle cry went up from behind them. Turning, they saw the mass of Dark Warriors charging. They desperately tried to judge the distance to the Proliate line.

"It's going to be close," Friar said, motioning to Lidenskap. He, in turn, gestured to Storlax, who nodded and yelled, "Advance! Keep shield wall!"

With blistering precision the wall of Proliate shields moved forward.

"That's a well-drilled unit," Ritari said appreciatively. Then, turning to Friar, he whispered, "Sounds like that conversation with Lidenskap didn't go so well."

"No," he answered sternly. "I fear the situation is progressing from bad to worse."

Ritari and Friar turned with swords drawn, carefully walking backwards through the littered battlefield with uneasy eyes on the attacking Dark Warriors.

"We'll make it?" Sorea asked as the advancing Dark Warriors sprinted with unbridled passion.

Scroll 2: Nice Kick

Gimelli looked behind to see the Dark Warriors charging the dismounted Proliate line. *Suicide*, she thought, seeing their impressive red shield wall and massive spears porcupining out. *Soon, we'll have our chance to break away. First, I need to butter them up.*

"I wanted to thank you *amaaazing* Magicians for all you did for the Tournament. You had things running so smoothly," she complimented.

The tall, thin Magician smiled. "You are most welcome and thank you for noticing."

"How long does it take to become a Master Magician like you?" she asked, smiling brightly.

"Jumeaux, why don't you come over here? You would be interested to hear this," the Magician declared.

Gimelli frowned. *This Magician is taking way too much of an interest in him.*

"My name is Fino, by the way," he said when Jumeaux was next to him.

Gimelli blushed with anger as the reality that he was the sallow Magician who had been in the back of the room as the Knights' weapons were being enchanted hit home. However, as the Magician started talking, Gimelli pushed the rage out of her mind.

She had bigger problems.

Gimelli stopped listening as the Magician droned on about all the years it took to become a Master. She did not notice how intently Jumeaux was listening and how proud he was of all the attention Fino heaped upon him.

Gimelli heedlessly nodded her head until the two armies collided with a thunderous crash of metal versus metal. Feigning shock, Gimelli screamed. "Oh, my! Thank you sooo much for rescuing us from that horrible battle. I am so glad you got us out of there!"

"Big Baby," Jumeaux claimed, too busy reveling in her perceived cowardice to doubt her sincerity.

Gimelli pulled up to move back next to a portly Magician and grabbed his arm as if she were frightened. She smiled broadly at him, and with a twinkle in her eyes said, "Sorry. Those sounds frighten me."

The plump Magician couldn't help believing her smile. In reality, she yearned to be back there in the thick of the battle with her Knight, Sorea.

The portly Magician patted her arm. "It is okay, dear. We'll protect you."

"Oh, I know you will. I saw you head into battle with your crosiers," she said, releasing his arm and gesturing as if she were holding one.

"Oh, give it up, Gimelli," Jumeaux said in disgust. "Don't be such a wimp!"

"I can't help it," she said, squeezing the chubby Magician's shoulder.

"My name is Trolleri," he said reassuringly. He adjusted his dark blue robes as if to emphasize he was a Master Magician.

"I'm Gimelli, just a simple squire." Slowing even more, she moved closer to Lontas and mouthed, "Get ready."

"What?" he whispered. Gimelli didn't reply but raised her eyebrows and had "that look" in her eyes that Lontas recognized. It was the same gaze Bellae got right before she led him into trouble. *Uh-oh!* he thought as Gimelli looked around furtively.

With the Magicians all looking away, she stood up in her saddle, leaned over and kicked Lontas as hard as she could. He looked at her with sad, helpless eyes as he flew off Klaufi. She sat down innocently as he soared feebly towards the ground. She pretended to be looking away as he cried out in pain, holding his right shoulder.

Trolleri reared his horse around as the thin, sad-looking Fino galloped over, looking suspiciously at the scene.

"Lontas, you are the biggest klutz in the world," Jumeaux said, laughing hysterically. The thin Magician looked up questioningly. "He does this?"

"Are you kidding? He falls literally all the time! Lont-loser is what we call him at Liberum. Being clumsy is what he's known for."

Gimelli dismounted and walked towards the writhing Lontas as Klaufi stood with cataract-obscured obliviousness.

"Trolleri, would you help me, please? Lontas seems hurt, and I can't pick him up alone," Gimelli said sweetly.

"Certainly," the Magician replied, grunting to dismount.

"I'm not that hurt. I…" Lontas said, attempting to stand-up. Gimelli quickly gave him the evil eye and put her knee in his side to prevent him from moving.

"Ow!" Lontas howled, stunned by what was happening.

As Trolleri neared, Gimelli mentioned to him, smiling, "Why don't you send the others ahead? I know you can handle this, and then we can catch up."

He hesitated, so she put her arm on his shoulder. "I am so immensely grateful you are here to protect us," she said, turning her head to the side and smiling innocently.

Trolleri adjusted his blue headband and nervously flung his ponytail around, obviously hesitating, unsure of what to make of the flattery.

Just then, the gaunt-looking Fino said, "Look! Our reserves are coming from the north. Get that klutz of a boy up so we can ride out to greet them properly."

Around fifty Master Magicians were riding towards them. All dressed in blue robes and riding horses. In the sky above, several Magicians were traveling on griffins.

"Ugh!" Lontas squealed as Gimelli dug her knee into his stomach.

Seeing her chance, Gimelli raised her eyebrows expectantly at Trolleri. "He might need a minute to lie here," she suggested. "He seems hurt, pretty bad." When Lontas was about to talk, Gimelli flashed him a deadly look and dug her knee into his ribs.

"Ahhhh!" he moaned, in real pain.

"Why don't you ride out to meet them," Trolleri advocated. "The boy needs a moment to gather himself. He may have bruised his rib the way he is holding them. When he's ready, this nice young lady and I can help him up and meet you shortly."

Fino hesitated, looking between the approaching Magicians and the two dismounted squires.

"We are a safe distance from the battle," Gimelli whispered to

Trolleri, encouraging him with another broad smile. There was no way they could escape from fifty Magicians.

"We are quite the distance from the battle. We'll be safe," Trolleri echoed.

"Very well," Fino declared. "You," he said, pointing to Jumeaux. "You stay with me. For your own safety, of course."

Jumeaux smiled brightly and nodded eagerly, loving being the center of favorable attention. All the Magicians, except Trolleri, rode off towards the advancing reinforcements with Jumeaux. Lontas lay on the ground, feeling hurt, literally and figuratively, still confused as to Gimelli's sudden abuse. He started to say something, but Gimelli cut him off with an admonishing glance.

"Trolleri, could you take that side to help him up?" she asked charmingly.

They both grabbed an arm and started to pull.

"Ow!" Gimelli said, suddenly elbowing Lontas' ribs and pushing his shoulder back, sending him falling again. He winced in pain as he landed on his already sore right shoulder.

Trolleri let go as Lontas' body twisted to the ground. The Magician stood up and looked at Gimelli in surprise.

Wincing in counterfeit pain, her expression changed to an apologetic one. "Sorry, you two. I think I pulled a muscle. Silly me," she said, holding her left shoulder. "I'm such a wimp! Trolleri, could you help him up by yourself? So sorry."

Trolleri set down his crosier, bent over, and grabbed both of Lontas' hands and heaved him up.

Gimelli made a deft move to grab the crosier but the Magician moved with surprising speed to snatch it himself. She outwardly smiled, while inwardly groaning as he eyed her suspiciously.

Lontas was feeling dumbfounded and insulted by the way Gimelli was acting. "I demand to know what has…"

He did not get to finish as Gimelli squealed again, "Oh wow, look at that battle raging!"

Lontas and Trolleri looked to see the fierce action as she moved towards the horses.

"Seriously, Gimelli, what…" Lontas started. This time he was interrupted by a loud neigh of pain coming from Trolleri's horse. The horse reared up and bolted towards the retreating Magicians and Jumeaux. Trolleri stood in shock while Gimelli sprang into action.

"Quick, Master Trolleri, run after your horse. Run! We can catch him," she yelled.

Trolleri seemed convinced and began running after his bolting horse. Gimelli deftly kicked his leg, tripping him and sending his paunchy body soaring through the air. He fell hard, and she purposefully landed on top of him.

"Ugh!" the Magician cried as the wind was knocked out of him, his crosier rolling harmlessly away.

"Get on Klaufi, now!" she yelled to Lontas. Trolleri started to rise, so Gimelli jammed the point of her elbow into his upper spine. He howled in pain and dropped back down to the ground with an *ooompf*.

The stunned Lontas began to protest, but Gimelli gave him a harsh look as she stood up. He mounted the oblivious Klaufi as fast as he could.

"Quickly! We ride for the forest," she said, smacking Klaufi in the rear.

"Aren't you coming?" Lontas squeaked helplessly as his horse bolted toward the forest.

"I'll catch up," she replied, running for the dropped crosier. Picking it up, she pointed it at the dumbfounded Trolleri.

"So much for a pulled muscle," he said dryly.

"Sorry about that, but my sister needs me," she answered, circling back to her horse.

"You can't use that crosier, silly girl," Trolleri said.

"Silly girl?" Gimelli raged. "You mean the girl that fooled you into thinking battle scared me? I am a squire of Liberum, bred to fight! Silly girl? You mean the one who just dropped you, and is standing over you, holding *your* crosier?"

Trolleri huffed in contempt, starting to rise.

"Ah-ah-ah! Stay on the ground and I will leave your crosier halfway between here and the forest. Otherwise, I break it," she warned, mounting her horse.

Ignoring her, Trolleri rose. "You have no chance. Give me my crosier, and we'll go easy on you. You can't defeat fifty Magicians," he said, walking towards her.

She stood up in her saddle and hit him on the head with his crosier. "Right now, I just need to beat you!" she thundered as he howled in pain.

As his arms reached up for his aching skull, she kicked him right in the chest, sending him tumbling backwards. Kicking into the flanks of her horse, she raced off towards the woods as the angry Trolleri began to scream for the other Magicians.

Gimelli's horse quickly caught up to Klaufi. "Come on," she chided, grabbing Klaufi's reins and pulling on the struggling old horse.

"What about Jumeaux?" Lontas asked.

"He'll find a way to come, if he wants to." With several hundred yards until they reached the section of forest behind the battle, she turned to see the Magicians charging hard.

"They're gaining!" she cried in a panic.

Lontas swiveled. "I didn't know you had it in you to be…so violent and deceitful."

"I'm sorry. I had to sell that you were hurt to get us separated from the other Magicians. He was right—we can't beat fifty Magicians. I hope you're all right, but this is my baby sister we're talking about. Time to get mean."

"Okay, but pushing me off my horse? Then, I saw you elbow, club, and kick that fat Magician guy."

Gimelli looked at him apologetically. "For you, sorry, but him? Not so much. Anyway, he should have let me go after my little sister. If they hurt her…" she stopped, letting Lontas imagine what she might do.

Lontas swallowed hard and said nothing for a moment. "I guess I was the logical choice to take a fall," he continued. "I mean, no one in the world has more practice falling than I do. Plus, that was a pretty nice kick."

Gimelli burst out laughing before turning to gauge the Magicians. She let out a gasp as a piercing squawk stabbed through the air above them.

Three griffins with Magician riders were streaking down from the sky.

Scroll 3: The Peaceful, Panicked, Pained, and Plagued

Back on the battlefield, Ritari slashed down with his sword and sliced into the chest of a Dark Warrior. With blood gushing from the flailing wound, he fell. Ritari stepped over him to attack another.

Sorea slashed up hard with a talon blade and caught a Dark Warrior under his chin. The blade gouged up through his skull and into his brain. His eyes popped open in wide-eyed terror before he went flying backwards into the next Dark Warrior, a savage stream of blood showering out. To add insult to injury, Sorea riddled his chest with a series of lightning-quick strikes from her talon blades.

Moving in close to any and all attackers, she could negate their reach advantage. She blocked the next Dark Warrior's axe attack with her left talon and dropped to her knees. With her free right talon she coated his legs in blood-gushing wounds thanks to a blistering barrage of impaling strikes. She severed both of his femoral arteries, and he quickly collapsed.

Lovag was using his scimitar sword to fend off three attackers, as the center of the advancing Proliator line was about to drive a wedge between the enemy's ranks.

"Reserves, to the center! Hit them noooow!" Storlax raged. "Follow me in," he screamed, charging into the back of the centerline. The pressure of the new forces helped break through the Dark Warriors' line. With their forces divided, the Dark Warriors did not retreat but responded with fierce cries and continued to fight.

Storlax signaled one of his commanders. Within moments, the spraks had been unleashed. The lizards slashed with teeth and claws around the flanks of the enemy line, creating chaos by biting and carving into the backs of the faltering Dark Warriors. If blood loss didn't kill them, the toxin in the spraks' saliva paralyzed the falling warriors.

This allowed the spraks to feast on their victims' flesh while they were still alive.

Taking advantage of the confusion, the Proliate completely encircled the beleaguered Dark Warrior army. It was now divided and surrounded.

"Surrender and end the bloodshed!" Storlax yelled.

The Dark Warriors laughed at the idea of surrender and threw themselves at their attackers with reckless abandon. Those without weapons simply flung themselves onto the spears and swords of the Proliate. To the last man, they fought and died.

A cheer rose up from the Proliate as the last Dark Warrior fell. The celebration didn't last long as the efficient Proliate began stacking the bodies like wood for a bonfire to the annoyance of the yearning scavenger birds. Still breathing deeply, the Knights clasped each other's arms, happy to be alive.

"Spread out and look for the squires and bodies of Arquero and Finn," Friar ordered, unsure if Bellae ever came out of the woods. As his few remaining Knights left, he gazed around the battlefield and whispered, "There are only four outcomes in war, and solely the first involves any serenity: the peaceful dead, the panicked dying, the pained wounded, and the nightmare-plagued living."

A groan went up about three feet from him. Turning, Friar saw a young Proliate warrior struggling to crawl. His helmet was off, and a large gash bisected his face. It started above his left ear and traversed his entire face, slashing through his cheeks, lips, and jawbone. As he crawled, his lip flapped helplessly, and you could see his shattered teeth and splayed-open tongue. Blood spurted out of his mouth in a shower of red that was littered with tiny white fragments of teeth and bone. He looked towards Friar with his mouth agape, and his eyes filled with pain and horror. As he struggled to talk, nerves and blood vessels swung from the shattered and jagged stumps of red-stained teeth as his nearly severed tongue dangled in agony.

"Healer!" Friar screamed, motioning to Lidenskap.

From skies teeming with hungry buzzards, expectant shrieks joined the groans and agonizing cries from the bloodstained ground. They circled the battlefield, looking for an opening to feast on flesh. A dark heaviness soaked the air, a signal death had joined the buzzards circling above, waiting patiently outside the crumbling door of life for the severely injured.

Scroll 4: Something Cooking?

"Stay here, Jumeaux," the Magician Fino said, looking with disgust at Gimelli and Lontas bolting towards the forest. "I should never have trusted them with that bloated fool, Trolleri."

Jumeaux looked from the gaunt face of Fino to his sister and Lontas. A battle raged in his heart and mind. Should he go fight for his sisters? Should he stay with the Magicians? He couldn't help thinking of all the disgrace and humiliation he had suffered as a squire, the times he tried to add humor, only to be rebuked.

The seeds of self-serving resentment sprouted to squeeze his heart. *It's precious Bellae and "sunshine" Gimelli everyone loves.* The invisible, but palpable, forces of jealousy and self-aggrandizement easily, and mercilessly, drowned sympathy and murdered love. He turned to Fino, who nodded respectfully, as if he had heard Jumeaux's thoughts.

"You can do amazing things with us, great and wonderful things. Veneficus knows you have a huge role to play in the future," Fino said.

Without realizing it, he had been leaning forward in the saddle apprehensively. Jumeaux smiled and relaxed—he was not going anywhere. He saw his twin turn. Their eyes locked, a small seed of uncertainty and guilt cracked into his mind. Jumeaux felt a twinge of anger and shook his head as if he could throw off his doubt. Anger quickly crushed hesitation.

Jumeaux smiled as his consciousness quickly created a sticky psychological web to catch any dissonant thoughts from rising. The suns seemed to shine brighter with the shadow of his sisters fading away from him.

Gimelli looked at the distance between the griffins and main forest—still a hundred feet to go. No way could they make it before the griffins descended upon them.

"Look, Lontas," she said, pointing to a closer crop of trees separated from the main Forest of Creber. "Let's head there."

As the two squires pushed their horses hard, the piercing and closing cries of the griffins stung their ears. Nearing the cluster of trees, a beam of hot light sliced in front of them. Startled, Gimelli's horse stopped suddenly, tossing her up and over its head. She landed with a hard thud, gasping as the wind left her lungs.

Klaufi continued to trot forward, unaware of the danger. Lontas pulled hard on the reins, but Klaufi stumbled right into the Magician's blue light. He jumped off just as a sickening *TTSSSSSSSTTT* sound erupted.

Lontas rolled and came to a stop near Gimelli. In a flash, she was on her feet and lifting him up. The sickly smell of burning flesh seared their noses. Poor Klaufi's body lay crumpled and headless on the ground, his singed and blackened flesh sizzling. Lontas started to throw up as Gimelli pushed him into the small grove of trees. The three griffins circled above as Lontas emptied his stomach. Occasionally, a burst of blue light from one of the Magicians riding overhead would scorch the earth around the grove as a warning.

The griffins were tannish-brown. They had large beaks and piercing black eyes. Large, diamond-shaped ears pointed up off their heads. All around their faces, thick, shaggy, brown manes flowed before coursing over their muscular chests and upper backs. Magician riders sat up front at the base of the beasts' woolly manes. Each one had his crosier pointing down at the ground.

Gimelli heard a loud neighing and turned her attention from the skies to her horse. She moved over a few feet to get a clear view.

Twitching in pain, her horse had obviously been hit by one of their shots of light. Its right side was sheared off with steam drifting skyward.

"Hurting horses? Cowards!" Gimelli screamed.

"What are we supposed to do now?" Lontas trembled.

"No idea," Gimelli admitted as panic started to rise within her. She ran through the thick underbrush to the other side of the small group of trees. There were only thirty feet separating them from the main body of the forest.

"Can we make it?" Lontas questioned.

"I'm not s—" A blast of blue light interrupted her as it raked back and forth over the blackening earth between them and the larger forest.

At that moment, her horse was hit again, the hot light slicing the animal in two.

Running to the other side of the grove, she saw her bisected horse. "What sort of horrible person kills horses?"

The Magicians on horseback were gaining quickly. With a burst of energy, she shattered Trolleri's crosier against one of the trees. "We'll have to risk it. Who knows what they will do to us if we are caught. They obviously don't seem to care if they kill us. They only seem to care about Jumeaux."

"I know…why?" Lontas asked as Gimelli shrugged her shoulders.

A loud squawking cry went up. This time it was full of pain. Gimelli crossed back to the side closest to the forest to see a horde of arrows zooming towards the circling griffins. The griffin and Magician rider closest to the forest were riddled with arrows. Their bodies recoiled from the innumerable hits before hurtling towards the earth, ending in a stomach-churning splat.

"Traitors!" one of the Magicians screamed to the concealed Elves.

"Now," Gimelli cried, grabbing Lontas. They crashed into the open as another round of arrows zoomed from the forest. The two remaining griffins clawed the air with their front talons, desperately trying to avoid the arrows as the Magicians fought to maintain control of the powerful winged beasts.

The Magician closest to the arrows yelled, "Orbis proteger contego!" A large orb of blue light surrounded both griffin and rider.

The Magician nearer the squires was more concerned with their death than his personal safety. "Faire incendie!" he yelled over and over again. Each time he did, bursts of blue light shot down and left streaks of scorched earth around the sprinting children. They were constantly forced to change direction, scampering to avoid the deadly fire.

The Magician who had been maintaining a shield was distracted by his griffin arching back violently to escape the arrow-riddled sky. With his concentration broken, the shield disappeared. His attempt to resummon the shield came out as inaudible gurgles courtesy of Elven arrows. His crosier plummeted towards the ground, spinning wildly end over end. He fell forward, over the left shoulder of the beast, his hands still clutching the reins, which jerked the griffin to its left.

The griffin frantically pulled its head up to dislodge the weight of the dying Magician. Shaking its head, the griffin veered into the blue light streaming from the other Magician's crosier meant for the squires. It cleaved through the griffin's back leg. Shrieking in pain, it convulsed, violently clawing empty space. The Magician rider was tossed into the air so viciously he slammed into the last unscathed griffin and rider before plummeting towards the ground. His loud scream was silenced with a mortifying thud.

The last airborne Magician sent a faire incendie spell scorching the earth right in front of the squires. Gimelli cried out in pain as her feet came into contact with the smoldering ground. Lontas let out a weak cry as the bottom of his feet began to burn. Gimelli tightened her grip on Lontas' shirt, pushing and pulling the terrified squire, desperately zigzagging to avoid the next shot.

Suddenly, the light from the crosier abruptly stopped as dozens of arrows shredded into the last circling griffin. The Magician had only been hit in the legs but was bucked off by the thrashing beast. He began tumbling towards the earth, his robe billowing violently and his arms waving wildly. He somehow managed to point his crosier towards the ground. After chanting, his descent slowed. He zoomed over to land directly in front of the squires.

His eyes blazed with rage as he pointed his crosier at them. Before he could speak, the front of his robe was pocked with dozens of arrowheads piercing through his body. Surprise replaced rage as his eyes widened, his crosier dropped, and blood began to hungrily saturate his clothes. A blood bubble squeezed out of his mouth as he fell. Gimelli and Lontas shrieked and sprinted around his body towards Creber.

As they smashed into the forest, they could hear shouts of rage from the newly approaching Magicians. The squires stopped to catch their breath, doubling over with their hands on their knees.

"That was close," Lontas panted.

"Where are the Elves that saved us?" Gimelli questioned.

"Don't know," Lontas huffed. "Up in the trees?"

"Let's move deeper into the forest," she stated, gently pulling Lontas. Each step provided additional security, but sacrificed light.

"This should be far enough."

The two stood for a moment, letting their eyes adjust to the darkness of the forest.

Scritch-scritch-scritch-scritch-scritch.

"What…is…that?" Lontas asked anxiously. The faint grating sound was coming from all around them and getting louder. It reminded Lontas of Grym and Borb scurrying across the wooden floors of their barracks. Lontas turned to the tree just to his right as a shadow moved across it. *That's odd.*

A strange voice startled them, "Keep moving into the forest, just to be safe."

Gimelli gasped, and Lontas jumped. They quickly scanned the forest for the source of the voice. Lontas' eyes were drawn to the tree with an unusual shadow. He stepped forward. The tree had four odd half-moon green marks on it. As he slowly reached out to touch them, they disappeared. His hand froze, the spots re-appeared, his hand started forward again. They vanished once again. His hand hit the tree, and he let his fingers run over the rough bark, probing for the source of the green spots. On moving down, they got stuck in two small holes.

"Dhat iss my nnaowws," an annoyed voice rang out. The green dots unexpectedly returned as the bark of the tree suddenly flew off and then flipped over. Lontas' hand fell away, his mind struggling to comprehend what was happening.

Figure 3: The Elves of Creber blend in with their trees.

"Don't ever stick your fingers in my nose, boy!" the voice rumbled to a chorus of laughter. Suddenly, Lontas saw the Elf in front of him. The bark hadn't fallen off. It was an Elf who had crawled down the tree, hanging upside down, then flipped over to stand on the ground.

Instead of the robe-like material of their battle kilts and leather armor worn at the Tournament, these Elves were bare-skinned save for small covering constructed of shed bark over their privates.

"Thanks for your help," Gimelli said, finally able see the innumerable Elfin warriors clinging to trunks and branches all around her, their forms perfectly blending in with the forest.

The camouflaged Elf reached out for Lontas, who promptly fainted.

Scroll 5: It Shall be Done

Back on the battlefield, Sorea yelled, "Finn's here!" The other Knights were still within shouting distance, but due to the number of dead and dying strewn unceremoniously on the battlefield, they could not run.

Ritari, Friar, and Lovag slogged their way over the legion of corpses to join her. Only Finn's wrapped feet were showing. The canopy had been destroyed, but his sled was intact. They immediately began to clear the dead bodies and debris away.

"Keep an eye out for Arquero," Friar advised.

Sorea let out a yelp—one of the Dark Warriors was still alive. His face was ashen and sickly looking. His left hand was completely cut off, and blood was streaming from the stump. A dagger was lodged in his right shoulder. He glared at the Knights with a weird expression that almost seemed relief. With his injured right arm, he slowly foraged for a weapon, eventually stumbling upon a discarded sword. With an odd wheezing sound, he heaved it ineptly towards Sorea with a grimace of pain.

"You have got to be kidding me," she said, stepping on his right wrist to pin the sword. The Knights looked in wonder at the ferocious warrior. He looked to be about nineteen or twenty. "He's just a kid," Sorea lamented.

"Paradise!" he gasped in a raspy voice.

His dark brown hair was matted with sweat and blood. His black eyes stood in stark contrast to his pale complexion. His large, high cheekbones dominated his face and made the other features appear small. Fresh crops of sweat beaded on his forehead as he glared at them, struggling against Sorea's foot. Looking as if he were going to speak again, he abruptly lunged at Sorea's leg with teeth bared.

"Nutcase!" she yelled, jumping back.

The exertion made him cough, and red-streaked sputum splattered over his thin black armor. As soon as he stopped coughing, he struggled to lift the sword again.

"Enough!" Ritari yelled, drawing his sword.

"The White Wizard is always watching," the warrior wheezed. "This is for you, Mom," he said, smiling broadly.

Ritari drove his broad sword through the weak chest plate. It sliced through his heart before severing his spinal cord. All movement instantly stopped.

"What did he mean, 'for Mom'?" Sorea asked.

Friar shrugged his shoulders. "No idea."

"Griffins," Ritari called. "Over by that outcropping of trees, there are a dozen or so circling with riders."

"You," Friar called to a Proliate soldier. "What's going on over there?"

"Nothing that concerns you. Just a few Dark Warrior scum who were trying to escape into the forest, likely to join up with the Elves that are helping them. The Magician reserves have come up and will quickly put an end to them."

Without replying, Friar commandeered a horse meandering by.

"Ritari, let's get Finn back on his sled and hooked up to this horse. Sorea and Lovag, go get Luchar from the healers. We're getting out of here. Wait, first, let the healers clean any major wounds," Friar said.

Once they had gone, Friar leaned over to Ritari. "Something's off. The squires should have returned to us by now. Someone or something is detaining them."

"What are you thinking?" Ritari asked.

"I think the squires are over there," Friar said, pointing to the circling griffins. "I think all of this may be related to Bellae and Jumeaux. I don't buy that story. Dark Warriors don't run unless they are setting a trap."

"I'm worried about Gleoi Dea. If she had made it to the forest, we should have heard from the Elves."

"There are too many questions that need answers," Friar said softly.

Ritari shook his head. "Let's find out." The two worked silently, preparing Finn's body to move it into the Forest of Creber. All the while, worry over the squires grew in their minds. Suddenly, they heard a loud neigh as Musta-Yo trotted up. Smiling broadly, Ritari ran to greet his horse.

"Use Musta-Yo to carry Finn instead of this one," Friar recommended. Once Finn's sled was hitched up, they waited for Sorea and Lovag to bring Luchar back.

"What are the chances we'll find Arquero's body?" Friar asked Ritari in a tired voice. With the adrenaline rush of battle gone, fatigue was settling into his aging body.

Ritari gazed around the battlefield. The chaos was overwhelming. Several teams of Proliate guards were making their way around a ground soggy with streams of blood, collecting their dead and killing any dying Dark Warriors.

"Storlax!" Friar yelled as he saw the High Commander walking by. He had an elite group of Red Guard around him.

"HK," he replied curtly.

"We are going to take Finn into Creber to be buried. We are missing a supply wagon and can't locate Arquero, one of our fallen Knights."

"I see," he said in a disinterested tone. Having hundreds of his own dead and thousands of Dark Warriors to be dealt with, the matter seemed trivial.

"Can you keep a look out? We don't want Arquero ending up in the Dark Warriors' mass grave," he requested. The Dark Warriors never came after their own dead. Whether this was another indication of their frank disregard for life, or a ploy to spread disease, no one knew.

"It shall be done," Storlax said, nodding to one of his lieutenants.

"Did you find the minotaurs' bodies?"

"Minotaur?" Storlax asked incredulously.

Yes, they fought just north of here..." Friar began.

"We found a pile of ashes and Elfin arrows. Proof your 'allies' are helping the Dark Warriors. Fairytales and myths belong in children's narratives. I have much to attend to and no time for nonsense."

"We will be coming back out in several days," Friar stated resolutely.

"I will have Arquero's body prepared and leave a detachment to guard him until you return," he said, nodding. The issue obviously decided in his mind, he immediately went back to surveying the battlefield.

Scroll 6: Truth of the League

The next morning, inside Creber, Bellae was beset by exhaustion and uncertainty. "Thank you again, for your help."

"That's my life's mission," the Eaglian said.

Bellae scrunched up her face and blushed at the notion she was important enough for such attention.

"I'm your protector, sent to watch over you by my father, Aquila." His head suddenly perked up and began to turn from side to side. "You are not the easiest person to keep track of. Trouble seems to stalk you."

Bellae laughed. "It seems that way lately. Why didn't you just come and introduce yourself to Friar and the Knights?"

"I had specific instructions not to…to make sure Eaglian involvement stays hidden. Plus, you know, adults."

Bellae laughed, but Arend turned serious. "Adults often let emotion overrule logic, and reason overrule passion." The Eaglian nodded as if that should be enough of an answer. "These Dark Warriors smell like rotting flesh even before they die."

"Yes, they do." She paused and smiled warily. "Do you live here?"

"No, no. I live with the giant red woods of the west. Well, I was born there. I have been mostly training for this moment or watching over you," he said, looking up. "These trees are like babies compared to ours."

Bellae nodded, having a hard time imagining trees so big.

"We need to get moving. The others will be waiting for us."

"The Knights?"

"No. The others sent by the League of Truth to protect and guide you. You are more important than you realize."

Bellae shook her head in bewildered frustration. "I am so sick and tired of hearing how 'important' I am."

She stared up at the awakening light struggling to pierce the forest's thick armor of branches and leaves. Her heart longed for the normal routine and familiar surroundings of Liberum. Out here, uncertainty grew like a weed.

Crann stirred, and she stood. Noises were coming from all around the forest.

"We have to go, now," Arend declared urgently. "The League is waiting."

"Crann, are you okay?" she asked, ignoring the Eaglian.

"Water," he croaked.

"Arend, do you have any water?"

"No. Eaglians rarely need water," he replied. "Those I travel with do. They will have some. Let's move."

Bellae and Arend helped the large, but shaky horse up. *"I'm not as young as I used to be,"* Crann neighed. *"That devil horse hits like Luchar's war hammer."*

"The League is this way," Arend directed.

"What League?"

"The League of Truth," he said, his words cultivating impatience.

"This bird-boy is crazy. Let's go find Friar and the Knights," Crann neighed. *"Let's get home."*

"At least meet them," Arend pleaded, sensing Bellae's hesitation. "Kainen, the Elf, is there. You know him and his father, Kempe."

Bellae paused, her heart aching at the thought of Finn. "Kempe was Finn's friend."

"They were best of friends."

"We should go with him, Crann. We can meet up with Friar and the others in a while," she said. In reality, she was sure of nothing.

Crann obediently limped behind her, moving past the mangled body of Honey in silence. Bugs were already buzzing friskily around the shredded horse, and the smell was horrific. Arend moved clumsily in the forest, his wings a constant problem with low branches.

"Ow!" Arend cried as he snagged one of his wings. "Did I mention I hate walking on the forest floor? We make our homes in the top of them where it is more comfortable."

"This forest hasn't exactly been fun for me," Bellae commented.

"Compared to…" the Eaglian was cut off and sent flying to his left after a darting figure plowed into him. As his back rammed against a tree, a scream pierced the air, but not Arend's.

"I know that scream," Bellae howled with joy. "Lontas!"

"Bellae?" Lontas questioned.

"Excuse me!" Arend protested.

"Oh, sorry. Lontas, get up now." She couldn't help smiling as the well-rehearsed phrase slipped effortlessly off her lips as she thought of the countless times his feet could not keep up with his brain.

"Bellae," Lontas said blissfully, quickly standing and swarming her in a hug.

Arend stood, rolling and twisting his neck in ways no human could. He uttered a peculiar screech, "Yee-weeent-weeent-weeent-yee-weeeent." The noises seemed to reverberate out from deep within him, terrifying Lontas. Seeing Arend for the first time, he jumped back, pulled on Bellae, and swiveled to flee.

WHAM!

He slammed into a large tree. His head bounced back, hung upright for a second before his whole body fell backwards. Moving swiftly, Arend caught him as Bellae moved to get into Lontas' line of sight.

"It's okay. This is Arend, an Eaglian, and our friend."

"Our friend?" he repeated shakily.

"Yes. The one I told you about."

"Our friend?" he restated with a generous helping of disbelief.

Bellae grimaced at the growing red spot on his forehead. "Arend's the one we met at the cemetery."

"Is that supposed to make me feel better?" Lontas replied.

"It should. He's been watching over us: saving you on the bridge and me just now."

Arend clasped Lontas' forearm and easily lifted him to his unsteady feet. "Arend, Eaglian and Bellae's protector."

"Lontas, appalling squire, expert klutz."

"Where are Gimelli and the other squires?" Bellae questioned, giggling at Lontas' response.

"Right here!" Gimelli said, nearly shouting with excitement.

The two sisters clasped each other in a warm embrace. "A forest wolf scared Lontas, and he ran," Gimelli said pushing her sister back, carefully examining her while Bellae rolled her eyes.

Cautiously keeping his distance from Arend, Lontas recounted what Gimelli had done to get them away from the Magicians. He also described how they hadn't been able to find her and so they were forced to spend the night in the forest with a group of Elves watching over them. While listening, Bellae tended to Crann, giving him some of the water from Gimelli's flask and seeing to his wounds, while Arend cleaned off Honey's blood.

"So this morning they told us how to find you," Lontas finished.

"The mentioned Arend, and that we're supposed to meet two Elves, Kempe and Kainen," Gimelli added.

"Where's Jumeaux?"

Lontas and Gimelli exchanged a sideways glance.

"He didn't get away from the Magicians," Gimelli said diplomatically. Bellae didn't have to be told. She knew he went willingly.

Two figures slid down from the trees around them. One was much larger and muscular. Bellae recognized him as Kempe, the large Elf from the tournament. The second was smaller—Kainen, his son. Their rough Elfin hands and tough fingernails gave them an excellent grip for climbing, fitting into the fissures of the bark, allowing them to glide down with friction controlling the slide. As soon as Kainen landed, he immediately went up to Arend, and the two boys embraced fondly.

Kainen spoke to the Eaglian in his native Elfish tongue. The Eaglian obviously understood, as he clasped his friend once again.

"We don't have much time," Kempe said. "Friar, Ritari, Sorea, Lovag, and Luchar are coming with Finn's body. They camped just inside the forest during the night with an Elf guard watching over them. After working through the night, the Proliate have finally finished cleaning up the battlefield."

"Arquero? The rest of the squires?" Bellae asked.

"Unfortunately, Arquero is dead. Jumeaux went off with the Magicians, and Scelto was taken by the Proliate." Turning to Gimelli, the large Elf smiled. "The Magicians are irate after your little 'stunt.' The plump one is still throwing insults into the woods."

Gimelli blushed but could not help smiling.

"Yay, Friar's coming!" Bellae said, joyfully.

Kempe frowned. "Listen, we must leave *before* he arrives." As his words were leaving his lips, Bellae's head snapped towards Gimelli.

"Of course, your sister, Lontas, and Crann can join you," Kempe said, satisfied these words would placate the terror building within her.

Leave Friar? Not attend Finn's burial? It all seemed so absurd but for the fact that she was in the middle of Creber with an Eaglian standing three feet away, Honey's betrayal, Finn's death, and the Dark Warrior battle. It was all too much. Bellae began to cry, burying her face in Gimelli's stomach.

"What are you talking about?" Gimelli challenged in total confusion.

Kempe shook his head. "Time is too short and the tale too long," he said in a tired voice. Bellae stopped crying. Something about his tone reminded her of the talks with Friar.

A soft vibratory sound distracted her. Letting go of Gimelli, she turned to find herself staring at an amazing, quivering figure.

Scroll 7: We're Going Where?

The size of a small dog, the fluttering figure blended in exceedingly well with the dark brown woods. Fragile-looking, brown, bifid wings beat furiously, and it was moving towards them with surprising speed. Long, coarse hair framed a sweet and pretty face. "We better head out," the creature said in a melodious tone.

"What news, Sankari?" Kempe asked.

"The Knights are moving with the dead Elf and will pass by soon. All the Dark Warriors are dead—literally none survived. The Proliate have several squads amassed on the border of the forest but have not given any indication of entering," the Fairy reported, finally seeming to notice the children in front of her.

"How charming—humans. I'm Sankari," the fluttering creature said while zipping back and forth between the squires. Her dark eyes inspected them with wary curiosity.

"This…little girl is…the One?" The Fairy laughed. "Not impressed."

Gimelli harrumphed before turning to Kempe for an explanation.

"Sankari is a Fairy, from Cappadocia. She's going with you," he said.

"You mean the talking butterfly is going to Liberum with us after we bury Finn?" Gimelli interrupted, but instantly blushed, embarrassed at her spiteful words.

The Fairy's face contorted in rage, and her wings buzzed violently. Arend grabbed her and moved her away just before she could lunge.

"Sorry," Gimelli apologized. "I'm feeling overwhelmed and frustrated. I just want to go home."

"Sankari, she apologized! Calm down," Arend said, still clutching the Fairy.

"Calm down? Calm down! Does that expression actually ever help anyone?"

Kempe examined the young squires closely before speaking. "I know you have questions, and I promise answers will come. However, right now I need you to accept this and follow us."

"We have to bury Finn before going *home*. Running away on some frivolous whim with complete strangers is *not* on our to-do list!"

"A bunch of strangers?" Kempe challenged, more than a little hurt. "I would have you know the League of Truth is an ancient order that has been watching over you since your birth. Our order was conceived to serve and protect—"

"What even is this League of Truth?" Gimelli interrupted skeptically.

Kempe sighed, suddenly regretting keeping the League a secret from Bellae, even though it was to keep her safe. A heavy look fell upon his face under the weight of so much to tell and no time in which to tell it. "It would take a lifetime to tell you the whole story. I can inform you we have guarded the sacred prophecy scrolls for hundreds of generations, and against all odds have managed to hold off the evil cycle,

Na Cearcaill, from swallowing Verngaurd again. This prophecy is the key to the survival of every living creature on the planet. After countless centuries, it is finally time to have the prophecy fulfilled."

"By 'hold off evil,' do you mean the Dark Warriors? We just ran into them, and the Proliate killed them," Lontas stated. He was tired, frustrated, and wanted to go home.

"Things are not as simple as they appear," Kempe answered. Seeing the confusion and mistrust growing in their eyes, he added, "The Dark Warriors are part of the problem, not the underlying force that needs to be destroyed. The larger and more important source of the evil is the subject of the prophecy."

Overwhelmed, Bellae leaned heavily against Gimelli, who cradled her younger sister. "This all sounds really interesting, but what does it have to do with us?" Gimelli asked.

"It has everything to do with Bellae. She is likely the Chosen One who can unlock the prophecy and save everyone," Kempe added, contrite and incredulous they knew so little.

"Are you crazy?" Gimelli lamented outwardly, but internally couldn't help thinking of Bellae's gifts, and the spirit reading at the Jaa kotatu. "She's a little girl! Are you sure you want to put the pressure of saving the world on her?"

Kempe moved to stand right in front of Bellae. "Each gift is a responsibility. It is your right to utilize the gift given to you, no matter how heavy the burden. I know you are confused, but trust this: Finn is like a brother, and I ask this of you simply because there is no other choice. The greatest sign of goodwill I can offer is sending my only son, Kainen, with you."

"Gimelli and Lontas can come with Sankari, Arend, and me," Kainen stated.

Kempe held up his hand before Gimelli could speak again. "Bellae, search your heart. You know the right thing to do. There's no going back to your previous life as a squire, no matter how much you want that to be true. The Magicians, the White Wizard, Watchers, the Dark Warriors, and the Proliate are all looking for you."

Bellae ignored the chattering protests of Gimelli and Lontas and focused on the reality that everything had, in fact, changed beyond repair. There was no going home with or without Finn. Part of her realized this, but an equal part fought with the truth crashing in on all sides, knowing whichever path she took would be laced with regret.

"There is no destiny," Kempe stated. "We are all born with infinite potential courses for our life. Some make their existence ordinary, others toil for the extraordinary. Very few are lucky enough to be able to see those two roads so clearly defined before them. It's your decision. I encourage you to choose the remarkable."

Crann nudged Bellae, pricking his ears at a faint neighing sound. *"It's Musta-Yo."*

Bellae could see two staggeringly different paths spreading before her. Even if she went back to Liberum, each corner of her former world would be marred by the bitter memories of her father, Finn. Liberum was no refuge, only a reminder of what was lost. *I might even be putting everyone there at risk.*

She focused her mind, trying to think. *Finn trusted Kempe, and I trust Kainen and Arend—especially Arend, my guardian.* Bellae knew the door to the future, *her* future, had opened, letting in an icy storm that froze any chance of going back to Liberum.

"I'll go."

"What? No!" Gimelli yelled as Lontas mumbled.

"Arend, lead on. Gimelli, Lontas, I hope you come," Bellae said stoically, but in reality she just needed to leave, to not see Finn's body.

"Thank you," Kempe said, gratefully. "I'll catch up to you later, but my presence would draw far too much attention right now. Sankari, Kainen, and Arend will lead you to your first trial. If you pass, you will go and see the Master Elf in exile. I can't tell you where yet, since there have been many attempts on his life."

A rough grating sound could be heard up in the trees.

They turned to see dozens of Elves easily swinging from tree to tree using their rough hands and feet. A muscular Elf gracefully slid down a tree near Kempe.

"Sir, General Lidenskap is at the border asking for permission to attend Finn's wake. He says he wants a truce to any hostilities to pay his respects."

"A way to spy on us and see who else is in here, you mean," Kempe seethed. "Let him in. If we refuse, he will use that as a pretense to charge in with his divisions and say we assisted the Dark Warriors. They are itching to declare war."

"One other thing," the Elf said. "Lidenskap stated the Magicians were upset someone had been shooting at them and their griffins."

Kempe rolled his eyes. "I suppose the fact that they were attacking *children* with rays of magical fire just outside our forest never came up?"

"No…they didn't really mention that."

Spinning towards the squires, Kempe said, "Go quickly." Looking at Kainen, emotion swelled in his eyes. "Remember what you have learned, my son, and make me proud. Work together and stick to the plan. Aquila will meet you where we discussed."

"Yes, sir," Kainen replied, with both the lack of enthusiasm of someone who had heard the plan so many times its grooves were deeply engrained in his mind, and the immaturity of child, unable to grasp the magnitude of such a goodbye.

Kempe and the other Elves quickly disappeared into the forest.

"Let's go," Kainen requested.

"No, wait. Get down and freeze," Arend instructed. Crann moved behind a few trees that had grown close together while Kainen, Arend, Sankari, Gimelli, Bellae, and Lontas ducked behind trees or lay down on the forest floor.

Bellae couldn't resist taking a peek. Ritari was navigating Musta-Yo and Finn's wooden travois slowly through the forest while the other Knights: Sorea, Lovag, Luchar, and Friar followed behind them. Bellae let out a small cry of pity at the sight of Luchar, blood-stained bandages all around his head and shoulder. *Poor Luchar.*

Briefly, she caught sight of Finn's shrouded body. An intense yearning to give him one last hug exploded in her mind. The finality of never seeing him again punched into her gut. Then, he was gone. Next, she studied the faces of the Knights and Friar, the only family she had known, as flashing images dancing in and out from behind trees. Her mind fought the feeling she would never see any of them again.

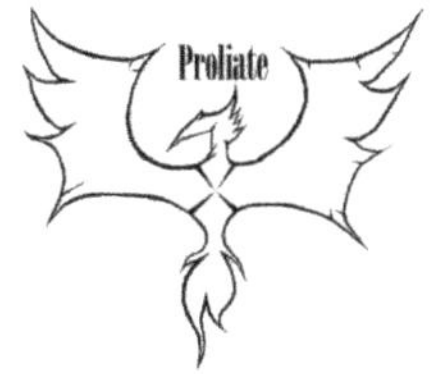

Scroll 8: Red Knight

Scelto gazed up into the clear blue sky, wondering about his friends. He erroneously assumed they were snug in their routines at Liberum, not knowing they too were scattered far from home.

Scelto looked back to Velox, the speedster from the Tournament of Flags. They had dismounted and were holding onto their grazing horses. Velox had taken Scelto under his wing since they rode into the Proliator outpost of Ragorsaf. Following Velox's eyes, Scelto could tell he was looking out over the fields of wheat, which flowed all around the wooden Proliate outpost.

Although everyone had been utterly welcoming, every question Scelto asked was often echoed back as another question. They had been quite vague about why he had been taken here and what Friar and the rest of the Knights were doing. They promised word would come soon about when they could be reunited.

"What are you looking at?"

Velox grinned. "What do *you* see?"

"I knew you were going to do that," Scelto said, smiling.

"You're smart enough to know how things work. If I give you the answer, it's a handout. Handouts are for beggars, not warriors. Soldiers scrap and fight for everything in and out of battle."

Scelto stared at the field, pretending to examine it. In reality, he was contemplating how impressive the Proliate were: their strenuous training, humor, intelligence, and camaraderie. They were not the mindless lackeys he had been led to believe. Finally focusing on the endless ocean of wheat, he said, "It seems to go on forever."

"Good. Does it?"

"No, of course not," Scelto answered.

"So there is more to what our small perspective gives us. Now, what else?"

As he looked again, Scelto noticed the light tan tops of the crop rows contrasting with the rich and dark chocolaty brown of the earth. As the wind swayed over the field, it seemed to breathe vitality into the grain, making it move as if it were one enormous beast dancing with undulating rhythm. "It looks as if the whole field is…" Scelto hoped his words did not sound ridiculous, "…alive."

The Proliator stared, imploring for more.

"When the field moves, it does so together."

"Yes!" Velox said excitedly. "Individually, the stalks of grain are weak and useless. Stand them together in unity, and they become powerful. That's our strength, many soldiers coming together to create something vastly superior to what we could be individually. All glory to Tallcon." A look of peace washed across Velox's face.

Later that day, Scelto and Velox were returning from patrol when their commander suddenly stopped and shouted, "Oval up!"

"Just stay to my right," Velox advised.

The Red Guard warriors quickly formed up around two of their comrades. One was Fenik, the commander of the Red Guard that Scelto remembered seeing at the Tournament. With all eyes upon him, Fenik pulled out a package from his saddlebag. In reverential silence, he removed a red silk cloth to reveal a well-worn book.

"That is the raamattu, it holds our daily prayers," Velox whispered. "Every day we pray from it at least three times. We also read the Sanctus Kirja Flamma, our bible, an additional two times per day. The only exemption is if you are directly engaged in battle. Fenik is renowned for staying up all night reading and praying."

Scelto had seen many prayer services since he had arrived. The Proliate seemed determined to give him a clear understanding of their lives, especially as it related to prayer and Tallcon.

Fenik began, "To the wicked, beware. The lava flowing from the eternal springs of Ainoa is an earthly sign of my blood and shall swallow you in bitter agony. For the righteous, it shall flow before you like a protective shield against your enemies. It shall bathe you in its warm embrace and at the hour of your death transport you to eternal life. If any stand against you, it will angrily smite them down with a dreadful vengeance. Those who follow my way shall come to perfection in my sight and gain great favor. Those of weaker lineage who fail to keep my ways shall be swallowed in the fire of pain." Fenik closed and carefully put the book away.

"All praise Tallcon!" Fenik suddenly shouted with such fervor it startled Scelto. Velox calmly grabbed Scelto's arm to steady him as he responded in unison with the other Proliate, "All praise Tallcon!" The Proliate went back into formation of two equal lines with Scelto riding next to Velox.

"Ainoa is the largest and most active volcano of the Proliate Islands. It is the birthplace of Tallcon and through him, all existence. It's the lifeblood of communication between his eternal paradise and our earthly domain," Velox stated. "You're in luck. Tonight you will see the Paradox of Fire celebration. It is observed every four weeks."

That night Scelto found himself sitting next to the other Proliate Warriors dressed in solid red robes. In front of the soldiers stood three Master Clerics in dark blue robes.

A tall and portly Magician with flowing red hair stood with his back to the other two. On either side of an altar, four sizable pillars held large metal bowls.

The red-haired Magician spoke first. "Welcome to the Paradox of Fire, the foundation of our religion. On the one hand, there is a great poverty in the sacred fire, as it crackles with a lonely and cavernous hunger, a parched emptiness, thirsting to consume. And yet, the all-powerful fire from mighty Tallcon takes away only that which is impure. It can only consume the trappings of this paltry earthly realm. But in those of clean spirit who follow Tallcon, fire is salvation. He emblazoned a path of eternal life, destroying the physical world to release the immortal soul within."

He finished nodding to the two Magicians behind him. They clapped loudly, and two wooden buckets were brought forward. "To confirm this is water, drink," they said. Taking a ladle from the wooden buckets, they had two nearby Proliate drink. They did so, nodded, and returned to their seats.

"We now add simple water to the sacred bowls," they stated, pouring the water from the wooden buckets into the four large metal bowls.

The redhead loudly said, "Oh mighty Tallcon, in your infinite power and wisdom grant us this day to see a miracle. Instead of water putting out fire, let it be the birth and fuel of your holy and purifying fire of life. This fire is sent from heaven itself, realm of Tallcon, our almighty protector."

The metal bowls suddenly burst into flames, sending Scelto jumping in amazement.

Velox whispered, "In the center of the bowls sits quick lime, and around that are several things: sulfur, coals from Ainoa, and naphtha. When water is poured onto it, the quick lime heats up, and the sulfur starts on fire. That lights the naphtha, and then, there is literally no way to put it out despite the water."

Scelto nodded but continued to stare at the fire from water. It was hypnotic and amazing even after hearing the explanation.

"Prepare the Kirous!" the red-haired Magician shouted.

As a flurry of activity erupted, Scelto studied the man's face. His jaw jutted out much farther than it would seem prudent. Its position forced a persistent, dimpled smile upon his face. His green eyes were fierce, and his eyebrows arched in a scowl, yet his lower face radiated the appearance of good cheer.

A dozen Proliate soldiers began dumping something behind him. "Today is a reminder for some, a wake-up call and invitation for others. The path of Tallcon has been clearly laid out. It is an unforgiving life but promises a precious gift in death—eternal life." He motioned to the other Magicians.

A short, thin Magician moved to the front, carrying a book. Scelto presumed it was their bible, the Sanctus Kirja Flamma. The Magician trembled slightly. "Liii!" His voice cracked, and he swallowed before continuing, "Live by these seven fires and you assure yourself everlasting life. Fire of sacrifice, fire of service, fire of bravery, fire of stoicism, fire of victory, fire of servility, and fire of endurance."

He closed the book and returned to stand behind the seemingly perpetually smiling, red-haired Magician.

"Rise," he said, flipping his ponytail over his right shoulder. "Tonight we take the oath of purification to commit ourselves to Tallcon's path, the oath of Kirous."

"It's okay, Scelto. I'll go first. Stay right behind me. Don't stop or jump off the path. Don't panic and do *not* run ahead or they'll kill you," Velox said. He put his hand reassuringly on Scelto's shoulder as if he hadn't just mentioned being killed.

"What path?" Scelto asked fearfully.

"Those are hot coals from the mountain of Ainoa," Velox said calmly. Sweat was actively jumping out onto Scelto's forehead. The red robes suddenly felt itchy and foreign. *I am getting sick of these little surprises.*

"Remove your boots. Prepare for purification," a soldier said as Scelto moved forward in line. Sweat stained his clothes under his arms and lower back. He strained to see around Velox and the other Proliate in front of him.

"What happens with the hot coals?" Scelto asked.

"You walk across them," Velox answered calmly.

Before Scelto could speak, he felt someone tug at his feet, nearly tripping him.

"Off with your boots!" one of the soldiers commanded. Scelto fumbled to remove them. The crackling heat from the large bowls and the hot coals combined with the smoke to make him feel disoriented and groggy.

"Let us be grateful to walk this path, becoming stronger in service to Tallcon. It is an oath to follow his way and to be reborn in his eternal fate," a Magician said.

Much too quickly, Scelto found himself in front. He could see those ahead of him drinking from a wooden bowl before entering a path of red-hot coals.

The long straight path consisted of grey rocks glowing a menacing orangish-red. Steam rose ominously, and he could feel the heat angrily radiating from them.

Velox whispered, "You must take the sacred drink before you go on the coals."

"What is it?" Scelto asked, fearing the answer.

"The entire sacred text of the Sanctus Kirja Flamma is written on wooden plaques. The boards are then washed into these bowls, and you have the honor of drinking the sacred words."

Walk on hot coals and drink ink? Bugger! Scelto had to smile, relieved it was just ink. His mind had been racing with all sorts of disgusting possibilities.

Suddenly, the bowl was thrust up to his mouth. Closing his eyes, he drank it quickly, swallowing the slightly bitter taste with no problem. Finishing, he opened his eyes and handed the cup back to the woman.

Velox wheeled around. "Follow me, now!" he said with an odd mix of concern and encouragement.

"Welcome," the Magician who had done the reading said. "Embark on the path to purify yourself. These embers are what are left from Tallcon's last rebirth at Ainoa. Walking across them purifies any weakness and, if you are worthy, you will emerge reborn in strength and loyalty," he said, waving his hand invitingly towards the coals as if it were the entrance to a party.

Scelto hesitated. *This is crazy.* Everything was happening too quickly. His breath felt labored—the smoke and his anxiety clogged his airway.

"Move, now!" Velox said with such intensity, Scelto started following him.

He immediately felt the heat bore into his feet. It was admittedly uncomfortable, but not the searing pain he envisioned.

Velox continued to throw encouragement back to Scelto without turning around, each step bringing a new phrase. "Follow me. Don't stop." His words were just loud enough for Scelto and those right around them to hear.

Steadily, Scelto walked, careful to stay close to Velox without running into him.

"Ignite my sacrifice to you," the Master Cleric said. "Burn the old and give rebirth to a purified soul. Draw out the toxins in our lives and refresh your eternal spirit."

For some reason, the words touched a chord with Scelto. He found himself being drawn into them.

"If Tallcon is to have the whole, there must be aught of me. There is nothing on this earth that can fill your soul. Only Tallcon's everlasting fire can quench that nagging longing in your heart. Everything on this earth is finite. Only through the healing fire of Tallcon can your soul reach the infinite."

Scelto no longer felt the heat. Velox was abruptly facing him. Panic welled up in him. *I can't stop!*

"It's okay. You did it!"

Scelto scanned the area intensely, and started laughing. "I'm through!" He felt pats on his back and noted many nods of approval. He shuddered with joy at those small acts of acknowledgement, which seemed to resound within him louder than the roaring cheers at the Tournament. Full of euphoria he embraced Velox.

"Congratulations. You did it."

"I would have appreciated a little warning."

"Ah," Velox scoffed. "The anticipation would have eaten at you."

"I don't know about that."

As the last of the Proliate made their way across the coals, they began to form up in rows. Once in formation, they began to sing hymns. Scelto scanned the faces of the Proliate while gently swaying with the calming music. It was hypnotizing.

"Giving yourself to Tallcon breathes into you a tranquility that the guilty pleasures of this world never can," Velox whispered. "Accepting he controls everything frees you from worry in this life and beyond."

Scelto closed his eyes and let the power of the moment resonate within him. With every crevice and corner of the world filled with such uncertainty, the carrot of control, even if by a greater power, provided warm security and cozy comfort.

Scroll 9: Realm of Elves

Ailante, the head Archerian ruler of the Elves, waved his hands, "We are about to leave the outer ring of trees and enter the sacred part of our forest." Where the Knights remained, the trees were medium sized, ranging from fifty to eighty feet high. They had rough, dark brown bark. There was nothing special about them. Behind Ailante, however, the trees changed drastically.

"These are arbor breith trees. Our birth trees," he said, looking up. "We have a strong, sacred, and ancient attachment. Stepping on them is like stepping on our soul."

Ailante motioned for the Knights to stay as he turned and walked towards one of the trees. Friar was troubled by his old friend's response when questioned about Gleoi Dea and Bellae. The head Elf had replied, "Both are safe, and you will see Gleoi Dea soon."

Ailante gently ran his hand up and down bark of the massive tree. It was several hundred feet tall and extremely wide. The lower section of the arbor breith tree is what made the Knights catch their breath. Large portions of the massive roots were above ground, arching out to create a dome with considerable space underneath. The wood flooring under the roof of tree roots was white and smooth.

As their eyes moved to the upper portion of the tree, they could see the bark becoming thicker and more grooved. The color also darkened to brown with heavy black grooves. Various shades of green moss clung to the dark brown trunks. Like the outer ring of trees, the resemblance of the bark to the Elfin skin was striking.

Ailante continued, "The bottom portion is called the brionn. This is where our connection to our birth trees is deepest. It is our home, where we sleep and live. Do *NOT* enter this area unless specifically invited to do so. The wood underneath the tree is actually part of the root system—it is alive, not cut and placed there."

The living space under the tree looked as if there were an imprint of an Elf fashioned into it. A blanket and a few wooden possessions were spread around.

"The impression matches our bodies, changing as we grow and age, and is where we sleep," Ailante said.

Ailante pointed to a solitary, long, and smooth branch sprouting from the lower portion of the tree. "This is a vestigial branch. We call it the uhri. Its white wood is a gift from our birth tree so that we do not have to cut down any trees. Just like your fingernails, it grows continually, and we simply cut and trim it back with no pain to the tree. It is the source for all of our weapons, utensils…really everything."

A thin Elf with a long narrow face approached. He walked hunched over and staring down as if he were either humble or ashamed. He quickly glanced up to examine the Knights and give them a chance to see him. His eyes were light green with silver streaks striking out from them like lightning. Deep furrows ran through his rough tan and green skin as if he were in a perpetual state of deep thought. His nose and mouth were small and inconspicuous, like his uncertain demeanor.

As the newcomer drifted towards Ailante, his light tan robes billowed out around him like a sail. It seemed as if he would float right out of the baggy cloak.

Finally noticing him, Ailante motioned to the man. They talked quietly in Elfish for several moments.

"I apologize for speaking in Elfish—it has made quite the resurgence since…"

He didn't need to finish. They all knew that once the Knights had failed in the Dark War their insistence on the common tongue lost its authority in all countries.

"Anyway, this is Beriglor, one of our chief Prete, or priests. He will be conducting Finn's Scaoileadh ceremony. I have a matter to attend to, so he will be your guide from here. If you need anything, let me know."

The two Elves whispered for a few moments before Ailante walked to the right of the Knights with an obvious look of concern. Just then, a dozen Elves slung down from the trees and moved around Ailante with such vicious speed that Ritari was startled into beginning to draw his sword.

Friar calmly put his hand over the pommel to prohibit it from being drawn out completely. "One thing you can count on when you enter the sacred part of their forest, you are *always* being watched. There are at least twenty Varna watching us. They are the defenders of the forest."

"Their army," Sorea commented.

"Yes. As you can see, they are incredibly at home in these woods. I pity the army that tries to enter here. I bet Ailante is going to see Lidenskap. We should join our Prete, Beriglor," Friar added.

"Oh, hello!" he said in surprise as Beriglor had moved right in front of their faces. The Prete still had his head down, but his eyes were arched up, secretly scanning the Knights.

"Yes…hello. Um…I will be showing you around," he said in a hushed voice. "Please…follow me."

As they moved deeper into the forest, two dozen Prete in green robes materialized.

"I wish they would stop doing that," Sorea stated as Luchar growled.

"These Prete will be taking Finn's body to prepare him for the re-unification ceremony we call the Scaoileadh," Beriglor whispered.

The Knights exchanged uneasy looks as they instinctively moved to block access to their friend's body. The reality, the finality of Finn's death, punched into their stomachs. Despite his throbbing headache, Luchar's heart rumbled with misplaced anger. He fought the urge to grab his axe and start swinging at anyone, everyone, the world.

After an awkward moment of silence, Beriglor stepped forward. "Your feelings for Finn are clear. It warms our hearts to see your love for him, but the time for us to take him has arrived."

Tears born of equal parts exhaustion and sadness welled up in Sorea. She turned to Ritari and buried her face in his cold, dirty armor. He closed his eyes, letting the soup of emotion digest in his gut.

"We will return your horse after we care for his needs," Beriglor stated in a calm tone. The compassionate and deferential mannerisms of Beriglor endeared him to the Knights. "Let's get you to where you will be staying so you can clean up and rest before the ceremony tomorrow morning."

"It will be tomorrow, then?" Friar asked.

"Yes…tomorrow. This way, please."

The small group moved silently through the enormous forest. Tomorrow they would bury Finn. The thought reverberated in their heads with desperate agony. Even ten years from now seemed too soon.

The Knights and Friar felt off balance. From the time they left Liberum, they had been greeted by one disaster after another. Now, with Finn's body off with the Prete, the squires missing, their horses and supply wagons gone, they were feeling overwhelmed and vulnerable. Beriglor led them to an area where three arbor breith were adjacent.

"This was Finn's tree," he said, pointing to the middle brionn. The Knights instantly noticed all of the tree's leaves were gone. It looked scared and naked, with all of its neighbors clothed in golden leaves of autumn. Beriglor answered their question before they could ask. "Although Finn had been gone for a long time, his tree still felt and mourned his death by shedding all its leaves. Some say we connect one last time with our birth tree right before we die.

"That tree belonged to Finn's parents, who are also dead. Unfortunately, the third is empty since his younger sister died in a tragic accident," Beriglor said as Sorea gasped.

"You will sleep here tonight. There is a well right behind these trees for your use. We invite you to wear the robes we provided while we wash and repair your clothes and armor so it will be ready for tomorrow."

"Sleep there?" Sorea asked.

"Yes, is that not acceptable?" Beriglor questioned, almost offended.

"More than adequate. In fact, it is such an honor. Our hesitation is born from the fear we are being an imposition," Friar said.

"Nonsense. You are his family," Beriglor said, smiling. "We have communed with the trees. They know who you are and are willing to allow you to sleep within their roots. After you have had a chance to clean up, I will be back to bring you to feast. We will eat in the arteria, which is our sacred eating-place, where we share food once per day. If you find yourself in need of assistance, just call out. As long as you stay within the inner sacred forest, help is always just an asking away," Beriglor said, looking and pointing up.

They could make out the image of several warrior Varna staring down at them.

Their presence is comforting and menacing at the same time, Friar thought.

"I have a question, Beriglor," Sorea said.

The Prete turned to stare with a surprised expression. "Of course."

"Why are there no mosquitoes in here?"

"No mosquito can penetrate our skin—it's too thick." Beriglor hit his hand against his forearm with a wood-like clunk to demonstrate. "If it is mosquitos that interest you, try the Mohado Mire."

"It must be nice to not have to deal with them."

"Yes. However, many would trade mosquitos for our reikas." He finished with a little laugh as if everyone would know about them. Seeing their confused expressions, he continued, "Reikas are boring bugs that infest the Forest of Creber."

"Boring bugs?" Ritari asked, cautiously.

"Yes, as in, they bore through our skin. They look like a sleek version of a caterpillar and crawl along the ground, searching for flesh. Once they burrow into our skin, they suck our blood and live there until the person is de-barked in that area and they are dug out. It's incredibly painful to have them removed, and it will forever leave a scar." He shuddered.

"Can they get into us?" Sorea asked, her face pale with worry. In fact, all the Knights felt an intense urge to scratch suddenly perceived itches as their eyes and feet searched for crawling creatures.

"Unfortunately, they can easily infest your fragile skin," Beriglor said.

"Lovely," Sorea commented sarcastically.

"Great! Did you want us to sleep at all tonight?" Luchar added angrily.

"However," Beriglor said authoritatively, "before you get too worked up, know that reikas cannot survive for long in your delicate skin. It confuses them, and they tend to worm their way into your muscles and die." Despite a chorus of "Ewww's!" he continued. "Or they get engorged on your readily accessible blood supply and puff up so large they are easy to remove. That is, if they don't burst before we can get to them."

"Ahh! They die inside our muscle or get really fat and explode. Well, that makes me feel better. You?" Sorea questioned jokingly.

He waved off their concerns and pointed them in the direction of the well. "Please, wash up and rest before the meal. Our healers will come tend to your wounds before you rest. Unless there is anything else I can do for you?"

"No, thank you." Turning to say good-bye, Friar saw he was already gone. As they headed towards the well, several Elves were standing near an uhri or vestigial branch. A Prete in his green hooded robe stood in the middle of two other Elves, who were wearing brown robes.

"The ones in the brown robes are hintels. They are the craftselves who use wood from the smooth vestigial branches to make everything they need, from cooking utensils to weapons. The Prete, or priest, is performing the preparatory ceremony of thanksgiving before they cut a portion of it off," Friar explained.

Several children were watching a little distance off. "They call the kids students of the forest or opiskelli. When they are fifteen, they must choose a profession to study and test for."

"Let me wash up, then I'll take a look at your wounds, Luchar." Sorea said.

After sleeping just inside Creber the night before, she was feeling incredibly filthy. She instantly started to wash herself in a ritual all warriors performed after combat. Washing off the blood and grime of battle was the easy part. The memories mired in how the splatters were obtained take much longer for time to slowly chip away, with some psychological trauma impossible to be cleaned off or forgotten.

"Friar. Friar!" Beriglor said, gently shaking the sleeping man's shoulders.

"Yes," Friar replied, expecting to see the castle steward, Baiulus. Instead, the tan, bark-like face of the Elven Prete greeted him. Friar could feel the comforting wood of the brionn gently swaddling his body. It was incredibly cozy.

"Sorry, but I thought we had agreed to have you eat with us tonight," the Prete said. "I started to wake the one with the bandaged head and shoulder," he said, swallowing hard and pointing to Luchar, "but he swung his axe at me and growled."

Friar chuckled. "Yes, he has a tiny problem with his temper." Sitting up, he remembered they were in the brionn that Finn had grown up in and wearing cloaks the Elves had provided. The wood was firm but softened as he lay down on it. Luchar lay to his left and Ritari to his right. Lovag and Sorea had moved into the section near the well.

"Why don't you let me wake the Knights up?"

Beriglor bowed slightly, looking relieved. "I'll be back in a few minutes to escort you to the meal." Once again he quickly disappeared into the forest. When they were all awake and ready, the Prete rematerialized.

A short time later, they began walking single file behind Beriglor. The tall trees blurred together, and the Knights were soon hopelessly disoriented.

"I hope you'll escort us back," Ritari said, gazing at the bewildering number of massive trees.

"Yes. Of course," Beriglor answered, stopping to gaze at them. "To many outside Creber trees are just 'objects' to be used like tools. For us, we hear their sweet music, feel their humble power, and see their glowing beauty. If you pay close attention, each tree is a poem. If we listen closely, we hear their melodic wisdom as we pass by."

After walking for an hour, they came to a wooden bridge that was ornately carved with relief pictures of Elves, animals, trees, and mountains. About every four feet, a large wooden pole with a different carved theme stood with a covered torch.

The group stopped to admire the craftselfship of the bridge and the scenery surrounding it. The banks of tall grasses and various wild flowers along the river served as a reprieve from the massive trees inside Creber. Even the small swath of more open space allowed the Knights to breathe easier, while having the opposite effect on Beriglor. He missed the comfort of the towering trees and crowded forest.

"This is the Kaksi River," Beriglor said, pointing southeast. "It leads to Lake Qualitas. From there, the Abhainn River flows to the Mires."

He paused and looked curiously at the Knights, gauging their response to see whether they recognized the importance of that path. When it was obvious they did not, he continued, "Finn took this path the day he left. You should know, Finn is considered a hero, as are all who have become Knights."

"We could use more of you," Friar said, pointedly.

Beriglor looked down. He seemed to be thinking of a reply and finally said, "It is hard for us to leave the forest, and times are different now. The ranks of our Varna have swollen with all the turmoil outside our forest."

After an awkward silence the group crossed the bridge and reentered the forest on the other side.

"You look tired today, Beriglor," Friar said.

"I had a conaisc ceremony yesterday. It is the most draining responsibility we have as Prete," he said with a heavy sigh.

"The Knights probably don't know what that means," Friar said.

"Conaisc is our marriage ritual," Beriglor explained. "Getting married is a complex issue. It is much more than a simple ceremony joining two Elves. We have to separate one from their birth tree and join them together to one. In fact, the Prete class developed thousands of years ago to assist in the difficult process. It is physically and mentally demanding. We have to prepare the entire tree, from leaves to roots. For one, it is a connection severed, for the other, it must be cajoled, guided to accept becoming a marriage birth tree. It can take an entire day or up to several weeks."

"Does the process ever fail?" Lovag asked, intrigued.

"Rarely—maybe once every few years."

"What happens then?" Lovag probed.

"The marriage is off."

"Wow, that's tough," Sorea commented.

"I suppose it is…on everyone."

"You okay, Luchar?" Ritari asked.

Luchar looked up with his eyes glazed in pain and slight confusion. He nodded, but his far-off gaze and heavily bandaged head spoke otherwise.

Lovag was still asking questions when the woods started to change. The massive birth trees started to be interspersed with the smaller trees they had seen on the outer ring. Families of Elves could be seen moving quietly through the forest around them. They carried ornately carved wooden bowls covered by leaves that had been sewn together into something that resembled fabric. A din of conversation could be heard. The woods abruptly ended, and they entered a large clearing.

"Amazing!" Lovag said. In front of them were a series of intricately carved tables laid out in a living, interlocking spiral pattern that weaved its way all around the clearing. Occasionally, it would loop around a tree. The chairs around the table varied greatly. Some were simple stumps while others were intricately carved with backs and arm rests.

"Welcome to the arteria," Beriglor said proudly. He waved his arm to showcase the thousands of Elves mingling about, many nodded or waved. Some were setting out food.

The Knights followed Beriglor through the intricate helicoidal pattern of tables, which flowed to a central ring. Inside that circle sat a giant fire pit. The aroma of roasting flesh made its way to the hungry Knights, who started to salivate. As they drew closer, they saw deer, wild turkeys, and boars on large spits.

It was the first time they had seen metal since entering the forest. Around the fire pit were stone ovens, each tended by several Elves. An unusual but delicious smell wafted towards them.

"Ah, mushroom and root bread," Friar said, inhaling excitedly.

"Outstanding, Friar. We sit here," Beriglor said, pointing to seats around the center ring with large and ornately carved chairs. The Knights suddenly noticed a solitary figure wearing a hood, slouching at the table.

"Each family makes its own chairs and brings food to share. My family is well known…" Beriglor was interrupted when the seated figure looked up, squealing joyfully.

"Friar!" Gleoi Dea said, pushing her hood back and running towards him. She hugged Friar and then stepped back to address the Knights.

"The Archerians wouldn't let me return and refused to send troops!" she proclaimed frantically, as if she had been practicing the opportunity to explain. "I tried, and pleaded, sir."

"I'm sure you did everything within your power."

"The Archerians thought the Proliate would accuse the Elves of working with the Dark Warriors if they sent out their army. They assured me they would have been out there immediately if the Proliate had not been on their way," Gleoi Dea continued, shaking her head from side to side with regret.

"It was a wise choice. Storlax was ranting he would kill all Elves that emerged," Friar said reassuringly. Gleoi Dea embraced Friar again.

"Ritari, your head…"

"I know. The Elves gave me some sort of Elfish salve for my burned scalp."

"It looks…"

"Ridiculous," Ritari answered for her. "I realize how it looks, but it feels fantastic."

"Luchar, please, I beg you, start protecting that brain of yours," Gleoi Dea advised.

"I'm fine," he insisted despite the pounding in his head and the fog that seemed to be sitting stoutly around his mind.

"Sorea!" The two embraced and whispered for quite some time.

The Knights sat down just as several musicians came out. Some had lutes, an instrument peculiar to the Elves of Creber. The four-string instrument had an oval body and long neck. A group of Elves raised several long, square, metal poles of different sizes and began playing them by tapping thin metal rods against their sides. The vibrating sound was hypnotically calming when joined by the strumming of the lutes.

Singers in light brown robes came out and began to hum and sing gentle melodies, while bells of various sizes started to ring.

As the food was served, several of the musicians walked up and down the arms of the spiral tables. The effect was relaxing yet disorienting, as the source of the sound was constantly changing. The Knights ate in relative silence, listening to the deep and tranquil music. Occasionally, they would look to the open sky, which was now dark and pocked with brilliant stars and moons. It was only after darkness had washed over the sky they noticed the innumerable bioluminescent mushrooms sprouting and spraying a soft, friendly light around the forest.

"I was just starting to relax," Luchar growled. "Now that dimwitted Lidenskap shows up?" The general and several of the Proliate guard were being seated at the ring of tables about thirty chairs away.

"Should make for an interesting ceremony tomorrow," Friar said.

Scroll 10: Don't be a Bump

After a couple days of hectic and rough travel, the fledgling group from the League of Truth had finally made it to the Tingij Mountains. Their route had been circuitous to avoid Watchers and Proliate warriors searching for them. Sankari and the squires had passed out from exhaustion.

"I don't like this," Arend said, looking up claustrophobically at the looming cliffs behind him.

"Once we sneak past the Way of Trepas and head north for a bit, we can head away from the Tingij, not before. The Watchers and Magicians riding griffins are patrolling the skies over the open plains," Kainen said. "Just look at Bellae and the other squires," he said, pointing to their sleeping figures. "We've been pushing them too hard."

"We shouldn't be so close to the Way of Trepas. The Magicians and Proliate will be coming back through soon. We should either move past it or find a deeper cave."

Kainen thought for a moment then nodded. "Agreed. Do you mind looking?"

Arend let out a little squawk and stretched his muscular, feathered legs. He wrenched his neck around to scan the horizon. "I will first fly high enough to scout around to see whether I can spot anyone approaching. Then I will look for a better resting place."

"Thanks," Kainen said, turning back to the fire as Bellae's eyes fluttered open.

"Hey, hope you had a good nap," Kainen said, just as Arend exploded upward. Bellae watched him circle several times before heading off.

She immediately went and looked Crann over before changing his bandages from the supplies Kainen had brought.

"Did you sleep?" she asked.

"Not as much as you."

"With all your injuries, Crann, you could use some extra sleep."

"I slept a whole four hours yesterday, most ever."

"Wow, think of all you missed," she replied sarcastically. When his wounds were re-dressed, she hugged him for a long time. *"We'll get through this together, Crann."*

"We could use some attention, huh?" the gritty voice of Grym scratched out. *"We are dying in here, and yet Old Bucky the Beaver-toothed horse gets all the attention just because of a few scratches? What if I told you that Borb bit me?"*

Bellae swallowed a laugh and gave them a half-hearted scolding look. After providing them some food and water, she went back to Crann.

"We're doing the right thing, right?"

"I trust your instincts…this time." Crann said, glaring at her. *"I hope this one turns about better than…"*

"Sorry about Honey," Bellae broke in, blushing. *"Go ahead and say it again."*

"I told you so."

"Are you finally feeling up to telling me everything?" Gimelli asked.

Bellae recounted her entire ordeal, becoming tearful at the retelling of Honey's betrayal.

"Wow. I'm so sorry I wasn't there for you, and understand why it was so hard to tell me."

Bellae leaned in to lay her head on her sister's shoulder as Arend returned, looking worried.

"What is it?" Kainen asked.

"A column of Proliate is moving up towards our position. If we hustle, we can be north of the Way of Trepas before they get here. Also, a few Watchers were hovering and chanting."

"Did they see you?" Kainen asked in a panic.

"No, my eyes could easily spot them before they could see me. They seemed to be putting out some sort of magical web. I'm guessing to detect flying creatures, so I stayed fairly low."

"Let's move!"

After covering their tracks, the League traveled quickly along the Tingij Mountains until they were north of the Way of Trepas. After walking through the night, they turned west into the Rebelde Plains. Despite their exhaustion, they continued to slice their way into the ocean of grass through the early morning of the next day.

"When's breakfast or lunch or tea time?" Grym whined from Bellae's pocket.

"Soon," she giggled, gently patting his head back into her pocket. *"Arend went hunting and he'll be back soon."*

They traveled in single file to make moving through the thick and lofty grass easier while hiding their numbers. For Bellae, her view was Lontas' back and a wall of grass.

"What news?" Kainen asked as Arend nimbly landed.

"We are several miles from the mountains. There are no Watchers, Magicians, or Proliate troops in the area. If we keep heading due north, we shouldn't have any problems making it to Lake Glasere."

"Any locals?"

"There are no villages around here. I saw a few small trees that could be used for firewood to the east. It's far enough that I should fly."

"Any food?"

"I saw many clusters of ravinto plants, all west of here."

"Awesome."

"Ravinto?" Bellae asked.

"An edible plant native to the plains of Verngaurd," Lontas answered, going into scholarly mode. "You eat the leaves and boil the roots into a thick soup, like potato. A few small berries grow on each branch."

Seeing everyone staring at him, he blushed.

"I have one here for you to look at," Arend said, handing it to Bellae. "If you guys collect some, I'll get the firewood."

Bellae examined the five-foot-tall branch. The light tan stick was firm but compressible, almost spongy. Thick, meaty leaves branched off from small, stubby limbs all along its length. At the end, there were two small red berries.

"Let's make camp then split up. Lontas and Bellae, head due west. Gimelli and Sankari, head northwest. Arend will get firewood. Crann can stay here while I head southwest," Kainen suggested.

With hungry stomachs, everyone but Crann set off in their assigned direction.

"I still don't understand why Arend didn't just come up to us at Liberum," Lontas said as they walked.

"He was ordered to keep his distance unless we were in trouble."

"Still, he didn't have to scare us."

"He didn't mean to," Bellae said sincerely.

"Look, a log," Lontas said. The two approached a small clearing devoid of the tall grass with a four-foot section of a thick rotting log. The dark brown fallen trunk had areas of black and orange where it appeared to be decomposing.

"I bet we can see better on it," he said. Running to jump on it, his right foot hit the top and skidded, sending him reeling backwards. His buttocks hit the log, his back and head, the ground.

"Are you okay?" she said, rushing to help him sit up on the old log.

He nodded, glad it was just Bellae who could see him. Arend and Kainen had already seen him slip and fall several times on their journey north.

"The top is slippery," he said, sighing. He noticed several six-inch black spots on the top. Touching one of them, his hand quickly recoiled at the warmth.

"You rest here while I look for the plants."

"Okay," he agreed, adjusting himself on the log. "My butt feels sore, and I don't feel like walking."

"I'll be right back," she said, heading into the deep grass.

He started to feel a tingling sensation on his bottom where it touched the log. *That's weird. I didn't think I fell that hard.*

"Ow!" he cried as his backside began to burn. He tried to stand up but couldn't. "What the…" Panic gripped him, and sweat began to oval up on his forehead. Looking at his legs, he could not see anything snagging them. They straightened and bent easily. Feeling around his buttocks, he felt a ring of wet warmth. The tingling sensation was replaced with intense heat and pain as numbness began creeping down his legs.

Wetness oozed out from around his bottom. "Is this blood?"

Gazing at the thick red liquid oozing over his hand, he began to scream.

Panic gripped him as he once again tried to stand. The muscles in his legs contracted and strained, but he could not stand up. The log shook a little and then rolled forward a few inches on its own. Looking down, he saw several sections of the log bulging out, as if reaching for his legs, and he quickly stretched them out and away. The log trembled again, shooting out tentacle-like feelers, hungrily extending for his legs.

This isn't happening! His mouth felt dry, and his throat seemed to freeze. Mouthing "Bellae," no sound came out. The log rolled forward again, and he started to actively push with his legs to prevent the log from flipping him forward. Bulging projections from the wood stretched eagerly towards the flesh of his legs while thick strands began clawing up around his backside.

The log surged forward, overpowering Lontas and throwing him onto his knees while his backside was still stuck on the log. Finding his voice, he screamed.

His feet were now trapped under the log as the bulging sections converged over them. He began to feel the warm tingling sensation flow through his covered legs. The pain in his buttocks was deeper, beginning to blaze like a hot fire.

"Bellae!" he yelled. He could hear her darting through the tall grass.

She burst into the small clearing, holding several ravinto branches. Both her jaw and the plants dropped as she stared in horror at the scene. The log seemed to be alive. Large swellings were surging, reaching, extending. At the same time, undulating waves were heaving across its entire length. She could see blood flowing freely and an oozing white substance bubbling out where the log touched his body. Unsure of what to do, she screamed as loud as she could. Just then, an intense grumbling sound echoed from deep within the log.

"Lontas!" she screamed. Drawing her dagger, she slashed at the bulging sections. The log rumbled angrily in response.

A high-pitched shriek filled the air. The whoosh of Arend's wings could now be heard beating furiously. Without landing he swooped down and began pulling on Lontas with his powerful talons. Lontas let loose a blood-curdling scream of pain.

Using all her might, Bellae began stabbing savagely at the log.

A ghastly, flesh-ripping sound made Bellae drop helplessly to her knees as tears began flowing down her face. Lontas was wrenched away from the log. His scream descended into silence, but his face continued to be locked in a ghastly contortion of pain.

Bellae could see layers of Lontas' flesh sizzling on the billowing log. A trail of blood led from the log to where he and Arend were now flying. Lontas looked at his backside and screamed before passing out from shock and pain.

"Get away from that thing and get back to camp!" Arend cried while flying off.

Bellae watched in horror at the trail of blood leaking from Lontas as he flew. Several large sections of his pants were gone, revealing exposed, weeping flesh up and down his backside and lower legs. Movement from the log suddenly caught her attention. It lurched towards her. She cried out in surprise and quickly scooted backwards. The log growled as she quickly grabbed the plants she had collected and ran, giving the deranged log a wide berth.

Entering camp, her lungs ached from running so hard. Lontas was lying unconscious on his stomach. Bellae closed her eyes and turned away from the horrid sight of his raw flesh. Arend and Kainen talked, glancing nervously at Lontas.

"My dad said not to make contact until we reached Lake Glasere," Arend said, sounding powerless.

"I know, but…" Kainen said, pointing to Lontas.

Arend nodded, "This is bad."

"We were stocked up on bandages before we left, but with Crann and now this…mess, we will quickly run out," Kainen added.

"Listen," Arend announced, "I will fly to the Fada River. Willow trees and the bota plant grow on the east bank. I could fly high enough to avoid detection by the Rebelde Plains people."

"Go!" Kainen cried out tensely.

Moments later, Gimelli screamed and dropped her ravinto branches as she and Sankari entered the camp. "What in the world happened?"

"Lontas sat on a lihumari," Kainen answered numbly.

"A what?" Gimelli questioned.

"It's a creature that looks like a fallen log but eats the flesh off anything that comes near it," Sankari stated impassively, as if it were common knowledge.

"What?" Gimelli repeated as she knelt beside his exposed flesh.

"It secretes an acid that liquefies your flesh while millions of little barbs dig into any good tissue to hold you down. It then digests your body. The pain is intense," Kainen added soberly.

"Are you okay, Bellae?" Gimelli asked.

"Yes. It just looked like a log. He was just going to stand on it and fell."

"Did you guys notice there are hardly any trees around here? Hence the name, Rebelde *Plains*? Not forest," Sankari said in a somewhat snobby tone.

"Please, Sankari," Kainen said. "There is no way they would know about the lihumari. We should have warned them."

Bellae explained to Gimelli what it looked like.

"The black spots were animals it had recently eaten. It's a hideous death. In fact, those who commit horrible crimes in the plains die by being tied down on one of those things. As you can imagine, there are not many serious crimes around here."

"We better clean his wounds before Arend returns," Gimelli said.

"I already doused the wounds with water to get rid of any acid."

Kainen and Gimelli used the remaining water to gently clean Lontas' exposed flesh. Just as they were finishing, Arend came streaking down from the sky, holding reams of vines. Both the vines of the bota plant and its small leaves were blue. He and Kainen quickly began to cut the leaves off at the base. Each time they did, a small amount of milky white fluid dripped out. Once they saw how to do it, Bellae and Gimelli began to help extract the milky fluid and spread it around Lontas' wounds.

Grym popped his head out to see what they were doing. One glimpse of the raw flesh, and he went back into her pocket, for once refraining from any comment. After what seemed like hours of extracting the fluid, they gently laid the blue leaves directly on Lontas' wounds. On top of those, they added some wet cloths from Kainen's satchel.

"I hope he likes sleeping on his stomach," Sankari said, raising her eyebrows.

Next, Arend and Kainen set to work on the bark from a willow tree.

"What are you doing?" Bellae asked.

"The inner bark of the white willow tree dulls pain," Kainen answered, rousing Lontas. "Later we can make a tea, but for now, here, chew on this."

Lontas took several strips of the bark and began chewing.

"Will this work?" Bellae asked, kneeling over her friend.

"We Eaglians use the bota for all sorts of injuries. It works to heal and stop infection, but with this injury, it will take a while," Arend said, letting his voice trail off. Looking up, he spoke again, "I'll get some fresh water."

"Thank you so much," Gimelli said, smiling and handing him the water skins.

Bellae sensed hunger in him and gently held his wrist. "Please, eat something first. Here, take some ravinto leaves. When you get back, we'll have the fire ready to start making some soup."

"Thank you," he said, wearily.

"Lontas only woke up once," Bellae informed Gimelli after breakfast the next day.

"You should have gotten me up."

"It's okay. Arend helped me change the dressings and build up the fire."

"So…" Kainen said sheepishly. "What should we do about your friend?"

Everyone exchanged quick glances before Lontas startled them, "Leave me."

"That's not happening," Bellae roared.

"You can't even walk," Kainen commented. "We're *not* leaving you here."

"Crann, can you carry him?" Bellae asked.

Crann neighed. *"I can try,"* he said, alternating putting weight on his various hooves. His own injuries were healing but still sore.

"No way can I sit!" Lontas exclaimed after Bellae translated for him.

"But, you could lie across him."

After much ado, Lontas was finally propped up on Crann, lying on his stomach over a few blankets on top of a saddle.

"This hurts my stomach, and all the blood is rushing to my head," he said, looking pathetic, laying his cheek dejectedly on Crann's side. "Just leave me."

"Lontas, seriously stop. We're not leaving you," Bellae said firmly.

They worked together to get him down again. No matter how carefully they moved him, screams of pain rang through the air.

After a moment of silence, Arend said, "I can carry him."

"Oh, Arend, you sure?" Gimelli asked.

"No," Lontas replied before Arend could respond.

"Why?" Arend asked.

"Me, up there?" he said pointing up to the sky. "Not happening."

Ten minutes later, Lontas was screaming, "AHHHHHHHHH!" at the top of his lungs while flying through the air in the gentle clutches of Arend's talons.

"Heeeeeeeeewlp!"

"He's giving our position away to everyone in Verngaurd," Sankari protested. "Realistically, maybe leaving him is not such a bad idea." Her little wings vibrated incredibly fast as she hovered with clenched fists.

"Sankari!" Kainen chastised.

"We'd put him out is his misery first…of course," the Fairy said.

Kainen put his hands on his head and gave her an exasperated look.

"He's coming back," Bellae said as Arend struggled to bring the wriggling Lontas down.

"It's okay, Lontas, you're down now," Bellae reassured.

"You don't understand it…makes me…" Lontas gurgled, the rest of his words were covered in retching noises as he vomited all over Bellae.

Scroll 11: Another Try

"The stench of Lontas' vomit is less repugnant. Some nice suns light and good wind should take care of the rest," Kainen said as he gingerly held up Bellae's cloak. "I am going to look for more ravinto plants. I'm hungry."

"Okay, Kainen," Bellae said, grateful, even if it was too big, for the extra cloak the young Elf had brought until hers could dry.

"You guys decide what we are doing?" he called out.

Bellae nodded and turned to Lontas, who was lying on his stomach with his eyes closed. She knew he was not sleeping but mentally beating himself up.

"Let's give it another try."

"I threw up on you, and you still want me to fly?" Lontas rambled, desperately trying to come up with an excuse to avoid floundering in the air again.

"You know what Friar says. With practice, anything is practical."

Lontas had to look away from her genuine smile. He did not want to disappoint his friend, yet again. Who else would smile and encourage him after wearing his vomit? The idea was so funny Lontas began to laugh. Soon, Bellae joined in.

I can't say no to such a good friend, he thought.

"Arend says that with a little conditioning, you'll get used to flying."

The Eaglian had just landed with the replenished water skins. Bellae had used it all to wash herself and her outer cloak.

"If it's okay with you, Arend, I'll try again."

"Wonderful. Let's have a go before Kainen returns. When we land, I suggest everyone give his mouth a wide berth."

Lontas nodded but looked like he would throw up if anything had lingered in his stomach.

Scroll 12: Big Tree-Bigger Stench

"That has got to be the biggest tree in the world," Lovag said pre-dawn of the next day. The Knights stared in awe at the Tree of Life just south of the center of the Forest of Creber.

"It makes the hours and hours of walking in the dark worthwhile," Sorea added.

Feeling disoriented while gazing up at the height of the giant tree in the middle of the Elfish temple, or chyfys, Sorea grabbed Lovag's shoulder to steady herself.

Like their communal eating area, the chyfys was actually an open field, not a building. However, the canopy from the massive tree covered most of the temple space giving the illusion of a roof. More of the tall and skinny mushroom-like plants grew sporadically under the large canopy, providing bioluminescent light.

The behemoth Tree of Life was over five hundred feet tall, with a circumference of over two hundred feet at the base. Directly around the tree there was a rim of solid ground, fifteen feet wide. For the next thirty feet, there was a moat-like ring made up of a substance that resembled wet sand. Several ornate wooden bridges spanned the slushy-looking moat to give access to the tree trunk. Unlike the arbor breith trees, the Tree of Life's roots were underground and it had rough bark all the way up its massive trunk.

Moving away from the tree, after the halo of wet-looking sand, there was solid ground again, which was raised up about three feet. Several sets of stairs led up to the higher ground where a series of concentric benches traversed all the way around its massive girth.

"This is the Edelia Arbor Breith. It is the birth tree of our nation," Beriglor said in an awed tone. On seeing their confused looks he added, "Outsiders know it as the Tree of Life, although that is not a great translation of its meaning to us. Our histories tell us it has been this size for at least three thousand years and probably much, much longer. Could you imagine a grander temple ever being constructed by mortals?" Pointing, he added, "Your seats are all the way up front." He then led Friar, Ritari, Sorea, Lovag, Gleoi Dea, and Luchar to their bench.

"Will you join us?" Friar asked.

"No, I have the great honor of presiding over the ceremony. I will meet you afterward," he said, before hurrying off.

He suddenly whirled around. "Don't worry—someone will come to help you through the ceremony. Everything will be fine," he said, smiling. This time he did not return. The circular seating in the temple area was starting to fill up with Elves of all ages.

All the Knights but Luchar were scanning the crowd and the monstrous arboreal form in front of them. It was intimidating being so close to the towering tree.

"That stuff's moving," Luchar abruptly said.

"The sand-like ground is called caith. It is excreted by Edelia Arbor Breith…the Tree of Life as you might know it," a whispering voice advised them from behind. "It is the source of all life in the forest. It's me, Kempe, but keep looking forward. I can't be seen. Lidenskap will be arriving shortly."

Kempe wore the green robes of a Prete, but his muscular military body looked woefully out of place crammed into the ridiculously stretched fabric. With his hood up, he leaned towards Friar and whispered, "Gimelli, Bellae, and Lontas are safe with the League of Truth. They will visit Stralande, the oldest living blue dragon, to confirm Bellae as the Chosen One. We have deliberately kept their group small and inconspicuous. Between the White Wizard, Watchers, Dark Warriors, wyverns, Proliate, griffins, and Magicians, there are many who seek them."

Friar nodded and asked, "Jumeaux? Scelto?"

"Jumeaux is with the Magicians." In spite of himself, Friar turned around, wide-eyed—he suddenly recalled visions of Jumeaux as a malicious Magician.

Kempe held up his hand. "It's okay."

Friar faced forward as Kempe continued, "After reviewing some of our ancient documents, the League is satisfied with this turn of events. A trap was laid many centuries ago to mislead others about the Chosen One. However, we're pretty sure Bellae is the One."

"Pretty sure?" Friar asked incredulously.

"These matters are eons old. We're all doing our best. If we are correct, it means our false prophecies are still in circulation stating it is the brother, Jumeaux, who is the One. The Magicians apparently fell for this ruse. The blue dragons…" Kempe paused as Lidenskap walked to a seat about thirty feet from them.

"…no time. Just know that Aquila and I will try to watch over them from a distance. Updates to follow," Kempe whispered.

"Scelto?" Friar asked, nervously.

"Scelto is safe with the Proliate. Good-bye, old friend," Kempe whispered as around twenty Prete in green robes descended out of nowhere to surround the Knights. They then quickly made their way over to the Proliators and greeted them warmly. By the time they had passed, Kempe was long gone.

Friar pretended not to notice Ritari's intense stare and nodded towards Lidenskap. The general nodded back before methodically scanning the surroundings.

"No doubt he's looking for Kempe and the others from the tournament, the weasel," Luchar said gruffly, but quietly under orders from his throbbing head.

Friar leaned towards the Knights. "The squires are safe. More later." Closing his eyes didn't stop the images of Jumeaux in Magician robes or Scelto in Proliate armor. *It's all happening as my visions foretold. Should I be comforted or terrified?*

After several more minutes, the temple seating was packed. The turnout was so great that some Elves had to stand around the outer edge as a hushed calm settled on the forest in the soft glowing light of the swelling morning. It was that special time of tranquility that briefly settles upon the forest twice a day in the recurring, and temporary, swap of power. That intermediary time of truce between the forces of the day, sun-adoring diurnal animals, and the nocturnal legions of the night as they transfer control.

A few crepuscular fireflies were impersonating twinkling stars under the mammoth canopy. The serenity of the moment had all the Knights relaxing, their minds drifting soothingly away from the reason they were there, Finn's funeral. Several gongs rang out, bringing them back to reality as everyone stood. Beriglor and hundreds of other Prete filed into the space just in front of the seats but before the bridges leading over the sand like caith.

"My name is Ith. I will guide you through the ceremony," the Prete closest to the Knights said. "This first part is giving honor to the forest and the Edelia Arbor Breith."

The Pretes in front began to chant rhythmically. With their arms raised towards the tree, they began to sway. The Knights could not make out any of the Elfin words. The caith began to undulate, and the louder they chanted, the higher it seemed to rise and fall in smooth, flowing waves. A strange glow began to shine up from below the caith, which made the surface emit an eerie greenish light.

Young Elves went up to the Pretes and handed each of them either a sizable branch with a multitude of leaves or a large rectangular wooden box on top of a wooden staff. Holding them straight out in front of their bodies, the Prete began to shake the branch or pole as the pace of the chanting picked up. Wooden balls within the rectangular boxes made a haunting, drum-like beat. It stood in sharp contrast to the soft, almost desperate rustling sound made by the shaking leaves.

"Of course, we are strictly forbidden from ever damaging a tree. Those are branches which have fallen of their own accord," Ith stated.

The younger Elves stood behind the Prete, and each took out an instrument consisting of two small turtle shells attached to a wooden handle. Wooden balls hung from strings between the two shells. As they began to briskly twirl the handles back and forth, the wooden spheres rapidly collided with the turtle shells, making a frantic cadence that prompted the chanting to quicken even more.

The previous calm of the dawn was now thoroughly shattered. Adrenaline rushed through the amphitheater. The chants seemed to be changing to focus on one word, a word which soon became evident to the Knights.

"Finn, Finn, Finn, Finn, Finn, Finn, Finn, Finn!" they repeated.

The bioluminescent mushrooms all around the chyfys began to gleam and sparkle in tune with the hectic chanting.

They could smell, before they saw, his body. Despite the preservation wraps, some decay had set in. Several younger Elves swiftly carried his body wrapped in a simple cloth sheet down towards the base of the tree.

"The first two parts of our process of returning home were completed at the Citadel: the Ullmhú and AnFilleadh. This part is the Scaoileadh, the release, or return. Normally, there are not this many days between death and release, but obviously the circumstances dictated it. The preparatory sealant and plant leaves have been removed," Ith said.

Figure 4: Prete Beriglor leads the funeral service for Finn, where his body is returned home.

Beriglor stepped forward and was handed a large wooden staff with a beak-like hook on one end. As the other Prete kept up the feverish chants and music, Beriglor made his way across one of the long wooden bridges spanning the caith and moved to stand on the rim of solid ground immediately next to the trunk of the massive tree.

The rippling caith was glowing bright green as he slammed the wooden hook down. It pierced the surface of the unusual material, and with considerable effort he began to pull. It barely moved despite the fact that he was tugging with all his might.

"That's obviously not just sand," Luchar wheezed.

Several Prete crossed the bridge and joined in behind him. They pulled together to yank on the top of the caith. Finally, they began to take a few steps backward, as if in a tug of war. Bending at their knees, they put their full weight behind the task. An edge slowly began to pull back. The luminescent mushrooms were not only glowing but swaying. Several began to wrap their stalks around the legs of the Prete.

"The upper coating must be removed," Ith said, keeping his eyes focused on the top layer of the caith being pulled away.

Once removed, a frothy and whirling green liquid glowing brightly was revealed. Occasionally a bubble would form and pop, sending the green liquid splattering onto the nearby Prete.

The chanting and beating of instruments intensified as a section of the top layer was completely skimmed back. Ghostly vapors rose from the exposed caith. Beriglor's rough brown skin looked odd, reflecting the eerie green light. With unblinking concentration, he started to lean forward, and it appeared as if he might jump into the rippling liquid.

He did not. Instead, he motioned wildly for Finn's body. A strong smell invaded the nostrils of the Knights, a smell of acid and death. Now that Beriglor was in his element, any measure of previous meekness melted away to reveal a fiery passion. The young Elves brought Finn's body to him. Beriglor got on his knees, right at the edge of the surging green liquid. The younger Elves carefully hoisted Finn's body high into the air. The chanting and thumping instruments picked up the already blistering pace. Beriglor raised his hands above his head and they lowered Finn's body onto them.

With well-practiced efficiency Beriglor lurched forward, and Finn's body was cast into the green liquid. His cloth garment was pulled away to reveal him sinking into the frothy fluid. The green liquid lapped up, hungrily swallowing his body, as if it were conscious, famished, and welcoming home a long-lost part of itself. All chanting and music abruptly stopped. With the powerful music terminating, the pounding silence was deafening.

All Elves present breathed a faint, "Reeeeeeelease to return." Then they delicately exhaled, "Filleadh abhaile."

"Return home," Ith whispered.

The eerie silence grabbed a hold of them again. The frantic music was still ringing in their ears and the sight of Finn's stiff and pale body submerging into the sentient caith burned into their retinas.

Friar winced and turned away, grateful Bellae was not here to see this. A flash of orange light shot out of the sentient liquid before the color faded to a pasty green.

Suddenly, a deafening scraping sound filled the outdoor temple. Hundreds of Elven Warriors scurried down the sides of the massive tree. The grooves were so large they fit within them as if they were trenches. When they were almost to the bottom, they abruptly stopped and let out a howling scream that embraced both sadness and passion.

As the yell died away, they began to sing a mournful tune. Even though the Knights could not understand the Elfish language, the deep heartache resonated through them.

"This is the song for a fallen warrior. It is only bequeathed to those who give their lives for our forest. It is a great honor," Ith said.

When the song ended, the warriors scurried back up the massive tree.

As the warriors faded from view, Beriglor slowly stood up. He handed Finn's covering to the younger Elves, who folded it precisely. Several Prete had set down their instruments to roll the top layer of the caith back into place with wooden rollers. Once it was covered, the pale green, bubbling light went out completely. Slowly, the rolling undulations died away as well.

Next, all the Prete and the younger Elves cleared out, leaving a tired-looking Beriglor. He slowly trudged across the walkway leading back to the temple seating. His deferential demeanor back, he moved with his head down. It was only once he was across and had reached the top step near the benches that he looked up. His gaze traveled directly to Friar. He raised his hands and spoke.

"It is always tragic to lose a friend, to lose family. However, to an Elf, we can say we are incredibly proud of Finn and all his glorious accomplishments as an Elf of Creber, and as a Knight. We will miss him greatly."

As he was talking, a large leaf began its long and lazy journey to the earth from the massive tree. Beriglor smiled, seeming energized. Shaking his head he remarked, "Right on time."

After pausing to watch the lazily drifting leaf, he looked at the gathered crowd to make sure they were watching it fall. He smiled as if it were the most amazing event one could possibly witness in all of Verngaurd.

"This time of year the leaves are falling quietly, and quietly descending away from all they have known to rejoin the earth. A day they could not have fathomed when emerging as a bud, with so much potential and life in front of them, yet they tumble down without resistance or complaint about the massive change. The only flutter of protest is at the bidding of the wind. We all undergo this change, from birth to life to death. Such is the way of nature. We owe our gifted life to the earth, and we all shall return to it, paying our debt. All of us should strive to accomplish as much as Finn with our time, to give our best each and every day while being true to family and friends."

A chorus went up from the crowd, "Finn! Finn filleadh abhaile."

Beriglor pulled the hood of his robe up, looked down, and walked towards the Knights. "Spend as much time as you need. I'll be at the edge of the chyfys, waiting to take you back to Finn's arbor breith tree," he said, slowly sauntering away.

Friar closed his eyes, wondering about the future. As much as he wanted to return to Liberum, he was apprehensive. There was too much uncertainty, too many variables swirling around. He wondered if his extraordinary preparations for war were enough, or too much? A waste of precious and shrinking resources, or salvation for the Knights? Tears welled up behind his eyes as the thought of never seeing Finn again tugged at his heart.

Scroll 13: Nice Landing

"You can do this, Lontas," Bellae encouraged as Arend spun him around. "Stand with your arms straight out."

"You do know he's going to hurl on you again?" Crann neighed. Gimelli was on the other side of Crann. Sankari rested on Kainen's shoulder.

"Have faith," she replied. *"He did okay when Kainen was gone."*

"All I'm saying is you should have more clothes on hand if that boy is going to fly."

Bellae laughed. *"He can do it."*

Arend used his muscular legs to run and then vault up into the air.

"Taking off from the ground is hard for Arend. It takes a lot of energy," Kainen said. "That is why he likes to be airborne and then fly around before coming to get you."

"Uh-huh," Lontas said, a cavernous pit of doubt gnawing at his gut.

"Flying near the mountains is awesome when the wind gives you a big updraft and you can just glide."

"Sounds as if you have flown with Arend before," said Bellae.

"Of course. He's like my brother." Kainen's eyes had a far-off look as if reliving the experience.

"Here he comes," Bellae said, scampering away. Lontas' arms shook with nerves. His eyes closed and mouth clenched as if he were about to be hit in the face with a bucket of freezing water.

Arend swooped down and deftly grabbed him under the arms with his claws. His massive wings beat forcefully as his face scrunched into a grimace. Lontas jerked forward, and his legs skidded and bopped along the ground.

"Oh!" Bellae sighed.

"Arend's tired, but he'll get off the ground," Kainen reassured, nodding as his friend took to the skies.

"Lontas looks frightened, but not as dreadful as before," Gimelli said.

Bellae nodded as Arend and Lontas' outline disappeared, blending into the long shadows of the Tingij Mountains.

The wind beat upon Lontas' face and body as the muscular whoosh of Arend's wings pulsed against the air above him. As they rose higher, Lontas felt as if his bones were rising but his brain, organs, and skin were being pulled back down towards the earth. Opening his eyes, the fading earth made his head spin while a feeling of nausea punched into his stomach. He peered up at Arend's wings, fascinated with the powerful and rhythmic movement. With short strokes the vast wings stayed fairly straight on the way down. When he pushed hard, they folded to wrap around Lontas' body.

I wish I were reading about this, Lontas lamented, missing his favorite seat in the library. It had faded green fabric that while almost completely worn off, fit his body perfectly. A sense of calm came over him as he imagined the rows of scrolls and books.

Arend was gliding closer and then farther from the ground. Lontas stared in wonder as their shadow grew larger and more ill-defined, then smaller and sharper against the blur of green racing by.

"Arend?" Lontas wasn't sure how well he would be heard.

"Yeah."

"I never thanked you. So, well, thanks a lot for getting me off that log, tree…thing."

Arend craned his neck down to look at him. "The lihumari, and you are most welcome."

"Why does your neck move like that?" Lontas asked.

"It keeps my eyes locked on prey. Even if my wings are beating or a gust of wind turns my body, my head stays stable, keeping my eyes on target. I need it if my prey tries to use obstacles like trees or something, and my body is whipping around them."

"It's good to stay on target."

Arend's answering laughter was pierced with an occasional screech. "Yes, in all things, it is good to stay on target."

Lontas felt a rush of warm air rise up and wrap itself around them. Arend let out a squawk and spread his wings. The warm air forced his feathers apart, especially at the tips so there was quite a distance between them. Lontas could see hints of the bright blue sky and drifting wisps of white clouds above them.

Arend chuckled. "Enjoying yourself?"

Lontas held back his impulse to scream. "No." Instead he looked up into Arend's large yellow eyes. "I think so?"

Arend squawked with laughter. "You are either enjoying it or not."

Lontas chuckled but said nothing since it felt like a little bit of both. Enjoyment laced with a sharp edge of terror and nausea. Arend glided over the mountains, and they could see the eastern sunlight gleaming off one side of the mountain, highlighting the uneven crags and roughness with black pocks and streaks. The rows of sharp peaks looked cold and uninviting. Suddenly, Arend's eyes turned towards the Rebelde Plains.

He lashed into a turn before diving swiftly. Lontas winced as he felt his body whip downward. It felt as if someone were squishing everything inside him up against his back and tailbone. It was particularly acute in his head where it felt like fluid was sloshing up and hitting the top of his skull.

"I see food!" Arend's windswept voice said.

"At the moment, 'going down' and 'dinner' both sound particularly unappealing," Lontas said weakly.

Arend ignored him, tucking his wings for speed. They zipped downward, frantically accelerating. Lontas felt his feet tip up and the wind abuse his face as they dove—the skin on his cheeks stretching and flapping towards his ears.

Nearing the ground, Arend let his wings out and their speed slowed with a snap. Without coming to a complete stop, Arend tossed Lontas down before shooting up into the sky. Lontas rolled, graceless and painfully, in the tall grass. With his backside aching, he fought nausea, beckoned by his whirling brain.

Moaning, he looked up to see Arend diving for a large buck. He was quickly gaining on the zigzagging prey. When he was close, his transparent inner eyelid closed to protect his eyes while allowing him to see his quarry. Arend used his left talon to grab the buck's right set of antlers while his right talon grabbed onto the deer's upper back. Using his wings to help swivel his weight, he shifted his body into a wringing motion, which violently twisted the deer's neck until a brutal snap could be heard. The deer instantly went limp, crashing to the ground. For good measure, Arend put his talons through the buck's carotid arteries and jugular veins, showering blood everywhere.

The smell of roasting deer was actually making Lontas hungry.

"Sorry about the rough landing," Arend said sheepishly. "You need protein to heal."

"It's okay," Lontas replied stiffly. "It all worked out."

When the meat was ready, Bellae and Gimelli took turns helping Lontas eat while he continued to lie on his stomach. Suddenly, a loud boom startled them from the other side of the Tingij Mountains. Arend turned his head almost completely around to look.

"That still weirds me out," Gimelli said, clenching her teeth and shivering.

"Thunder," Kainen said.

Sankari rolled her eyes. "Oh great, we're going to get wet."

"The mountains will probably take most of the moisture," Kainen said.

Bellae stared at Arend as he ripped off a huge chunk. "You eat the bones?"

"Actually, all Eaglians do."

Kainen laughed.

"What?" Gimelli probed.

"You'll see," the young Elf said, laughing again.

When they all had their fill, they sat around the campfire in the foggy postprandial haze that comes after engorging yourself.

"Thanks for the meal, Arend," Kainen said. "Ravinto soup gets old." The others all murmured their appreciation. Bellae stared as Arend stretched his wings.

"Do you want to touch them?" he questioned.

"What?" she asked in surprise.

"It's okay."

Bellae slowly rose and self-consciously reached out to gently feel his feathers. They had a silky soft texture, and yet were tough. Her eyes were drawn to his massively muscled back.

"I have extra muscles to power my wings. They are totally separate from the rest of my back muscles."

"Thanks. Your wings are very nice," she mumbled, still embarrassed.

"Sankari, can you take first watch?" Kainen asked.

"Suppose so," she said, fluttering up and out of camp in a huff.

"Everyone else, get to sleep. Tomorrow we need to hustle. It seems as if we are finally ready to go." He nodded to Lontas. The group took their places around the fire.

After several minutes, a retching sound jerked the dozing companions fully awake.

"Lontas?" Bellae asked, groggily assuming it was him.

"Not me," he replied sleepily.

"Sorry," Arend said.

Kainen began to laugh. "I told you guys to just wait and you would understand why I was laughing earlier. Eaglians vomit part of what they eat."

"I *regurgitate* the parts I can't digest. It's actually quite efficient."

"You can try to pass vomiting off as 'efficient regurgitation' if that makes you feel better, but it's throwing up. Hey, get rid of that disgusting thing, will you?" Kainen said jokingly.

Arend picked up a grayish-brown oval mass. Parts of bone and what looked like fur were tightly packed within it.

"And people call mice disgusting?" Grym sneered. *"I'm going back to sleep."*

"It's called a pellet," Arend said. "I have this pouch in my esophagus called the crop. It's where I can store food, and then I form this little ball of waste and cough it up," he said, throwing it into the fire.

"Like any of us want to hear about your freaky personal digestive problems," Kainen said, laughing. Arend gently kicked him with one of his talons, careful to not let his claws cut him.

Kainen looked closely at the burning pellet. "Have you been eating rabbits? That looks like rabbit fur in there. You better be not be holding out on us, big guy."

Arend ignored his jibe, pretending to be asleep.

Lontas closed his eyes, but his stomach churned with equal dashes of excitement and fear. *I wish I were in Liberum, sitting in class. Oh, no! Not sitting!* He smiled. *Plus, Jumeaux would certainly have a lot to say about my little accident.* Lontas wrinkled his nose, imagining Jumeaux's goofy laugh, silly jokes and inevitable comments, *"I always knew you were a pain in the as—."* Lontas covered his mouth to keep from laughing.

He finally managed to stop giggling. Still on his stomach, he craned his neck to stare at the largest moon, Stor-Manen. It looked calm and peaceful floating through the dark sea of night. He visually traced the craters and what appeared to be mountains. *How would it be to walk there?* he wondered sleepily, slowly giving himself up to slumber.

"Ready?" Kainen asked the next morning after Lontas' wounds had been cleaned and dressed with the milky white liquid of the bota plant.

Lontas nodded faintly and showed a stifled smile as Arend flew around. Lontas' head rolled forward slightly. He pursed his lips tightly as if he were holding in vomit. The ground, so comfortable, so familiar, made the anticipation of flight horrifying.

Suddenly, his body lurched forward as the wind began to rush into his face and flip his hair upwards. He sucked in a deep breath as they gained altitude.

"How is it?" Arend asked.

"Good," Lontas said calmly, surprised to find his stomach spinning with equal excitement and nausea.

"Glad to hear it. Let's try this." Arend suddenly broke into a series of dips and turns.

Lontas let himself go, getting lost in flight, surrounded by the blue sky and threads of clouds, seeing it for the first time not as prison but an experience. Relaxing, he let the world flip and spin as the Eaglian danced across the sky.

"Well?" Arend asked.

"Fun!" Lontas remarked in a windswept tone, his hair jumping with the excitement he felt.

"Urgh-spphhhh-sppt-tttttttttaaaa," Lontas spat.

"Are you vomiting again?"

"Ssppt-tttttttt-no…bug."

"Excellent source of protein!" Arend laughed.

Lontas tried to use his tongue to scrape the tiny residual bits of the bug out of his teeth but couldn't help swallowing parts of it.

"I know Kainen wants to make it to the Lake today, but I don't think we will," Arend said as he made huge arcing circles around the others walking below.

"Can the Watchers' net catch us?"

"No, we are not flying high enough for that."

Lontas could barely see the tiny detail-less forms of his friends. "They look like little smudges."

"To you. I see them just fine."

"Eaglians are amazing."

"Wait until you see my dad, a full sized Eaglian."

Lontas gazed at the massive talons and impressive muscles. *Not sure I want to.*

Chapter Three

War–Magicians–
Proliate

Scroll 1: Death of Waiting

"Are you ready?" the Elf priest, Beriglor, asked, hunching timidly the next morning.

"Yes," Friar answered. Although it was early, he felt tired, and resigned himself to hard day's journey towards home. Visions of Finn sinking into the caith, Jumeaux as a Magician, and Scelto as a Proliator stung his mind, poisoning his sleep.

"Thank you for the ceremony yesterday," Sorea said.

"We greatly appreciated your sincerity and kind words," Friar added.

Beriglor whispered something that sounded like a choked-up "You're welcome."

"Where's Musta-Yo, my horse?" Ritari asked.

"He's waiting for you," Beriglor answered, sounding relieved to talk about something else. "I have good and bad news. We also found another of your horses."

"One?" Friar asked.

"Actually two," he faltered. "One of your horses was found shredded and killed by animals. It was likely forest wolves, as we found many of them eating its carcass."

"Which one?" Friar asked.

"It was the largest horse we have ever seen…"

"Honey!" Sorea said worriedly.

"We know the squires are safe. Kempe told us yesterday," Friar reassured.

"I apologize. It would be alive if our forces had not been distracted by the battle. The good news is, the other horse we found is waiting with your supply wagons," Beriglor stated.

Friar, Ritari, Sorea, Lovag, Gleoi Dea, and Luchar trudged behind Beriglor with minds racing. The mood was low as they walked through the morning forest. The chatter of the birds and beasts seemed far off, but intermittently they could clearly hear trees creaking and bending as the Varna warriors escorting them moved high above. After many hours, the forest began to thin, and their pace quickened as they neared the edge. Suddenly, shadows emerged from the trees surrounding them.

"Ambush!" Luchar yelled.

"Hold!" Friar ordered. "Hello, Ailante. Elegant entrance as always."

"Sorry for the surprise. The Varna and I wanted to catch you before you left our forest," he answered, motioning to the Elfish warriors around them.

"We appreciate the chance to thank you for your hospitality," Friar stated, bowing.

"I wish you could stay, but I understand you are anxious to return home given the uncertain times," Ailante said. "Friar, may have a word in private?"

Friar and the head Elf of Creber moved off.

"I want to emphasize that your squires *are* safe. However, there is now no doubt that the White Wizard knows about Bellae, Jumeaux, and the prophecy," Ailante advised. "This attack outside our borders was designed to capture Bellae and Jumeaux."

Friar raised his eyebrows questioningly.

"We found many Dark Warriors in our outer ring of trees. An Eaglian, Bellae's protector, had mutilated them. Thank goodness the League thought to have Bellae watched."

Friar rubbed his forehead. "One more complicating factor for us to worry about."

"This incident taught us valuable lessons about where to place our resources when faced with a threat to our forest. We are embarrassed we did not rescue Bellae sooner, and will never let this happen again. We placed most of our forces around our sacred birth trees," Ailante stated. He then moved even closer to Friar and whispered, "I want you to know, we're with you."

Friar nodded. "Thank you. Regrettably, war is hurtling towards us."

Ailante nodded sadly as the two of them joined the rest of the Knights. "On a happier note, the Proliate have been true to their word. They have a squad guarding your warrior's body, secured horses for all of you, and restocked your supply wagon."

"Wonderful."

"Sleazebags," Luchar snarled.

Friar embraced his old friend one last time. It contained extra intensity, the kind born of friends in anxious and uncertain times when any measure of security and familiarity is yearned for.

Ailante spoke in Elfish. "Sorry," he said, waving away the words they could not understand before repeating it in the common tongue. "Good luck, Knights."

They paused in the relative darkness of the forest, a tinge of remorse hanging over their thoughts at leaving the well-protected and magical world of Creber.

With a sigh, the Knights emerged from the forest into the blinding, two-sun afternoon. Shielding their eyes, they could hear the Proliate barking orders. Friar moved forward even though his eyes were still reeling from the bright light. With each step the emetic smell of burning flesh burrowed deeper into his nostrils.

"Sir, we have orders to turn these things over to you. Do you require anything else?" a Proliate sergeant asked briskly.

"No, we greatly appreciate your assistance."

The Proliate made a series of low guttural noises and with impressive precision headed off to the northwest towards their outpost at Ragorsaf.

"Talkative bunch," Sorea said sarcastically. "Oh, what a smell."

Friar and the Knights surveyed the residue of battle carnage. Despite the tireless work of the Proliate, the ground was marred by the blight of blood and disfigured with body parts and fluid, which the scavenger birds and hordes of flies labored to devour. A scorched mound still smoldered over the blackened bodies of the Dark Warriors.

"So much blood."

"This blood, I fear, is just the first payment in a war where much more will be due," Friar said.

Ritari rushed to Musta-Yo and cradled his neck.

"Behalen!" Lovag yelled, running towards his horse. The two put their heads together as Lovag whispered inaudibly.

Friar nodded in approval while examining the wrapped body of Arquero. The preservative salts and linens, the tradition of the Proliate, had been applied, and he rested on a well-made sled.

Ritari stepped forward. "I'd like to claim eximus-nex."

Friar raised his eyebrows. "The exception to the practice of burying Knights in our cemetery? That means no monuments or grave markers to make sure his remains are not disturbed."

"We all love Arquero, but we are a long way from home, riding without an advance or rearguard though hostile territory. If we are attacked, we will have to outrun them."

"Everyone agrees?"

The Knights nodded.

"Alright, let's move away from Creber to prepare his grave. How about the small grove of trees over there?"

"You mean, where the bloody Magicians tried to scorch our squires?" Luchar grumbled. While his shoulder injury was feeling better, he still had a constant headache, souring his already foul mood.

"Yes, near the sight of the Magician battle. However, I told you they are safe and on their way to play a role in the future."

"Our squires should be with *us*!" Luchar howled.

"Agreed. I can't understand this 'greater purpose' you mentioned. They're just kids," Sorea added as Luchar grunted approval.

"I can't control that which is out of my realm. Sometimes fate and circumstance decide things without my express permission," Friar said, half in jest and half in frustration.

Unsatisfied, the Knights deferred to bury Arquero. Upon finishing, they observed a moment of silence over his makeshift grave. Lovag took the longest time with his old friend. Once loaded up, they headed northeast towards the Way of Trepas. With war looming ever closer, Friar was anxious to do a little reconnaissance there and at Temple Ovest.

"Can you tell us more about the squires?" Sorea asked anxiously.

"There are deeper issues at work here. Rest assured they are safe and where they can do the most good."

"Jumeaux may be a cocky heel of a squire but he's my cocky heel of a squire," Luchar growled, unable to comprehend anything deeper than the feeling that they were abandoning their own.

"No one misses them more than me. However, these are difficult times, and I ask you to accept that they have a part to play in our future and that role is not with us."

"Friar, that makes no sense. I love Lontas, but he is the clumsiest person I have ever met. We can't leave him out there by himself," Lovag declared.

"That is where the trust part comes in."

A groan of dissatisfaction went through the Knights.

"Trust the skill of your squires and our allies who help them. With his love of learning Lontas has a mind as sharp as anyone twice his age.

He scored higher than any other squire on his mental tests, even better than you, Lovag," Friar said, laughing.

"Gimelli can charm a dragon with her smile and positive attitude. She is responsible, caring, and can make friends with anyone. Scelto is mature and strong as a trompe from Ager. Bellae, well, we have all been amazed by her heart, curiosity, and unique aptitudes. Jumeaux…" Friar started. He was interrupted by several grumbles.

"Now, now," he said. "Jumeaux has passion and a strength that needs to be channeled and developed."

As the Knights chewed on his words, Ritari said, "Friar, we are being followed."

"Proliate?" he questioned as the Knights began to scan the horizon, their eyes hungrily eating the landscape for signs of attackers. The small size of the group made them feel, paradoxically, like a large target.

"Looks like Red Guard." He squinted at the barely visible line of soldiers. "Wait…silver shields and helmets—Proliate Ultor Division," Ritari answered.

"I expected company. They were likely sent to watch, but not engage," Friar said. "Let's pick up the pace and see if they can keep stride."

The Knights rode hard the rest of the day with the Proliate shadowing them at a consistent but non-threatening distance. As the third sun tucked itself away for the night, they had made it towards the Tingij Mountains, whose pitch-black silhouettes looked angry against the darkening sky.

After an uneventful night, they arose before the Mardin sun had climbed high enough to clear the eastern horizon. Lovag sat hunched over, with his back to the others.

"What are you doing?" Luchar growled in his traditional morning ill-humor.

"I had good luck," Lovag said, holding up two large, skinned rabbits.

"Saddle steak for lunch," Friar said gleefully.

They divided the rabbit meat and carefully wrapped the pieces in leather and placed the packages under their saddles. After tending to the horses, they ate some bread and preserved cheese. As they rode, heat from the horses and the friction from the saddle tenderized and broke down the meat so that it could be digested. They rode in silence, and time seemed to drag along.

"The Proliate force has grown and is closing," Gleoi Dea stated calmly. The others turned to see a force of two to three hundred Proliate riding hard towards them.

"These pansies are Red Guard, not the ones who have been tailing us, and they have Magicians with them," Luchar growled. Never fond of them, his dislike had blossomed into hatred after the Tournament and Finn's death during the dragon battle.

"Not just Magicians, Veneficus himself," Ritari said. "Friar, orders?"

"Keep weapons sheathed. Let's slow up."

"Let's attack!" Luchar howled. He was leaning forward, his eyes ablaze. Sorea began to winch back her crossbow.

"We hold," Friar said in an even, unruffled tone, despite the churning of his stomach. As the Proliate drew closer, Friar held up a hand to say 'hello' and convey they did not have weapons drawn. About fifty yards from the Knights, the main force of the Proliate came to an abrupt stop. Veneficus, General Lidenskap, an elderly looking Magician, and several Proliate Red Guard continued towards them.

"Greetings Veneficus, general," Friar said, staying cheerful despite the pretentious and condescending attitude radiating from the Proliators.

"We have disturbing news," Veneficus said.

Yeah, you showed up, Luchar thought, fighting the urge to swing his battle-axe.

"There have been five new massacres," Veneficus continued. "Piscium, Ager, the Kingdom of the Southern Dwarves, and for the second time, Jaa experienced attacks."

"This is concerning," Friar stated anxiously. "First, the Dark Warriors attack us with a huge force, and now this? They are becoming emboldened."

Lidenskap laughed mockingly. "The Dark Warriors are not responsible."

"It was Elves of Creber and Northern Dwarves," Veneficus said in a dejected tone.

"Lies!" Gleoi Dea yelled, standing up indignantly in her saddle.

"Lies?" Veneficus roared, his eyes ablaze in anger. His crosier glowed crimson, and Gleoi Dea sat down in her saddle, Veneficus' face slowly softening. "I have seen them myself."

"You saw the fighting?" Friar asked.

"No," Veneficus admitted.

"He didn't have to," Lidenskap interjected. "There were a few small details, such as *the ground littered* with innocent villagers courtesy of the Dwarf and Elfin weapons *sticking out* of *them!*"

"General, you were with us in the Forest of Creber. Surely, you can't believe the Elves are capable of these atrocities? You know their only wish is to stay within the borders of their forest, living in peace."

"The only thing I know is that the Northern Dwarves and Elves of Creber have been attacking innocent villages, creating havoc to aid the Dark Warriors and destabilize the Proliate."

"Have you captured any of the Elves or Dwarves?"

"This must be hard for you to accept since the one leading these massacres is your longtime friend, Kempe. He and his band of murderers escaped with the aid of the White Wizard," Lidenskap said, absorbing the glares and scoffs from the Knights who knew that Kempe was at Finn's funeral and clearly could not have been involved.

"This cannot be," Friar said.

"Why? Why can't it be? What more proof do you need? You heard Kempe implicated at the Tournament, and we get the same story over and over again from different villages in different countries."

"These are staged attacks," Gleoi Dea declared in exasperation. "Kempe would never be involved in murder or plunder. Elves don't value money or gold, only nature."

Lidenskap ignored her. "Be careful who you consort with, Friar. The Elves of Creber and the Northern Dwarves are destroying Verngaurd to the delight of the White Wizard."

"I *will* choose carefully," Friar answered. "The Dark Warriors and White Wizard are clearly staging these attacks in an obvious attempt to divide us. That you are falling for it is what I cannot believe. Veneficus, surely you can tell the White Wizard is behind these attacks?"

"Ridiculous!" Lidenskap shouted. "What proof do you have?"

Friar looked to Veneficus to interject, to provide some reason in this insanity.

"I have personally seen the battlefields and heard eyewitness accounts. The evidence is overwhelming," Veneficus said in a reluctant and sympathetic tone.

"Surely, in all your wisdom, you can see this doesn't add up," Friar pleaded.

Veneficus shook his head slowly. "I can see darkness closing in. Unfortunately, much of it appears to be coming from within our own borders."

"That is precisely why now is the time to consolidate all forces still loyal to Verngaurd. It appears that, so far, you have not gone over to the Dark Warriors," Lidenskap declared. "Only after we secure the rebels can we face the increasing hordes of Dark Warriors. Time is up, Friar. Make your choice. Join our Confederacy in the fight to secure our homeland, or we will take it as a declaration of war. Sitting around wishing for rainbows while Verngaurd implodes is no longer an option. Decide where you stand!"

"By securing our homeland I am assuming you mean attacking the Northern Dwarves and the Elves of Creber?" Friar asked caustically.

"Right now they are the greatest threat to Verngaurd. We must neutralize them quickly in order to concentrate on the Dark Warriors. Without the support of the traitorous insurgents, the Dark Warriors will flounder," Lidenskap replied. His face softened at the thought of Tallcon's request that the Knights join the Proliate.

"My offer for the Knights and Proliate to unite still stands." He handed Friar a scroll outlining an alliance between the two states.

"You are wrong about this, and one day, probably when it is too late for Verngaurd, you will realize it," Friar said, tossing the scroll back.

"Then it is settled. In the name of Tallcon, and the ultimate peace and safety of our lands, we are formally at war," Lidenskap said, entirely too casually.

"You're an old fool, Friar, and just signed the death knell for the Knights," the elderly Magician next to Veneficus stated. He turned his horse and rode for the main Proliate army.

"I afforded the Knights every opportunity to survive," Lidenskap alleged. Deep lines of disgust were painted in broad strokes across his face. "I made my offer out of sympathy for your wretched—"

Luchar interrupted with growling words, "Sympathy! Why…" A look and restraining hand from Friar silenced him.

Lidenskap continued, "…state and a fading respect for your tradition of protecting Verngaurd. We both know those days are long, long gone." He paused as if to let the Knights absorb his powerful words. Friar said nothing but stared amiably at him, as if he had just complimented them.

Frustrated at the lack of rise from Friar, Lidenskap continued, "The next time we meet it will be under less pleasant circumstances."

"I look forward to it," Friar said, smiling as if they were best friends agreeing to meet for dinner.

With a look of exasperation that only one in a position of power can wield, Lidenskap turned and rode off. He had only gone a short way when he turned back. "If you get into trouble, don't bother blowing the Horn of Kayda," he said, raising his eyebrows with a look of superiority, his expression physically helping to rub in the taunting words.

Veneficus waited while Lidenskap marched out of earshot then motioned for Friar, who nudged his steed forward.

"Oh, how far we have fallen—the opposite of what we hoped for. This link between Proliate and Magicians has proven troublesome of late," Veneficus said, motioning to the retreating Red Guard. "I hope we can still salvage this situation."

Friar smiled, happy to see such a powerful being moved by their plight. "I'm sorry to say, the days of waiting for reconciliation are long past."

"Perhaps, but the alternative is too vile."

Friar shook his head, as if it would help shake loose the delusions Veneficus seemed to have about the situation. "If peace comes without war, I will welcome it wholeheartedly. However, to be practical, I beg your assistance."

"Anything," Veneficus answered.

"I ask for safe passage to Liberum for myself and Knights."

"I'll talk to Lidenskap myself, and it will be done."

"Thank you," Friar said. The two exchanged an awkward embrace, hindered by too much baggage laden with dashed hopes and uncertainty of the future.

"I hope we meet under friendlier circumstances next time," Veneficus said, knowing it was unlikely, before swiveling and galloping back towards the Proliate line.

War. Back so soon, Friar thought. Catastrophic images of enduring the Dark War as a squire rose like fire but with hazy details manifesting as a smoky whisper. Chaotic reflections of battles, blood, and confusion grew only to quickly disintegrate given their remoteness and sheer brutality.

"Now the future is set," he said. "The planning I hoped we wouldn't need will pay off. The endless drills and maneuvers you endured over the last year seemed unnecessary, but they were for this exact moment. I can tell you we are about to witness the greatest moment in the history of the Knights, our return to prominence!"

A loud cheer went up from the Knights. Before it died down, Friar spoke, "We ride hard for Liberum."

The idea of war became so palpable the concept transformed into a savory flesh that their minds chewed over as they rode. As for Friar, he knew that the cataclysmic change that had precipitated the Knights decline, the Dark War, was nothing compared to what was coming. A new convulsion was about to rip through Verngaurd, and the Knights would either regain their previous glory, or all die.

Scroll 2: Crimson Overload

Scelto tossed and turned as the other Proliate slept. The small barracks were efficient, with beds stacked three high against the walls. The rest of the room was filled with storage trunks, tables, and shelves. Three fireplaces roared, seemingly crackling encouragement to his already racing mind.

Could I stay here? The unspoken, unwanted thought poked up, demanding that he pay attention. *Haven't I already been accepted?* Like unwanted baggage, pictures of Liberum rose and fell into a shuffling mix with those of the Proliate and Tallcon.

"Time to get up, lazy boy," Velox said in a good-natured tone.

"It's morning?" Scelto asked groggily, not feeling as if he had slept at all.

"Morning is the traditional time to get up, yes," Velox answered, laughing.

Scelto threw the covers off and stood up quickly, catching the back of his head on the bunk above him.

"If you are to be knocked out, let it be in battle."

"Funny," Scelto grinned, rubbing the sore area on the top of his head.

I wonder if this is how Lontas feels in the morning? He felt absolutely exhausted. The battle raging in his mind had taken a big toll on his stamina.

Velox stopped smiling, and deep furrows spread across his forehead.

"What's wrong?" Scelto asked.

"Today's a big day. Follow me."

The two made their way to the far end of the barracks. There, spread over one of the chairs and tables, sat a shiny new set of Rutilus Obitus red armor.

Scelto looked at his friend skeptically. Velox smiled and nodded.

"Here, this first." he said, handing Scelto a thin red robe. "We put this on before the padding or aketon."

Scelto nodded, not understanding the significance.

"It is our angladd, a burial robe," Velox said. Scelto snapped his head to Velox.

"Proliate wear our burial robe every day as a reminder that death, whether tomorrow or in twenty years, means life is gone in a flash. We should remember not to fear death but choose a life full of glory and honor. Fear of death on the battlefield pollutes your mind," he said solemnly. "Get dressed and hurry out. You get to participate in Morning Prayer today."

Scelto obliged. The armor was similar to Ritari's, and so he was able to put it on with help from several Proliate passing by.

"Hurry," Velox chided, breaking into a run and not turning back. Scelto ran after him. They burst through the outer gate of Ragorsaf. Waiting there was the entire garrison stationed at the outpost, all facing east. Scelto let out a little gasp as he gazed upon the skyline. The horizon was ablaze with deep blood red.

Velox leaned in and whispered, "This is a special prayer service acknowledging Tallcon as the source of the world. He shared part of his body and blood with Verngaurd. Each day this covenant is renewed as his gift of fire, in the form of the three suns, lights our world. The red dawn and sunset are symbols of his gift of blood that washed across the earth and initially breathed life onto the barren rock that was here before."

"Welcome," the Master Cleric in front of the group said. "Let us start our day by renewing our commitment to Tallcon."

"Eternal Tallcon, Tallcon Eternal.

Source of the World, the World's Source.

We Live by the Seven Fires, The Seven Fires Guide our Lives.

As the suns rise and set.

Our sacred oath is met.

Your sacred blood,

Sets across the horizon like a flood.
Sacred blood of life.
Guide us through our daily strife."

The men stood in silence with their heads bowed for several minutes. Scelto moved his armor around enough to test its flexibility but not enough to draw attention. The overlapping plates of armor provided protection with great suppleness.

"You will spend the morning with Temere," Velox informed. "Temere—Scelto. Scelto—Temere." The two nodded at each other. The man had a somber and serious look etched across his young face. His dark brown hair had a natural curl to it. His eyes were a light brown, speckled with grey.

Later that day, Scelto gazed up at the suns to see how much time there was until lunch. Mardin was high, and Luminos was peeking up over the horizon. He felt uncomfortably hot but smiled at the thought of Gimelli, sometimes called Lumi due to her sunny disposition. Temere had been working him hard in full armor. That wasn't as bad as his constant chatter about Tallcon. His stay at Ragorsaf had hardened him to their preaching, but this seemed different.

"A Proliate must know the infinite significance of Tallcon's name, while doing his best to spread his message. Tallcon deserves our honor, our respect, dedication, inspires us to bravery, to never quit, to go above and beyond, to never lose." Temere paused, staring at Scelto to gauge his response.

"What do you think about war with the Knights and their allies?" Temere probed.

"What?" Scelto questioned.

"There has been a huge spike in attacks by the Elves of Creber and

Northern Dwarves. It is only a matter of time before war is declared," Temere said, pausing to lean against the siege engine they were working on.

"I have equal fear war will happen—many of my brothers will die, and not happen—we cannot show Tallcon's power through battle. Of course, our victory is assured," Temere paused.

"So tell me more about the diezmar," Scelto asked, pointing to the giant siege engine. He was trying to deflect some of the uncomfortable feeling in his stomach. It didn't work, as Temere ignored him, continuing, unfazed.

"The raamattu tells us to delight only in the glory of Tallcon. It states that killing in the heat of battle is honorable only if in his name. The Proliate rose at precisely the right time to safeguard the innocent during the first Dark War. Now it is the Knights, Elves of Creber, and Northern Dwarves who join the Dark Warriors in wreaking havoc across Verngaurd. We will stop them." As he finished, his eyes were ablaze, his intense stare daring Scelto to say otherwise.

Scelto was feeling increasingly uncomfortable. Nodding, he repeated his question about the siege engine. Temere seemed satisfied with Scelto's interest in the machine and let the subject change. A large firing wheel with eight large slings sat in the center of a large, rectangular wooden building. On either side of the building were two running wheels used to raise a counterweight and add torsion force to spin the firing wheel.

"The main advantage of this siege engine is its ability to rapidly focus a massive amount of power on one spot. It uses a series of pulleys *and* torsion to magnify the power of the counterweight, which turns the large firing wheel. Each of the eight slings holds a projectile and then, look," he said, pointing to a large blade at the top of structure. "This lever pushes the blade into the slings path and cuts them as they spin past, releasing the projectiles to a precise location. New slings and projectiles are loaded, and it goes again."

Scelto nodded silently as Temere continued to smile in slick satisfaction. "When we get this lady humming, she will unleash eight bundles of destruction in less than thirty seconds to a single point. When you add twenty of these on a battlefield, forget it. When they all hit together, it generates deep vibrations that resonate within a castle wall until it starts to oscillate and boom!"

Scelto looked at the eight diezmar siege machines sitting out in the open plains. "What are these doing way out here anyway? There are no nearby castles to destroy."

Temere seemed pleased with the question. "Diezmar are helpful on any battlefield, not just a siege. Imagine eight projectiles heading towards an enemy's ranks. Chaos and destruction. We are setting up this outpost for the regular Ultor troops, who will relieve us while we head back to the Citadel. From there, who knows…" He paused, looking over the horizon as if the answer were somehow written out on the Rebelde Plains.

Scelto looked out to see the sparse trees, scarce and isolated enough they seemed lost, or abandoned.

He could relate.

"Can you smell that?" Temere suddenly asked. Scelto sniffed and shook his head. *Nothing other than my body odor.*

"War is in the air. It smells of a righteous war!" Temere said, inhaling deeply.

"It must feel good for you to be with an organized army like ours. I can't imagine being with the disorderly Knights. Their unorganized and nonconformist ways have made them feeble. They will fall quickly when we decide to move."

Scelto felt a burst of anger rise up within him. Looking down, he didn't answer. But what else was he feeling? Shame? Was there some truth in Temere's words?

"Hey, you two, target is ready. Wake up and get ready to fire," someone yelled. Scelto looked up to see several squads of Proliate approaching the various siege engines. Eight came directly towards Scelto and Temere.

"We're your runners," one said.

"Jump in the wheels and get this baby humming," Temere said as they began galloping in the two running wheels, which slowly groaned awake, and eventually began rotating quickly.

"Look in here, Scelto," Temere said, opening a door in the back of the rectangular structure and pointing. "See those ropes and pulleys? They help store energy. One wheel raises the counterweight while the second puts energy into those ropes by twisting them, like you see on a torsion ballista. As the counterweight falls, the pulleys and torsion combine with the counterweight to increase the energy that spins the firing wheel at absurd speeds. That unlucky wall in the distance is our target."

Scelto looked across the large field to see a solitary section of stone wall. It looked ridiculously out of place and a little lonely sitting in the field by itself.

"We built it just to blow it up," Temere said, chuckling. "How cool is that?"

Scelto was in charge of pushing the lever to engage the blade and release the rock projectiles. It had to be timed perfectly with the release of the other diezmars to get the vibratory power of resonance they sought.

"We will teach you the physics of the diezmar's inner workings later, and eventually, you can handle the angler that controls where and when the blade cuts the ropes and, hence, controls the aim."

Just then, their commander shouted, "Initiate firing sequence!"

With the Proliate runners out of the wheels, the counterweight began to fall, and the giant wheel whipped into action. It was spinning with increasing speed, and the giant siege engine swayed ominously. The eight slings with the boulders began to whip around. Temere and the Proliate were pushing and pulling levers frantically.

"The torsion ropes are taking over the powering now," Temere said excitedly.

The commander started shouting orders that Scelto didn't understand.

"Get ready, Scelto. We are number five. Wait for the order."

Boulders from the first diezmar began to slam into the wall of rocks. *BOOM-BOOM-BOOM-BOOM-BOOM-BOOM-BOOM-BOOM.*

There was no let-up as the projectiles from the second diezmar arrived in the exact same spot immediately after the first ones.

BOOM-BOOM-BOOM-BOOM-BOOM-BOOM-BOOM-BOOM.

The third and fourth siege engines followed, and Temere yelled, "Now!"

Scelto slammed the lever. Just above the frantically spinning wheel, the blade engaged and began cutting the massive ropes holding the spinning rocks in their sling. As the sword cut each one, the boulders were released towards the target.

"Now watch this!" Temere screamed with childlike fervor. A high-pitched *whhhhhhhhhhhiiiiiiiiiiirrrrrrrrrrrrrr* pierced the air as each projectile launched. As more stones soared into the air, the sound became deafening. The machine and the ground around it shook, and Scelto felt the vibration deep within his own body.

BOOM-BOOM-BOOM-BOOM-BOOM-BOOM-BOOM-BOOM.

Scelto watched as the boulders from their diezmar slammed into the target. It was quickly followed by the projectiles from the final three engines. The wall had sequentially received sixty-four projectiles and was surrounded by dust and debris. When the shroud of residue settled, Scelto saw that the entire wall had been obliterated and only fine particles of rubble remained.

"Woo-hoo!" Temere yelled as he jumped up and down. Turning to Scelto, he said, "Come on. We have more fun planned for the Knights and their allies. The euphorbia plant is a horrible irritant. We have figured out a way to grind it into powder and launch them in clay pots with a mangonel. Anyone nearby when the clay pot shatters will be out of commission. I want you to help—"

"Scelto," a gruff Proliate yelled, cutting off Temere. "Get to the commander's quarters in the outpost now. Someone's here to see you."

Temere looked disappointed. "What's going on?"

Scelto had visions of Friar, maybe Ritari.

"Interrupting our training for a girl! What's next? Regular bathing?" the gruff Proliate said in an annoyed tone.

Scelto smiled as visions of Gimelli flashed before him.

"Come on, ladies' man. I'll escort you there."

Scroll 3: Guests and Visitants

Bellae felt as if she could breathe deeply for the first time in quite a while. To finally see the end of the ocean of grass and massive mountains was like a weight being lifted. The League huddled against the sheer cliff that skyrocketed to the last peak of the Tingij range.

"This mountain range is enormous," Lontas remarked.

Bellae nodded, watching the icy water of Lake Glasere lap up to the base of the rocky cliff. "So the lake comes down around both sides of the mountain?"

"Yes," Lontas replied. "Lake Glasere loops down on either side of the northern edge of the mountains, making it impossible to pass into Eastern Verngaurd except the Way of Trepas, or going way far north around the lake and the Ice Falls."

Bellae shuddered. The wind seemed to whip over the lake and tear into them.

"You're sure we meet them here?" Sankari asked, her dark brown wings fluttering furiously. The squires had learned her wing speed served as a direct indicator of her mood. The tan spots on the wings created a weird strobe effect when she was upset.

"I'm sure," Arend said calmly. But, he too, seemed anxious as he scanned the horizon for his father. They were late, thanks to Lontas' run in with the lihumari.

The fierce wind called up memories of the Storten Flower Fields and the top of Castle Liberum for Bellae. Uncertainty tugged, sincere doubt pulled down, on her confidence. *They must be wrong about me. What can I do?*

"There!" Kainen shouted as the girls ran over. "Ha! Saw them first, eagle boy," Kainen asserted excitedly.

"I saw them. I just didn't say anything," Arend replied serenely.

"Yeah right!" he said, jabbing the Eaglian's shoulder with a good-natured punch.

Suddenly, Arend released a deep, ominous screech.

"Sore loser. I—"

"Those aren't Eaglians."

"What?"

"Watchers!" Arend replied.

"How many?"

"Three."

"Gimelli, Bellae, get to Lontas and stay out of the way," Kainen said, surprisingly tranquil. "Alright, brother, time to kill some Watchers."

Arend nodded fearlessly before exploding up into the air, zealously screeching.

Kainen quickly nocked an arrow and took sight as Arend rushed towards the Watchers.

"Stay back. Let them come closer!" Kainen begged.

The young Eaglian ignored the request. When he was about thirty feet from them, the lead Watcher thrust his hand forward, magically hurling Arend rearward.

Squawking loudly, Arend tumbled backwards, somersaulting through the air. Finally stabilizing his flight, he fought forward once again.

Laughing, the Watchers flew ahead while continually using magic to push Arend back.

After a few moments, Arend looped around, flying back and landing next to Kainen.

"Have I mentioned I love that fun trick they have?" he said breathlessly.

Kainen spoke to his Eaglian friend in Elfish.

Arend nodded before bolting back into the air, this time away from the path of the Watchers as if he was retreating.

"Your friend is easily discouraged," the first Watcher said once closer.

Kainen replied by loosing several arrows in rapid succession.

Rolling his eyes, the Watcher flicked his wrist, sending the arrows limply to the ground.

"Let's not play this game again." Small flakes of his arid skin seemed to crumble like dust from the Watcher's face as it curled into a spiteful smile. His blue eyes sparkled within their red sclera sea.

"Give us the girl and live. Resist and be immersed in pain."

Kainen wordlessly loosed several more arrows.

"You're not very intelligent, are you, stripling? I'll say it simply: remember, our magic means, 'arrows no hurt us.'"

Kainen began to laugh, which enraged the Watchers.

"Our command to avoid killing only applies to the girl, so I'd wipe that smile off your bark-rind face!"

Kainen stopped laughing and let a barrage of arrows fly. The Watchers magically knocked them down while flying straight for the young Elf.

Suddenly, Arend dropped out of the sky, slamming into the lead Watcher. The surprised Watcher grimaced as Arend grabbed his wrists to prevent him casting a spell and lunged with his vicious beak.

His massive jaws sliced deeply into the Watcher's skull, nearly severing it in two. Blood, dust, and blue magic exploded out from the massive laceration, instantly jolting Arend. Magically shocked, the Eaglian limply plummeted towards the lake. Kainen immediately sprinted towards his falling friend.

The injured Watcher tried to scream, but the deep gash cutting through his skull made it sound like a raspy gurgle. His hands desperately reached up to stabilize the top half of his head, which was still sending out an avalanche of blood and magic. Slowly, he began to fall while his flight became haphazard and erratic. The top half of his partially bisected head wobbled desperately until he eventually crashed to the ground in a heap.

"Above!" one of the remaining two Watchers howled as six black streaks plummeted from the clouds. At first, the forms were widely dispersed but quickly converged as they descended into three pairs.

The Watchers shot a series of fireballs at the streaking figures, six attacking Eaglians. With amazing flight dexterity they contorted, twisted, and spun out of the way. The flaming globes stopped, and the first two Eaglians to arrive were magically flung backwards. The next two diving Eaglians sped up their already incredibly swift flight, zooming past their two warriors hurtling backwards to crash into the remaining Watchers. Their immense momentum snapped the Watchers' heads back, and the two pairs of combatants hurtled and spun through the air.

The Eaglians wrestling the Watchers abruptly hurled them away. The Watchers' snide smiles evaporated as the fifth and sixth adult Eaglians arrived and sunk in their massive talons before lashing the desiccated creatures around three hundred and sixty degrees. The Watchers slammed into each other with a loud *crack*. Dazed, they limply fell towards the ground.

The recovering first and second Eaglians hurtled back into the fight. Closing in, they inverted to fly talon-first. Their sharp claws shredded into the tumbling Watchers' wings. They, too, did a midair somersault and catapulted the Watchers skyward. The second pair of Eaglians had come back around and their blade-like talons ripped into the chests of the Watchers. Blue, almost glowing, blood and magic erupted from their trunks.

Kainen had reached Arend's still-flaccid body, struggling to keep his head above water while desperately dragging his friend through the icy lake to shore. Gimelli, Bellae, and Crann arrived to help.

"Thank goodness he landed in the lake," Gimelli said, while shivering from the near-freezing water.

Two sets of screams stung the air—the Watchers having their chests gored, and the Eaglians exhilarated to inflict damage on the evil creatures. Their long claws insulated against the magical shock. The cries of the Watchers quickly turned to maniacal laughter before they began to briskly chant something inaudible.

The wounded Watchers suddenly seized the two attacking Eaglians, violently ripping them close in a tight clasp. As soon as their mouths stopped uttering the incantation, their bodies erupted into flames of self-immolation.

Even while burning, their dried faces twisted into evil smiles. "We die, you die!"

The ravenous magical flames quickly spread to the shrieking Eaglians within the Watchers' clutch. Engulfed in desperate pain, the Eaglian-Watcher pairs began to plummet downward.

"Stay away," a massive Eaglian yelled.

"But!" Kainen screeched in horror, having pulled the now-recovering Arend out of the water. "They're burning!" he screamed as Gimelli and Bellae tended to Arend.

"If we try to help, we die. Those magical flames are worse than dragon naphtha."

The wings and arms of the Eaglians were smoldering nubbins as the corrosive magic flames eroded their flesh. First one, then the other Eaglian launched their ferocious beaks at the Watchers' heads. With a savage snap, the spiteful, fiery smiles of the Watchers quickly turned to an explosion of flesh and blood as the sharp bills sliced open their faces. A black mix of blue magic and red blood, some of it on fire, erupted out like a volcano spewing lava.

The four fused bodies thudded loudly to the ground in a revolting clump of blood, bone, and flesh. The hungry flames of the Watchers' enchantment seemed to advance over the Eaglians' bodies as if sentient, devouring, ingesting, corroding until two burned-out fleshy masses remained.

Soon only blackened clumps, with only an occasional recognizable body part, remained. The blazing pile seemed to be sinking, eating its way through the earth itself.

Three of the massive Eaglians remaining went and gently helped the still-disoriented Arend. The fourth made sure the initial Watcher Arend had attacked was dead before joining them.

"I am Aquila, Arend's father."

The massive Eaglian Aquila caught sight of Bellae and gasped, staring through sad, culpable eyes.

Intimidated, Bellae turned away while tattered bits of an old memory bubbled up within her sister. Gimelli had a vague notion it was Aquila, carefully hidden, who had tearfully carried Bellae to Liberum after their parents had died.

The brown feathers on their muscular legs rustled in the brisk wind as did the snowy feathers of their heads. Their massive wings coiled behind their human backs.

Two of them unslung large sacks full of supplies as Aquila made several hand signals up towards what appeared to be an empty sky. Shortly after his gestures ended, three small dots began to descend, slowly converging and enlarging.

Scroll 4: We're Off to See the...

The three figures floating down were other Eaglians. Once alighting they set about covering the congealed heaps of blackened flesh, which had finally stopped sinking. They first put a layer of rocks then used a crude wooden tool that looked like a hybrid of an oar and a shovel to cover it in dirt.

A fourth Eaglian carrying a large fia asteikko joined them shortly, making the total adult Eaglians number eight.

"I'm sorry for your loss," Gimelli said, breaking the tense silence.

"Thank you, child," Aquila replied. *I'm sorry for your loss so many years ago when Bellae was born,* he thought, choking back tears while remembering the painfully long walk to Liberum as he carried the newborn Bellae.

After introductions, they cleaned and prepared the fia asteikko. While the animal roasted over a pit, Aquila said, "It's nice to officially meet you, Bellae."

He looked away, woefully hiding the tears forming in the corners of his massive yellow eyes. "The League of Truth has been waiting for you for a very long time."

A look of recognition flashed in Bellae's mind. "That was you under the cloak with Kainen and Kempe."

"Yes, that was me," Aquila responded. "There is so much I want to say…"

He turned his majestic head away again, wiping the tears staining the corner of his eyes. "However, that expression of regret will have to wait for another day."

Utterly confused, the squires said nothing. Eventually, he continued, "Although the League has been waiting for thousands of years for this moment, it still seems as if time has snuck up on us."

"It would be nice to get details," Gimelli stated somberly.

"I know a lot has been thrown at you in a short stretch. There have been forces moving across Verngaurd since time immemorial. They would see *everything* destroyed in the cycle of Na Cearcaill. It took courage for you to come this far, but make no mistake, any semblance of your former life is gone—forever. That previous quiet was nothing but an illusion, and there is no returning to that fabricated dream."

"Get to the details!" Sankari prompted with irritation.

Aquila glared at the Fairy, who raised her eyebrows and returned his stare with unblinking scorn.

"Understand this prophecy is countless generations old, and that innumerable members have died protecting it. We must confirm you really are the One in the prophecy with the Council of the Kirvella Dragons."

The mention of dragons provoked memories of Finn's grisly death, leaching Bellae's face of all color.

"Dragons?" Gimelli said, feeling overwhelmed by the prophecy, Eaglians, Watchers, and being away from their Knights.

"These are the Kirvella Dragons—not the large Saatana," he said with urgency. "They are extremely intelligent and trustworthy. If the blue dragons confirm you are the Chosen One from the prophecy, you will meet the Master Elf."

Sankari perked up. "Cappadocia!" she said, smiling broadly.

"Sankari! You are not supposed to speak of his location."

"Wait," Gimelli said. "We are supposed to traipse all the way east to the dragons, then turn around and head back to Cappadocia on the other side of Verngaurd?"

"If she is confirmed, yes," Aquila said. Seeing their disappointment, he continued, "Sometimes we can't control what happens to us, but we can make the decision to control our attitude and determination to do what is right. We're getting ahead of ourselves. The Kirvella first have to give the okay. There is so much at stake…"

Bellae's head was spinning. Part of her had hoped for a nice and neat answer with some dream of her old life and the security it brought.

"After we eat, we'll fly you over Lake Glasere. From there…" Aquila started.

"Why not just fly us to the dragons?" Gimelli questioned.

He solemnly pointed to the mounds that were once two of his friends, now a grave of congealed, charred flesh. "We have learned a grim lesson, paid for with the lives of many Eaglian warriors. The Watchers magically track the skies via some sort of enchantment detecting flight. Initially, we thought we could fly erratically and avoid them, but despite trying to throw them off, they always anticipate where we are headed.

"It is only when we fly solo, or spread far apart, that we can evade their dark magic. Add to that the griffins and Magicians looking for Bellae…" his voice trailed off. "As safety allows, we will help. However, we have our own preparations to make, and battles to fight."

"Arend saw the Watchers casting that magical net," Kainen said.

Aquila nodded before continuing, "If Bellae is the Chosen One, you will learn what's next, one step at a time. Each of us within the League knows only their role in their small section of this ancient plan, all designed by her ancestors, the Ainmhi Caint. We…"

"You mean *our* ancestors?" Gimelli interrupted.

Aquila looked away, obviously hiding something. "Of course. We have kept the overall path of the prophecy hidden for security reasons. Once you have embarked on your mission, we will rarely know where you are, or where you are going.

"Once on the other side of Glasere, you will skirt the border of Jaa, but do not cross into their territory. There have been many more staged attacks made to look as if the Elves of Creber and Northern Dwarves were responsible, and Jaa is now frequently sending patrols south of their border."

"What?" Gimelli questioned, knowing the implications of such attacks. "That means all-out war! Where's Friar, and what does he say about this?"

"Last I heard, he was heading for the Way of Trepas," Aquila replied. "We need to talk to him."

"Not possible."

"Not possible?" she repeated. "If we could just…"

"There is an important distinction here. I am telling you we absolutely *should* not go. I am not saying you *couldn't* go. He has his responsibilities, and you have yours. Kempe told Friar where you are, and he understands you have a bigger role to play. While you do have a choice, trust us a little longer and see the Kirvella dragons."

The color had returned to Bellae, and she took a deep breath, looking down to deflect some of the potency of everyone staring at her. *I doubt I can do anything important and wish people would stop saying things about me as if I wasn't here.* "I want to go home and don't understand this prophecy. But I am certain Finn and Friar would tell me to do what's right. If I can help…" *which I doubt* "…I will. When do we leave?"

Aquila let out a small shriek that sent Borb and Grym to shivering. "Wonderful. We leave after we eat."

Gimelli sighed and put her hands on top of her head.

"You must avoid Temple Aon Intinn at all costs as you near the Hino Mountains. Your old friend Abhac will meet you and lead you to the Council of Kirvella dragons."

"Abhac?" Bellae said excitedly. The Dwarf Dragon Rider made her think of her favorite green dragon. "Will Soma be there?"

Aquila laughed. "I don't know. We'll keep a distant eye on you when we can. We don't want to draw too much attention to your party and must fly in small numbers spaced apart to avoid the Watchers' net. Secrecy will be your greatest weapon. We will try to throw off those on your trail with diversions."

Aquila turned to Lontas. "Let's have a look at your wounds before we eat."

Bellae and Gimelli helped move Lontas away from the others and turned to leave.

"No, stay. I may be able to give you some advice on the care of his wounds," Aquila said while undoing the dressings. "It's good we thought to bring fresh supplies."

As each bit of fabric was removed, Lontas winced in pain.

"You need new dressings," Aquila commented. "Hey, Sankari."

The Fairy looked annoyed and rolled her eyes. "Yep," she huffed.

"That doesn't sound like you want the sart cake I bought. Do you?"

Sankari screamed in excited yips. "Yes, yes, yes, yessity-yes!"

"*After* you get me that healer's bag."

"Sankari quickly flew up to Aquila, slugging him on the shoulder. She then kissed him on his cheek before zipping off faster than anyone had ever seen before.

"Fairies are peculiar folk," Aquila commented with a smirk.

"What are sart cakes?" Gimelli asked.

"A delicacy from Effeus Woods. It's a delicious mushroom cake. Well, at least according to Fairies, Sprites, and Elves," he answered. Suddenly, Sankari zoomed past Aquila, who just avoided being hit by leaning backwards.

"Oops, overshot there," she declared, turning in midair and whipping around to head back to them. "Here you go," she said with a smile and a wink. It was the nicest the squires had ever seen her act.

Aquila grabbed the leather pouch. "Thanks. Ah, here we go," he said, rummaging through. "Now, Sankari, I do need some space to work here," he added as the fairy buzzed around his head.

I wish more people were watching so I could feel extra humiliated, Lontas thought.

"This medicine, laak-htua, will help, and hurt," the Eaglian said, scrunching up his eyes at the sight of the horrid-looking wound. It was covered in a thick yellow layer with oozing clear liquid seeping all over. He felt the back of Lontas' neck and his forehead.

"No fever—that's good. This yellowish layer is granulation or healing tissue, not infection," he said as he examined the edges of the wound with his honed eyes. "You are starting to get some of the red sickness, but it is, fortunately, early. Your friends have been doing a great job taking care of this."

"So you think it's getting infected?" Gimelli questioned.

"Yes, but its early and this salve will help."

Lontas was intimidated by Aquila and afraid of someone touching his wounds, but he was more afraid of infection, fever, and death. He had seen even the strongest Knight die from a relatively minor wound once infected.

"How do your wounds feel?" Aquila asked.

"Um," Lontas cleared his throat. "Itchy with occasionally tingles."

"Okay," the Eaglian said. "Those sensations sound like healing with the start of infection. Considering the attack you have suffered, it's healing wonderfully." He let out a little squawk before continuing, "This wound is more like a burn. You were lucky to survive a run-in with the lihumari. They are powerful and dangerous."

Aquila dipped his fingers in a leather pouch and came out with a whitish emollient. "The laak-htua salve oozes from blighted trees in the Effeus Woods. It originates from a flowering mold-like illness that kills trees. However, we discovered that it secretes an anti-infective substance that prevents the red sickness from spreading. It's bad for the trees, but we always let a little of the blight simmer to keep this stuff coming."

"Nature's law: what is bad for one is a savior for another," a short and stout Eaglian said.

"True. Alright, here we go," Aquila warned, spreading the whitish ointment on the wound.

"It stings a little, but the itch feels better."

"Unfortunately, tonight is the second full moon this month for Stor-Manen. A blue moon can be a bad omen for healing," the stout Eaglian said.

"Actually, there's no correlation between celestial movements and my wellbeing," Lontas said. "Moons are rocks in orbit around our planet. Seeing blue has to do with dust particles, say after a big volcanic explosion, high up in atmosphere…"

"Lontas," Bellae whispered with no effect.

"…Likewise, a red moon occurs when one of our sun's light bends around the curve of the world and reflects on them as they, of course, have no intrinsic light source…"

"Lontas," Bellae said, trying to get his attention as the stout Eaglian looked at Lontas wide-eyed with his fierce beak open menacingly.

"…and you are correct, the second full moon in a month can also be called blue, but in terms of affecting my healing…"

"Lontas!" Bellae yelled. This time he stopped, looked up, and shuddered, finally realizing he had offended the massive creature as the portly Eaglian huffed away.

"The salve and new bandages are on. Let's eat," Aquila stated. "By the way, best not to antagonize an Eaglian you don't know extremely well."

Lontas nodded aggressively.

"Here," Aquila said, but Sankari was already trying to rip the sart cake from his hands. "Slow down, Kari." The circular sart cake was ten inches in diameter. The outside was flaky brown with a dusting of a rust-colored, powdery substance. Aquila broke it in two. The top had a series of vertical lines that were a creamy white color. Underneath were woody-looking, copper-colored strands.

They had just started tearing into the fia asteikko when Aquila craned his neck up and laughed. "Old Chum." The Eaglians glanced up before nodding. It was still several moments before the squires could make out a barely perceptible dot on the horizon.

"What is it?" Gimelli asked, nervous about Watchers.

"A tree hugger flying." Aquila laughed. It was apparently terribly funny because all the Eaglians burst into laughter as Bellae and Gimelli exchanged a questioning look. "Before they arrive, Lontas, let's get you up and taking a few steps. You must stretch and walk every day to prevent your skin and muscles from tightening up as they heal."

Lontas wheezed weakly as Aquila flexed his giant muscles and snatched him up off the ground. He grimaced with each stiff step. Aquila's muscular arm easily supported Lontas as the two hobbled around. Occasionally, Aquila's wings would open up, making a crisp snapping sound, startling Lontas.

"Take a few small steps on your own." Lontas felt shaky and off balance as Aquila slowly withdrew his arm.

"You've got this, Lontas," Gimelli said.

"Hey!" Bellae said, wrinkling her nose and shaking her head in mock anger. "That's my line."

Lontas' arms were outstretched and fluttering up and down like a baby bird learning to fly. His left foot skimmed the ground and caught on the heel of his right. Aquila quickly steadied him.

"Let's get you more to eat, big guy. Protein helps healing," Aquila said.

Bellae followed anxiously. Once he was back on his stomach, Lontas motioned for her to come closer.

"I'm sorry for being clumsy. I hate it," he said, choked up. She sat down to block his tearing eyes.

"Look at it this way. The Lontas Trip Counter is only at one!" she said in a cheerful voice. Little spasms of laughter jumped into his sobbing. She rubbed her friend's back until he quieted.

Scroll 5: I Already Told You, It's a Temple!

Gleoi Dea urged her horse forward, catching up to Friar. His eyes seesawed across the landscape that led up to the Tingij Mountains in agonized concentration. As they neared the Way of Trepas, her horse lurched before she managed to rein him in.

"Sorry for the loss of your Kameli," Friar said sympathetically.

"Thanks. Riding a horse is an adjustment," she said, tears welling in the corners of her eyes. "I want you to know, I'm sure of what I saw. Veneficus and the Proliate are wrong!" She recoiled, embarrassed at the intensity of her words. The measured approach she practiced in her mind vanished under passion's command.

"I believe you," Friar said, pulling up. Turning to Gleoi Dea, his expression mirrored her own confusion and doubt. "What troubles me is Veneficus' conviction. I have a hard time believing he could be so easily fooled."

"He admitted he didn't see the Elves or Dwarves in battle and the forged weapons are excellent."

Friar nodded as the other Knights joined them. "Here is the high ground we need outside the Way of Trepas. Sorea, this is where we need your skill."

"Yes, sir," she said excitedly. "This ground will work." A part of her felt a tiny pang of sympathy for the Proliate and their allies in the coming war.

"It will be hard to keep our troops, equipment, and preparation secret," Ritari challenged. "There are bound to be Watchers and Magicians with griffins circling overhead."

"Prestidigitation shall prevail," Friar said, smiling. "Pumilus and the loitsia sticks will be here."

"We are relying too heavily on them," Ritari said.

"No more than they are relying on us. We are all connected and responsible in this plan. Everyone has their part, and, as in any battle, we need a healthy dose of luck and faith in our allies."

"An elaborate plan with many participants only aware of a fraction of it? Dangerous," Ritari said.

Friar smiled. "As long as each leg of a table does its part, the table will stay up regardless of how well they know what the others are doing."

Ritari shook his head as the others groaned.

The group eased their way into the Way of Trepas, scanning the claustrophobically steep walls as they moved cautiously through the rubble-strewn pass.

"This narrowing is a murder hole," Luchar said as several small- to medium-size rocks plummeted down the steep rock face.

"Watch yourselves," Friar advised as Lovag deftly moved Behalen out of the way of falling stones. Behalen neighed, frustrated at the closed-in space and falling debris.

"We need Bellae to calm them," Luchar said in a surprisingly soft, caring tone.

"Whatever happens, we can't afford to get bogged down in here," Ritari said.

They continued through the pass until a narrow slit of light finally began to open up in front of them. Soon they began to make out a massive building. With each step forward, the details of the immense Proliate Fortress of Ovest took shape.

"Technically," Friar said, "this is a temple and therefore guarded by the Red Guard, Sanctus Divisions. It's so large there are a fair number of Ultor as well."

"The Proliate tailing us have not entered the Way of Trepas," Lovag informed.

"They must be stationed west of the Tingij. We will surely have someone from Ovest start following us," Friar responded. "Let's hope they received the message to let us pass unharmed."

"That's a massive castle," Luchar said.

"Temple! It's a Temple," Ritari said, smiling. Luchar groaned, unappreciative of the humor.

"It is a concentric castle, er…temple," Friar said, smiling. "The outer wall is sixty feet thick at the base and thirty-six at the top. The inner wall is a mere sixteen feet thick."

The flanking towers on either side of the massive gatehouse were circular and immense in their own right. Embrasures, openings for the archers, lined the height of each tower. The top battlements looked like formidable teeth. There was no moat, but the earth had been dug down so that only a narrow walkway led into Ovest.

"Sorea, as we discussed, we will want to attack the embrasures in that area there," Friar said, pointing to an area right of the gatehouse. "We cannot predict how much time it will take to draw them out. We have a number of contingencies ready."

"I'm ready to hammer that wall right now," Sorea answered, salivating.

"I have to admit, when you were talking about these plans, I didn't think we would ever need them," Ritari stated.

Friar nodded. "Despite our wishes, war on two fronts has found us."

"Our new tail," Friar said, waving to a group of Proliate outside Ovest.

The castle was whitewashed, and the Knights could see thousands of Proliate lining the walls in full military dress and banners.

"Show offs," Friar said, his face hinting at a smile.

"Not many weaknesses," Ritari said gloomily. "This will be hard to take."

"Not our goal," Friar said.

Scroll 6: They Said You Would Say That

"We should be coming up to Bocht," Sorea said, sleepily.

"I'm not surprised you're tired. You've talked in your sleep the last several nights."

"I haven't slept well since they declared war," she replied.

"It will be nice to see Svika and Vanalia, but I sure miss Lontas," Lovag said.

"Vanalia's no Bellae," Luchar rumbled.

"Still, it will be nice to get a new stablemate," Friar said.

After riding for several hours, Lovag sat up in his saddle. "What's that?"

What now? Friar wondered as black smoke billowed in the distance.

"Permission to ride ahead," Lovag asked.

"Scout only. Keep your distance."

After several moments, Lovag came galloping back. "The town is torched."

Friar shook his head. With the abundant dangers roving Verngaurd, they were severely understrength. "Any sign of Dark Warriors?"

"Nothing obvious, but I kept my distance."

Friar looked into the faces of the questioning Knights and nodded. "Let's go." Urging their horses forward, they broke into a gallop.

"Is it Bocht?" Sorea asked. In her heart, she already knew the answer but was not keen on what that reality meant. The others remained silent.

Sorea whimpered with urgent sadness as they drew closer. The charred outline of burnt-out and burning huts of Bocht began to take form. Smoky black plumes streamed up across the horizon like inept and tardy pleas for help.

"The mark of the Dark Warriors," Ritari said, pointing. They all turned to see the black flag with a White Wizard's hat and a staff fluttering in the wind.

Suddenly, they saw a solitary figure moving next to the flag. Friar drew his sword. Without need for an order, the others followed.

"Stay in line. Stay together," Friar ordered. "Watch our flanks, watch our backs."

Lovag and Sorea had their bow and crossbow out respectively. The lone figure standing by the insignia of the Dark Warriors collapsed.

"It's an elderly woman!" Gleoi Dea said.

Now that they were on the edge of the town, the smoke trailing up from the individual fires was congealing into a swirling black swarm, which was choking out most of the sunlight. The Knights started to feel its sting in their eyes and lungs.

"Wrap your mouths in cloth," Friar ordered. The Knights tied lengths of white cloth around their mouths. Ritari gingerly removed his helmet, carefully tying the makeshift mask over his bandaged head. The pain he had felt was giving way to a sharp tingling sensation as his burned scalp struggled to heal. Luchar, feeling vulnerable with no helmet, also navigated a mask around his heavily bandaged head.

"Gleoi Dea, tend to the lady," Friar said as they drew near.

She dismounted as he surveyed the devastated village. Several of the buildings and huts were burnt to the ground. There was no sign of movement except the burning embers and rising smoke. A portion of the outer right wall was the only undamaged part of the village.

"Ritari, Luchar, and Sorea, head to that portion of the wall. Make sure no one is hiding behind it, then perform a sweep around the village and check for any survivors or hostiles," Friar ordered as they quickly moved off.

"Lovag, keep an eye out. Watch our backs," Friar said, dismounting.

Gleoi Dea was giving the lady water. Her trembling hands were covered in yellow callouses, which were in turn blanketed in the relentless grime that comes from daily hard labor. The soot and ashes covering her face highlighted the adversity her years had endured, creating inky slashes within the permanent lines and wrinkles. Like rings on a tree, each furrow marked a bygone burden or year.

Her features were stubby and rough, resembling chisel marks from a clumsy carpenter. Gazing up at Friar, her lips pursed in sadness, sending an aftershock of well-worn lines flowering through her lower face.

After enduring a coughing fit, she asked with labored breath, "You...Friar?"

"Yes," he answered tentatively.

"Got...a message," she huffed.

She went into another, longer, coughing fit, and Gleoi Dea helped her take another drink. To Friar, her face seemed hardened from a harsh life, emerging compact and toughened instead of broken.

"What happened?"

"The Dark Warriors told us...you and the Knights...ordered them to come and...destroy the village," she said, wearily struggling with deep breaths in between words.

A groan of disbelief arose from Luchar, Ritari, and Sorea, who had just returned.

"All clear, Friar. What in the world is she talking about?"

"The Dark Warriors said...you were mad...that Svika wouldn't let you...have Vanalia as a squire," the woman said. The audible wheeze from her chest was growing louder.

"We were coming to get her because they *had* agreed," Luchar growled angrily.

"That's what the parents…kept trying to…tell them," she huffed. "But, it didn't stop…the torture or burning…of the village. The Dark Warriors said they…wuz lying. Eventually, once the nasty…winged monsters came…the parents…finally said…they had told you no."

"Torture?" Gleoi Dea inquired.

The woman lifted up her cloak and sleeves to reveal alternating lacerations and burns.

"Tssssst," Gleoi Dea exhaled in disgust.

"Ritari, get the medical supplies," Friar ordered.

"They left me…alive and…told me…you would come by shortly. I guess…" She gasped, her breathing growing more labored. "…they wuz tellin'…the truth…after all.

"I'm…supposed to…tell you…Svika…his wife…and Vanalia will continue…to be tortured…as you requested."

Luchar whipped his head to the sky and let out a primeval yell. "The Dark Warriors are all gonna die!" He instantly regretted it as his brain pulsed with pain.

With her chest heaving, the woman looked up at Luchar and said, "They said…you would say…that…to throw…us off. You've…been… help'n 'em."

Her breathing became erratic before stillness silently wrapped itself around her. She went limp in Gleoi Dea's arms. The Knights' thoughts raced like the festering smoke from the burned-out village.

"We didn't even know her name," Gleoi Dea said, gently laying her on the ground.

"Where are the other villagers? Why did they take them?" Ritari asked.

"How did the Dark Warriors even know about Vanalia?" Friar asked.

"They might have seen us traveling to the Tournament together," Sorea suggested.

"Perhaps."

"Sir," Ritari said with quiet desperation as the insignia of the White Wizard magically transformed to the Knights' symbol.

Friar attempted to take it down, but it was protected. "Black sorcery. There is no way for us to remove it."

"Another set-up, this time against us. Things are deteriorating," Ritari said.

"Someone is thrusting us towards war with vengeance," Friar said, looking up at the smoldering sky. "I don't like being pushed."

"Once word of this spreads, we are going to have every army and farmer in Verngaurd trying to kill us," Lovag said.

"They're boxing us, the Elves of Creber, and Northern Dwarves into a corner with these staged attacks. Everyone else will soon stand against us," Gleoi Dea added.

"It seems quite the coincidence that you reject the Proliate and then *we* are set up. Do you think *they* are the ones working with the Dark Warriors?" Lovag asked.

Friar shook his head. "The more we try to gain control of this situation, the less we seem to have. I do believe someone within Verngaurd is helping the Dark Warriors carry out this plot to divide us.

"Sorea and Gleoi Dea, change of plans. You two head back through the Way of Trepas to the Rebelde Plains. Contact Teyol, Kelig, and Vakava to keep their support. Then you and Pumilus head to the ground we scouted west of the Trepas. I will have Baiulus send the materials and personnel you need for the traps we will be setting."

Sorea and Gleoi Dea looked at each other.

"I know there is the matter of our tailing Proliate," Friar said. "We will all set out towards Liberum. Once concealed by the smoke, double back around them."

"We should go," Ritari said with uncharacteristic uneasiness.

"Who will bury her?" Gleoi Dea asked.

"We'll take care of it," Friar said. He nodded to Luchar, who lifted her up and threw her into the closest fire. Sorea and Gleoi Dea gasped, looking crestfallen.

"Under the circumstances, it's the best we can do."

Halfway through the village, the Knights stopped to add some wood, a few barrels, and hay to several of the smoldering fires.

"That should add some good cover," Lovag announced.

"Be ready to break off," Friar ordered.

The Knights moved between two huts with roaring fires. As the stamping hooves of their horses roared through, the smoke billowed angrily, forming swirling lines resembling angry snakes curling to strike. Once they had passed, a smoky curtain seemed to close behind them.

Sorea and Gleoi Dea broke right, heading south for the portion of the wall that was still standing, while Friar, Ritari, Luchar, and Lovag continued forward.

"Let's pick up some speed to draw the Proliate after us," Friar said as they cleared the burning village and urged their horses into a sprint.

Sorea and Gleoi Dea anxiously peered through the cracks in the fence until the Proliate Warriors zoomed by in hot pursuit. Several commented on the Knights' symbol.

"Let's go," Sorea said, and the two Knights headed back towards the Way of Trepas.

Scroll 7: Target? Rise above...

Only burnt edges of flesh, scales, and warm bones remained of the fia asteikko. Sankari lay bloated and sedated from the massive quantity of sart cake eaten. The "tree hugger" that Aquila had laughed about was the Elf Kempe being carried by an Eaglian. Kempe and Aquila had been talking privately since his arrival.

"What do you think our dads are talking about?" Kainen asked.

Laughing, Arend said, "How the Eaglians are always carrying the sluggish Elves!"

"You're just mad I spotted the Watchers before you. That *has* to be embarrassing for an Eaglian," Kainen quipped, jokingly hitting Arend's arm just as their parents started walking toward the group.

Aquila moved next to the sisters. "The prophecy has a long and erratic history of control and deception. Eons of scheming games have cast a shadow on it, leaving it open to interpretation. Most of us are convinced we have the authentic copy, but forgeries had been floated out there to throw off our enemies. Only those long dead truly know. Some say it is, in fact, your brother who is the one spoken of in the prophecy."

"Jumeaux?" the sisters said together.

"It's possible," Kempe said. "The point is, in light of recent events, we need to get you to the Kirvella Dragons and seek their counsel."

"What events?" Lontas asked.

Kempe sighed. "There has been a formal declaration of war."

He paused as a gasp went up around the campfire. "On one side stand the Allies: Knights, Elves of Creber, Rebelde Plains, and Northern Dwarves. Opposing them are the Proliate/Magician Confederacy including the Western Elves, Ager, Jaainians, and Southern Dwarves."

The group exchanged questioning looks.

"It is with great urgency that you journey to the council of Dragons. You must travel light and quick to avoid the Proliate while evading detection by the Watchers. Every nation will be forced to choose sides, and this conflict will grow until it swallows all of Verngaurd," Aquila announced sadly.

"All of Verngaurd is at war?" Gimelli asked.

"The whole world is at war," Kempe repeated. "It is only a matter of time before the Dark Warriors from Ifrean cross the Dark Sea in even greater numbers."

"During war, a squire's place is with their Knight," Gimelli said, burying her face in her hands. The idea of her Knights under siege from the Proliate and the Dark Warriors was overwhelming and nauseating. "We're going to Liberum."

"Did you not hear what they have been saying?" Sankari asked. "You have to…"

"We don't have to do anything but go to our Knights!" Gimelli shouted.

"These are frightening times," Kempe said. "However, as I told you in Creber, finding the Chosen One is vital to Verngaurd, and the entire world. Whether it is Bellae or Jumeaux, *they* will decide the outcome of this conflict, not the Knights, the Proliators, or Dark Warriors."

Gimelli huffed. Her head was spinning, desperately wanting to be with her Knights. At the same time, her heart jumped, wanting to be home with Scelto.

Aquila's wings flapped briskly. "The future has the impressive ability of coming whether you want it to or not." His head torqued to the side, and he stared at Bellae with his large, piercing eyes. "Your past life is gone forever, no matter how much it hurts or you may wish it was not so. Even if you head to Liberum, there's no going back, for any of us. Evil has stirred us into a war greater than you can imagine."

Gimelli's brain twisted his words and made them hollow and fabricated. "Get up, Bellae. We're leaving."

Gimelli's declaration gave Bellae a flash of hope she could go to Liberum. However, she knew it was a false wisp of a dream that would only temporarily shelter her from the future. Tears welled up in her eyes despite her mind's protest.

"May I speak to you alone?" Kempe asked, pointing to Gimelli.

She reluctantly moved away from the others with the muscular Elf.

"You don't know us, but we have been watching you since you were little."

"That's super creepy," Gimelli said.

Kempe laughed. "I guess that came out wrong. I meant to say I'm aware you are known for your cheery disposition and I realize the situation seems terrifying, but do not let the precarious nature of the world transform your virtue."

"I get what you are saying. But this pressure you are putting on us, especially my *little* sister, is absurd."

"Time, circumstance, and the condition of the world are not within my control." Kempe paused and looked down, as if lamenting the truth of his statement. "Did you know I was with those who brought you to Liberum?"

Gimelli paused then nodded her head. "I remember."

Kempe smiled. "I'm glad. That was a tough time for you."

"Aquila was there too?" she asked.

Kempe paused before speaking, "Yes, we tried to keep him hidden…to not scare you."

"Why is he so sad around Bellae?"

The brawny Elf flinched, almost as if in pain, "That is for him to tell another time. When nearing Liberum, my father, Patuljak, said something to you about the death of your parents, 'Acceptance isn't easy, but it does start the heart to heal, and maybe, eventually, allows you to move forward.' If you accept your sister's situation, and stop fighting it, you may be able to move forward."

Gimelli looked into his deep green eyes. "Change is hard."

"Change is here. Change always happens. It's the acceptance of it that allows us to move forward."

"Blaming this on the artificial and inanimate concepts of 'time, circumstance, and conditions' doesn't change how unreasonable it is. Maybe I'm sick of being 'cheery' all the time."

"I understand. Perhaps my father should have come, for I am merely here to battle to my last breath, to leave the earth better off than what I was born into."

"Still unfair."

"You're right, and make no mistake, there are grueling and bitter days ahead, and your sister needs you. Every day the world will throw out challenges and obstacles, daring you to fall into despair. Rise above the storm.

"It's easy to get stuck in the tempest, but if we can rise above the blizzard of emotions and get a better perspective, maybe we can appreciate the beauty and purpose of the gale."

Gimelli shook her head doubtfully.

"A storm can be terrifying but provides water for our forest. A storm in our lives, even an intimidating one, can be the fuel we need to grow. Choose to be the light gleaming within you, even when the world tries to snuff it out. The darkest times are exactly when we need to smile, even when we don't feel like it. Don't lose yourself because of the rising whirlwind. Help her by holding on to the best parts of you."

Gimelli nodded, sighed, and forced a smile.

Bellae stood up, slowly, as Kempe and her sister returned. She could feel everyone's eyes boring into her. "I-iii…" she squeaked. Clearing her throat, she declared, "I will go. I'm not asking anyone else to."

Lontas reached up and squeezed her hand. "I'll go." Blushing, he continued, "That is, if Arend will carry me."

Everyone laughed. As they did, the young Eaglian moved close to Lontas. "It is good to stay on target," he said as the two laughed.

"What target?" Gimelli asked.

"An inside joke for us fliers," Arend said, patting Lontas on the shoulder.

"There is no chance I am letting my lil' sis go without me." Gimelli paused, thinking of what she could say that would make any sense in a world that seemed to be spinning out of control. Smiling, she settled on, "Let's avoid all the creatures trying to kill us and go see some blue dragons about a prophecy."

Magicians

Scroll 8: Jumeaux is Finally the Show

"Room thirteen? Amazing," Kaveri said. "Room thirteen is the most famous in all of the Academy of Magic."

Before Jumeaux could ask why, Kaveri started talking. "This huge area is called the Triangle," he said, holding up his hands and shrugging at the square indoor chamber. "Obviously, not in the shape of a triangle. Not really intelligent considering the Magicians are supposed to be brainiacs, huh?"

Jumeaux nodded, staring open-mouthed around the unbelievably enormous and spotless room. Everything, even the floor, was a pristine white. There was no dirt, no clutter—not even scuffmarks. People of all ages and different colored robes scurried past. Most carried scrolls or books. From time to time, one of them would nod at the two boys.

Am I dreaming? This place is amazing, and everyone is so friendly.

Kaveri continued, "Okay, this entire complex within the Citadel is called the Academy of Magic. All Magicians are trained here. This Triangle is the heart of it all. You can get to the dorm hallways from here," he said, pointing down each of the four hallways that led away from the central square.

"What about that center area, with the light?" Jumeaux questioned, pointing to a bustling area in the center of the hall with light glowing from ceiling to floor.

"Let's talk about the hallways first. We call them zaals. They are magical and make things super easy. Each one has a specific color that matches the robes you wear, so it's not hard to remember. The hallways appear short but in reality, are incredibly long. When you enter your hallway, you say your name and room number, then presto, it's magically the first one. It also works if you want to see a friend. You step into their hallway and say the person's name, and their door appears across from you. Pretty cool?"

"Definitely," Jumeaux said. As he peered down the fresh-looking hallways, he thought of his dingy barracks in Liberum and smiled.

"The lighting here is magic, so no candles or torches needed, which is cool, but they are strictly controlled until you reach the Adjutant level. They turn on automatically at five o'clock in the morning and off at ten o'clock at night. If you want to get up earlier or stay up later, just ask the Master assigned to be in charge of your hallway, but you better have a good reason. Questions?"

"Not yet," Jumeaux said, despite the fact he was feeling overwhelmed.

"Each hallway denotes your rank in training to be a Magician," Kaveri said. "The red hallway is for novices like you—red hats and robes. You do not get a hood on your robe, which stinks when it gets cold. Most of the kids are between two and ten.

"Next, in the green hallway, are the Apprentices, wearing green robes with a hood. Plan on spending several years there. You finally can grow your ponytail and get a green tie for it. No headbands, though," Kaveri said, smirking in mock disappointment.

"You graduate from green to yellow hooded robes *with* blue stars," his friend said in faux excitement as he pointed to his own outfit. "Yellow headbands and ponytail holders are also provided for you as an Adjutant. So I live down that hallway," he said, pointing to the yellow corridor.

"Why the ponytails?"

"It may be a fabrication, but the old thinking goes that a magician who cuts his hair has bad luck. Something about flowingly long hair and increasing the flux of your magic—plus, taking your long hair and restraining it in a ponytail represents discipline.

"Last, but not least, are the big dogs, the Masters who wear the blue robes, and, drum roll, can you guess it? They live down the blue hallway! Amazing, isn't it? They wear blue headbands and a long, blue fabric tie for their ponytails. Like him." He pointed. "The standard Master has a yellow star in the middle of his headband. The ones with the red phoenix in the center are clerics who live and help provide the worship at the Temples of the Phoenix for the Proliate.

"You don't take classes on Temple Magic until you are a green-robed Apprentice. Temple Magic is a highly sought after job that requires knowledge of science and mathematics. They say it is nine parts creativity and one part Magic."

Jumeaux was not sure what to make of the creative part, or the fact he completely left out faith in Tallcon.

"Are you with me?" Kaveri asked.

"I think so," Jumeaux replied.

"Great. Let's talk about the friend or virkelig hallway. It's a way to have instant contact with your friends. If we both sign up with our hallway Master, we can be in the same friendship hallway."

Jumeaux shook his head, confused.

"This is hard to explain." He paused and wrinkled his face. "Once you are physically standing in your room, there will be two doors. One is white, outlined in the color of your robes, and the other glows a soft blue. If you open the white one, you are in your physical, colored hallway, and that is the one you use to go to class or meals.

"If you open the blue door, you are in *your* virkelig hallway. It's actually more of a common area. Think of it as a magic back alley that is filled only with your friends. You can have as many people as you want, but you *both* have to sign up for it. You will see the doors of everyone in you virkelig group complete with images of their faces. You start knocking on doors, and if they are there, you can hang out with just your friends. If someone knocks on your blue door, and you open it, you are in *their* virkelig room."

"That's cool," Jumeaux said.

"Yeah, it's as awesome as it sounds, but you can only open it during free time, not during classes or study hall. There are definitely advantages of magic. Another one is the instant Message Board."

"The what?" Jumeaux asked.

"During free time you have a picture frame that looks like a smooth white board. If you want to send someone a message, you say their name and room number and then write with your finger. As you do, the person you are messaging sees them on their board. Once either of you swipes with your hand, it disappears. It is supposed to be used for questions and help with homework. Yeah, that happens…never!" Kaveri joked.

"What about Veneficus?" Jumeaux asked.

"Ahh. The biggest of the big guys. He lives in the great tower. We don't get to go there, pretty much ever. He does have an office in the Citadel that you potentially could go to. I have heard it's pretty dull compared to the office near his living quarters." Kaveri answered while motioning for Jumeaux to follow him.

A steady stream of colored robes blurred by as they stopped about twenty feet back from the glowing center of the square. Jumeaux could see some entering the lighted area.

"What the…" Jumeaux gasped as he watched them get swallowed by the light. He had been too distracted by the commotion and newness of his surroundings to notice the people vanishing in the gleaming center.

"Let's say you have to get to class. Well, this campus is gigantic so, wherever you need to go, you walk to that central lighted area and it transports you there. I…"

"No way!" Jumeaux interrupted, taking a step back in disbelief.

"Yes, way," Kaveri said, slapping him jovially on his back. Jumeaux stared at him. Kaveri was being so nice to him—he could hardly believe it. At that moment, despite the stress tenaciously squeezing across his head, he finally felt at home. As the two moved closer, the soft glowing blue light became more dazzling.

"What does it feel like?"

Kaveri was about to answer when a bulky young man wearing yellow robes bumped into him. His sleeveless robes revealed large, muscular arms. He was carrying four books in his right hand and a large apple in his left. The skin below his mop of disheveled black hair was chestnut brown. A playful but fierce look radiated from his dark brown eyes. With a mouthful of splattering apple he muttered, "Hey, Cave Boy. Where you going?"

"Cave Boy?" Jumeaux questioned.

"This big brute is Chyhrau-Nghyhyrau. When you have a name that sounds like you are vomiting a squawking chicken, you compensate by trying to make fun of other people's names. It's his pathetic way to cover up the fact that he's a freak," Kaveri said, laughing. When he stopped, he added with a sly smirk, "Kicked out of class *again?*"

The large boy ignored Kaveri. "Call me, Chy," he said. "My humor has a sophistication that sometimes needs explaining. You see, I took this pathetic guy's funky name and played with it: 'Cave' from 'Kaveri.' Then I added boy because he's as tough as a wet noodle. Pretty funny, huh?" Chy probed as juice and small projectiles of apple sprayed out from his mouth. Jumeaux laughed at the fruit bath as much as his bantering while using his sleeve to wipe off the fruit shower.

"Now see, I like this new kid. He has a sense of humor," Chy proclaimed.

"Chy, meet Jumeaux. He came to us from Liberum," Kaveri said.

Chy raised his eyebrows before storing the apple in his mouth and squeezing Jumeaux's forearm in a death grip complete with plenty of apple juice. "Gaad ooo errr ear," he said with a mouthful of drooling apple dampening his speech into blather.

Jumeaux laughed and said, "Thanks, I guess."

"Get out of here! You did *not* understand that?" Kaveri questioned.

"He said he was glad I was here," Jumeaux guessed.

"Ahh, smart boy. Didn't I already say I liked you?" the mouth-free-of-apple Chy said. Looking to Kaveri, he added, "Anyway, my plan worked. I got kicked out of class for 'uniform violation,'" he said, chuckling and looking down at his sleeveless arms.

"What? Kicked out for that? They are definitely picking on you," Kaveri joked. "Sure, the sleeves are a *tiny* bit short, but it's hardly noticeable!"

"Thank you, I know. Can you believe I am *forced* to go to my room and chill while the rest of the suckers are stuck in class? What a punishment," he said, laughing. "Where are you guys headed?"

"Jumeaux needs his robes and books. Then we are heading to room *thirteen*," Kaveri said, emphasizing the room number.

Chy raised his eyebrows. "Really? Does he know about that number?"

Kaveri placed his hand on Jumeaux's shoulder reassuringly. "The story is that hundreds, if not thousands, of years ago, long before there was an Academy of Magic, there was an apprentice who studied with Magician Thirteen. The original one hundred Master Magicians each had a number that would be assumed by their apprentice when the master died. This made sure there were always and only one hundred Masters. They stopped referring to Magicians by numbers when the Academy of Magic was founded. Anyway, this apprentice became Magician Thirteen and was not exactly the most loved guy in the history of magic. Once—"

"Not the most loved guy?" Chy interrupted. "The guy is hated and feared by everyone, even Master Magicians. No one has ever used room thirteen before because it was considered unlucky. However, they do say the dude was brilliant and on his way to being more powerful than Veneficus."

"Ah, who…" Jumeaux started.

"No one knows his real name. Now he goes by none other than the White Wizard," Chy exclaimed excitedly.

Jumeaux's mouth dropped, and his eyes widened.

"Enough, Chy," Kaveri declared. "Anyway, when he was still an apprentice, he killed his Master, Magician Thirteen, claiming that putting someone so stupid out of their misery was an act of mercy. He is said to have used a new spell that he, as an apprentice, had developed. They also contend he is the only one to have ever used, the kiduttaa rajahtaa enchantment."

"Yeah, this apprentice, aka the White Wizard, made the old Magician slowly implode on himself over several tortuous hours. Then, when he was a shriveled mess…boom! He explodes!" Chy exclaimed, throwing out his hands like a mock explosion.

"Nice, Chy. Eloquent and subtle as always," Kaveri chided, giving him a friendly punch. "Get the heck out of here and go get dressed, you delinquent."

"What? This is high fashion!" Chy said. "Hey, Jumeaux, watch out for Cave Boy and put me on your virki list so we can hang out," he said, walking away.

"I will help you set up your virkelig friend list when we meet your Hallway Master later," Kaveri said, smiling. Jumeaux returned the smile and followed him towards the glowing light where steady streams of people were disappearing.

"Don't worry. The transporter doesn't make mistakes," Kaveri said as they both stepped into the light. "At least, not that often."

"What?" Jumeaux said, frantically looking around. On every side he could only see brilliant light that seemed to be alive, slithering around him before attaching to his skin. Slowly, it crept and crawled up his hands and legs. His body started to shiver, and it seemed as if he were transforming into white light. Raising his buzzing hand, the light clung to it like white fire. He looked desperately for Kaveri, but his eyes were blinded by the brightness.

The white light bolted forward, engulfing the rest of his body. Feeling airy and buoyant, he could feel and see nothing but a warm prickly tingle and glaring white light. Suddenly, he smashed to the ground, feeling unbelievably heavy. The white light was gone, but his overwhelmed retina still saw bright flashes.

Jumeaux felt a hand slip under his shoulder and help him up.

"Great job," Kaveri said. "You did it, buddy."

Standing on wobbly legs Jumeaux uttered, "Thanks?"

"No, really, most people pass out or vomit their first time."

"You forgot to mention that."

"I didn't want you worrying. That makes it worse." Kaveri chuckled.

Jumeaux shook his head, and the room started to take focus. Especially after having been in the transporter, this new room lined in ebony wood seemed incredibly dark. A handful of torches cast a pale, defeated light about the gloomy room. There did not appear to be any doors leading out, and Jumeaux assumed you could only enter via transporter.

A grumpy-looking man sat behind a chest-high counter directly across from them. He looked up from a large scroll, thumping his fingers impatiently on the counter.

Behind him stretched innumerable rows of hanging garments, mostly robes but some formal wear, and casual clothes as well. In between each line of clothing were small walkways with unusual circular metal bars hanging from the ceiling.

"What are those metal bars for?" Jumeaux whispered.

"You whispering about me, boy?" the man behind the counter yelled.

"No," Kaveri answered, gently elbowing Jumeaux into silence.

Letting his arms smack loudly on the desk in front of him, the man yelled, "You sight-seeing or what? Maybe you came down because you need somethin'? Or did you come to gawk at my beautiful face?"

"We need something, Gretten," Kaveri said in a surprisingly friendly tone.

"Hey, the tall one can speak! I'm astonished! I guess I can put my best quill away and skip the written invitation to stop wasting my precious time. Get on with it!"

Smiling, and ignoring his comments, Kaveri continued, "We need to outfit our new friend here, Jumeaux, and to get his books."

"Jumeaux?" the man repeated. His tone changed, and he seemed surprised. He raised his bushy black eyebrows to take a closer look at the new arrival. "Well, well. You must a-done somethin' right to somebody *very* important."

Gretten suddenly launched his body upwards and grabbed a metal bar above his head with surprisingly muscular arms while mumbling,

"Another hotshot. Great, just what this place needs." He then began to traverse around by swinging from the circular bars hanging from the ceiling. His long and disheveled black hair waved wildly above his pasty pale complexion as he swung around the street-like rows.

Kaveri seemed surprised that Gretten recognized Jumeaux but shrugged his shoulders and walked towards the counter where the man had been reading. Kaveri slapped Jumeaux on the shoulder and, smiling, pointed to the scroll Gretten had been reading: "Ten Spells Anyone Can Master!"

In small print below the title it said, "(Even Without a Crosier)." Jumeaux smiled, and the two kept reading. "Learn to impress your friends, family, and even strangers. In this first of our twenty-five-course series, you will learn to stand up to the conceited and aloof Magician."

"You boys better not be looking at my scroll. It's personal!" Gretten growled. The boys exchanged a snickering glance while taking a small step backwards.

They watched the greasy man swing from bars strategically placed in between each of the various aisles. Jumeaux now saw that the back area consisted of more than clothes. Row after row of shelves over-flowing with a menagerie of goods disappeared into the distance of the stunningly large room. The back area had once been painted green but now stood timidly faded and peeling. There were no labels on any of the rows, and there did not appear to be any organization.

"He won't let anyone, even the Magicians, down here to clean or fix it up," Kaveri said, almost apologetic about the appearance of the room. "The only way in or out is via transporter and a small ladder in the back that leads to Gretten's residence.

Jumeaux nodded. That explained the room's disheveled state.

Gretten's bushy eyebrows stood guard over small and beady eyes. His pale face sprouted a thick, beefy nose and a plump, jutting chin. His arms were as thick as small trees and covered in bristly, abrasive-looking dark hair. His forearms were twice as large as his immense biceps. His legs were stunted, disfigured to the point it seemed impossible they could even bear weight. They dangled loosely and dysfunctionally as he swung his short and stocky frame around.

When Gretten found what he was looking for he grabbed a package wrapped in cloth and latched it to one of many hooks around his belt before swinging back onto his grimy little chair. It creaked in weary protest as his stocky body flew onto it, teetered, but did not fall. The chairs legs were slightly warped from his constant flopping. He unhooked the package from his belt with his right hand while his left grabbed the counter to stabilize himself and the chair. With well-practiced fluidity, he flipped the package to Kaveri while thrusting a piece of paper on a thin board into Jumeaux's face.

When Jumeaux hesitated, Gretten growled, "Ya sign it, bright eyes!" Turning his head slightly, he spoke in a muffled voice, "Another child prodigy."

"Just put your right hand on it. There on the bottom," Kaveri said calmly.

Placing his right hand on the bottom of the paper, Jumeaux felt the now-familiar tingling sensation as the paper seemed to crawl up onto his hand.

"Just relax and hold it there for a moment," Kaveri said.

Seeing Jumeaux's trembling panic, Kaveri grabbed his forearm to steady it.

When the tingling feeling left, Jumeaux quickly removed his hand, only to see a perfect imprint of it on the page, including his fingerprint lines.

"Okay. Well, sorry to stress your juvenile brain out with the tough task of putting your hand on a piece of magical paper so early in the day," Gretten said sarcastically.

Kaveri simply smiled at his ill temper.

"Ah, you geniuses can leave now," Gretten said cantankerously. "I work for a living."

"What about his books?" Kaveri asked.

"Already in room *thirteen*!" Gretten sniveled.

He kept pushing on the counter and lifting himself up with his arms. There did not appear to be a reason for this, and with each thrust, he set his midsection girth swinging, displacing fat rolls and stirring up an odor of decay.

Stopping, he rested his elbows on the counter and put his head into well-calloused hands. He mumbled, "Snot-nosed kids. Get to wear a ponytail and fancy robes and think they can run the world. Not down here, they don't!" The rest of his rant transformed into an inaudible mutter.

"Bye now," Kaveri said.

They walked to the spot they had landed, and Jumeaux noticed a small section of the floor glowing a faint light.

"When you want to leave a location, if the gateway is large, you just walk into it, and it takes you away," Kaveri explained. "In a small place like this, you have to tell it where to go."

"Hey, Kaveri!" Gretten yelled. "Tell that oaf of a friend of yours, you know, the big shot Chytentutten or Cheesyhead or whatever he calls himself…"

"Cheesyhead?" Kaveri said as he joined Jumeaux in laughter.

"Don't get smart with me. Don't you even start with me! His parents should pay for naming him something so ridiculous. You know, I was in a fantastic mood until you little snots showed up. Anyway, your friend, Chippy-Chy or something equally ridiculous, tell him that if he cuts up one more of *my* robes, I will personally use his hide to a make a shirt for myself. Although, as you can see, this one still looks nice, I could use a new one."

"I will hhhmmp tell him," Kaveri said, trying not to laugh.

"Very, very funny, you bonehead. Better have the silent genius try on that robe. I hope you will take offense at what I have to say next: I don't want to see you again till he needs a new robe."

The two boys unwrapped the cloth to reveal green robes.

"This is wrong, Gretten. He's just starting and needs red robes," Kaveri said.

Gretten rolled his eyes, muttering obscenities. Shaking his head side to side, he said, "Oh, you know sooo much don't you, Mr. 'I wear big fancy yellow robes and have been here a few years.' I've been wiping the snot from kids like you for decades. I don't make mistakes. Veneficus himself came by and specifically told me to give green robes to Jar-moo the mute boy over there."

Jumeaux looked at Kaveri questioningly, and they both shrugged their shoulders.

"As nice as it is to hear two such articulate young men, get the blazes out of here and spread your manure load of inconveniences somewhere else! I have to study. You're not the only ones who can get an education, you know."

Kaveri pulled Jumeaux into the light streaming gently up from the floor. "The Triangle, please," he said as the now-familiar light rose up before turning a blazing white, engulfing the boys. This time, Jumeaux only went to his knees and was quickly helped up and moved away from the teeming square of light.

"Well, that was interesting." Jumeaux laughed.

"I'll say. You do have to be nice to Gretten, though. He can make your life miserable," Kaveri answered, wearing a smug smile. "So what do you say, big shot?"

"Hey, I didn't ask for these green robes."

"I know. I meant, what do you say about your nickname being Jarmoo?" Kaveri burst out laughing. Jumeaux just shook his head.

"Ah, you didn't think I caught that, did you? Nothing gets past me. Just think of it, Jumeaux. You can carry a nickname given directly to you by the one and only legend that is, Gretten! Very nice. Very prestigious."

"I'll pass."

"Don't worry. We'll keep that little nickname between us. Starting off with the greens is a pretty awesome compliment. You must have done something to impress Veneficus."

Jumeaux shrugged his shoulders, honestly unsure. "Do I keep room thirteen?"

Kaveri nodded. "Yes, your room number is yours for your life. Just the hallway changes. Apprentice classes could be incredibly difficult for you since you don't have the background." Seeing the panic on Jumeaux's face, he added, "We'll help you. Don't worry."

"Thanks," Jumeaux replied sincerely.

Magicians

Scroll 9: Two Roads Diverge

Later that night, Jumeaux lay in the darkness of his small, whitewashed room. There was a bed, a desk, and a dresser, all white. The only color was the green trim around the white door. The pale blue friendship door had vanished with lights out. The day's events tumbled rapidly around his mind. He found himself happily tracing along every crevice of each occurrence in vivid detail.

Eventually his thoughts drifted into an unwelcome image, his two sisters smiling. It brought back his sworn allegiance to the Knights and family. The negative memories and feelings he had for his family and old friends stood in sharp contrast to the wonderful experiences with the Magicians. He felt at home for the first time in his life.

His mind did not hesitate at the mental fork in the road: living in the shadow of his sisters or staying with the Magicians with an endless stream of possibilities. He effortlessly discarded thoughts of Liberum and those who inhabited it. *I have more good memories in my brief time here than the years there. My destiny is here.*

"Okay, Jumeaux. I'll meet you for lunch," Kaveri said the next day. A big smile spread across his face. "All your professors have been informed of your situation and they will look out for you, Mr. Big-Shot-Green-Robes. You start with Temple Magic, which is good. You are not behind in that class since you can't take it until you are an Apprentice."

Smiling, Jumeaux nodded and headed off for the lighted section of the triangle.

"Chy…I mean, Cheesehead, will make it to lunch as well," Kaveri called out before doubling over laughing at Gretten's pet name for his friend.

Jumeaux began laughing so hard he lurched into the light, which quickly whirled to dazzling white. Luckily his eyes were squinting from laughing. The warm embrace of the milky glow began its tingly creep up his legs and arms until he felt himself floating in the encircling light.

With a thud, he slammed heavily into a circular counter. He looked up, still seeing flashes of white, as ten people descended upon him. He was barraged with a series of 'Hellos' and 'You must be Jumeaux.' His eyes glistened with happiness, and his smile was so genuine, so deep, he felt it might last forever.

Scroll 10: Fanged Sheep Bouquet

"There, the commander's quarters and the giiirl waiting for you," the Proliate said, sounding annoyed.

Wow, so funny, Scelto thought as he knocked. The door immediately flew open, and two massive men moved up into his face. He instantly recognized them from the Tournament. Their heads were shaven except for a single long ponytail of black hair. Tattoos of barbed designs rolled up and down their ample muscles.

Scelto caught his breath as the face he had been seeing in his dreams glided between the two gigantic men. Her large dark eyes pierced into him from behind a thin white veil. Her dark hair stuck up from the top of her white fur hat and spread in the shape of a fan. Even through the veil he could see her silky soft, perfect skin.

"Blessings upon you," Princess Hamaza said, pushing her way through the two overly solicitous guards.

Scelto racked his brain for the correct response. Just as the silence became noticeable, he said, "Blessings upon you and your house."

She smiled widely, and he had no choice but to return it. His heart skipped a beat. A quick image of Gimelli popped up in front of him. He felt the interruption rude and mentally waved it off.

"Those are big pillows," Scelto said as he entered a large room with two rows of large cushions on the floor.

He soon found himself sitting across from her. After several minutes of adjusting the large pillows, he finally felt comfortable.

"These pillows are…so big," Scelto observed.

"So you said," the princess replied.

"Colorful, too."

"Koddi are sacred pillows used in Jaa due to the lack of wood for furniture on the frozen tundra."

"No chairs?"

"No."

"Tables?"

"No."

Desks?"

"Um, no."

Scelto pretended to study the room but felt uneasy under the princess' gaze.

It's so quiet in here, Scelto thought some time later. *It is so super helpful to have the two hulking guards staring at me, and their boring eyes are so relaxing.*

Time clunked awkwardly forward as the stillness became increasing painful. Scelto couldn't think of anything to say, his mind fixated on a country with no furniture.

Finally Hamaza nodded through the confining strain to a guard who went out the back of the building. The door was left open, and Scelto could see him descend into a below-ground icehouse before returning with a medium-sized barrel and two glasses.

Scelto's thirst seemed to increase as much as his nausea as the guard poured an exceedingly thick white liquid into two drinking vessels.

"Thanks a…thank you," Scelto said nervously. Despite coming from the icehouse, the vessel felt hot. Feeling his mouth drying up, he took several gulps of the thick white liquid.

He blushed but nodded his approval at the disgusting liquid under Princess Hamaza's expectant gaze.

The thick drink seemed to do more to increase his thirst than quench it. His saliva was hastily absorbed by the viscous drink. What was left turned thick and pasty. As he smacked his lips, he could feel the dry saliva entwining with the mucousy, white liquid and straddling his mouth in gooey bridges.

What should I say? Scelto thought. The longer the silence went on, the weightier it became, making it increasingly difficult, and awkward, to cut into.

After a long, bulky span of muteness, she finally spoke, "The milk is from the Torahammas, or fanged sheep. They are not domesticated, and milking is a massive undertaking, so it is a sign of great wealth and prestige to drink it."

Prestigious? More like egregious, Scelto thought, saying out loud, "Oh?"

"Yes. Yes it is."

Fanged sheep! Fanged sheep? Scelto's mind spun on the animal. *What do I say about that? Shouldn't I be talking? Fanged sheep-fanged-sheep.*

Time once again struggled forward, slowly striving against the strained, mired silence settling into the room, each second stretching out to make the uncomfortable tension more unbearable. Scelto cleared his throat awkwardly. He glanced at the intimidating and omnipresent guards. Their constant attendance and aggressive stares had been a thorn in his side. He felt uncomfortable and nervous around them, as though he were on a stage, expected to perform despite never having seen the script. They definitely made talking to the princess infinitely more arduous.

Stop drinking, you fool! I have to pee sooooo bad, Scelto thought.

He had been drinking large quantities in an attempt to combat the unpleasant dryness in his mouth and cover the embarrassing stretches of silence—each gulp only serving to make his mouth more parched and increasingly arid. The afternoon had been punctuated with periods of hushed and stifling stillness followed by even more uncomfortable conversation. He longed for the easy friendship of the squires in Liberum.

"So…your mother," Scelto started, but the giant guards growled. "I mean the, your Queen, *the* Queen, came here on business?"

Princess Hamaza paused and tilted her head to the side. Scelto imagined she was wondering why she was ever infatuated with him.

"Yeees, as I declared earlier, she came on diplomatic business, and, also as I said previously, I decided to join her," Hamaza eventually said.

Scelto tried to clear his throat, but it was thick with mucous from the meaty, greasy milk. Knowing it would only make things worse, as if the milk was his personal nefarious tropism, he took another drink.

"You obviously enjoy the Torahammas milk."

"Yes," he answered. In truth it was bitter, with a thick and sludgy texture, complete with the occasional foul congealed curd. It was so full of fat, he felt bloated and gassy. That, along with his need to urinate, made him dreadfully uncomfortable.

He cleared his throat loudly to cover the churning of his insides as they tried to consume the fatty beverage. He imagined his intestine flipping around like the spinning wheel of the diezmar. He was afraid if he belched or farted, he would completely lose control and relieve himself from both ends, all over the sacred pillows. He was no scholar of Jaa, but he was pretty sure urination, defecation, and regurgitation upon the Koddi pillows was seriously frowned upon.

He held in a chuckle at the thought of his vomit and stool all over the hallowed fabric. The pressure in his bloated stomach lurched, and he abruptly felt nauseated.

Oh, great! A new discomfort.

He looked around the room for what seemed like the millionth time. He knew the exact number of support beams, and which ones had cracks and knots visible.

After enduring another burdensome hit of uncomfortable silence, she spoke, "Have you seen a Torahammas?"

"No," he answered. *Think. Say something else. Fanged sheep-fanged sheep. Is that a song? Should be. Say anything. Fanged sheep-fanged sheep.* "No…no…never…never really seen them. Not been in…not…the seeing them." *Holy crap, have you forgotten how to speak?*

"Oh," she replied before the room sank exhaustedly into another unpleasant silence.

"Yeah, no, never did have the chance to ah, see them." *Stop repeating the same stupid answer,* Scelto thought to himself. *Fanged sheep-fanged sheep.*

One of the hulking guards shuffled his feet and coughed. The seemingly innocent gesture seemed to draw attention to the deafening silence closing in around them.

"Are they nice?" Scelto asked when the stillness became unbearable.

She cocked her head to the side as if he had just asked her if she could remove her head from her body. "Uh, no," she said sarcastically. "They have really large fangs and are generally considered the meanest creatures on the planet. You know they are carnivores?"

"Oh. I…no…no," Scelto replied as his face flushed. *You're such an idiot!*

"Did you not learn about them when you visited our kotatu in the Citadel?"

Scelto blushed. He vaguely remembered Seestya, the trainer serving as their guide, talking about them and some sort of wolf-bear. However, he had been too busy staring at the breathtaking features of Hamaza to pay attention. "Uh, perhaps…maybe he…might, he possibly could have talked about them?"

"Many people die each year in our country from their vicious attacks, especially when trying to harvest their milk."

Scelto spit out the milk he had been drinking, sending it showering over his armor and a bit of the sacred pillows.

The two guards huffed angrily while springing into action. After snatching his glass, they grabbed, and whipped, the pillows out from underneath him, sending Scelto tumbling backwards, rattling in his armor. Once stopping, he quickly sat up.

"Sorry," he murmured as his face turned a darker shade of crimson. The guards methodically wiped the pillows down with white towels while chanting a prayer. After finishing, they carefully put the pillows aside before turning their attention to Scelto.

Using the same bits of cloth, they dabbed his armor and face.

Bloody Helvetti. I feel like a baby being cleaned up after his first solid food.

His intestines reeled and gurgled loudly as he struggled to hold in the gas desperately trying to escape from both ends, thanks to the nasty, apparently killer, milk. He was beset by a surge of anger at being offered a drink people had to die to obtain, and guilt for drinking so much.

More awkward silence followed as Scelto continued to struggle for something to say. His nerves were so frayed he felt on pins and needles. The hushed air felt still and lifeless.

"That armor looks good on you," Hamaza said for the third time.

"Thank you," he replied. "It's…a…nice…and…" *think* "…red."

"I see that," she said, annoyed at the obvious comment.

Scelto's mind feverishly searched for any topic to discuss. He sighed loudly. The guards and Princess Hamaza looked up expectantly as if that was a signal he had something to say. His face flushed anew, and he raised his eyebrows helplessly.

"Do you enjoy it here?" she finally asked.

"Yes," he announced loudly, obviously a little too excited at having something to say. "Everyone is…nice…and so…dedicated." His stomach suddenly lurched with fresh vigor and pain. He was forced to re-swallow a surge of bile and vile milk as it re-assaulted the back of his throat with acid-laced revenge. He cringed and shuddered at the tart, acerbic taste. He felt like he was going to explode if he didn't get to the bathroom. His gluteal muscles burned from the effort of holding in the volatile gas thrashing angrily to escape.

"Princess, I sincerely beg your pardon, but I must excuse myself for the night," he said, gingerly rising while squeezing his legs to maintain control of his bodily functions.

He turned to shuffle out when one of the massive guards gruffly cleared his throat. Scelto turned his head with desperation etched on his face. The guard put both of his hands in front of his chest and bent one at the knuckles. Just to emphasize the point he mouthed, "Bow to her!"

With the pressure building in his intestinal tract, he smiled in quiet desperation and slowly turned to face her. He was pinching his backside in an anguished attempt to slow the exit of the gas. He gingerly walked towards her as she approached. Attempting to step over a pillow while holding in the rippling gas, he tripped forward, his left foot landing on the edge of her dress.

A loud *riiiiiiiiip* shrieked through the air as her dress split.

"Oh, so sorry!" he cried, desperately reaching out to hold onto her for balance. He ended up tearing the sleeve of her dress. She wrenched the dress sleeve up and jerked his foot forward. The next thing he knew, he was on his back and the two guards were on top of him, rudely lifting him up. They shoved him backwards. He winced from equal parts embarrassment and strain at keeping the slowly leaking flatulence, stool, and urine in.

"I'm okay," he said as he began to back up. Gas was constantly squeaking from his rear as his stomach lurched in bloated agony, demanding to release its load. Scelto quickly bowed. "Thank you and I… must go," he moaned at the double meaning.

"Good night," she said, nodding.

"Yes. Good night…urp…Princess," he said, quickly backing out of the room while maintaining a slight bow.

Bathroom! Bathroom! Bathroom! his mind kept screaming with critical urgency.

"Hope to see you tomorrow," she called, but he was already sprinting towards the latrine, gas spurting and erupting its way out from both ends, belching and farting as he ran. Scelto burst out laughing, but it could not overcome the sound of pent-up gasses breaking free with a vengeance.

He burst through the outhouse door. For once, the stench did not seem so bad, his own contribution to the smell trailing behind him. He sighed repeatedly as he alleviated himself with a colossal sigh of relief.

"What's going on over there?" a Proliator asked as minute after minute the pressurized urine, gas, and dysenteric levels of diarrhea flowed out with seemingly never-ending force.

"Cursed Torahammas milk! That stuff is wicked," Scelto said, laughing in relief. The Proliator wrinkled his nose in disgust and left as the cloud of gas continued to expand in a toxic bouquet. Scelto's smile vanished as he thought of the squires and Knights back at Liberum. It was an easy and comfortable memory. A place he could just be himself without putting on airs. He began to chuckle as he imagined Ritari and Luchar laughing hysterically at his loss of bodily function.

I soiled my death robe, he thought. *My funeral will really stink!* The thought sent him into a fresh convulsion of laughter.

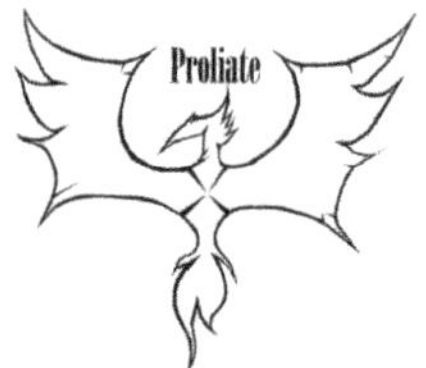

Scroll 11: Airy Impression

Later that night, Scelto lay on his bunk, sighing heavily at the invisible but deadly stench clouds his backside continued producing.

"Let me guess, yet *more* repercussions from the Torahammas milk?" the Proliate from the latrine asked as he walked by, holding his nose.

Scelto laughed.

It had been a whirlwind day. He wanted time to think about his options and fought sleep. He strained his ears, his mind jumping and clinging to each strange sound. He brought his mind to Princess Hamaza, desperately trying to see himself in her world. A prince! He could be sitting in the famous Palas Frusen, or Ice Palace, with the most beautiful creature in all Verngaurd.

I wonder if my farts would freeze? The thought sent him into a fresh fit of laughter that he vainly fought to suppress. His eyes fluttered heavily. He smirked at the horrible impression he must have made. He sputtered a laugh. *What a sight as I ran to the latrine.*

As if on cue, his stomach lurched and retched. *As long as I live, I never want to see a Torahammas or its dreadful milk. She will want to see me tomorrow.* The thought was dreadful and made his stomach flip in vigorous protest.

Despite the strength of his will, his eyes fluttered and the swirling images of the day began to blur as the sovereign of sleep overruled his determination, overwhelming his conscious mind.

Is it Lontas? How bad is he hurt? Scelto thought as his eyes fluttered open. He had trouble recognizing the face in front of him. Slowly the realization of where he was set in, and he recognized Velox's face. His mouth was moving, but he could not understand what Velox was saying. Looking around, he saw the barracks were a hive of activity.

"Is it morning already?" Scelto asked. Fatigue and a white frothy dryness from the massive quantities of Torahammas milk combined to make his words thick and heavy. His esophagus burned, and his throat hurt from all the acidic reflux.

"No, it's the middle of the night. With the Princess coming, we did not perform the piada yesterday. It's way more fun than sleep. After that, we undergo the clarification process. Hey, I heard you made quite the impression with her."

"You heard about it?"

"Everyone has heard, *and* smelled, your impression!" Velox answered, laughing.

"Oh, great."

"Don't worry about it. Anyway, put on this hakama," he finally stated. He handed Scelto a deeply pleated fighting kilt. "Put it on over your angladd."

Scelto obliged. His angladd was still wet from washing out the backlash from drinking so much dreadful Torahammas milk.

A circle of Proliate soldiers gathered around a roaring bonfire. The flames' flickering light highlighted their faces as they huddled for warmth under the starry night air.

"This is our piada, mental sparring, where sarcasm and double meanings are the rule," Velox told Scelto.

Exhaustion had floated away, flowing off with the smoke from the campfire, replaced by a surge of excitement. A tall, thin Proliate stood up and walked toward the fire. Lighthearted groans erupted around the group.

"Thank you, thank you. I appreciate this support and encouragement. So, ladies, let's start with a riddle. What is of different sizes in every man and…"

Laughter erupted as the previously stoic and quiet Proliators came to life with radiant and relaxed expressions. Their serious eyes twinkled expectantly.

With a look of mock annoyance the tall Proliate continued. "As I was saying, different sizes in men, *women,* and *children*!" he continued. "Even within the same person, it is never set in its proportions. It can grow and shrink over time."

"What was that about women being around and something of different sizes?" someone shouted as laughter rolled through the group.

"Mind out of the latrine, boys. Those in whom it grows to gigantic proportions tend to be the smallest of creatures, in reality, and often full of a deeper doubt. They are not seeing reality as others do."

"Is that it?" someone asked. "We need more!"

"That should be all you need," the Proliator said, warming his hands over the fire.

"Is it fear?" someone asked.

"No, but decent guess."

"Happiness?"

"Loneliness!"

"No, no. Listen. It is often the loser of the race who had one too big. As it grows, you would want to spend less time with them."

"Ego!" several answered as once.

"Finally. Egos come in different sizes and change over our experiences, and the loser usually starts with a larger one," he said, sitting down.

Without moving toward the center, another stood. "In a debate does the argument of a person who is incredibly thin carry the same weight as one who is fat?"

Lighthearted boos went up around the circle. "That's an old one!"

"A lesson for our new friend from Liberum," another said. "Come here, boy."

Velox nodded encouragement and helped Scelto up as the crowd roared with approval.

"Don't worry, I have no sheep-milk for you!"

Scelto blushed as they laughed heartily. He moved towards the Proliate who was holding a large shield.

"Stop there. Now come halfway to the shield," the man said as Scelto guessed at the halfway point.

"Good. Now come halfway again," he instructed as several Proliate chuckled. Confused, Scelto once again made an estimate of the halfway point and walked to it. After the fourth try, he was exceedingly close. The Proliate asked him two more times to come halfway. Laughter rang out as Scelto was butting up against the shield.

"I can't really go halfway anymore," Scelto said. A fresh round of laughter was followed by catcalls and yells.

"If you do things halfway you can, mathematically, never get to your goal. Have in your mind to do it one hundred percent, and you can accomplish anything."

Scelto smiled and sat down. Velox nodded and whispered, "You were a good sport. They were not laughing at you, just having fun."

Another Proliate stood up. "Okay, Okay!" he said, putting his arms out to quiet the crowd. "I have a statement for your reaction. The only constant in the world is change."

Even before he finished, a howl of grumbling went through the crowd.

"Another old one," someone yelled. "We did it last month!"

"I guess some things never *change*," another screamed out to howls of laughter.

Another Proliate stood up. "If change is constant, that is something that never changes, and therefore, the statement must be false."

The tall Proliate from the beginning stood up again. "What is a hat?"

"That's weak!"

"Is it? Try answering."

"Something you wear on your head!" one answered jovially.

"So, if you were to wear your braies on…"

"You mean underwear?"

"I was trying to be civil!"

"He never wears underwear. That's why the back of his angladd is stained."

"Anyway! If you were to wear your underwear on your head, does that makes it a hat?"

"Don't be ignorant—of course not!"

"That was your answer, not mine," the asker of the question said.

"What about a metal helmet? You wear that on your head!" He spoke louder to continue the point above the racket of opinions, "What of the hood of a cloak? Is that a hat?"

After multiple rounds of this banter, the commander came and yelled, "All right, piada has to be cut short. It's time for the clarification process."

Scelto was amazed at the transformation. The smiles disappeared like a fire doused with water, and the stoic faces he was accustomed to returned. *I don't think the clarification will be as much fun as the piada.*

"I have to go out on night watch. I asked Gozador to look out for you. Here he comes," Velox said, patting Scelto on the back.

"Thanks, Goz!" Velox said as he left.

The two slid into the darkened back part of the outpost.

"At night things are crisp and clear, literally and figuratively," Gozador said. "With the deceitful distractions of the day stripped aside, we collide with our true, inconsequential position in the universe. The night is an undressing of the false diversions of the luminous day. Darkness peels away the warmth of suns, coziness of family, amity of friends, and even part of your sight. Thus exposed, you are forced to rely on your soul in experiencing the world.

"You will enter a small courtyard ringed with trees where you can think about your place in the world in general, and more specifically, with Tallcon. You should meditate on how well you are following his teachings, clarifying your priorities. Night is the time given to us by Tallcon to allow us to appreciate him more fully. When he shucked away part of himself to make the suns, he commanded them be out but half the time. The night, the darkness," he said, raising his arms up into the starry sky, "is here to humble us and make us realize how cold the world is without his light."

Scelto nodded, but Gozador was not looking directly at him. "This allows us to abandon the arrogance of the warm and lighted day and focus our mind into the night sky and the seemingly billions of stars."

Gazing around at the awe-inspiring view, Scelto realized he had never stopped to truly appreciate the night sky. He could hear Friar's words in his mind, *A feeling of insignificance on your part does not necessitate something of great significance on the other end. A dog would seem awe inspiring to an ant, but that doesn't mean the dog cares for it.* Scelto started laughing.

"Just as I suspected," Gozador said coldly.

"What?" Scelto questioned, his laughter thawing.

"The openness and lack of enthrallment rampant amongst the Knights drowned your discipline, respect, and unity. Proliate have deep roots of faith to keep us centered, balanced. If unchecked, freedom breeds unrestrained uncertainty, which leads to egotistical chaos instead of following the true path of Tallcon. Sooner or later, unchecked freedom strips respect and awe for Tallcon. Your laughter is sacrilege."

Despite his blood boiling, everything suddenly seemed clear to Scelto. He stood up. "I need to go."

"What's wrong?" the startled Proliate asked.

"For the first time in a while, nothing. Everything's clear. I'm going home." Even before the words trailed out of his mouth, he felt a rush of relief, a weight lifting. He would take the disheveled Knights over the supercilious Proliate.

He walked to the barracks. Upon entering, he saw two Proliate getting into full armor. "I'm not sure we need to double the guard. They won't attack us in a fortified position," one said. "They like to prey on the defenseless."

"Who?" Scelto asked innocently. Without looking up the Proliate blurted, "The Knights, Elves, or Dwarves, of course. Don't you know we are at war?"

"War?" Scelto said in complete confusion.

"Yes, it's official. For the glory of Tallcon and the safety of Verngaurd," the Proliate replied, oblivious that Scelto was from Liberum.

Scelto froze, overcome with emotion. Even though he knew he was doing the right thing, the Proliate had been incredibly welcoming and friendly. He had come to respect them, their dedication, hard work, and even flashes of being incredibly funny. Yet the Knights held a much greater emotional investment. They were family. Either choice would require him to gut part of himself and leave it painfully behind. Without another word, he walked past them and pulled out his dingy and drab squire's shirt, vest, and pants. He smiled. They held a feeling of comfort, of home.

Velox rushed into the barracks. He and Scelto stood, staring at each other for a moment, before Velox smiled. "Did you have another accident? Perhaps too much fanged-goat milk?" he said, laughing. "I knew you had a problem. I should have searched your bunk for a hidden stash. Pretending to not like it to lull us into inaction. Shameful..."

Scelto did not, could not, smile. The sadness of leaving someone so nice overshadowed the humor.

"Come on, that was funny," Velox said, moving closer.

Scelto embraced him warmly. "Thanks for all you have done. I shall never forget you, but I need to go home. I'm not waiting for them to come any longer."

"You are home," Velox said earnestly.

Scelto shook his head. "Don't make this any harder than it already is."

"We were sincerely hoping you would join us," Velox stated quietly. "I'm also sure Princess Hamaza will be crushed if you leave. Don't be afraid of following your dreams. Make sure you are living your life, not following what someone else wants for you."

"That's just it. For the first time, I *am* going after my dreams. I know where I am supposed to be."

Velox's smile was weighed down by disappointment. "If you change your mind, you'll always be welcome. We'll keep some warm Torahammas milk waiting," he said, laughing despite the look of sadness and betrayal in his eyes. "I'll be outside when you're changed."

Outside Scelto found Velox arguing with the two guards who had been talking earlier, both wearing deep scowls.

"They got you a horse and will take you to Temple Aon Intinn. From there they will turn you over to the Northern Dwarves and let them get you to Liberum," Velox said.

"Thank you," Scelto replied. In silence, they walked to the gate of the outpost. There, Velox and Scelto embraced one last time. "Thanks again."

"Take care," Velox answered. "We shall miss you."

Scelto swung onto the back of a stunning white steed. The two Proliate guards shifted in their saddle restlessly as their annoyed eyes darted around. Before the three were through the gates, Velox sprinted to Commander Fenik to let him know Scelto left.

The screeching of the closing gates made Scelto feel mournful, knowing he would never see Velox or the outpost again. The reverberation as they slammed shut announced another chapter in his life was over. The same pang of sadness that struck as he left Liberum reared up, but this time a small seed of anticipation started to blossom. Thoughts of the Knights, Friar, the other squires, especially Gimelli, flowered. He nudged his horse forward to keep up with the Proliate guards. He did not even know their names, but it was obvious they were in a hurry to get rid of him.

"Keep up, boy! We don't appreciate having to babysit a snot-nosed squire," one of them said gruffly. "We ride through the night, and no complaints."

After riding all night and day, they finally stopped to rest the next night, but only for several hours. Scelto was roused while it was still dark. They roughly pushed the still-groggy squire into his saddle.

They had been riding for many hours when something flashed in front of the ninth moon, Himmel.

"What was that?" Scelto asked, nervously.

"No talking, ride," one replied apathetically.

The three rode hard for another hour.

"There it is again," Scelto said, noting several dark streaks flash in front of moons. "Guys, something huge is flying up there," Scelto appealed, fear creeping through his spine. He stopped his horse, letting them continue forward.

Suddenly, a sizable black shape started to grow larger right in front of them.

"Hey, uh, there is definitely something up there, and it's coming right towards us!" Scelto yelled.

Looking up, the two guards saw the shape about a hundred feet away and closing quickly. They shared a look of concern before turning back to the approaching figure. Scelto veered his horse left in a full sprint.

"For Tallcon!" the two Proliate shouted, while continuing to advance.

WHHHOOOOOOOOOOOSH, and all at once, the night sky exploded in crackling flames.

"Dragons!" the Proliate yelled.

Chapter Four

Dragons Blue

Scroll 1: Blue Battlefield

Aquila and the other Eaglians had flown the League over Lake Glasere, using a special harness for the skeptical Crann, and well into the Siochain Pass before departing. The pass was an open stretch of land sandwiched by Jaa in the north and the Teorainn Mountains to the south.

"Arend, I wish your dad could have taken us a little further," Sankari complained.

"How many times do we have to go over this?" Kainen answered defensively for his Eaglian friend. "You know how many of them died just getting us here. You've seen how many Watchers and griffins are patrolling the skies. Plus, they are preparing for the upcoming battle."

As if on cue, the piercing shriek of a griffin bit into the air. Some ran to a tree for cover. Others scurried over to a large boulder.

"Hold perfectly still," Arend whispered. "Any movement will alert the griffins."

223

Siochain Pass had sparse, but consistent, cover. Arend's father, Aquila, had advised against crossing into Jaa, as Jaainians didn't take kindly to strangers, especially with tensions so high. Eventually, the griffins cleared the area.

"Should we just stay here for the night?" Gimelli suggested as the third sun, Pheobus, drifted lazily into the western horizon. "We need a fire and hot food."

"We should keep moving. Our goal is to meet the Northern Dwarves in a couple of days. We can barely see the Hino Mountains, and the griffins are constantly on us," Arend said.

"I agree with Gimelli," Kainen offered. "This far north at this time of year is miserable. We could use a hot meal and a decent night's sleep."

"We should stop for Lontas. He walked half the day for the first time," Gimelli finished with a smile. Raising his eyebrows, Lontas smiled sheepishly at the attention.

"You did great today," Arend commented. "That laak-htua salve is working to heal your wounds."

"Wait a minute," Gimelli said. "You didn't trip once today."

"Lontas!" Bellae said loudly. "What in the world?"

Arend let out his Eaglian half-squeal, half-laugh. "Maybe accidentally sitting on the flesh-eating log wasn't such a bad thing. It only seemed like it at the time."

"What the heck are you talking about?" Sankari asked.

"He lacked a sense of balance and body position. Flying helped both," Arend answered. "We should celebrate Lontas' return to walking with a warm fire and hot food. I'll be right back."

"I hate to say it, but I'm getting sick of the ravinto plant," Bellae lamented.

Later that night, after they had finished eating an arctic fox, everyone but Arend, who was standing away from the others, was enjoying the warmth of the crackling fire.

"What's wrong?" Bellae asked.

"I have never seen the Northern lights before. It was incredible. Plus, I got a glimpse of the Palas Frusen, which is also amazing," he answered.

"What's the Palas-thingey?" Gimelli asked.

"The Ice Palace of Queen Antiopay and Princess Hamaza," Arend replied. "They were lighting it up as I was flying over. It was breathtaking."

Gimelli bristled at the mention of Hamaza. Her thoughts immediately rushed to Scelto as she gazed to the eastern sky. It was still a friendly blue, but turning dusky as an early warning of the impending darkness. Despite the fire, she shivered, dreading the coming night.

With teeth chattering, Bellae looked over at Gimelli. She was smiling but obviously feeling the cold as well. The flimsy hints of orange and red within the charred embers offered only a hint of heat. Crann neighed loudly, fully rousing all those still slumbering in the cold early morning.

"We should move," he told Bellae. *"The griffins have been swarming all night."*

"What's Crann upset about?" Arend asked.

"The griffins have been busy, and we need to go."

"Did you notice anything, Kainen?" Arend asked.

"Yeah. The ugly buggers have been buzzing around my entire watch. The good news, I did not see any Watchers, and none came close enough to need to douse the fire."

Gimelli was the first to physically rise. "Walking will get the blood flowing and help us warm up as well," she said, smiling through a deep shudder.

"Do you have to be so blessed cheerful?" Sankari asked in an irritated voice.

"Seriously, Sankari?" Arend questioned. "Did you honestly get on her for being cheerful?"

The Fairy rolled her eyes. "I'm guessing this means more wonderful ravinto for breakfast? Do you realize how much energy I burn flying?" Sankari asked, pointing to her wings.

Kainen looked up at the Fairy, thinking of his harsh training to be in the League, including the days he went without food. "My father has an ancient Elf saying he repeats to me frequently. If enough is not enough, it is doubtful that even avarice and gluttony will be satisfying."

Sankari huffed, annoyed, "Not the same thing! I have a mind to take down a dumb griffin!" She brandished her sword made from the tusk of a peccary from Cappadocia as the others stifled their amusement.

Their progress was slow and tedious. The heavy sightings of griffins, Magicians, and Watchers meant Arend often had to walk and they constantly had to hide.

"The griffins are as thick as mosquitos in the Mohado Mires," Gimelli commented.

"I know my dad said to avoid Jaa." Arend fluttered his wings, as if shaking off his father's presence. "However, the griffins and Watchers aren't patrolling north of the border."

"Really?" Kainen asked, scanning the skies. "Why? Has Jaa really sided with the Proliate?" Kainen asked, pacing restlessly and making animated gestures with his hands. "They insult the Elves of Creber. We have always had an excellent relationship with the Jaainians."

"They are probably just concentrating their forces around Temple Aon Intinn," Arend offered.

"Watch out!" Crann neighed to Bellae.

"Down. Now!" Bellae cried, and they scrambled for cover. They remained still for what seemed like an excruciatingly long time as a flood of griffins streamed above.

"Some of the griffins have Magicians on them," Kainen said, looking helplessly at Arend. "There are way too many to fight. They must know we are here."

Arend laughed. "Maybe, but right now they seem more interested in them." He pointed to three rapidly approaching green Vioma dragons.

"Wow, that one must be thirty feet long," Gimelli said in awe. The shiny green helmets of the Aer Ridire dragon riders glinted in the dull morning light. Fierce cries from the Dwarves and bolts from their crossbows could be heard zinging above.

Ten griffins without riders moved into formation with two rows of five, the outer griffins falling back into an aerodynamic "V" pattern. With their fluttering feathers, they looked like the fletching on the back end of an arrow. The other three griffins hung back as their Magician riders barked orders. The three Vioma dragons slowed and began to fly in a disorganized manner. The squires could see the frantic movements of the Aer Ridire Dwarves struggling to control the dragons as the two aerial groups moved towards a collision.

The griffins were gaining speed as the Vioma's flight pattern grew even more mercurial. When they were about thirty yards apart, the Vioma abruptly straightened their formation into a vertical "V," one on the bottom and two above. The air between the two forces exploded into flames, disintegrating the first four griffins. The three Magicians immediately used their crosiers to make magic shields around themselves.

As the charred chunks of dead griffins fell, the Vioma dragons broke off in different directions. One Magician and two of the griffins without riders wheeled and followed each of the dragons to attack from behind. Understanding their strategy, the dragons turned and flew headlong towards each other in a crisscross pattern, drawing the trailing griffins into the line of literal fire of the dragon approaching from the other direction. The sky was intermittently lit up with bursts of flames as the dragons tried to take out the griffins.

Bolts from the Aer Ridire also filled the skies. The griffins clawed and snapped at the Dwarf riders and dragons as the Magician's crosiers alternated between blue fire and magical shields. A griffin managed to rip his claws into one of the Aer Ridire Dwarves, lifting him until his harnesses snapped taut before decapitating him. Several bolts from his Dwarf brothers slammed into the griffin. One Dwarf freed himself from his harness, punching his two swords deep into the creature's neck. With blood surging out from the wounds, his left talon shot forward and pulled the Dwarf out of the wooden carriage. Both quickly fluttered to the ground, thudding hard, rendered lifeless.

Without warning, a griffin broke formation, and one of the Vioma turned to follow.

"It's a trap!" Arend warned, knowing the dragon riders couldn't hear him.

As the dragon whipped around to follow the griffin, blue magic from one of the Magicians sliced into the dragon, shearing across its neck, instantly setting its head free from his body. Immediately the disjointed body hurtled downwards with smoke swirling in an ebony trail from its sizzling neck. The riderless griffins took the chance to attack the hapless Aer Ridire on the dead and plummeting dragon. Using their claws to hold onto the wooden carriage, they ripped and slashed savagely at the Dwarves. The griffins broke off their attack just before the flayed dragon smashed into the ground.

The initial thud was joined by the sounds of bones crunching and wood splintering against the unforgivingly hard earth.

The bigger of the remaining dragons headed east with two Magicians and two riderless griffins trailing after it. The smaller dragon headed west, towards the huddling League with one Magician and three riderless griffins following.

"They are coming really close," Bellae said.

"Crouch and be still," Kainen directed.

The dragon was diving incredibly fast straight for them. Its body seemed to shudder as gravity assisted its speed.

The overlapping sheets of spiked armor were clearly visible on the neck of the dragon. The driver seemed to be staring down at them while the other three Dwarves had their attention focused on the pursuing griffins. The front griffin had a Magician rider while the three trailing griffins were without riders, set back to make a diamond shape.

"That dragon is coming right for us!" Arend said, his muscles tensing. Bellae stole a glance at the Eaglian. Desire to get into the fight radiated off his face, reminding her of when he had taken out Honey. She shuddered at the unwelcome memory that was crowded with Honey's betrayal. Turning back to the dragon, she saw a fluttering right ear.

"Soma!" she cried out.

"It's going to crash! Should we run?" Lontas asked with surprising calm.

Despite the tension, Bellae smiled at the changes in Lontas since his injury and time flying with Arend. No longer a picture of fear, he even seemed older. Turning back to the approaching dragon, she felt calm. *Soma would never hurt us.*

"Abhac! Soma!" she called, waving. Gimelli quickly pulled her down.

The movement was enough to catch their attention, and a moment of recognition passed between Abhac, Soma, and Bellae.

Abhac barked orders to Soma, who pulled up and somersaulted backwards with incredible aerial agility. Abhac was shouting as flames suddenly burst from Soma and scorched the griffin on his right. The entire body and wings of the griffin burst into flames. Bellae and Gimelli shrieked loudly, but it was drowned out by a horrific scream from the griffin burning alive. The screeching creature immediately began to spin towards the ground as the other three griffins banked to their right to avoid the approaching dragon. Soma managed to kick the sputtering griffin as it plunged.

"Yes!" Arend cried, his face a picture of intensity. Seeing the look of horror on the girls' faces he added, "The griffins and Magicians deserve no sympathy. They have been handing out worse."

The blackened figure hurtled helplessly towards the ground as a trail of smoke streamed upwards. Just above the ground, the shrieking stopped, replaced by a bone-jarring crunch as it crashed into the ground with a series of teeth-rattling cracks. The barely recognizable creature flopped about in bursts of violent, helpless spasms as its charred flesh continued to burn. A nauseating sizzle punctuated by an occasional crackle echoed in their ears. Bellae doubled over, feeling its pain sharply.

Even Arend showed sparks of softening at the sight of the pathetic shape. Vicious shrieks ripped the air as Abhac and Soma tried to draw the three griffins away from the children. The griffin carrying the Magician had taken the bait and was chasing Soma. A blue light burst forth from the Magician's crosier and struck the tail of Soma, who quickly rose upwards. The two creatures without riders were circling above the children in small rings.

"Hold very still," Kainen said with his beaked kama weapon drawn.

Soma performed an aerial backflip and picked up blistering speed downward. A series of five fireballs shot out from the Magician. The first one missed. The second one glanced off Soma's abdomen. The third scorched right into one of the Aer Ridire just as Soma started to spiral away. The Dwarf burst into flames, his screams still powerful in the already reeling ears of the League. The carriage and the Dwarves strapped onto it burst into flames as shards of wood and smoke exploded.

"Oh, no," Bellae whimpered. The Dwarf who had been hit directly came loose and began a meteoric descent.

Bellae made a move to run towards him.

"No," Gimelli cried, pulling her down.

"Incoming!" Kainen yelled as one riderless griffin headed straight for them.

"You guys make a break for it! I will fly to fight him," Arend squawked. He stood up and made a move to open ground just as a disgusting splat and hiss came from the burning Dwarf colliding with the earth.

Sankari cried out, "Ewwww!"

"We should stick together and run," Lontas cautioned.

"There's no time," Arend replied as he squatted down low before bursting upwards with his powerful legs. His wings beat furiously just to maintain his height at first. Then he started to move up with increasing speed.

"Let's go," Kainen said.

"Not going to happen. We don't leave anyone behind," Gimelli said, drawing out her bow and nocking an arrow.

Soma had pulled up and was heading right for the diving, riderless griffin. A three-way collision was shaping up: Arend heading up, the griffin down, and Soma horizontally. Bolts and arrows were flying from the Aer Ridire Dwarves clinging to the shattered and burning carriage. Two struck into the griffin but did not faze it. One went into the back left flank, the part that resembled a lion. The second entered its front leg just above the talon and below its shaggy mane.

Figure 5: Arend flies up to fight an attacking griffin.

Arend moved his sword down by his leg. As he neared the griffin, he slashed upwards with it. The griffin, aided by gravity, was going incredibly fast and with lightning reflexes used his good talon to gently deflect the sword. Arend's body and head were now exposed, and the griffin headbutted him. Arend's neck snapped backwards, and he somersaulted rearward, his sword falling uselessly downwards.

The griffin snapped with its ferocious beak at the flailing Arend— the first bite barely missed. Just as it neared Arend's head and prepared a second chomp, Soma slammed into it. The enormous size discrepancy became obvious as the green dragon was easily five times the size of the griffin. In perfectly timed execution, Soma sank in his vicious teeth and claws before wrenching his legs out and ripping the griffin apart in an awesome display of power.

With blood and feathers still fluttering in his teeth, he turned and dove for Arend, now plummeting unconscious. Soma managed to grab him. With blood-stained claws, he gently cradled Arend and headed down towards the other children.

Suddenly Abhac yelled, "Fire! Fire! Now!" The Magician riding one of the last two griffins was in a steep dive and gaining on the dragon. A blue light shot out from his crosier and shattered what was left of the fractured carriage, rendering the crossbow shots of the Dwarves useless. Wood splintered out in every direction, and Soma howled in pain. Abhac flailed wildly, barely holding onto leather straps near Soma's neck. The other two Dwarves were blown off. One was nearly cut in two by the hot light and dropped lifelessly. The other had several blackened areas on his green tunic and began screaming while careening horizontally. Eventually he began flailing wildly while plummeting down.

Soma let out another roar of pain but continued downward as the destroyed carriage rained down around him. Abhac was screaming orders and pointing to the living Dwarf. Soma made a move to rescue him just as the Magician yelled "Eldur hnottur!" A series of fire balls burst from his crosier. The first four blasted one after the other into the floundering Dwarf. Only fine dust and smoke were left as the fifth one sailed through the obliterated soot that was once a body before zooming off into the distance. A howl, this one of anger, burst from Soma, who turned towards the Magician and his griffin.

The crystal on the Magician's crosier sputtered blue, but nothing came out. His eyes widened apprehensively, and he quickly fled the battle, deciding fighting a dragon without magic was unwise. This left one lone griffin without a rider circling above.

Arend was now conscious and hammering on the dragon's claw, screaming, "Let me go! I'm ready to fight."

Seeing he was coherent, Soma threw Arend up into the air. Abhac yelled, "Decoy, to your right, hard and fast." He then gave several commands to Soma: "Gilla, sivu hyokkays! Ween!"

Understanding the command, Arend was already flying up and began to hurl his sleek, black throwing darts. If thrown with enough force, the entire four inches of the double-sided dart would be buried in the victim, making it impossible to retrieve. The griffin screeched in horrible pain as the first two throwing darts impaled its body, causing it to fly erratically, zigging and zagging desperately to avoid the darts. It proved effective, as the next three went wide. Shrieking, the griffin soared closer to Arend.

Two more misses, the griffin closing quickly.

Frustrated, Arend tried again. Two more darts zoomed past the griffin, the last one barely missing his head.

Whoosh! One of Gimelli's arrows zoomed just past the griffin's right shoulder.

"Only one dart left," Kainen said, as much to himself as the others.

Arend swayed side to side, imitating the bobbing of the now rapidly approaching griffin. Its front talons were only feet away from Arend. Blood was dripping from one of them as well as several places on his body.

"He's too close to Arend now," Gimelli said anxiously as she lowered her bow.

Arend pulled back and let loose his last dart, which sailed straight into the griffin's right shoulder, causing it to stop and shriek. Shaking its majestic head, it lunged for Arend, who was now weaponless.

The griffin's razor-sharp beak was inches from the retreating Arend when its eyes shot wide in a mix of terror and surprise. It emitted a strangled cry before being ripped backwards by Soma's powerful jaws. Soma wrenched his neck backwards with incredible force and violently shook griffin from side to side until it became limp.

Abhac, still barely holding on, was barking orders as Soma and Arend landed.

Bellae stared at the lifeless griffin caught in Soma's jaws. Bellae was glad Arend was safe and knew this griffin would have killed him, but the crumpled and hemorrhaging body evoked an intense sadness and regret within her heart as nausea at the griffin's pain rose from below. The waves of conflict sloshed against each other in her mind. Its majestic head feathers arched back into a lion's mane, the muscular chest now crumpled and fragile looking.

The griffin's eyes suddenly snapped open, and it lurched towards Bellae. She fell backwards, screaming. Soma began savagely, and repeatedly, slamming the griffin against the hard earth, continuing the assault long after the crumpled body had gone limp. Its inert body resembled a sack of shattered bones and hemorrhaging bruises.

Gimelli and Lontas were instantly on Bellae, helping her up and showering her with questions to make sure she wasn't hurt. She nodded, indicating she was okay.

"Since war was declared, the skies have become insane. I'm glad you're safe," Abhac said, sighing. "Even if Soma was healthy and my carriage wasn't smashed, I don't think I could get you back to the mountains safely. More griffins or Watchers are sure to come. You guys should cross the border into Jaa and head due east. We'll try to pick you up before you pass Temple Aon Intinn. The closer you get to the temple, the more Proliate patrols you will have to deal with on the ground."

Soma released the griffin and let out a soft howl. Its lifeless and tattered body rolled to a stop a few feet in front of the dragon. "We better go. Soma's pretty beat up. Get to safety and good luck," Abhac said. He secured himself with what was left of the leather straps before yelling, "Huun sisu koti!"

The dragon groaned as he squatted for takeoff. Jumping to get momentum, he lurched violently to his left and howled in pain. Abhac talked soothingly to him before calling out for the dragon to get up in the air, "Huun! Huun!"

Soma squatted down once more, his legs coiled and both wings ready to assist in the liftoff. Grimacing, he shot up into the air. Once again, he lurched to his left, but this time, Arend appeared, flying up and under the dragon's left underbelly. Straining, he pushed, and slowly Soma gained altitude.

Arend flew back to the ground, looking exhausted. "Here," Sankari snapped.

"What?" Arend said, still out of breath.

"I found four of your darts that missed the griffin," she said in a softer tone. "Kainen got your sword."

Arend leaned against Kainen, his breaths heaving and deep. The two lifelong friends talked softly to each other.

Silently, the rest of the League surveyed the charred and splintered residue of the battle. Several of the griffin's remains were still sizzling and popping thanks to the merciless dragon naphtha. The first griffin killed by Soma resembled a crisply burnt log, indistinguishable as a living creature. The mortally wounded Vioma dragon lay in a crumpled heap, surrounded by fragments of the Dwarf riders, their green armor scorched and dented. Splashes of blood were shoddily framed by shattered pieces of the Dwarf carriage.

The sickly smell of overcooked flesh filled their noses while their eyes began to tear from the stinging smoke. An unspoken thought laid heavy on everyone's mind.

War.

They knew this was just the beginning. The fight outside Creber, near Lake Glasere, and this skirmish had more than quenched any desire for conflict. Curiosity for battle had been replaced by the stark reality of its cold, unfeeling embrace. Gone were any delusions, leaving the naked image of a ravenous beast with an unquenchable thirst for blood.

"We should bury the Dwarves," Arend stated.

"Sorry, we can't risk getting caught out in the open," Kainen said. "We head north, into Jaa."

Magicians

Scroll 2: Temple Magic

"Come in," Jumeaux said in response to the knock.

Kaveri and Chy burst through. "You *still* studying, man?"

Jumeaux smiled. "They assign a lot of work."

Chy threw him an apple and plopped himself on the bed. "You're taking this way too seriously."

"I like studying this stuff."

Chy and Kaveri exchanged looks of mock horror.

"It's worse than I thought," Chy said. "I'm going to have to cut the arms of your robe off. It's the height of fashion these days."

"Fashion and you? That's funny," Kaveri joked. "By the way, in case you didn't notice, at this school they have a strict dress code, and if they ever let you graduate, you will be wearing robes of the color and fabric they tell you until you die."

"Ah," Chy sputtered, waving the words off with a swat of his hand.

"Ah, yourself," Kaveri said earnestly. "Listen, Gretten is really mad about his robes. You better get serious."

"You want me to get more serious? You mean like the study-oholic over there?" he said, pointing a thumb over at Jumeaux.

Kaveri laughed. "Well, on second thought, maybe a happy mix of your antics and his overachievement."

"What's so interesting?" Chy asked, absently flipping and catching his apple.

"This semester I have astronomy, mathematics, crystals, temple magic, anatomy, and alchemy. They want me to consider picking up griffins, healing, and herbalism…"

"What?" Chy asked, exasperated. "If you let them, Jumeaux, they will walk all over you and work you to death. There is no way…"

"I told them no, so don't worry. But I do like what I am studying."

"Oh, boy!" Chy said, slapping the palm of his hand up against his forehead and flopping back on the bed. "You're too much, Newbie."

"That's a heavy course load," Kaveri said with a serious look upon his face. "Especially since they're all new."

"Actually," Jumeaux answered, "I've studied astronomy and mathematics already. I know a bit of alchemy as well."

"What are you working on?"

"Temple Magic. I have a tour tomorrow," Jumeaux said.

"I will talk to the Prof and see if it can be me," Chy declared, smiling.

"No way. With the trouble you are in, forget it. You stay away from him," Kaveri advised. "I'll see to it you get the best."

"By best, do you mean yourself, Cave Boy?"

"You'll have to wait and see," Kaveri said, turning away to avoid letting them see the mischievous look in his eyes.

The next morning, the automatic lights flipped on and startled Jumeaux. Despite feeling tired, he jumped out of bed and went right to his Temple Magic book.

After studying through breakfast, he rushed towards the triangle. The light looked inviting, with no hint of fear creeping up into his mind. Stopping just short of the glowing light, Jumeaux abruptly and unexpectedly thought of Liberum. *I wish they could see me now,* he thought, straightening his robes and striding into the transporter.

"About time you made it, sleepy head."

"What's this? Did you stay up partying last night, Newbie?"

Jumeaux laughed as Chy and Kaveri came into focus. "I think you know better."

"Your robes are scrunched up, and your hair looks like Veneficus' abundant nose hair," Chy joked.

"Hey, I was in a hurry," Jumeaux replied. "Are you two my guides?"

"We are indeed. Thanks to me," Chy said as he turned his nose up in the air with a snobbish expression.

"Well, I'm honored that you decided to wear a real robe just for me," Jumeaux said as the three laughed.

"Don't encourage him," Kaveri said, pushing into Chy. Despite using all of his weight, he barely managed to move his much larger friend.

"Having fun, are we?" a deep voice startled them. The three boys turned to see Veneficus looking relaxed, leaning heavily on his crosier.

"We, um," Kaveri started.

"No harm in a little fun. Perhaps now, however, would be the appropriate time to head back to work?"

"Yes, Supreme Master," Chy and Kaveri conceded while bowing deeply.

Veneficus acted like he was going to turn and leave but stopped to face the boys again. "Jumeaux, I hope everyone is treating you well. I may call on you later to see how things are going, yes?"

"Yes, sir. Thank you."

With a nod Veneficus turned and disappeared.

"That was just plain weird," Kaveri said. "He never shows up like that. You must be somebody really important."

Jumeaux blushed and shrugged his shoulders. They stood in uncomfortable silence for a moment while the two older boys stared at him with a mix of awe and uncertainty. Finally, Chy grabbed his shoulder. "Come on. We have a lot to show you."

They walked up to a large double gate and stopped below a sign, which read, "Templum Palaestra."

"So this is the temple training area," Kaveri said. "The things here are modeled after the Great Temple, so when you assist at service, they will seem familiar. For example, check out this gate." Kaveri began waving his arms wildly, pretending he was casting a spell.

Chy laughed at his antics.

Clink! a loud sound echoed, and the two doors began to swing open.

"Cool magic," Jumeaux said.

The older boys chuckled. "It isn't magic. You may not know there are two types of crystals. The ones for the crosiers are mindre-minor crystals, which eventually lose their magic. The Power or Macht Crystals can refill the mindre, but were stolen. Until we find the Power Crystals, we ration the mindre where possible.

"This gate has a trigger in the floor that kicks over a suspended container below. That dumps water into a bucket attached to the door by a series of pulleys and weights. When the bucket fills with enough water, it becomes heavy enough to open the door."

They walked through the gate into a massive area. The ceilings were enormous and held up by a series of large columns and arches. A number of smaller wooden buildings dotted the immense chamber. Several Master Magicians from the Clerics Division were moving around the space, checking on other groups of students.

All the students had scrolls floating over their right shoulders. When they had something they wanted to remember, they would simply say the words and they would appear on the scrolls.

One of the Magicians eyed the three suspiciously. "Ah, the famous Chy and Kaveri, just what I need on a morning when I am already in a bad mood!"

"Orior oriri ortus crosier!" he said reluctantly. Still wearing a doubtful look, he paused before handing the crosier to Kaveri. "Remember, only the bare minimum spells."

"Oh, come on. Can't I turn Kaveri into a turtle or some-um-mpppfffff?" Chy huffed as Kaveri elbowed him in the gut.

"Notice who I handed the crosier to. I know about your hijinks," the Cleric said.

"Who says hijinks? I mean, seriously," Chy said sarcastically as he pushed Jumeaux through the door of the first building. They entered what looked like a long hallway painted pitch black.

As Jumeaux took a step, he heard a high-pitched click, like the one he had heard before the gates opened. Suddenly, a fierce howling noise filled the dark hallway.

"Clarus lux murus!" Kaveri yelled. Suddenly, the wall on their right began to glow brightly. "Look at this," he said, swinging open a panel in the wall.

"These same howlers are used in Glanha Hallway of the Great Temple entrance. See the rhomboid-shaped howler?" Kaveri yelled over the howling.

"It's spinning rapidly because of the same principle of torsion on ballistas. The ropes get cranked and locked into position. All of the energy is stored until someone steps or presses on the right spot. The metal rhomboid spins around this central wood pivot. If you put a few well-placed holes in the metal, you have got yourself a terrifying howler. No magic, but huge effect."

Shutting the panel, Kaveri said, "Desino avta, clarus lux!" The light vanished, and as the boys walked further, Jumeaux noted a strange relief sculpture of a fantastical beast with glowing, fierce eyes and four large horns upon its head.

"The eyes are white phosphorous, which glows when exposed to air, so they keep it covered until right before people enter. It's called chemiluminescence and needs to be replaced periodically. That's on your test," Kaveri said as another "click" pierced the air. Jumeaux froze, unsure what would come next. He jumped as a high-pitched wail erupted from the mouth of the creature.

"Clarus lux virgam!" Kaveri said. This time, only the crosier glowed. It was still enough for Jumeaux to see Kaveri unlatching the front half of the relief carving. Once opened, he saw a series of metal vessels, one on top of the other.

"This top one is full of water. When you trip the switch, the water starts to siphon into the airtight container below. As the water comes in, the air in the bottom is pushed out through these pipes with holes and you get wailing," Chy said. Winking at Jumeaux, he pinched Kaveri. "You can also get that wailing by pinching a girl like Kaveri."

"Ow!" Kaveri said as he mock punched Chy. "Are you two or something?"

Kaveri kept the light on the crosier until they came to a floating image of Tallcon.

Jumeaux stepped closer to the suspended statue and heard a series of all-too-familiar "clicks" before it began to spin.

"A magnetite lodestone is under the statue," Kaveri said, moving the crosier closer to the brownish black rock with a metallic sheen. "They're rare. This one came from the storm fields south of the Teorainn Hills."

"They have nasty storms up there. Lightning showers down like rain. Our Master shielded us through the storm but used so much magic it burnt out his crosier while we were searching for a lodestone," Chy added.

"The magnet keeps the metal statue floating. Sometimes…" Kaveri was cut off by a horrific noise vibrating from above. Jumeaux crouched below the thunderous roar.

Chy reached down with one of his powerful hands to help Jumeaux up. "Imagine how regular people feel."

"The click started water flowing into a series of propped-up bowls filled with rocks. Once they are full, they tip over and the rocks spill across the floor. Each one requires a different volume of water before it tips for a prolonged rumbling."

"I see," Jumeaux said.

"You mean, *hear*?" Chy said. Jumeaux laughed. Finally, someone who appreciated his type of humor.

For the better part of an hour, the three boys wandered the great hall. Chy and Kaveri explained each new device until Jumeaux had to leave for class.

"See that guy? That's Heron, the greatest inventor of these devices." Kaveri said. "Step on the transporter so you're not late. Master Peraakon is less than understanding."

As the white light crept up his body, Jumeaux's skin began to sting. *This isn't right!* Suddenly the light started to swirl and lurch, taking a misty physical form. In front of his eyes it began changing into the likeness of a face—it was Veneficus' visage. Panic started to grip Jumeaux as it disappeared along with the white light.

"Welcome. You're a little late," Master Peraakon said cheerfully as Jumeaux appeared in the classroom. Jumeaux smiled and nodded but was still disturbed by the impression of the Supreme Master.

Peraakon's tall frame held old and tattered robes. He had small circular spectacles that looked funny on his round, plump nose. "You didn't miss anything, so soon enough is as good as early. I was talking about the mindre crystals that power our crosiers.

"Each Magician is given a certain amount of mindre crystals to use over their lifetime. While they last a long time, it's not forever. When a Magician dies, his leftover crystals are recycled. If his crystals run out before he dies, he is given a job as a Master Clericus, not utilizing magic. Of course, you can choose temple magic as your solitary career and be assured your allotted crystals will last.

"Be careful without being stingy. The story of these crystals is complicated…yes, Blino," Peraakon piqued, pointing to a boy with his hand up and standing on his tiptoes, looking more like he had to urinate than ask a question.

"In battle you get more!" Blino stated with an enormous, self-satisfied smile straining across his face.

"Ah, excellent, there are hundreds of crystals designated for just such occasions, like the new war."

Looking around in confusion, Jumeaux could tell the other students seemed to already know about the war. He decided to hide his uncertainty and ask Chy and Kaveri.

"Be advised, basically no one in the world can touch the actual crystals without getting severely burned. This is why they are in a crosier instead of say, around our necks. Don't worry, these are just models to give you an idea of what they would look like. Everyone gather around and examine them. You can see there are various sizes and colors. Your class rank determines the order you pick your crystal on graduation, a good reason to study. Who wants to be first to touch the models?"

"Sir, Jumeaux would like to be the first to touch them, and that's okay with me," Blino said in a loud but oddly monotonous tone.

Jumeaux turned to the smiling Blino, instantly noticing Blino's eyes were glowing a soft white and staring through, not at, the former squire.

"I love your enthusiasm, Jumeaux," Master Peraakon said. "Come up and pretend you are picking out your crystal at graduation. Think of this as a lifelong companion. You will spend more time with it than any other person or object. A special bond will form between you."

Jumeaux slowly made his way through the harsh stares of the other students, resisting the urge to shout that Blino was lying. When he gazed back, Blino was shaking his head, looking confused. *Was he enchanted to volunteer me?*

"Look at the crystals, soak up their color. When picking your real mindre crystal, you will feel their power with your soul. When you feel a connection with one, because these are just models, pick it up. The real ones would severely burn you."

Jumeaux scanned the twenty or so crystals. His eyes kept being drawn to a large, bluish crystal.

"Now, I should say a word about shape," Peraakon said. "Each one is determined by Master Cutters, who decide the most efficient shape after the large, rough crystals are cleaved or broken apart. All of this is done with magical gloves and lots of healing enchantments. I see your eye on that one. That's interesting—I don't remember that model. Anyway, go ahead and pick it up."

Jumeaux reached for it. As his hand drew closer he felt a pressure, pushing his hand away, like two magnets in the wrong orientation. Jumeaux could hear Master Peraakon talking but did not comprehend his words. Pushing harder, he suddenly felt his hand break through the invisible barrier and shoot towards the now-glowing crystal. The crystal suddenly began sucking his hand forward.

"Uh," Blino said. "Is it supposed to shine like that?"

"What?" Master Peraakon said, turning to stare at the crystal. "Oh, no! This can't be. Jumeaux, don't…"

It was too late. Jumeaux's hand was pulled forcefully to the crystal. It flashed a brilliant, blinding, bluish light. A feeling of calm and serenity enveloped Jumeaux. He closed his eyes and enjoyed the feeling of peace. Suddenly, a tinge of pain began to rise from his hand. Flashes of Gimelli raced through his head. She was walking beside Bellae, an Elf, and… someone who looked like… *No, that couldn't be,* he thought. But it was, in fact, Lontas. He looked different, more confident. The intensity of the discomfort exploded exponentially. Opening his eyes, he was immersed in white light and moving like in the transporter while screaming in pain.

Squinting, he found himself standing in an office and began jumping up and down from the agony radiating from his hand. His head swiveled to take in the details, slowly realizing he was in Veneficus' office. The Supreme Master was staring at an extremely old scroll levitating in front of him as ten Valo lights hovered anxiously around his head.

Jumeaux moaned and grabbed his right wrist as excruciating pain pulsed out of his hand. Veneficus held his palm up to silence Jumeaux and continued reading the scroll. Staring at the angry red skin on his hand, Jumeaux bit his lower lip as pain from the burn exploded.

Scroll 3: He'll Swerve?

The squires in the League of Truth huddled in cold silence around a feeble fire. Even though their camp was behind a rock, the wind stretched out to bite at them with its long, icy tendrils. They had been marching along well north of Jaa's border for several days, and the temperature was steadily dropping. The Hino Mountains were directly to the south, and the towering Koori Mountains were visible to the east.

Frost was now a constant, unwelcome companion with the inhospitable ground making sitting or sleeping an extremely disagreeable experience.

"More ravinto root soup?" Lontas offered.

His question was met with a universal groan. Shrugging, Lontas helped himself to thirds. Bellae smiled at his newfound coordination and growing confidence. A few weeks ago he would have assuredly spilled some over himself and everyone else. The skin where he had been burned was raised, red-pink, and wrinkled, but as long as he did his stretches and applied the salve, he was moving well.

"They are starting early tonight," Arend said, using his superb eyesight to scan the southern sky. The others turned in time to see the hint of flames in the distant sky.

"The Vioma are rocking it!" Kainen said as the sky lit up with dragon fire.

"There are about twenty or thirty of them in one line," Arend said, pointing to something the others could not see.

"Ooo!" Arend said, his body leaning and dodging as he acted out the battle. "I've never seen so many griffins." Arend looked longingly at Kainen.

"Ab-sooo-lute-ly not!" Kainen said. "No!" he added for emphasis.

"I'll be back by morning," Arend pleaded. He had been lamenting his performance in the previous skirmish and wanted revenge on the griffins.

Kainen shook his head firmly. "We need you here."

"Are we just supposed to keep walking until we freeze to death? Let me help in the battle and then get one of the Vioma to come get you. The firewood is not lasting through the night, and I am having a harder time finding any."

"Arend, we're all frustrated, but we have to trust Abhac and the Northern Dwarves. Our fathers believe in them, so should we."

"So much for picking us up before Aon Intinn," Sankari moaned.

A tense silence resulted. Lontas, Gimelli, Bellae, Grym, and Borb all huddled together and combined their blankets. Sankari seemed to be suffering the most. Her wings were constantly freezing. Kainen sat poking aimlessly at the delicate fire, as if hoping it would magically enlarge. Arend continued watching the distant battle only he could see.

Bellae stood up and went to Crann. *"How are your wounds, dear one?"*

"Better."

"I wish we were back in the warm stables."

Visions of Star purring and food from Cookie made her smile. There was a coziness in the images, but she stopped grinning at how distant they seemed. The old memories felt smudged and faded. Their loss of focus arising more from the depth of her recent experiences than the physical distance or time apart from the castle. *"Good night,"* she said, giving the horse's neck a big squeeze.

"Everything all right?" Gimelli whispered.

"Yeah, he's okay."

"Good, then get your warm little body under here, it's colder without you," Gimelli said, struggling to keep smiling.

"Okay, but why are we whispering."

"Look." Gimelli nodded to a peacefully sleeping Lontas.

"Impressive," Bellae replied, raising her eyebrows in surprise.

"Normally, he would be fearfully begging to go home."

"The fresh air is doing him good," Bellae said. The two girls laughed quietly.

They abruptly stopped under the weight of Arend's icy stare. They felt embarrassed for laughing when a savage battle was raging so close by.

"Hey, Arend," Kainen probed. When the Eaglian did not answer, he continued anyway, "Let us know if the battle moves closer, okay?"

"This is insane!" Sankari grumbled the next morning, frost clinging to her wings and hair. Even though Lontas seemed stiff, he jumped up, looking incredibly refreshed for having slept on icy rocks.

"I can go look for some firewood," Lontas offered with a smile.

Gimelli and Bellae looked at each other, shaking their heads in disbelief. Both were wondering who this guy was. Offering to go into hostile territory to look for wood?

"We don't have time," Kainen said as he twisted his upper body in a vain attempt to work some of the kinks out of his icy back.

"We can spare half of an hour to warm up. Look at us. We look like snowballs! Seriously, I'm not some pea-brained snow Fairy," Sankari said testily.

"A fire would be nice," Bellae said softly, nudging closer to Gimelli for warmth. The idea of getting out from underneath their blankets seemed loathsome.

"I'll go," Arend said grumpily.

"Do you want me to…" Lontas started, but Arend was already in the air.

"I guess he's not in the mood for company," Bellae said. Crann neighed, and she reluctantly stood up and moved towards the horse.

"Arend was up all night pacing and shaking his fist at the flames in the sky. I couldn't see what he did, but I can tell you the battled raged most of the night."

"Thanks, Crann." Bellae looked south towards the scene of the previous night's fight. The skies appeared calm and tranquil, but she could imagine the carnage on the battlefield.

"Lovely chat, but um, what about some serious breakfast? Are you trying to starve us?" Grym asked, wobbling his head, feigning as if he were going to pass out.

"I know, I'm hungry too."

"When do you think we'll get some real food?" Borb asked.

"See, even righteous Borb is feeling it. We're starving here."

Bellae absently rubbed the black patch of fur around Borb's right ear. *"I'm sorry, but I'm not sure when we'll eat well again."*

By the time the League had been walking for about two hours, the Mardin sun had stood up in the sky far enough to push back the frost, which was now relegated to hiding in shadows. Arend was constantly scanning the skies. No one realized he had flown south until he came back with blood on his talons and hands.

He wouldn't speak of what he saw, but they knew there were no survivors. After what they had witnessed previously, they could imagine the carnage of a larger battle. The only good news: he had found a lot of wood from wrecked Vioma dragon carriers. They had more than enough, thanks to Crann's willingness to carry it. Sankari was resting on top of the pile, eagerly soaking up the stingy sunlight.

"Oh no," Arend said. He said something else, but it was inaudible.

"What do you see?" Kainen questioned.

"Griffins—three. One has a Magician. They're circling." He strained his eyes. "Three Dwarves are holed up behind a large boulder," he said, pointing straight ahead. "With no dragons they are sitting ducks. Let's go!" Arend howled, taking to flight.

"Stick together," Kainen implored. Arend shot his head around, obviously anxious to get into the fight. Gimelli and Kainen readied their bows.

"Let's move," Gimelli said as the group broke into a run. The details of the scene gradually took shape for the rest of the League. Time seemed to slow down, and it felt like they would never reach the Dwarves.

"Is that Abhac?" Bellae asked in a panic.

"I think so," Gimelli answered.

"Soma! Do you see a dragon?" Bellae called breathlessly to Arend circling eagerly above. They had been running long enough for her leg muscles to ache and lungs to burn.

His face scrunched angrily at acquiescing to stay together. "I see him. He's moving but hurt pretty badly. The…"

"Noooo!" Bellae screamed. Adrenaline and fear pushed away any soreness, and she moved into a full sprint. The small sword given to her by Friar was drawn and glistening in the late morning sun.

"They're keeping the griffins away," Arend said, trying to reassure her.

They were close now, and Bellae could clearly hear Abhac's voice. Three Dwarves huddled behind a large rock. Two were firing crossbows while a third was loading them.

"Be careful of that Magician!" Kainen yelled. He seemed fresh, with no hint of breathlessness. He ran in easy strides beside Lontas, who was more than keeping up despite the scars and tightness on the back of his legs.

"Head for the boulder," he continued. "Gimelli and I will use our bows. Everyone else, keep a lookout, but stay down. Arend, you…"

Without waiting to hear anything else, Arend streaked up towards the griffins. He let out a piercing screech to let them know he was coming, and furious.

The griffins startled. The two without riders charged towards him. With the griffins distracted, the Dwarves took advantage and hit one with their bolts.

The wounded griffin continued charging Arend.

"Ready your bow, Gimelli," Kainen instructed as he did the same.

"But Arend's in the way."

"He'll swerve at the last second to give us each a shot. We will have to loose before he swerves. He always remembers…well, he hopefully will."

"Are you sure about this?" Gimelli questioned anxiously.

"He'll swerve," Kainen repeated, but seemed to waver.

Gimelli took a knee while Kainen stood, both had arrows ready to loose.

"Come on, Arend! Come on!" Kainen coaxed, his heart pounding with excitement. Suddenly, Arend kicked out his left leg.

"Loose, now! Aim a little to the right—he's rolling left," Kainen yelled as his arrow departed the bow.

"Are you crazy?" Gimelli yelled. Just as she was about to chide Kainen, Arend banked hard to his left and Gimelli let her arrow fly.

The injured griffin swerved to avoid Kainen's arrow, watching it whizz by uselessly. The griffin turned his attention back to Arend just as Gimelli's arrow slammed into its chest. A heart shot. The wide-eyed creature went slack and hung in the air for a split second before plummeting towards the ground.

"That was a big-time shot, Gimelli," Kainen said. "Come on, let's get to the Dwarves."

"We have to keep that bloody Magician away from that young Eaglian, or he will murder him," Abhac said as the League of Truth huffed their way behind the rock to join the three dusty and exhausted Dwarves. "The magical oaf already took out Soma. Your boy has a fighting chance if we can make it a one-on-one fight with the last lone griffin."

Gimelli and Kainen immediately prepared to fire. If the griffin carrying the Magician went towards Arend, they loosed their arrows. If the Magician stayed away, they held their fire. The Dwarves did the same with their bolts.

The Magician was older, his flowing gray beard and ponytail encircled the wrinkles of age and worry. He had been battling dragons, Dwarves, and fatigue for two straight days. Even though he had been given a new crosier, it was already starting to act up. The rumors about the desperate shortage of mindre crystals had been circulating for years, but the wizened Magician finally believed them. Unwilling to drain his crystal of all its magic, he settled into an uneasy, implicit truce. The two groups waited for the outcome of the battle between Arend and the riderless griffin. Whichever side won would have a huge advantage.

This time, things are going to be different, Arend thought as he and the griffin sped towards each other. Just before they were going to collide, Arend banked hard to his right, narrowly missing the charging griffin, who lashed out with his front talons. They passed so close that Arend had to use his hands to push off of the beast.

Follow me, Arend pleaded. "Yes!" he said, seeing the griffin whirl and start chasing him out of the corner of his eye.

"Soma," Bellae said hopelessly, staring at the injured green dragon and the crushed wooden carriage.

Abhac gently pulled her back. "Leave him, for now. Wait for the Eaglian."

Although Arend was flying swiftly, the griffin was gaining. *Good,* Arend thought. Closing his eyes to heighten his other senses, he listened to the wing beats and breathing of the griffin chasing him. As the distance between them began to close, Arend started to fly evasively, giving the griffin the sense he was panicking.

"Come on, Arend," Gimelli said tensely.

"Arend knows what he's doing. He's about to unfurl the ribbon," Kainen said.

Before Gimelli could question his meaning, Arend began a well-practiced maneuver, the rolling ribbon. It was designed to turn the tables on a faster opponent coming in on your tail. He abruptly flew up and to his right. As the griffin banked to follow, Arend flipped over and dove downward. The faster griffin tried to counter each move made by the Eaglian to keep on Arend's tail. The two crisscrossed through the blue, their flight paths looking like two ribbons dancing across the sky. On the third time circling around, Arend abruptly slowed and came down behind the charging griffin.

With the tables turned, the surprised griffin slowed right into Arend's waiting talons. His sharp claws ripped and tore savagely at the screaming griffin. Arend repeatedly torqued his leg muscles with all the force he had within him, wrenching the increasingly limp griffin left and right as feathers, splattered flesh, and blood rained down. Arend was spurred on by visions of the previous night's battle he had endured helplessly. As the two creatures started to plummet towards the ground, the griffin's scream turned to a muted gargling.

"Arend!" Bellae screamed as he accelerated towards the ground. With stunning grace, Arend released the lifeless griffin, letting out a fierce squawk, which even startled the League, before spinning towards the Magician. Unnerved, the Magician quickly conjured a shield spell. The light from his crosier flickered ominously, and the shield sputtered.

The Magician, seeing he was badly outnumbered, quickly steered his griffin into a hasty retreat.

Scroll 4: Cloudy With a Chance of Sun Beam

"Let's move now!" Abhac cried out. "If we head towards the Koori Mountains, we will run into our reinforcements that are surely on the way."

"What about Soma?" Bellae asked.

"He can't fly, so we leave him. He took a shot from the Magician to his right wing. We need a sling and dragons to fly him back."

"I'm *not*…leaving…Soma," Bellae said deliberately, and defiantly.

"Look, we have been fighting since dusk two days ago with no food, water, or a moment's peace. The griffins will be back and in greater numbers to finish us off," the Dwarf explained. "The only way they can kill us is if we are foolish enough to stay."

"You can leave if you want. I'm staying!"

Bellae and Crann stormed off towards the writhing dragon. Gimelli, Lontas, and Kainen quickly followed. Arend flew down to join them. His young face beamed with excitement at his victory. Using a robe from a previously killed Magician, he wiped the griffin's blood off as the others congratulated him.

"You had us worried," Gimelli said. Arend smiled but said nothing. If they hadn't known him, they would have run away screaming. He looked fearsome with his sharp orange beak, wide grin, and blood-spattered body.

"It's going to be okay. It's Bellae," she said, sprinting towards the injured dragon. Soma responded by fluttering his eyelids weakly as Bellae began to cry.

"So what exactly is your plan here, Bellae?" Kainen asked. "Let's not forget our mission. You are likely the Chosen One. It's *essential* we get you to the blue dragons."

Abhac and the weary Dwarves staggered over. "Bellae, listen to your friend." She shook her head and clasped Soma's neck, burying her head in his rough scales.

Abhac sighed angrily. "Can't you see these Dwarves died to bring you to the Kirvella dragons safely? Don't let it be in vain. What if you die or you are captured?"

"Here are some ravinto roots and some water," Lontas offered the Dwarves. "We're going to be here until the relief comes to get Soma." The strength in his voice was so surprising that Bellae lifted her head to make sure it was her friend.

Arend nodded his approval before starting to preen himself. After tasting victory, the idea of fighting more griffins was thrilling. Frustrated and exhausted, Abhac said nothing. He grabbed the water skin from Lontas. With the imminent threat of death removed, he finally felt the parched dryness in his mouth. A drop of sweat trickled down over his beard, and his dry tongue heedlessly swiped the briny, dirty drip.

"Go ahead and drink," Lontas encouraged him.

After a dusty swallow, he nodded in appreciation and drank vigorously.

"We should build a perimeter. There is no cover here. We can gather wood to construct a little wall and use Soma as a back guard," Abhac said.

Seeing Bellae's anger at the idea of using Soma as a shield, he quickly went to retrieve a leather bag. "Here, Bellae," he said. "Maigre, my wife, sent this for you. We were on our way to find you when we were ambushed."

Bellae eyed Abhac suspiciously while reaching for the satchel. She peered in cautiously, a smile spread across her face. She inhaled deeply and removed a bundle of pink and purple flowers. They had been smashed by the journey and ensuing battle, but to Bellae they looked and smelled magnificent.

"Thank your wife," she uttered, soaking up the aroma. It blocked out the stench of scorched death wandering aimlessly, but oppressively, around the battlefield.

Yawning broadly, Abhac sat down. "Maybe I will sit here and rest for a bit."

Seeing a potential ally, Kainen moved next to Abhac. He could imagine his father chiding him for endangering Bellae to protect a half-dead dragon. "Take charge," his father would say. *He doesn't know Bellae's strong will.*

"I agree that we should get moving," Kainen offered.

The Dwarf wiped the sweat from his forehead. His thick hair was matted to his head, and the swipe served only to smear the layer of dirt and grime left over from days of battle. He turned to look at Kainen with heavy eyelids. "They must be using Magicians or magic to track us. If we move, the griffins are on us. Now, Watchers and wyverns have joined the fun. Plus, someone has done a great job framing us for village massacres. Any day now the Piscinians or army of Agerians will be marching on us along with the Proliate and Magicians."

"You mean the staged killings?"

"Yes. It's got to be the bloody Dark Warriors and the black-hearted White Wizard. They are tearing Verngaurd apart. Plus, there are other things…"

"Like what?" Kainen pressed.

"Take the Saatana that killed Finn," Abhac replied. Bellae felt a chill go up her spine at the mention of Finn.

"What about it?" Gimelli asked defensively. Her eyes glued on Bellae.

"We found out one of our guards was taking bribes," he growled. "The sleazeball admitted some guy, who looked like a beggar, gave him a ton of gold to keep quiet about the torture of the dragon, Hullus, which you guys would end up fighting."

"We heard one of the dragons howling when we were making our detour to the Tournament," Gimelli informed him.

"That would have been some magical force torturing Hullus, whipping him into a raging fury for the Dragon Battle to ensure a dreadful outcome. Whomever is setting us up to be villains was likely the one trying to kill off the Pantteri squad and get the Knights to hate the Proliate even more than they already do. Could be the Dark Warriors or the Proliate."

"We met Trenalai. Was it him?" Bellae asked quietly, as if she were talking to herself. No one had noticed her get up to stand right in front of them.

"No, but he was furious because it was one of his underlings. He still hasn't forgiven himself for Finn's death."

"What happened to the traitor?" Sankari asked.

Abhac smiled. "Let's just say, he became intimately acquainted with the working end of a volcano."

Bellae fell to her knees, feeling sick to her stomach. This time it was not memories of Finn but the jarring, repressed images and sickening feelings from Hullus. She remembered the pain of the Saatana dragon the night he killed Finn. It was a deep, searing pain mixed with bitter betrayal. She closed her eyes. *That's what I was feeling. That's what the dragon was telling me. Someone had been torturing him for a very long time each and every night.* She scolded herself for the combination of forgetting and not understanding. *Who was it? Didn't he tell me who had tortured him?*

An image of Finn's face, pale and lifeless save for spattered blood, hit her. The rush of emotion overwhelmed her senses. Bellae felt strangled by an overwhelming sense of sharp loss and acidic grief. After crying for a long time, she drifted into sleep, curled next to Soma as they waited for relief.

The tickle of one of her mice friends in her pocket woke Bellae. She tried to stretch her arms and realized she was tied down. A rush of frosty wind poured over her. Her dry throat protested as she tried to swallow. Her mind struggled to remember what happened.

Are my eyes open? Bellae wondered, bathed in a dreary gray that seemed thick enough to be a blanket.

"Ahh!" she suddenly cried out, blinded by a flash of sunlight before being re-immersed in the thick gray fog.

"You're safe on a Vioma dragon, and he's flying through some thick clouds to help avoid griffins or Watchers," Gimelli said.

"I'm flying!" she whispered in awe. She shivered against the cold, biting wind whistling past her as she caught glimpses of giant blue gliders in the shape of a triangle.

"What are those?" she asked, nodding towards the gliders. Each one had a lone figure holding on underneath the wings.

"Those are gliders piloted by the special forces of the Northern Dwarves, their Vasama division. They're escorting us to the Kirvella dragons," Gimelli replied. "You were so fast asleep when help arrived that we loaded you on this nice Vioma dragon and strapped you down in case we ran into trouble. We're almost to the mountains."

Scroll 5: Blue Sky–Blood Rain

"Prepare for impact," one of the Northern Dwarf warriors under a glider said. His face was absolutely calm as he glared at an approaching enemy. The group had started to descend and was now out of cloud cover. Calmly, he reached up to the underside of the glider and pulled down a large weapon roughly shaped like a crossbow but loaded with a massive sword-like projectile.

He latched it to the crossbar he had been holding onto and took aim.

"What is it?" Bellae asked.

Gimelli peered over the wooden carriage of the dragon carrying them and grimaced.

"Untie me!"

"Stay put, darling," Abhac said as he ratcheted back the crossbow mounted onto the wooden structure they were riding in. "This is going to get ugly."

"Lontas! What is it?"

"A whole lot of Watchers and wyverns lined up in a long row."

"Hand over the girl or suffer agony!" a Watcher shrieked.

Bellae blushed as everyone stared at her. A Nishi appeared just under the clouds above her, gesturing rudely before running her finger across her throat and pointing to the young squire.

"Maybe you should just give me to…" Bellae started.

"Maybe they should all die! Suck on this, you desert-skinned freaks!" Abhac shouted.

The dozen or so Vasama warriors fired the massive weapons attached to their gliders. The gliders only mildly shook as the colossal sword-like projectiles raced through the sky due to an inert piece of metal shooting out the back, to minimize recoil. The majority missed, but five managed to rip into the line of wyverns. The massive blades lacerated into the beasts, most were instant kill shots. The rest incapacitated and, stealing their competency for flight, condemned them to plummet to their death.

"Unwise choice!" a Watcher screamed as streams of magic light suddenly lit up the blue sky. Six of the Vasama warriors were blasted. The one closest to the League had his head blown clean off and the glider obliterated. The headless body immediately went into a tailspin along with a shower of blood.

"Keep them off the gliders!" Abhac yelled as a swarm of wyverns dropped down from above.

"You're not the only ones who can use cloud cover!" a Watcher sneered as several Nishi maliciously urged the wyverns onward.

The few bolts streaming from the Dwarves on the Vioma Dragon were no match for their overwhelming numbers. The remaining Vasama warriors were quickly torn to shreds in their clumsy gliders.

"Do NOT kill the girl!" a Watcher yelled as the wyverns flocked around the carriage and dragon.

"Hyokkays! Hyokkays!" Abhac screamed. "Pyrros!"

The squires could feel a rumble from deep within the dragon before a cavernous growl ended in a plume of flames arcing across the sky. Several wyverns right in front of them were instantly bathed in fire. Shrieks of pain grew more distant or stopped as their charred bodies dropped.

"Look out!" Gimelli yelled as a wyvern precipitously dove and snapped at Abhac. His wolf-like face snarled savagely.

Abhac dodged, but the Dwarf next to him was not so lucky. The wyvern used its back claw to impale the Dwarf's head before ripping off his helmet. A sickening crunch followed as his sharp snout gnashed through skull, shaving off half his face. Blood burst from his mouth and hailed from fileted flesh.

Abhac drove his S-shaped sword deep into the wyvern's chest. With a loud snarl, the wyvern slammed his claw into the Dwarf. Abhac was thrown backwards, off the carriage, but saved from falling by his restraints.

A deep roar came from the bowels of the mountain.

Abhac began to laugh despite his slashed fellow Dwarf flailing life-lessly against the wood of the carriage.

"We're getting battered, yet you laugh?" Gimelli questioned.

"Making their stand this close to our home? Unwise," Abhac said, laughing even more enthusiastically. In the face of the overwhelming number of wyverns closing in all around him, Abhac crawled back onto the wooden carriage and raised his hands triumphantly. "You're all gonna die!"

"He's lost his mind…" Lontas couldn't finish as sultry heat engulfed them on all sides. The Dwarves laughed heartily as shockwaves of flames were followed by three streaking Saatana dragons.

The squires gasped, forgetting how much larger the fearsome red dragons were compared to the green Vioma.

Using claws, horns, and flames the Saatana quickly decimated the wyvern as the sky became engulfed in crackling flames and wails of pain.

"Nuh! Nuh! Geiv nuh!" Abhac yelled, almost in a panic.

"What's wrong?" Gimelli asked.

"Hold on!" Abhac commanded as their Vioma twisted into a savage vertical dive. As they plummeted towards the mountain, they passed shredded and charred bodies of the plummeting wyverns partaking in their fiery free fall of death.

"You can fly away, you can try to hide, but we will find you, girl!" a Watcher shouted, his voice magically enhanced.

The League of Truth felt their intestines cramming into their feet as the Vioma wrenched out of the dive, landing hard on the unforgiving mountain.

Other Northern Dwarves seemed to materialize out of the mountain face, joining their comrades in detaching the safety restraints from those in the carriage.

"Get into the mountain!" Abhac shouted.

They ran into darkness and heat as they followed the Dwarves into a hidden cave entrance.

"Okay, we should be good," Abhac said. Sorry about that, but the Saatana were in a combat frenzy, and when they run out of wyverns to kill, they could turn on us. I will leave you here. Your guides will meet you soon."

"Wait! We…" Gimelli stopped, the Dwarves were gone.

"There's light a little further on," Kainen suggested. The League shuffled through the steamy darkness down the roughly chiseled passageway. The heat became more intense, and the walls seemed to glow orange.

"It's magma lighting the corridor and throwing off heat," Lontas said.

"Welcome to Koori," a strange voice said, startling them.

A bespectacled blue dragon, about seven feet tall, stood directly in front of them, pausing before cautiously reaching his hand towards Bellae. She was amazed that his three fingers and opposable thumb had no claws, only fingernails. The small blue scales glistened in the light of a large torch. His snout was proportionally much smaller than the other dragons. He moved his wide, flat nostrils up and down as if he could tell she was studying them. The scales felt smooth as his fingers brushed her cheeks. Adjusting his glasses, he turned to leave. Bellae noticed small spikes along his spine and the tiny, useless, wings flittering on his back.

"Come. We must move you through under-mountain passages to Mount Honoo. The Council of the Kirvella dragons will be waiting for you."

A narrow trench ran the length of the corridor to channel the hot orange liquid bubbling up from inside the earth.

"It's hot in here," Arend said.

"In a cold world, the mountains are always toasty," the dragon said.

"It's always this warm?"

"Yes, but we manage to make cool judgments all the same," the blue dragon said, laughing.

"What happened to Crann and Soma?" Bellae asked. She stopped so suddenly that Lontas ran into her back.

"Crann is safe, but we didn't have a way for the Vioma Dragon to carry him," Gimelli said, smiling. "We'll meet up with him later."

"Soma," a deep voice called, "is in the dragon infirmary. Now please follow us." They turned to see a Dwarf dressed in the blue of the special forces join the Kirvella dragon. "Many of my brothers died getting you here."

"I'm so sorry," Bellae said.

"They were very brave," Gimelli added.

He nodded but impatiently motioned with his hand for them to follow.

"We better go," Kainen said anxiously.

"They must not like introductions," Gimelli whispered. Bellae nodded as they began to follow the blue dragon and Dwarf.

Magicians

Scroll 6: Burn it, Fix it

Friar, Ritari, and Baiulus were making preparations for war. Bellae and the League of Truth were moving through the Northern Dwarves' secret tunnels at the same time Jumeaux was rubbing his right wrist, afraid to touch the blisters popping up all over his excruciating burn. His whole hand felt like it was on fire. Veneficus cleared his throat as if annoyed at his pain and continued reading the floating scroll. Jumeaux was starting to feel lightheaded from the discomfort, but fear kept him silent beneath the angry aura surrounding the Supreme Master.

A Valo floated over to Jumeaux. "That looks like it hurts, kid."

Jumeaux silently grimaced in pain, clutching and rubbing above his throbbing hand as time crawled. The discomfort reminded him of the heaped-up scars on his legs after his run in with the river monster of River Vita. *That was all Bellae's fault.*

"What? Is my *blistering* look bugging you?" the Valo said, chuckling.

Another Valo flew close. "I have a *burning* sensation this kid doesn't like us!"

Jumeaux closed his eyes against the pain, ignoring the grim jokes.

"Hey guys, give the stupid kid a break. Stop giving him the *third degree!*" a Valo said, his light quivering as he laughed.

After what seemed like hours, Veneficus spoke, "Despite the fact that only a handful of inhabitants of Verngaurd even know of its existence, I find this scroll tedious, having read and reread it a million times.

Many died acquiring and hiding this ancient prophecy. It involves those from whom you are descended, the Ainmhi Caint."

Veneficus walked around the desk towards Jumeaux. "The Ainmhi Caint were animal speakers. I thought, initially, they were wonderful people who served as trusted advisors. They had a magical bond with all of nature, but particularly animals. I think you may know someone who shares the gift of talking with animals?" he asked.

"The Ainmhi Caint were the only ones who could easily touch the magic crystals, and I appointed them as the keepers of the source of our magic," Veneficus continued without waiting for a response.

Jumeaux suddenly had a mental flash of a burn on his mother's left hand. It was an odd, vertical shape. She said it was a cooking accident from when she was younger, but he now knew she had, at some point, tried, and failed, to be able to touch a crystal. Several others from their village near the Giant Redwood forest also had such burns, everyone but Thysia. She had been a close friend of his mother. In fact, Thysia had been pregnant the same time as their mother was with Bellae.

"You discovered the pain of touching the mindre crystals, yes?" Veneficus paused, for the first time noting how pale and weak Jumeaux looked.

"Ex agito hic!" he cried, using his crosier to guide a chair until it was just behind the boy. "Sit."

Jumeaux let out a moan and sat.

"Your injury, of course," Veneficus said, roughly taking the boy's right hand. Jumeaux winced but suppressed a cry of pain.

"Interesting," he said, roughly poking his finger at the blisters. Each jab sent a shockwave of pain up the boy's arm.

Veneficus paused with his index finger still prodding into Jumeaux's hand. "You know, this presents me with an opportunity." He looked up at Jumeaux, who was biting his lip and sweating from the searing agony.

"This might work," he said, finally releasing his finger. "Parantua!" he yelled. His crosier flashed blue, and a cool wave washed over Jumeaux's right hand.

Jumeaux let out a moan as the throbbing in his hand exploded. Then, suddenly, all of his pain disappeared. His hand was red, but the pain and blisters were gone.

Veneficus stood up and walked back towards the floating scroll. Jumeaux smiled, his thirst and lightheadedness also disappeared.

"Feeling better," Veneficus said as a statement. "Let's get back to the Ainmhi Caint. They inhabited what is now the Proliate Islands, and I considered them the all-time greatest inhabitants of Verngaurd, and I have known them all. Magical, incredibly cheerful, hardworking, I have to admit, I was quite taken with them and even lived amongst them. As it turns out, I trusted them too much and failed to see their dishonor—that is why I thought they were just devious enough to make the Chosen One the brother of the last animal talker. While I was sincerely interested in all aspects of their life and wanted to protect them forever, they chose to betray me."

Veneficus slammed his crosier on the floor. The sound startled Jumeaux, who nearly jumped out of his seat.

"Never again," Veneficus mumbled, before turning to Jumeaux as if making sure he was still there. "I offered them a gift I have never offered anyone before or since. I told them things in confidence I had sworn never to tell any living soul, and they spit it back in my face. Their treachery set off a string of unfortunate events.

"Through their subterfuge the Macht Crystals were stolen. They used some crippled excuse that they had discovered some 'evil force' that would 'ravage Verngaurd.' As if I would ever allow that! I loved them too much, and that misplaced trust resulted in a massive, bloodthirsty war. All of Verngaurd was plunged into chaos. The eventual winners were the Knights. They rose to dominance because every country was broke and their armies nearly completely destroyed in the ferocious wars that ensued.

"The Proliators also benefited, moving from a savage existence on the highland fringes of the volcanic islands to taking control, wiping out the Ainmhi Caint. With the protective Ainmhi Caint gone, the natural balance of the Proliate islands was thrown off. The Tilkeri, saber-toothed cats, and Red Saatana dragons took off in unheard of numbers, decimating the food chain beneath them. This forced the Proliators onto the mainland. The world was in complete turmoil. It was I, and the one hundred Magicians, who rallied Verngaurd, saving it from plunging into icy chaos."

He glared at Jumeaux. "With the White Wizard and Dark Warriors on the loose, don't you agree we are still the protectors of this world?"

Jumeaux zealously nodded his agreement born from fear more than consensus.

"You saw firsthand the devilry of the Dark Warriors. It is vital we have the power to fight and keep Verngaurd free. We can only do this if we find the Macht Crystals that the traitorous Ainmhi Caint stole. They hid the crystals and developed an absurdly elaborate set of riddles and cryptic rhymes, known as the prophecy, to protect their location. As those entrusted with the locations began to die, the remaining betrayers formed the so-called League of Truth to protect their secrets." Veneficus scoffed, his face contorting into a demonic mask of hate.

"Stupid bunch of nobodies!" a Valo said.

"Yeah, in a contest of losers, they would surely win!" another chided.

Veneficus nodded. "League of Imbeciles, trying to rob the world of *my* protective magic."

"Excuse me," Jumeaux said tentatively.

Veneficus turned to him with his eyes ablaze in fury.

"I thought you had lots of reserve crystals. I read last night—"

"Ah, decidedly astute," Veneficus interrupted, his eyes softening. "However, the cursed Ainmhi Caint, in stealing the Macht Power Crystals, the ultimate source of magic, left us with only the mindre crystals, which, as you know, eventually lose their magic. Before the Macht were stolen, we simply incubated a used up mindre crystal and they regained their potency."

"Shouldn't you have been saving the mindre crystals? Since…"

Veneficus' eyes exploded with anger, and he leaned forward. "I had anticipated finding them by now! Your failure has put that objective back. I did not ration them because I wanted to avoid panic and continue the wonderful Academy of Magic. Never in the history of the world has such a set-up existed."

His rage dimming, Veneficus sighed deeply, and Jumeaux thought he suddenly looked exhausted. "I learned a valuable lesson the day the Ainmhi Caint betrayed me. Never underestimate anyone. Even a few rebels can wreak havoc on our world. Think of the death and destruction that needlessly resulted from their theft. Now the world is on the brink of another world war, and we are dangerously low on mindre crystals.

"I brought you here because I thought you would fulfill the prophecy and lead us to the Macht Crystals… Obviously not," Veneficus said, pointing to Jumeaux's previously burned hand. "The Chosen One should be able to touch the crystals. I had managed to get a copy of the prophecy from one of the last known Ainmhi Caint by being…let's say…powerfully persuasive." The smile that spread across his face had a sinister stroke.

Jumeaux shuddered.

"The Ainmhi have gashed me again, this time from beyond the grave. They planted this false scroll to deceive me. I'm glad I ordered my Magicians to bring *her* to me. I swear to you, this is the last time one of those halfwits gets the better of me."

"It's Bellae?" *My stupid sister once again gets the glory,* Jumeaux seethed.

"It appears so." Veneficus paused, studying an old memory within his mind. "I even used the truth enchantment on the prophecy so enough of these words must be correct to fool my magic, but which parts? Obviously the section about you being the Chosen One is wrong."

"I'm in there?" Jumeaux asked.

"Not directly. Understand, under pain of death, this is between you and me," he said ominously. Jumeaux nodded robustly. The edges of the scroll were frayed, and several larger rips staggered along its sides.

"Our ranks have dwindled low,
Time, sword, and magic made this so.
All began when a single secret did emerge.
What the One adored, we thought a scourge.

A battle did erupt, ·
We fought the One who is corrupt.
That power is too great,
Our victory will have to wait.

Thus was born the League of Truth.
All hence, written for a special youth.
Born in distant generation,
He, Chosen One, shall save every nation.

The skill of the Ainmhi Caint will reappear,
Look to the brother who is near.
If deemed true,
Forget what you thought you knew.

Move on to your quest.
Your strength it will test.
The power to hold the crystal he can attest,
With Grand Master Elf, the next scroll will rest."

Veneficus continued to stare at the scroll even after he had finished reading. *Patuljak, the current Grand Master Elf, where are you?* he wondered. Veneficus had been trying to find him for some time with no success.

"What's the difference between 'the One' and the 'Chosen One?'" Jumeaux asked.

"As always, the Ainmhi Caint love to confuse. The 'One' is the great, fictitious 'evil' they fabricated. The so-called 'Chosen One' is Bellae."

Jumeaux's face scrunched up. "So the Chosen One is supposed to fight some evil One?"

"Inane to the end, those animal talkers." Veneficus chuckled before whispering, "I should have known—their women were always more powerful with magic than the men."

"Those animal talkers took too many baths in the stupid pool!" a Valo shrieked.

Veneficus held up his hand for silence as a look of satisfaction spread across his face. "If I didn't know this was a fake, then there must be some uncertainty in the fools that make up the League of Truth. Their deepest relatives were not alive when this transpired.

"Your hand is healed, so I shall let it leak to my spies that my version of the prophecy is correct—you *were* able to touch the crystals. Let's see if we can't flush the League of Truth out with some misinformation. I want you to say nothing, to anyone. Don't mention being burned. Just go about your business."

Jumeaux nodded his understanding.

"How do you like it here?"

"I love it," Jumeaux said, brightening.

"Did they treat you well at Liberum?"

"No," Jumeaux said, his smile drying up. "I try not to think of it."

Veneficus smiled. "Unpleasant memories are peculiar. No matter your effort to hide them, they keep popping up. Since our minds are confined by our skulls, it is impossible for bad memories to ever truly fly away," he finished by twirling his finger around in a circle. "They may go out of sight for a bit, but they always circle back around.

"Speaking of Liberum, we asked the Knights to help us stop the massacres so we could deal with the Dark Warriors, but they refused. We are, therefore, at war."

"Wow," Jumeaux said. In reality, he was unmoved. The world of the Magicians was so all encompassing that the idea of war seemed remote and unimportant. He felt no affection for the Knights. He had been a fish out of water amongst them.

Veneficus sat down heavily. Many questions swirled in his head. He wondered what role the Knights still had to play and worried about balancing the attacks from within Verngaurd as well as those without—the Dark Warriors. The greatest thorn in his side was the blasted prophecy and the desperate need for Macht Crystals.

How can I fulfill my role as protector of Verngaurd? Veneficus wondered. Looking up, he seemed surprised to see Jumeaux. "You can leave now."

About half of the Valo stormed towards Jumeaux, all screaming.

"Yeah, get lost, scorched-hand boy!"

"Good *burn* my brother, Valo! You heard him—get out and stay out!"

Jumeaux turned to leave, ignoring the floating lights. As he was walking towards the door, the familiar white light of the transporter began to creep up his legs.

"By the way, for everyone else, no time has passed," Veneficus called out. "Plus, the real crystal you touched has been replaced with a fake."

Reeling from what had just happened, Jumeaux watched helplessly as the glowing light slowly overwhelmed him. *I knew Bellae was a freak of nature. We're related to the Ainmhi Caint, who betrayed Veneficus, so why can't Gimelli and I talk to animals?*

As soon as Jumeaux disappeared, Veneficus yelled, "Vanda!" The cursed scroll began to spin. Resting his head in his hands, he thought back so many centuries ago. He had been made to look like a fool then, and now. Without thinking, he stood up and yelled, "Scoppiare!"

The scroll stopped spinning for a moment before exploding into thousands of tiny pieces flying out in all directions. With tiny shards still flying everywhere, he yelled again, "Scoppiare!" The floating pieces of the scroll were blasted into minuscule bits.

"Scoppiare! Scoppiare!" he repeated over and over again, each time with more rage. With each scream the tiny shards were blown into smaller and smaller fragments, wafting around the office like a fine mist of loathing.

"Wow, boss. Nice!" a Valo coughed.

"Yeah, you sure showed that scalped piece of tree who's boss!" another added.

"Great job, if something is worth doing, it's worth waaaaay overdoing! Huh? Am I right?" a third added.

Veneficus shot the lights a fierce look, and they silently floated away through the fog of diminutive scroll pieces.

Sitting down, he watched the tiny specks drift quietly downwards. *Everything depends on the Macht Crystals.* He needed them to sustain his inordinately long life. While he had a secret supply of mindre crystals, they would not last forever. Snippets of his future plans flashed in his mind.

Veneficus spoke the summoning enchantment, "Arcesso, Prast."

"Oooaugh-oauagh, Supreme Master," Prast coughed, appearing in front of Veneficus. He began swatting at the mist-like pieces of the scroll. "I take it this was *not* the real prophecy."

Saying nothing, Veneficus slammed his crosier down on the floor.

"My apologies. I came as soon as I heard your summons. How can I be of service?" Prast groveled.

"Assemble ten of our worst spies, completely inept. Convince them we have the correct version of the prophecy and send them to non-existent contacts all over Verngaurd. Tell them if they return without delivering their message they will be tortured and killed. Since they can never arrive, they will surely be caught. If the Allies panic when we offer our deception, maybe we can find out where Bellae and that blasted Grand Master Elf, Patuljak, are hiding."

Veneficus paused, swatting at the smog-like residue that had been the scroll a short time ago. "Avoin!" he huffed in annoyance, ignoring the fact he was the cause. Instantly, the room cleared of the debris.

"Thank you!" Prast said, bowing.

Veneficus waved his hand in the air, batting away Prast's fawning.

"It shall be done," Prast said. "What will you do with the boy?"

"Not sure," Veneficus answered. "For the moment, wait. We need to keep him around until we see what happens when our spies are caught."

"There have been even more raids in Piscium, Ager, the Southern Dwarf Kingdom, and increasingly in Jaa by both the Dark Warriors and Verngaurd's own Northern Dwarves and Elves of Creber," Prast stated. "They seem coordinated to stretch the Proliate and the home country's military out thin. I think this confirms what we already knew. There is an unholy alliance between the Dark Warriors, Northern Dwarves, Elves of Creber, and Knights."

"I see," Veneficus said. His eyes drifted off, trying to see the possible outcomes of such an alliance. He had been in this situation numerous times in the past, but never without the Macht Crystals. He had a careful balancing act to perform if things were to turn out as he wanted, and Verngaurd needed.

"The skirmishes between the Proliate and Knights are small but intensifying," Prast continued. "The Knights are hurting. Someone is going after their outposts. They blame the Dark Warriors, but few believe such tales. They could even be destroying them to make people think they *don't* have an alliance with the Dark Warriors. Hatred and distrust towards the Knights is taking off among all the countries of Verngaurd. Our own squadrons of griffin riders are becoming involved in larger and larger battles with the dragons of the Northern Dwarves, especially around Aon Intinn. I have sent reinforcements twice already, and it is quickly draining our wartime reserve of mindre crystals."

"How are the griffins holding up?" Veneficus asked, raising his eyebrows.

Prast wobbled his head indecisively. "Considering they were never meant to battle dragons, they're holding their own. With each encounter we learn a bit more about how to best approach them. Storlax is itching to launch a full ground assault against the Northern Dwarves with his Proliate and end this."

"The Proliate won't be happy until every last dragon and Dwarf who trained them is dead."

"Hatred runs deep between them, that's for sure, but if we turned the Proliate infantry loose, it would help stop the draining of our reserve crystals."

"What's Storlax's mood towards the Knights?" Veneficus asked.

Prast chuckled. "He hates them about as much as he does the dragons."

Veneficus said nothing. Prast stared at his leader intently. The mental effort churning inside the Supreme Master's head was obvious even behind his steely gaze. Prast smiled and felt at ease. *With such a powerful leader, how can we lose?*

Scroll 7: Something Has to Change

Ritari burst through the door uninvited. "We need to talk."

Friar looked up in surprise. "Come and sit."

Ritari mumbled something, holding up a beautifully, but viciously, made sword. It had a beaklike hook near the tip. Its craftsmanship was undeniable. It looked like something their armorer, Hephaestus, would make.

"What happened?" Friar asked, fearing a deadly training accident. With war looming, their drills had drastically increased in intensity.

"On patrol we were attacked by a single unarmed villager with hatred in his eyes…" Ritari's voice trailed off. Friar could see he was shaken but willed him to continue his story.

"When he finally relented, he told us we were monsters. We followed him until we could see smoke. We moved closer…" Ritari choked back tears as horror gipped him. "A horrid scent greeted us, something no one should ever have to smell."

"What was it, Ritari?"

"Vanalia! Vanalia…" his voice trailed off as sobbing commenced.

"What about her?" Friar thundered, despite guessing the truth.

"She was tied to a post, tortured. On either side of her were her parents, Svika and Koniena, and then the rest of the villagers from Bocht. Half were on one side, half on the other. They suffered through many, many a scourge only to be slow-cooked to death," Ritari sobbed.

Friar sat down and sighed.

"You could tell by the difference in the fires and the degree of burning on the bodies that they started on the far ends and roasted them one at a time until they got to Vanalia. Can you imagine seeing your friends and family slowly burned to death? Hearing their screams and knowing your turn was coming…" Ritari's voice trailed off and he snorted, trying to get the smell out of his nostrils.

"Dark Warriors!" Friar roared.

Ritari looked up despondently, "Knights."

"Don't be ridiculous!"

"As far as everyone is concerned, we did." Ritari handed the sword to Friar. It bore the stamp of Liberum. "Our weapons and banners were everywhere, as was a message burned in the grass, "Traitors to the Knights.""

Friar shook his head slowly. "I knew the White Wizard and Dark Warriors were going to great lengths to divide Verngaurd, but this…"

Ritari sighed deeply. "I have to admit, it's ingenious. Not only has all of Verngaurd turned against us, our own troops are demoralized. When confronted with these scenes over and over again, it creates doubts in their minds."

The two sat in silence, letting the weight of the situation settle upon them. Turning his attention to his old friend, Friar broke the silence. "There's more I think?"

Ritari sighed. "Our patrols are getting pounded by ambushes from the Dark Warriors *and* Proliate. Both have superior numbers and I am sure would be content to slowly chip away at us. Our morale is battered so thin it's become translucent."

"The reports I have received from our Allies are, unfortunately, similar. The Northern Dwarves are in an even worse spot. The griffins and Magicians are constantly harassing them in the air, and the Proliate ground troops are skirmishing with their infantry on the ground. The Dark Warriors have left them alone, for now."

After a quick, superfluous knock, Baiulus entered. Ritari informed him of the news before continuing, "We are harassed on every patrol. Looking for game used to be the most excitement we had. Now the Dark Warriors are constantly baiting us. Usually there's just a few, but occasionally the force is large. This morning we ran into twenty and suffered two deaths. By the time we get reinforcements, they are gone.

"We had four deaths last week at the hands of the Proliate." Shaking his head, Ritari rubbed his short black hair, now growing through the previously burned skin. It was coated with sweat and grime. "How can the Proliate say we are in league with the Dark Warriors when they are attacking us?"

"They think we are lying about the attacks to deflect blame. Plus, they have seen the attacks staged by the Dark Warriors to make it look like we did it. The whole thing reeks," Baiulus said. For the first time, Ritari saw past his own fatigue, noting how worn out and exhausted the other two men looked. Heavy bags clung under their eyes, and deep furrows of worry coated their foreheads. Their haggard looks did nothing to curb his anger. Something had to change.

Friar nodded as if he could hear his thoughts. "I understand your frustration. Please, go freshen up and get something to eat. Leave us for a while to reason this out. We'll call you when we have a new strategy."

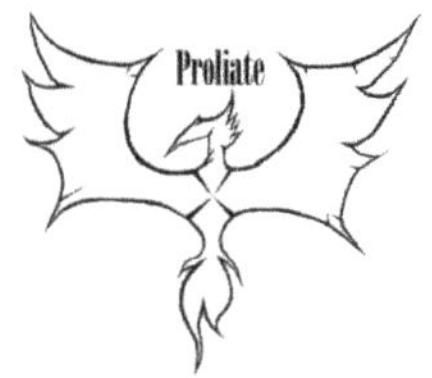

Scroll 8: Pax Passes

The next morning General Lidenskap paced in his office at the Citadel. A suspicious boat had been spotted working its way past the Proliate islands. It had finally moored south of Juopa Cavula, off the coast of Ager. *Our informant was certain it was an important ship from Ifrean.*

I sent enough men there from Temple Ensjel? he questioned. *What's on board that is so valuable?*

He continued to pace, having hoped for news by now.

At the exact moment Lidenskap was pacing, Friar opened the shutters of his office window in Liberum. There was no hint of the Mardin sun, and the cool air danced itself into his fingertips. He turned towards the door as Ritari and Baiulus strode through.

"You called?"

"Please, sit," Friar said, motioning to open chairs. Baiulus shook his head and went to stand at Friar's right side.

Ritari felt impatient for any news or orders. His muscular right leg jiggled nervously while he struggled to keep the rest of his body still.

"Last night I had another dream of catastrophe with our battle against the Proliate."

"A dream is not reality. We need to base our decisions on facts, not dreams," Ritari answered. "We are increasingly isolated, and even with your foresight, our reserve supplies won't last forever. We need a decisive move."

"I know," Friar said wearily, rubbing his face. "Our meager Knights stand on the brink of war between two massive armies, the Proliate and the Dark Warriors of Ifrean."

Ritari smiled and raised his eyebrows.

Friar smiled back. "Don't take that to mean I don't believe there is a chance we can win. With proper preparation and care choosing our battles, we have a chance. However, I want to send someone to reach a negotiated settlement with the Proliate."

Ritari nodded his head as Friar wondered, *Am I becoming my father, full of naive hope of peace? Like him, am I too full of doubt and appeasing missteps?*

"I would like you to travel to the Citadel. Seek out Veneficus and Lidenskap."

"I would be honored to try," Ritari said, with a hint of insincerity.

"Speak freely," Friar prodded, seeing his captain's hesitation.

"The simple fact is we are being played like puppets, likely by the White Wizard and Dark Warriors," Ritari said. "Is it worth the risk to go? It seems too late to overcome the influence of those framing us. The massacres we are blamed for have burned many bridges with former friends."

"While the odds are poor, there is hope for peace in Veneficus, and perhaps General Lidenskap. If we approach his reason, there's a chance." Friar sighed. "If nothing else, when we smash their teeth in during battle, it will be nice to know we did everything we could for peace."

"I like the optimism," Ritari smirked as Friar handed him the letter. Clearing his throat, Ritari set about reading it. After a few minutes he huffed, "Considering we are getting framed and most of our former 'friends' are throwing us to the wolves, this is a pretty honey-coated letter."

"Sweet honey catches more bugs than a mace."

"Are we trying to catch bugs?"

"Get out of here, deliver the letter," Friar said, laughing. "However, be careful," he added with a serious tone as his captain reached the doorway.

"Always," Ritari replied before disappearing down the hallway.

"Speak freely, Baiulus," Friar said, his eyes still fixed on the empty doorway.

"Your faith in Veneficus is misplaced. While he has done great things for the Knights in the past, there is too much hatred brewing. These massacres erase people's judgment and common sense. Perception is enough to overrule truth. Plus, the Proliate strength now matches their hunger for power and expansion."

Flopping down, Baiulus put his feet on the table.

"Comfy?" Friar asked, smiling at his old friend.

"Tired and frustrated."

"I can relate. Just don't let anyone else see you, or I may lose all credibility." Friar took out several scrolls and sealed them with melted wax before handing them to Baiulus. "Deliver these to the people listed on the front."

"What are they?"

"You really want to know?" Friar kidded.

"Yeeees," Baiulus said with mock annoyance.

"Marching orders for our troops and allies. One is for Sorea to let her know that everything is on schedule. We are pushing forward with battle preparations against the Proliate."

"So why send Ritari with a peace offering?" Baiulus challenged.

"It is possible to be realistic and optimistic at the same time, old friend."

"You are always one step ahead, boss."

"Am I?" Friar asked with somber sincerity.

"Once things get going, you will have the entire army and I will be left with a skeleton force and a bunch of stuffed dummies for wall sentries protecting Liberum."

Friar laughed. "Logistically, you have it easier—scarecrows don't complain or need food."

In spite of himself, Baiulus laughed. "Very funny. But if the Proliate don't take the bait and decide to march on Liberum, we're all dead."

"I realize this, but being so far outnumbered, we have to take some serious risks," Friar said gravely. "Losing Cumhacht was one of the most painful days of my life." He looked up, his eyes fierce. "I will not allow Liberum to fall while I am alive."

"I don't know how you're feeling about traveling by ship, but the boys and girls from this castle don't like traveling by sea."

"Well, they'll just have to suck it up," Friar said, laughing.

Later that morning, Friar watched from the ramparts as Ritari rode out with twelve Knights to serve as scouts along the increasingly dangerous routes of Verngaurd. "Good luck," he whispered to the wind. He resisted the urge to reach out and wave wildly at the formless shape of despair that seemed to be swarming around him.

Scroll 9: The Scarlet Scroll

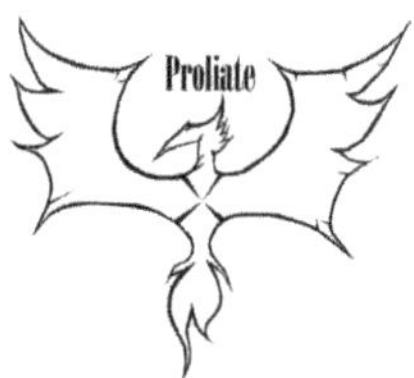

Days later, Veneficus yelled, "Come in!" on hearing a second knock. He had secretly hoped he imagined the first.

Lidenskap and two ragged Proliate Soldiers stumbled in, one clearly a sergeant. The two soldiers had dirt, grime, and dried blood splattered on their faces and armor. The sergeant had a large dent in his chest plate with a laceration in its center complete with a halo of blood.

Veneficus stood, quickly walking towards them. "What in the world?"

Ten floating Valo lights hovered around the mangled figures, casting sinister shadows on their savage appearance.

General Lidenskap spoke, "Weeks ago, an agent in Piscium was able to extract information from a suspected spy for the Dark Warriors.

Based on their intelligence, we carefully followed a Dark Warrior ship to the coast of Ager. The spy proved correct."

"My men and I hit them hard as soon as they landed," the sergeant said wearily. "Dark Warriors always fight fiercely, but there was something different in their savagery, and we knew we were onto something. A small group of Dark Warriors made a break for it while the rest tried to provide cover. I personally took a squad in pursuit of the breakaway group. We battled all across Ager. Their reinforcements kept appearing out of nowhere. They got away from us temporarily when they crossed the Azul River system. Our armor slowed us down," he said, pointing to his damaged chest plate. "We pursued them relentlessly. They didn't stop to rest, but neither did we. Praise Tallcon."

Veneficus studied the sergeant's eyes. They were glassy with sheer exhaustion.

"We finally caught them about four hundred yards from Liberum. We knew we had to overtake them then or never."

"They were headed for Liberum?" Veneficus asked. "What..." he let his words trail off as General Lidenskap handed him a bloodstained scroll. "Have you read this scarlet scroll?"

Lidenskap nodded with raised eyebrows. Resting his crosier against his chest, Veneficus unrolled it with a slight tremor. He cleared his throat as if he was going to read it aloud but did not. His eyes widened with each word. When he finished, he looked up in horror. Tossing the scroll to the Proliate, he leaned on his desk. "It can't be."

"It bears the seal of the White Wizard, and they defended it with a zeal unheard of, even for them. Clearly they were heading for Liberum," Lidenskap said solemnly.

Veneficus motioned with his arm impatiently. "Let me see it again." Sighing deeply, he skimmed parts of the letter again.

"Dear Friar,

...we look forward to our newly forged alliance and agree to your terms...we will support you financially. Working together...defeat the Proliate and their feeble minded Magicians.

Any who stand with them will be destroyed. You will continue to enjoy sanctuary from our attacks, as will your allies... Once all who stand before us are annihilated, your Knights shall regain their former glory, and your previous castles will be surrendered back to you as well as the surrounding territory needed to support them. We would help you with forced conscription to fill your ranks.

We will leave you at peace as long as you do not interfere with our territory—which would encompass the rest of Verngaurd."

Veneficus skimmed the remainder of the scroll before reading the last part out loud, "Sincerely, Troldmanden." He let his voice trail off in disbelief. "Troldmanden? That is what he is called in Ifrean, precious few know of it in Verngaurd." Next to the signature was the wax seal of the White Wizard (a wizard's hat and staff).

"Dico verum!" he shouted while placing his crosier over the scroll. The parchment glowed brilliant blue under the truth enchantment.

"I knew it!" Lidenskap exclaimed. "Look what the Knights and their allies are doing to Verngaurd. Relentless attacks on the helpless. After what they did to the villagers of Bocht, they have lost all perspective and decency."

A rapid-fire knock started them.

"Why do I even have a door?" Veneficus huffed. "Enter!"

"Yeah, what is this, a thoroughfare?" a Valo chided.

A young red-faced guard entered. "Sorry to interrupt."

"Speak, man!" Veneficus howled.

"There's Knights, a Knight…" the flustered soldier said.

"A Knight or *the* Knights," Veneficus asked.

"Just one. The others are outside the Citadel."

"Wait, there's more than one?" Veneficus quizzed with some urgency. "I assume you would tell us if an invading army was at our gates, boy?"

"O-o-o-nly one inside the walls and a few outside," he answered.

Veneficus rolled his eyes and looked at Lidenskap. "Well, I would love to see their reaction to this scroll. Which Knight?"

"Black armor, with a panther head," the man stammered.

"Ritari," Lidenskap said, nodding. "This should be good."

"Indeed," Veneficus said, sitting down heavily. "General, please stay."

"Sergeant, you and your man, get cleaned up and checked by a healer," Lidenskap instructed. The sergeant, his soldier, and the messenger left.

"What will you do?" Lidenskap asked.

Veneficus slouched in his chair. "I have a hard time believing Friar could do this."

"I did see them fighting the Dark Warriors quite ferociously."

"The further we travel down this path of war, the more uncertain I feel. Come in!" Veneficus shouted to a short, hard knock on his door.

Two rows of Proliate warriors quickly came in and lined up. Ritari walked in between them. As soon as he entered, he could feel the tension hanging in the air like a foul odor.

"Dismissed!" Lidenskap barked. After exchanging a salute, the soldiers left.

"Greetings, Veneficus, General Lidenskap," Ritari said, willing himself to smile despite the strain in the room. His words sounded hollow and muffled as they fought their way through the shroud of uneasiness encircling the room.

An awkward silence governed the room.

Ritari sighed, breathing in the heavy air. He nervously tapped the small scroll. The cumbersome silence was growing unbearable, so he spoke. "Friar, asked me to inform you we have never attacked any villages."

Lidenskap scoffed loudly as several hovering Valo lights snickered derisively. Ritari turned to glare at the general, anger rushing up within him. *I would rather be in battle,* he thought as Lidenskap returned his stare.

"Come now, hear him out," Veneficus said.

The weight of his doomed trip was springing to life in front of his eyes, encroaching on the already crowded room. "We are still the Knights and have the welfare of Verngaurd at the core of our actions. We want peace and to ensure everyone is entitled to a life full of opportunities, free from oppression and danger."

"I can stand this no longer!" Lidenskap blurted out. His face flushed with anger. "Lies and deceit! We are not the imbeciles you take us to be!"

"You could have fooled me," Ritari said as Lidenskap drew his blood red sword.

"Enough," Veneficus said quietly but menacingly. "Don't make me paralyze you." He walked around his desk to stand between Ritari and the general. He held his hand out towards Lidenskap who, in turn, handed him the captured scroll.

Ritari kept his eye on Lidenskap as he unrolled the blood-soaked scroll. Looking down to read the scroll, his face grew more ashen with each line.

"A look of guilt, if ever there was one. You are caught in the quagmire of your own treachery!" Lidenskap blurted.

"Yeah! Let the dirty rat of a Knight have it, you Proliate tight wad!" a Valo squealed.

"This…" Ritari paused in shocked disbelief. "…is unbelievable."

Lidenskap snatched the scroll and snarled in disgust, "You Knights are a wisp of your former noxious glory. This evil allegiance is an obvious ploy to turn back time and regain some scraps of what you once were. You, the Elves of Creber, and the Northern Dwarves have made your intentions clear, and this captured scroll confirms it all."

"Veneficus, please. This is not right," Ritari said, still unsettled.

"I admit, I have a hard time believing it," Veneficus said, sitting on the edge of his desk, leaning heavily on his crosier. "On the other hand, the evidence is overwhelming. There is a black cloud of doom over all of us." Turning to Lidenskap, he asked, "Please recount the tale of how we came to possess this."

After Lidenskap told him the story, Ritari shook his head in disgust. "Why wouldn't they just use their portals to Ifrean to transport it directly to us?"

"You made up these 'portals.' No one else has seen them," Lidenskap said.

"They do seem to appear and disappear at will," Veneficus added.

"The portals are real. This, all of this, is a ploy by the Dark Warriors, to divide us. Can't you see it? Don't be fools…"

"Fools?" Veneficus howled, standing up in anger.

"I meant don't be tricked by—" Ritari started before Lidenskap interrupted.

"Don't worry, we won't let *you* play us as fools. This confirms all of our suspicions about your alliance with the Dark Warriors."

"I see," Ritari said. "It seems this letter comes too late, but here." He handed Veneficus the scroll written by Friar and then turned to leave.

"Wait," Veneficus said. He went back to the other side of his desk and retrieved a small blue scroll. He touched his crosier to it saying, "Skrife upp!" Closing his eyes, he then spoke so rapidly his lips became a blur. As he did so, both his crosier and the scroll glowed softly. After stopping, he opened his eyes. "Carry this with you. It grants you safe passage to Liberum, but it disappears in four days."

"Lidenskap, see he is respectfully escorted to the gates," Veneficus ordered. "By the way, if you two fight on the way out, there will be no place for you to hide."

The two walked out, exchanging threatening looks as Veneficus slouched in his chair. He stared at the scroll for a long while before picking it up and reading it.

"Dear Veneficus,

I write to you with great urgency. Our current path will lead to the destruction of Verngaurd. The Dark Warriors are behind this evil plot to divide us."

Veneficus laughed. *The evidence certainly suggests otherwise.*

He continued reading. "I entreat you to use your considerable influence to place a hold on war. I call on all of our history as friends to use reason in the face of deceit. I am willing to accept Magicians within our walls to monitor our activity. A force of Proliate is out of the question.

"I fear for the future, my old friend. I miss our talks and would love to have you visit us at Liberum. Please help me secure the future of Verngaurd.

"Your friend, in great hope, Friar Pallium"

Veneficus sat back in his chair. *An act of utter desperation. The Knights are but a ghost of what they once were. This war is unevenly matched and could be over quickly.*

"Dico verum!" he shouted to check the truth of the scroll. It glowed a brilliant blue. *Friar's words are true.*

"Interesting, but I doubt it would hold much weight with the Proliate," he said. "If the future I seek for Verngaurd is to be assured, I will have to carefully manage this convoluted situation."

"Na Cearcaill is here again!" a Valo squealed.

Veneficus nodded. "True, and I feel the Knights still have an important role to play. I shall offer them assistance without seeming too obvious."

Yes, he thought. *I shall have to help even the odds a bit.*

Scroll 10: Where are the Defenses?

A hiss startled the League. The passageway felt like a catacomb, sizzling with stifling heat within a cocoon of claustrophobic black rock. Balmy perspiration blanketed their foreheads and slithered out to wet their clothes.

Arend let out a piercing squawk as steam shot out of a crevice in the wall.

Seeming irritated, the blue dragon with the glasses moved over to the crevice. "I'll cover the geyser, but I recommend running ahead."

The League rushed forward as the Dwarf traveling with them yelled, "Move!" Once they were past him, he spread himself out as big as possible to act as a shield. A loud gushing sound exploded behind them. The dragon was leaning against the sharp flow of steaming water exploding out around his blue scales.

"Turn away from the fumarole," the Dwarf yelled. The hot liquid blasting past the dragon shot around his outstretched body, misting the League.

"That will get your blood flowing!" the Dwarf said as the water ceased.

"Thank you," Bellae said.

"Ah, we're used to those steam baths."

"What's that hole?" she asked, pointing to an opening in the ceiling of the cave.

"Those vent the harmful gases from the fumaroles, up and out."

"They are not harmful to us," the blue dragon said, trying to sound casual, but his words dripped with pride.

"I'm Bellae," she offered. "That's Gimelli, my sister; Lontas, my friend; Sankari, the beautiful Fairy; Arend, Eaglian; and Kainen, Elf of Creber."

Sankari shot Bellae a questioning look. When she was satisfied Bellae was not making fun of her, both cheeks filled with a grateful red blush.

"Come out," she called while opening her pocket. "Grym has black fur, and Borb is the larger white one."

The Dwarf nodded his head. "Sorry if we seemed rude. We are under constant sleepless siege from those blasted griffins, Magicians, Proliate snakes, and now, as you witnessed, Watchers and wyverns."

"This chap is Sarskil, one of our top Special Forces operatives," the blue dragon said, placing his hand on the Dwarf's shoulder. "He has killed more griffins than any other." Pointing to the end of the Dwarf's white tunic, they could see a dozen blue "X's" sewn on it.

"Griffins!" Arend hissed angrily.

"My feelings exactly. They are not loved here—I can tell you that much for sure," Sarskil grunted.

"My name is Vlug," the dragon said, rapidly flapping his small, vestigial wings.

A harsh rumble struck through the cavern. "It's okay, just the mountains making sure we have not forgotten them or the power they hold." Vlug chuckled, pushing his glasses closer to his eyes. "Shall we get going then?"

The incline was increasing and the ceiling becoming lower as they moved along the passageway. The roughly chiseled walls were jagged in some places. Bellae ran her fingers along the stone, surprised at how sharp the angles were. They passed countless corridors veering off in seemingly limitless directions.

"Wait until we move into the main tunnels," Vlug said, sensing their growing apprehension. "It will be more comfortable."

The temperature was rising exponentially. Occasionally, Arend would flutter his wings to cool himself. As they moved along the rough path, steam sizzled out of small fissures and the distance seemed to increase between the torches.

A hint of cool air tickled their faces with a promise of fresher air before the stifling heat quickly swallowed it.

"You talk to them? Your mice?" Vlug questioned.

"I can," Bellae replied. Despite the steam all around them, the heat seemed to be drying out her nose and lungs.

"Curious. Perhaps the time of the prophecy is upon us," the dragon said, adjusting his glasses once again.

"Ah! Feel that? Hang in there, Arend," Gimelli said as a jet of cool air rushed towards them. The passageway finally opened up to the outside. Jumping up, Arend took off up into the air.

"Get back down, NOW!" Sarskil yelled urgently.

His pride wounded, Arend quickly landed.

"He was just shaking out his wings," Gimelli interjected.

"The boy was about to be shot down," Sarskil said defensively.

"Sarskil's correct," Vlug added. "We have positions hidden in the mountains with all three of our military branches watching the skies for griffins or wyverns. I'm not sure they would recognize you as an Eaglian given your species' long absence from the rest of Verngaurd. We must get out of here now," Vlug stated without warning.

Moving surprisingly fast, he rushed over to Bellae and Kainen. With astonishing force he lifted them, including their confused looks, off the ground and set them about four feet away.

"Sarskil, if you would be so kind as to lead," the dragon said as he rushed over to where the squire and Elf had been standing before he moved them.

The League could now see trickling orange-red lava flowing out of a crack in the mountainside. It was moving slowly but glowed menacingly. As it steadily oozed forward, it looked like orange blood flowing from a wound in the rock face.

"Start towards the main mountain," Vlug instructed as he used his feet to push the flowing lava away from the children—obviously impervious to its searing heat.

Surrounded by towering peaks, the group headed across an open walkway towards the adjacent mountain. Scanning the rock, they could see no opening at the end of the path.

"Look, Mount Honoo!" Kainen called out, pointing to a small opening between two peaks. The group gathered just as lava violently spurted out of the volcano, surrounded by a halo of steam and wispy clouds.

"Look there..." Kainen stopped as several barrages of lightning burst around the top of the mountain. "Lightning without storm clouds?"

"Ah. Very astute," Vlug declared. "It's caused by static electricity. You creatures with hair are particularly well suited to conducting a few experiments. Take you, Bellae, for example. Let me pull up your cloak and rub it on your head. It..."

"What are you talking about?" Gimelli asked. She was still smiling but moved over to stop him from pulling up her cloak.

"Oh," Vlug said, a little taken aback. "I was just going to show you how static electricity makes her hair stand up and apart. They are repelling each other and..."

"Move!" Sarskil yelled with such ferocity that Bellae and Gimelli jumped. He plowed into Bellae, tackling her to the ground. The other members of the League stared in amazement as he covered her body.

TWWWWWWWWHHHHHHHHOOOO! a blast of fire slammed right next to them. Sparks of flame and bits of rock showered up from the path.

The other members of the League looked up to see a Magician riding a griffin pointing his crosier at them. The Magician's arm recoiled slightly as another burst of flames erupted from his magic crystal.

The group scattered, spreading out across the rest of the track that led to the next mountain as a second fireball blasted onto the floor of the passageway. This one exploded near Lontas, slamming him backwards into a wall protecting those on the path from falling off. His back thudded painfully before he was jarred forward by the rebound. With surprising deftness he managed to jump over the debris from the blast, his ears ringing fiercely.

"Where are the defenses?" Vlug shouted, moving to help Sarskil cover up Bellae. Lontas did a forward roll and squatted down at Bellae's feet.

"Stay down, Eaglian!" Vlug yelled as Arend readied himself to spring up into the air. "Let our defenses handle this!"

After rising only twenty feet, Arend grabbed wildly at the air. It was only then they noticed he was flying to retrieve Sankari's struggling body. He quickly wrestled her close before flying back to the ground.

They turned to see the Magician's Crosier glowing a fiery warning that the third shot was about to rain down upon them. At that moment, several crossbow bolts stuck the Magician in the chest and neck. He rocked backwards before falling forward. The third fireball shot up and over the ridge they were on. The crosier tumbled downward as two more fireballs shot out harmlessly, gifted to the mountains.

With the Magician still limply attached, the griffin continued its steep dive. A large bolt from a ballista ripped into the griffin when he was only a few hundred feet above them. A startled squawk escaped its beak as its body jerked sideways. The griffin's shattered form bowed around the projectile in a crumpled "V." Just then, two ballista bolts tore into it from the other side. The force was so great that parts of the drooping griffin were torn off. The pieces gyrated wildly toward the ground before thudding lifelessly against the mountainside.

"Move, move!" Sarskil shouted. Standing, he lifted Bellae. "More griffins are diving."

Vlug started to run, his small wings beating rapidly. Arend was struggling to hold onto Sankari as they sprinted forward. The Fairy's face was contorted in anger and coated with tears of anguish.

"That Magician looked like the one that killed my parents!" she screamed.

Stunned, Bellae and Gimelli slowed to a stop, staring at the struggling Fairy.

"Keep moving," Sarskil nudged, his eyes scanning the skies nervously.

Eventually, they crossed the ridge and moved up to the next mountain. Vlug stepped off the path and seemed to disappear into the rock.

"Go to your left towards that outcropping. When you hit a dead end, turn to your right. You will see a hidden gateway," Sarskil called out.

Once they were inside, they found themselves in a large, stunning hallway. Smooth, chiseled relief images dotted the walls. The rock was the same black as the previous passageway but it was well lit with golden torches. Scenes of dragons, mountains, and ancient battles played out in relief upon the walls.

As their breathing slowed down, an awkward silence ensued. Sankari sat sobbing on the floor, her head leaning against the wall. The rest of the group huddled together. Bellae and Gimelli snuck quick glances at Sankari. They nodded and silently walked over to her. "I don't want you two freaks over here," the Fairy said angrily.

The two sisters ignored her ranting and sat down beside her. Gimelli smiled sympathetically and gently patted the Fairy's delicate legs. After several minutes, Vlug motioned for them to move up the hallway. Gimelli shook her head from side to side and gestured he should wait a minute.

"That's how it was when my parents died," Sankari sniveled. "I was out with them while guarding Patuljak, the Master Elf. The griffins came down on top of us. I saw the face of only one of the Magicians, and he looked a lot like the one that just died. It was horrible, the way the griffins tore apart my parents." She shuddered violently, retching as if she might vomit.

Silently wondering why Magicians would attack Patuljak, Gimelli continued to rub the Fairy's delicate legs. Sankari looked at the two girls with sad, drooping eyes. Gimelli returned a warm smile and leaned her head gently on the Fairy's. After a minute or two, Sankari pulled away. Her wings fluttering, she rose up into the air.

Holding out her arms welcomingly, Gimelli smiled. Sankari paused before dropping down into them. Used to her abrasive temperament, the others were speechless. Just to let them know she was still someone to respect, she shot them a fierce look before settling back into Gimelli's chest.

In surprised silence, the group followed Vlug up the slanting walkway. The clean and polished surfaces of the passageway added strength to the echo of their feet, the reverberation actually seeming louder than the initial step.

"I didn't used to be so angry," Sankari whispered to Gimelli, her soft voice seeming out of place after the monotonous, metronomic sounds from their footsteps. "I miss them."

They both cried softly as memories of their dead parents danced harshly in their minds.

"Here we are," Vlug said after they had traveled for several hours. He pointed down a hallway with thirty doorways. "Each one of those chambers holds bedding. We rest here for the night."

Several within the League were about to protest but realized how exhausted they were and acquiesced. Carved into the mountain were small rooms with a bed, complete with bedding, and small shelf. Most were asleep as their heads touched down.

After a quick breakfast of fia asteikko jerky, the League headed out through the seemingly never-ending series of indistinguishable mountainous pathways.

"Did you know that sleeping chamber was built by my Great-Great-Great-Great Grandfather Grafar?" Vlug asked, knowing they could not. "Think of how much these mountains have witnessed. They watch us with the restful patience that only a mountain can afford. While that should be admired in them, it should not be emulated by us mortals. We just don't have the time."

Vlug gently put his blue-scaled hand on Bellae, gazing at her with sad, thoughtful eyes he let the others move ahead down the passageway.

"Life is but a fragile slave to its master, time—it callously seizes us from the moment of our birth, ripping us forward remorselessly, constantly from moment to moment, whether we are ready or not, through the seconds we are given for our existence. The feeble believe the paltry time given us is predestined. The brave know it is a no-holds-barred challenge to get up, take the oars, and steer your life where you choose."

Bellae scrunched her nose, unsure what to make of the dragon's words.

"Sometimes, Bellae, the brave are not armored Knights fighting on the field of battle. Sometimes they are the timid that, against all odds, rise up to take on a challenge. Most people shuffle through life, half-dead, wasting priceless time, letting opportunities slip by with such frequency they become attenuated to lost chances," Vlug said, staring at her. "Living means collecting regrets like mud on a rainy day. If you are to collect regrets, collect regrets of action, not inaction. Seize your opportunity." Finishing, he gave her a quick hug.

Bellae looked up. "It's just…overwhelming."

The wizened dragon smiled, "Everything new becomes old. Everything old turns forgotten. All that seems glaringly important today decays to a memory before decomposing to the disregarded."

Bellae's face fell despondent at his bleak words.

"I did not intend to be depressing, but encouraging. Live your life for right now and don't let fear hold you back. Do not trouble yourself with how others, or the future, shall judge you. In the end, all of us are sliding down the same steep decline to our demise.

Bellae cocked her head sideways at the unsettling anti-pep talk.

"There are many definitions of courage, but the greatest one I have heard? Marching forward, even full of fear, headlong into the darkness of the future."

"Everything okay?" Gimelli asked, jogging back to check on her sister.

"Just a little chat," Vlug said loudly before whispering to Bellae. "Boldly face this challenge. When things seem dark, know that many, including me, will be thinking of you."

Despite feeling rattled, Bellae nodded, and they continued their journey.

Eventually the League came to a large, circular, and well-lit cavern.

"This is our splendid antechamber," Vlug said proudly.

Sarskil moved to talk to several other Dwarves who were already in the sizable hall. Each held a large halberd and, like him, wore a white tunic with a blue dragon. They greeted him warmly before settling into hushed conversation.

"Those Dwarves are the guardians of the Council of Kirvella. They are part of the Vasama Division of our army. It is the most difficult branch to get into. If it was me, I would like to be an Aer Ridire so I could fly on the green Vioma Dragons," Vlug said, dreaming of flying as his own undersized wings fluttered wildly but ineptly.

"Wing envy," Gimelli mouthed as Bellae suppressed a giggle.

"The council is responsible for governing the Northern Dwarves and Dragons. They work alongside King Abernan, of course," he added quickly. "I don't want to brag, but we Kirvella Dragons are widely regarded as the most intelligent creatures of Verngaurd.

In the center of the room stood three banners they recognized from the Tournament of Flags. Statues of Kirvella dragons were set around the impressive hall, each one housed within a beautifully carved arch.

"These are famous Kirvella dragons. There are philosophers, politicians, and scientists," Vlug said, smiling and raising his hands out to either side. "They have all made great contributions to the lives of all who inhabit Verngaurd. That one there is Stjerne. He was a great astronomer who developed and improved the telescope and armillary spheres. I'm sure you learned about him in your astronomy classes."

The blank expressions on their faces made his smile droop.

"Who's that?" Lontas asked, pointing to a massive statue in the room.

"Pugnatex, the one Saatana to make it into the circle of honor here in the antechamber," Vlug replied. "Only the green Vioma dragons used to live here with us. The red Saatana came relatively recently to escape persecution by the Proliators, who were, and are, bent on their destruction. Eons ago, the majority of the council had traveled to Cumhacht for a meeting with the Knights to discuss the war with

Figure 6: Bellae, Lontas, and Gimelli stare in wonder at the Northern Dwarves' antechamber as special forces guard the area.

the Proliate—they were just marauders at that point, bent on killing all the Saatana dragons. On the way back, a massive force of Proliate ambushed them. The Knights escorting us were badly outnumbered and cut off. Pugnatex was out for exercise and broke away from his trainers to fight the Proliate until the Knights reached the Council. It was a massive battle, the last major one of the conflict. The fire worshipers were badly defeated and crawled back to their islands. They left us alone after that…until the Dark War."

"What happened to Pugnatex?" Bellae asked.

"He died as the last Proliate was driven from the battlefield," Vlug answered. "You'll notice there is a statue of a Vioma dragon carved in the ceiling. If you look closely, you will see the Aer Ridire Dwarf on its back. It represents all the brave Vioma dragons, not one in particular.

Scroll 11: Blue Dragons

"It's time, Bellae," Sarskil called. "Only you may see the Council."

"She goes, we go," Lontas said, defensively stepping forward.

The Vasama Dwarves growled at the perceived disrespect.

"You realize only a handful of humans have ever been in the Council's chamber? It's reserved for Kirvella Dragons, King Abernan, and Vasama Dwarves. This is all highly irregular, and you should be grateful we are even allowing her in!"

Gimelli stepped forward. "I'm her sister. Why don't the two of us go together?"

"I'll be okay alone," Bellae said.

"Now, now. Let's not get too ahead of ourselves," Vlug said, raising his hands to signal everyone to slow down. "It's acceptable for the girl's sister to go. In fact, they may want her there. The rest of the League members will wait with me."

"Perfect," Gimelli said as the guards nodded their affirmation.

Moving close to the girls, Vlug bent down and whispered, "Just be yourselves and speak the truth. You'll be fine." Smiling broadly, he gently patted them on the shoulder before adding a tender nudge in the direction of the door.

"We'll be right here," Kainen assured. Bellae smiled and waved. If she was supposed to feel worried, she didn't. The honesty and kindness radiating from the blue dragons was calming. *Plus, they are so cute!*

As the two girls followed Sarskil into the new room, they were stunned by its dark simplicity. They stole a quick glance at each other before turning back to examine the room more closely. Large, worn rocks served as chairs and surrounded a table roughly chiseled from the mountain. Two torches were lit at either end of the room, and a few candles sat haphazardly around the table. All of the roughly twenty chairs sitting in front of them had gold nameplates, with both Dragonese and common-tongue writing.

As their eyes adjusted, they could make out rows of stone bookshelves carved into the wall, each one overflowing with well-read books and scrolls of various shapes, sizes, and ages. Each bookshelf had the strange writing of the dragons, a dizzying series of lines and flourishes, labeling the contents below.

Eight Kirvella dragons, their blue scales occasionally sparkling in the sickly light, were positioned around the room. Several sat around the roughly hewn table. Others reclined against bookshelves.

Sarskil leaned in, "You *must* be quiet. These are intellectual leaders, always reading and debating. They call it…" he paused, searching for the word, "…dialectic."

The Dwarf glanced around the room. Satisfied he had not disturbed them, he turned back to the girls. "It's your great honor to listen."

"I think we can all clearly agree on this point, knowledge is power and one of the greatest achievements one can strive for. We also seem to have agreed that knowledge is much stronger than opinion, or, of course, ignorance," the dragon with the nameplate of Eide said. He adjusted his glasses as the other council members murmured their approval.

The dragon Pistis held up a large and tattered book. "Also, we can all agree with the vaunted author that pleasure alone is not good, but knowledge is good."

"Yes, yes, good addition, Pistis. The real problem to tackle is the true form of the good," Eide said to murmurs of agreement.

"They sure seem excited about talking," Bellae whispered.

Gimelli giggled, quickly stopping under Sarskil's withering gaze.

"If more people set their heart to learning, then it would divert their life force away from evils, such as savagery, war, and hatred. The world today needs more education. I don't think it is coincidence that after the Proliate shut down the universities and libraries, we are bathing in massacre and war!"

"Here, here!" a few dragons muttered in approval.

"Not emotionless education, but a true devotion!" another added. "Now, if we may, let's return to these forms or paradigms."

"I think we should head our discussion back to the idea of revolution," one said. This word piqued Bellae's attention. Perhaps now they would discuss the impending war, the prophecy, and her role.

"We were discussing the idea of turning around, away from the traditional images of the world in order to see higher levels. The truth is in the form of it, not the specifics," Pistis said to great applause from the others.

"Yes, turning around to enlightenment, and realizing we have been only seeing shadow projections of objects, can be painful, but necessary for greater understanding."

"The problem," another dragon said, "is that when we try to spread this truth and reality, society may be too comfortable with their ignorance. Society may resist our philosophical journey."

The other dragons cheered as Bellae and Gimelli exchanged looks of confusion blending with annoyance.

"Still missing the point," a new Kirvella dragon, hunched with age, said. He shuffled in with a cane. A tattered-looking pair of glasses hung precariously on the end of his gnarled snout. "Remember, he is a *poet* mocking the philosopher with a stinging epic poem."

"Oh, please yourself, Stralande," Eide said. Eide was thin compared to the other dragons. Something must have happened to him, for the right side of his face seemed to droop and he wore a monocle on his right eye. He held his inept left arm bent at the elbow in front of his body. If he tried to adjust his weight, he hobbled on his left leg.

"His is philosophical journey, not a poem!" Eide said. "Surely you remember that the great Kirvella dragon, Plato, gave up the life of poetry when he met the great teacher on the way to present his tragedies."

"Oh, how tiresome," Stralande said. "He gave up writing tragic poetry for epic poetry to mock philosophy and its bickering. Don't you think he simply would have written a textbook or a set of laws or even a guidebook on philosophy if he was opposed to the arts and the 'false images' as you describe them?"

A murmur went up among the eight council dragons. Puffs of smoke could occasionally be seen escaping from the nostrils of the more irate council members. A few actually looked deep in thought as if considering the notion.

"Preposterous," hissed Eide. "The form is the perfect good. The so-called sun of all things. He argues this without a…forgive my pun…a shadow of doubt." Several of the other dragons murmured their approval.

"Ahhh, let's talk about his arguments." The old dragon smiled. "How does he describe his masterful outline of the idea of the good? Does he draw a diagram with labels? No! He crafts a story of prose and of the highest imagination: the parable of the cave. You must use your imagination to see his point. He specifically asks us to *imagine* this and *imagine* that.

"If it is so evil to use one's imagination, if it is so lowly to be a poet or writer, then why does the man use what he professes to hate, prose and poetry, to convey his points? Why does he constantly cast a web for our imagination to shine upon? If it is our imagination that emits the light to allow us to see the good, is imagination not the good itself?" Stralande suggested.

"Blasphemy! Imagination is merely the shadow used to mimic, to make truth easier to be understood."

"Is it not imagination that leads to all advances?" the old dragon asked.

"Imagination is *not* real. It is a first step in a larger process. He describes it as simply an offspring of the good because of the enormity of the topic."

"Ah, is it really fair to say imagination is not real? Is something you imagine really less than say, a memory of some great event? That said, imagination only gains into power if it stirs us to action, to create, to build. Living only in imagination simply like our dreaming at night."

Bellae glanced at Gimelli. "What in the world are they talking about?"

"Absolutely no idea," Gimelli mouthed back.

Bellae stepped away from Sarskil, loudly yelling, "Excuse me, dear council, I have a matter of the utmost urgency!"

An astonished silence burst upon the room. The Dwarf Sarskil blushed, a look of wide-eyed terror on his face.

The elderly dragon inched forward. "Is this the girl?"

"Yes, sir," Sarskil said quickly. "I did tell them to be silent. I apologize."

"Ah," he said, inching forward with his cane. "These clods are just playing around. I'm Stralande. Let me introduce the rest of the council."

He shakily pointed his cane at each one as he spoke. "This trouble maker is Eide. Then we have Noesis, Chiffre, Dianoia, Contatto, Pistis, Eikones, and that silent one in the corner who should be saying a lot more is Eikasia."

"Please, girl, speak in the animal language."

Sighing, she opened her pocket. *"Hey, you two. We need to put on another show."*

"What's in it for me?" Grym asked, pawing his whiskers.

"Do it for Bellae," Borb said with urgency, sensing the importance of the audience.

"I'm really sorry to ask you, but these dragons want to hear us talk," Bellae said, unsure of what else to say.

"Oh, dragons, is that all?" Grym said sarcastically. *"At least you're not asking me to do something, you know, dangerous. Just perform for dragons. Lovely. Overall, I have to say you have done a wonderful job planning out this vacation from hell."*

Bellae giggled.

"Fascinating. Wonderful!" the elderly Stralande said. "Come, come with me, and let's talk. Blast it all, can someone light some more torches?"

He whispered to Bellae, "They think the ambience helps their mental powers." He rolled his eyes mockingly. "I say, Pistis, would you get *the* scroll? I can trust you."

The young girl and elderly dragon walked to the far end of the room. Several Vasama Dwarves bolted in, quickly lighting torches as the portly dragon, Pistis, waddled out. When a few of the Council dragons made their way towards the pair, Stralande gave them a fierce look and waved them away. He sat in a cushioned chair carved into the mountain and surrounded by floor-to-ceiling bookshelves as Bellae stood next to him.

"What were they talking about?" Bellae asked.

"Ah, Plato likened those ignorant to the Theory of the Forms to prisoners chained in cave and unable to turn their heads. They were forced to watch shadows cast on the wall, and mistakenly took those shadows for reality. They are, of course, missing the truth—puppets are casting the shadows on the wall. Also, if they escape the cave, in the world they would see even greater realities.

"It is through education—thinking and looking beyond what we can see, trying to grasp the original forms of things in our mind—that can set us free. When we are open to learning, new ideas and thoughts, we truly ascend out of the cave."

"That's important?" Bellae asked, confused.

Stralande laughed, "Important to some, but not as many as it should."

"Why didn't those chained up struggle to escape and turn around?"

Stralande smiled at her. "It is easy to get stuck in the flawed comfort of the familiar, of what we know. Many in the world are not physically shackled but mentally restrained by their cozy, static view of the world. Some of those people really believe they see the truth but discern only a shadow reality."

Perplexed, Bellae shrugged her shoulders as he suddenly turned serious. "It is difficult to lift ourselves out of the mask of our own perspective. We can only see and experience a tiny fraction of what is happening in the world, our own tiny radius of perspective. We are limited by our viewpoint and time. We briefly grope around the universe with our puny little senses, trying to find meaning and purpose. Only when we stand on the collected knowledge and wisdom of our ancestors do we stand any chance.

"I know that does not make sense to you right now, but trust me, before this ordeal is over, it will. The inexperience of youth often deters the mind's ability to truly comprehend, or appreciate, the vital importance of the here and now. It is unfair, but I ask you to try to see, feel this moment's significance. Over the next several months to years, your perspective will explode thanks to the League and the path of your journey. Just like those chained in cave mentioned by Plato, you have to break the shackles of ignorance, stand up, and turn around to the truth. You will not want to see or learn most of it. In fact, the pain of awakening is why many are content to sit and watch shadows dance on the cave wall. Some of your journey will be downright painful, mentally and physically." He paused, sighing deeply.

"It does no good to try to gloss over the truth. It will, sooner or later, always break through."

Bellae stared at him in shock and confusion. If this was supposed to be encouraging, it wasn't working.

Stralande leaned close to Bellae. She could hear rattling and phlegmy breathing and smelled something foul on his breath. His eyes twinkled with life despite the tired-looking scales sagging around them. Some were cracked, others were curling at the edges, and some had large splits down the middle.

"Bellae, I have actually known you were *the One* for quite some time. I will tell you how in a minute, and I want you to keep it to yourself. The prophecy dictates that you come see a Kirvella dragon as your first step on the path of the prophecy. For the sake of the others, I will go through the formality of reading the scroll, and then I will put on a show, pretending to look you up and down and blah, blah, blah," he whispered. A satisfied smile spread over his wizened face, and both began laughing. His cackle turned into a hacking cough.

Bellae closed her eyes and held her breath as a blast of warm, fetid air washed over her face and tossed her hair back. His glasses fell off, and after shakily replacing them, he inched even closer and spoke softly, "After a splendid display of my showmanship for everyone else, I will tell you several secrets that you must swear to keep only to yourself. Plus, I was also hoping to give you a small nugget of wisdom."

He sat back and relaxed in the chair. Taking phlegmy, deep breaths, he turned to see Bellae staring at him expectantly.

"Darling, the nugget was already passed to you. It was the part about the mask of our own perspective, et cetera, et cetera," he said, waving his hands about. "Apparently, it was only a *very* little bit of wisdom."

Bellae tried to remember what he said, blushing under the heat of his gaze. She did not feel particularly special and did not like being called "the One."

"What does a dying old dragon have to do to get something to eat?" Stralande bellowed. Turning to Bellae, he said, "I love bats. You?"

Bellae shook her head vigorously. He began to describe the texture and tastes of their different body parts, and she held her breath to keep from throwing up. Bellae looked to Gimelli for help. She was standing up and staring over the shoulder of one of the seated dragons. Gimelli suddenly burst out laughing, the kind of contagious laugh that she was famous for. Bellae joined in, as did several of the dragons.

Stralande gave her a puzzled look and motioned her over. "What's so funny?"

Gimelli shook her head and waved her hand to signal she could not speak.

"Ah, now here we go," Stralande said eagerly as two Vasama Dwarves laid a tray down next to him. On the plate were four wiggling bats. Gimelli and Bellae stopped laughing at the sight of their struggle. Each one had its wings wrapped up in a large light green leaf. High-pitched squealing sounds were coming from them.

Occasionally, Bellae would pick up a word, but they were mostly crying. Their dark black eyes bore into her, pleading. She looked away and tried to make her mind think of other things. *How does he know*

I am the One? she wondered. Turning back to the salivating dragon, a wave of nausea washed over her again.

"The trick is to eat them before they wriggle loose," he said, hungrily rubbing his hands together, which, with his worn-out scales, made an irksome grating sound. Grabbing a bat by the foot, he dangled it over his mouth before dropping it in.

"MMMPPPPPPHFFF!" he mumbled, chewing and crunching. Sinewy black chunks and green ooze mercilessly tumbled around his mouth and yellowing teeth.

"We farm grow them in enclosed areas with lots of bugs to eat. Bats are fiercely loyal with a well-defined social order. If we only fed half, the ones who ate would share their food, by regurgitation. Did you talk to them?"

"Not when I knew they were going to be eaten," Bellae whispered. The pain radiating from the bat and the cries of the others weighed heavily on her heart.

"Well, quite right to feel a little bad, I suppose," he said, even as he licked his lips. "We have noticed they make sounds Dwarves and humans can't hear when they hunt—echolocation. Our dragon ears pick them up as shrill and rhythmic chirping. It's actually quite lovely to our more attuned ears.

"Our surgeons located the spot in their brains where this happens. When we remove that section..." Bellae gasped in horror. Stralande chuckled and continued without missing a beat, "...they can't hunt without it."

After he had eaten, the elderly dragon began to nod his head, and his eyelids fluttered heavily. Soon, he was fast asleep.

After a minute, Bellae moved closer to Gimelli, "What was so funny?"

"That dragon has a scroll with an ad for a kursted magma spa, where you can increase your naphtha production. It said, 'Kaelen's Kursted. The spa for Kirvella dragons to increase fire production to impress that someone special.'"

Bellae smiled but did not really understand why it was funny.

The elderly dragon stirred, his eyes fluttering open at the noise of Pistis entering. "Pistis, my good dragon," Stralande said, as if he hadn't just been snoozing.

Pistis was surrounded by ten of the Vasama Dwarves. All had swords drawn and fierce looks stamped upon their faces.

Bellae and Gimelli craned their necks to get a glimpse of the scroll through the fearsome guards. They could see a red glass case bobbing up and down in Pistis' hands. Stralande struggled to rise, and two of the Vasama guards rushed over to assist. The old dragon groaned while rising, his aged muscles fluttering in protest at the exertion. Grabbing his cane, he took a few doddering steps forward.

"Please set the prophecy down and remove the protective case. Guards, I want two of you at each of the entrances and the rest of you to the far end of the chamber. Other than Pistis, all Council members move to the other end of the hall," the elderly dragon said with surprising force.

As the others moved to their requested positions, Pistis carefully removed the red glass covering. The case had an ornate golden dragon-head staring out from the top.

"This is much older than me, believe it or not," Stralande said with a chuckle.

"How old are you? Bellae questioned. Blushing, she quickly added, "If I may ask."

He laughed. "I am three hundred and thirty-six years old."

"You mean three hundred and thirty-six years *young!* Don't you?" Pistis groveled, smiling.

Stralande did not look amused. "You can put as many bats as you want in a heap of dung, but it's still a pile of crap."

Bellae and Gimelli laughed.

"That was funny, wasn't it?" the elderly dragon said. "Okay, now we shall unroll the ancient prophecy. Please, Pistis, unfurl the scroll so I may examine it!" he said in a mockingly serious tone while adjusting his glasses.

Clearing his throat loudly, he stepped up to the scroll. It was yellowed with age and had blackened and shredded edges.

Far Forest Scrolls

"Our ranks have dwindled low,
Time, sword, and magic made this so.
All began when a single secret did emerge,
What the One adored, we thought a scourge.

A battle did erupt,
We fought the One, who is corrupt.
His power is too great,
Our victory will have to wait.

Thus was formed the League of Truth.
All hence, written for a special youth,
Born in distant generation,
She, Chosen One, shall save each nation.

The crystals have spoken true,
This is what you must do.
To avoid Na Cearcaill, never-ending cycle of doom,
Seek the girl in whom,
The skill of the Ainmhi Caint does reappear,
A chance for truth will be near.

If deemed true,
Forget what you thought you knew.
This is not a blessing, dear,
It will cost blood and tear.
Now start your quest,
Your strength to test.

Touch, for you, Macht Crystals allow,
Seek the Master Elf, if dragon avow.
With him, find the next scroll,
Be ready to sacrifice in this role."

Stralande rubbed his grizzled chin and squinted his eyes at the scroll as if studying it intently. He then turned towards Bellae. Pressing his face right next to hers, he asked, "Please open your mouth. Wider! Wider now!"

"AHHHHH!" Bellae sounded as she struggled to open her mouth. "AHHHHH-OHHHHHH!"

"I see," Stralande said, a concerned look flashing across his face.

Bellae and Gimelli shared a look of confusion as the elder Dragon turned back to the scroll. Nodding, he turned back to Bellae. Brushing aside her hair, he examined her ear and felt her neck. "Remember, just for show," he whispered with a wink.

Stralande shuffled to the closest bookshelf, letting his grizzled hand run across the spines of several codices. After taking and studying several books that he returned, he finally nodded enthusiastically and began flipping through one.

"Ah-ha!" he said excitedly as the other dragons nodded enthusiastically.

"Listen," Stralande said loudly. "Guards, thank you. Would you please escort Pistis back to the vault to return the scroll? I have the vital information I need."

As Pistis began returning the scroll, the guards helped Stralande back to his chair. The ancient dragon spent several agonizingly slow moments reading various passages from the book, intermittently looking at Bellae, and occasionally having the young squire look up, down, or spin around.

Finally, his ancient finger motioned Bellae to come in closer.

"Can you keep a secret?" he asked.

Bellae nodded.

"Even from your sister?"

She nodded again as he opened the book to show the title. Bellae began laughing hysterically.

Several of the dragons in the room made irritated huffs and vexed harrumphs.

"All part of the important process," Stralande said, waving off their annoyance.

"What does a book titled 'Exceptional Recipes, a Link to Our Past Through Cooking' have to do with the Chosen One?" she asked.

"Nothing. I will tell you another secret in a moment, but first, your sister. Come stand near me," he asked, motioning to Gimelli while looking up to everyone. "Now, I need time to examine and talk with the girls, *alone*, as I try to evaluate her for this momentous decision."

The two squires stood in silence as the room slowly cleared. Several of the Council members took their time, shooting hopeful glances at the old dragon, aiming to be asked to stay. Nodding at them, he pointed to the door.

"Who is the 'One adored' that did something bad in the prophecy?" Bellae asked as Stralande yawned.

"Ah, yes. Well, that is a tough question with an extremely complicated answer. But, alas, you, the Chosen One, must discover this for yourself on the journey ahead."

"So I *am* the Chosen One?" Bellae asked, confused at his answer.

He chuckled. "I know this is overwhelming, but all will become clear as you move forward on your quest. This scroll is just the first in a series that you must discover and unlock. But to answer your question, yes. You are the 'Chosen' that must recover the Macht Power Crystals."

"What's this 'cycle of doom' we keep hearing about?" Gimelli asked.

"Another good question. The answer as to the nature of the destructive cycle that is Na Cearcaill awaits you as move forward on your quest. It is tied into the formerly adored one that we talked about," he answered with a smile.

Gimelli did not return it. The two sisters exchanged frustrated glances. "That's it? The big reveal? I could have learned more by sitting on the scroll."

Stralande began laughing. He kept laughing until the girls finally started giggling themselves.

"It is hard to stay frustrated at you when you keep cracking up," Gimelli managed.

"My last advice is this," he said, turning serious. "Don't sit on scrolls."

They all began laughing again, this time even harder. They made such a ruckus that several of the Vasama Dwarves stormed in.

"Are you…is everything okay?" one of them asked.

"Yes," Stralande muttered, impatiently. Turning to Gimelli, his expression turned solemn. "Please stand over by the door. I wish to speak to Bellae alone, for just a moment. I want to tell her the great secret of how I knew she is the One. It is information just for her ears."

Gimelli turned defensively towards Bellae.

"It's okay."

"I don't really have a choice, do I?" Bellae asked after her sister left.

"Having a choice is the only true power we have. There's always a choice, until the last one, that we all topple to, death. Having that lingering finality hanging over us like forbidden fruit forces those awake to scrutinize each moment, each day, each decision. Choosing that hard option, pushing through when times are tough, just might give your life the meaning only a few can dream of.

"Walking away is *always* an option, just be aware that sometimes the problems that flourish from walking away are far worse than any that would be endured by facing your quest head on."

Bellae shook her head. "That is…this is all overwhelming."

His scales cracked as he smiled in a mix of sympathy—at the trials ahead to be laid on her untested youth, and envy—of the adventure such a grand plight would offer, an expression that can only be earned through aged wisdom. "Young lady, don't make things too complicated. Wake up each day and smile. Take that first step, and then the next. Then another. Be determined, do your best, and keep stepping forward."

His face scrunched in contemplation. "You might just find, when this is over, whatever the outcome, it was a grand adventure, a swirl of the best and worst of your life."

Bellae sighed, unsatisfied with the answer.

"Odd thing about knowledge is you have to earn it through study. Tough thing about wisdom is you have to go out and live, surviving the bumps and bruises, to find it. Troubling thing about truly seeing the reality of the world and our situation is you have to *want* to look beyond, turning around, rising above, the world's shallow veneer. Like in a cave, you have to turn away from the comfortable, the known, and search for more. Have no doubt that a person can be a promise, and we need *you* to be that promise to the world."

Bellae looked at the aged dragon, her face rumpling into her best pouty expression. She didn't want his words to have made so much sense. "But saving the world? It's a…lot."

"Saving the world is an abstract and cold motivation, which, in our mostly grounded minds, has no nobility, rarely stirs one's heart, seeming too overwhelming a task. Now saving a family member, a best friend, that is something capable of stirring the hardest of hearts. Move forward with your family and friends, taking one step at a time, for them. Let the outcome work itself out."

His smile creased deeper at her hesitation. "For untold generations in the future that will have a chance to live in peace, if you succeed, and countless masses whose lives are already over, many get stuck, from choice and circumstance, in the ordinary, only dreaming of adventure. They would look on this as an amazing opportunity. Now one could argue that from the safe distance of their prosaic life of routine and banal, far removed from the danger you will bear, they will not feel the fear or peril, or understand the risk.

"However, of the list of possible activities to do with your life, escaping the mundane to go on a grand adventure with great friends, is not the worst.

"But that's it—something, like this quest, can be unfair *and* exhilarating—terrifying *and* glorious." The elderly dragon flipped his trembling hand back and forth, "Two sides to the same coin. This goes back to perspective. The first breed of perspective is how we view what happens to us, and we can control it. The second category is how well we truly see the world, like those in Plato's cave. Think of life as ascending a giant mountain, as we live, grow, learn, we ascend a little bit and broaden our viewpoint of the world—how far we can see. Very few, if any, reach the top, but we should never stop improving our perspective of the world."

Bellae nodded, and Stralande motioned with his knotty fingers for Bellae to come closer. His warm breath spread over her cheek and ear, causing her to shiver with a tingle of uneasiness. To avoid upsetting

Gimelli, Bellae stayed and waited despite the sickly fermented smell trickling from his mouth and tickling her nose.

"I knew you were the Chosen One before you were born because of what happened to your mother when she was pregnant—magic began to flourish within her. The Ainmhi Caint have a special and powerful magic, and you are linked to that heritage. Their power is what made Veneficus fall in love with them. Their scruples are what led to their downfall. When all pure born Ainmhi Caint were destroyed, we hid the last straggling remnants with dilute ancestry to the animal talkers in the Giant Redwood forests with the Eaglians, waiting for their magic to coalesce and reemerge. They were safe there—no one messes with the Eaglians. That reawakening, that consolidation of magic, happened in you, dear!

"Now I am going to tell you how, and one possible way, this will end. No one really knows the future. Destiny is a myth of an idea created, for justification, by those in power who already have what they want. We can only hope to guide our futures in a good direction with our decisions and actions. I am asking you to commit your whole self to this cause with no promises other than hardship, sacrifice, and uncertainty."

Bellae shivered, reminded of the harsh words venting from the Nishi she kept running into.

He continued, "This information is good and bad, but it is all just between you and me. Share this knowledge with no one, at least until this is nearly over. Agreed?"

"Yes," she whispered breathlessly, an uncomfortable, ominous feeling settling upon her.

The ancient dragon leaned even closer. After several minutes, he stopped talking, and Bellae felt a rush of fear and uncertainty. Abruptly, she threw her arms around him and squeezed tightly. His scales felt rough, dry, and cool.

"Oh, my! We don't hug much, but from you, this means a great deal," Stralande stated, hugging her back. His gnarled hands gently patted her back, unable to grasp with their twisted knuckles. The two stayed frozen for several minutes.

When Bellae finally stood back, she quickly wiped some tears from her eyes and smiled brightly. "I can do it. I'm okay," she said quietly.

"Keep in mind that no matter what happens, many will die in the coming battles. I know you did not ask for this quest and it is an unfair burden, but realize there are no other choices. All of Verngaurd is calling out for you to succeed.

"No matter the outcome, things are going to change forever. More than the usual drifting changes that make up our lives. You, my dear, are in for a great evolution. If you succeed, Verngaurd will finally be able choose her own destiny. If you fail, the maniacal cycle, Na Cearcaill, that has plagued Verngaurd for countless, and I do mean countless, eons will continue."

Bellae had no choice but to laugh. She slowly shook her head from side to side. "Uh…that's a little much to put on me."

"True, it's a lot to ask. However, it's also an opportunity. Make your time here on earth count. Take a chance to do something exceptional. Either path you choose leads to the same place. It is only the middle, the days from now until your end, that will change through your decisions. Go, live an adventure. If you 'play it safe' and do nothing, you will still meet your death."

"You know I'm just a kid?"

"Some are born older, as you were, and some are forced to rise up and make themselves into a hero for all of us," he answered. "Rise above the storm of doubt, rise above the fear of hardship. Resist evil's ascent."

"No pressure, though."

"No, not really," he laughed. When he stopped, he grew serious, "Most afflicted with youth want to shout in vigorous ignorance, their words proving how little they know. You? You understand the value of listening, usually a trait of the wise. Now lean even closer, child." He then began to whisper, and as he spoke, her eyes grew wide and then narrowed as tears began flowing.

"I wish I didn't know that."

The wizened dragon smiled. "My dear, ignorance is not bliss—it is a drunken stupor of the apathetic." Bellae continued to cry until he finally handed her a special bag and waved to Gimelli.

She rushed over and inspected Bellae closely. Seeing her sister crying, Gimelli looked accusingly at the dragon.

"He didn't do anything. I'm all right. Everything will be okay," Bellae said firmly, hugging her sister. When they finished, so were her tears.

"You squires do love to hug, don't you? Well, all good things must come to an end," Stralande stated. "I am sincerely glad to have met you, Bellae. Say hello to my good friend Patuljak when you get there. Good luck."

Bellae hugged him once more.

"Sorry," she said, accidently snagging one of his wings.

"Ah, they are good for nothing," he said, coughing. Then, sighing heavily, he spoke. "Would you two guards please take these girls to see the babies about to break free?"

The two Vasama Dwarves exchanged questioning looks.

"It's all right. I don't feel up to going today. Take them instead. I need to sit here and rest a smidgen. Just a bit."

"Yes, sir," one of the guards said reluctantly. "Let's go, ladies."

Bellae looked back, waving at the old dragon. Stralande smiled and waved feebly. His eyelids seemed heavy as he slouched into his chair.

"He's seen every baby break free for decades," a guard said, nodding back to the sleepy looking dragon.

"He absolutely adores it," the other added. "You need to realize it's a rare honor to see a dragon break free. No one other than a Dwarf or dragon has *ever* seen it before."

"Is a dragon going to lay her egg?" Gimelli asked.

"No, that is their entrance day. Their birthday is when they hatch."

The two girls followed the guards through a maze of twisting and gently sloping corridors. Abruptly, the walls of the passageway became ornate with rough chiseled rock giving way to intricate patterns. The four approached two Kirvella dragons, deep in conversation, who were just entering a room off the main hallway. Steam was pouring out from the doorway, and the air was thick and humid.

Before the door closed, the two girls caught a glimpse of several dragons getting into what looked like a pool of magma. "Are they…" Gimelli started.

"Yeah. That's a kursted magma spa," one of the guards answered. He was shaking his head in disgust. "They think it makes them live longer if they take a bath in a special type of magma called carbonatite. It's a mere eleven-hundred degrees."

"Some of the sickest Dwarves will even try it out by wearing a special suit made of discarded dragon scales," the other added.

"Does that help them?" Gimelli questioned.

"No. They usually die."

Bellae and Gimelli exchanged looks of horror as they came to a dead end with a large door. One of the guards knocked loudly. Within a few seconds, a sliding slit opened in the door. "Yes?" a somewhat frantic and annoyed voice asked.

"Orders from Stralande. These two humans are to see the babies being born."

"Humans?" the voice on the other side of the door cried in a high-pitched squeal.

After a brief pause, grinding metal on metal could be heard as several bolts were unlocked. As the door swung open, they saw a dragon that looked identical to the blue Kirvella dragons except brown.

"Hurry up! Stralande must know what he's doing. You're just in time," the dragon said, quickly shutting the door behind them. "You were lucky you caught me up here. I was just heading back."

"This is Synty. She's in charge of the birthing ward," one of the guards said. Seeing their confusion, the guard explained, "The female Kirvella dragons range in color from blue to brown or brownish-red."

The four hurried after the brown dragon until the corridor they had been following abruptly divided into three openings. Ornate gold lettering hung above each doorway, but in Dragonese.

"We keep the three types of dragon eggs separate. Today we have some Vioma about to be born," Synty said, hurrying through the middle door.

With each step, the heat became fiercer. After they walked about ten feet, a fairly large chamber opened up with a partial wall dividing it into two equal parts. To their left a pool of magma bubbled and frothed angrily. Suspended about five feet above were badly scorched thick metal bars in a crisscross pattern. A dozen large eggs of different colors sat on the intersecting rods. Moving from left to right they changed from snowy white to yellow, and finally to a soft meadow green.

"This left side is our heated incubation area for right after their entrance day," Synty explained. "Once a dragon lays an egg, we take over its care and bring it here, placing them over the magma pit. It takes about forty-two days for Vioma eggs to hatch. The Saatana and the Kirvella take fifty-four and sixty-seven days.

"When they first come to us, the eggs are white. As they mature, they change. See how they turn green from the bottom up?" Synty said, pointing. "All green means it's ready to be brought to the birthing area."

The group walked to the right side of the room. There was no magma pit, and the temperature was noticeably cooler. Another brown Kirvella dragon was near two summer-leaf-green eggs sitting on a latticework of metal bars over an empty pit.

"The eggs of the Kirvella dragons are only eleven inches long. The Vioma eggs, like these, are at least two feet in length while the Saatana's are three to five feet.

"The last week before birth, the unhatched dragons become able to generate fire and this internal heat turns the egg a darker green. In old times, when food could be scarce, the cruder dragons, such as the Vioma and Saatana, would scorch the eggs and eat them before they hatched. As a defense against this, external heat to the egg in *only* the last week causes the outside shell to seal itself and become incredibly hard, keeping the baby safe. Even a Saatana isn't able to break it. The unhatched dragon then enters a stasis, trying again in a few weeks as the shell slowly softens."

Bellae moved closer to the eggs but suddenly jumped back. "Whoa!" Gimelli caught her. "What is it?"

Bellae pointed to one of the eggs as a burst of orange light erupted inside the top half. The squires looked to the dragons expectantly.

"It's close to hatching, and the baby has to burn its way out," Synty explained. They could see a dark shadow paddling inside it as the entire egg began to glow bright orange.

"They have a primary set of hard frizzen, one on top and one on the bottom. When they are slammed together, they create a spark and ignite the naphtha inside the egg until it starts to boil. When the heat comes from *inside* the shell, it becomes brittle and the baby can easily break through," Synty described as the other dragon hovered expectantly. "The frizzen will retreat inside the mouth of the baby and not reappear until they turn four years of age and start producing naphtha themselves."

A high-pitched cracking sound was followed by a small fracture at the top of the egg. Synty squealed, and tears flowed from the eyes of the dragons.

"Move back, move back, darlings!" the dragon shrieked excitedly. "Sometimes the naphtha sprays quite a distance."

The girls felt the guards pull them backwards. "Stand behind these." Each squire was handed a large shield made from wood and coated with dragon scales.

The girls ducked behind the shields just as a spray of the flaming liquid splattered around the room. A gush was followed by a loud sloshing sound as the baby dragon burst out of the egg. They set the newborn dragon on the floor while it was still engulfed in burning naphtha.

"There we go," Synty said, tears of joy streaming down her face. The baby dragon was wiped down with a cross between a towel and chainmail. When the cloth was saturated, they threw the still-burning piece into a large and well-charred metal barrel.

"Aw. Soooooo cute, but white!" Bellae said, surprised.

The baby dragon was indeed pearly white with large closed eyes. It yawned widely to reveal a green tongue but no teeth.

"Its color comes in around age two. This protects it from territorial fathers who might view the newborn as a threat."

Just then, the baby dragon burped loudly, and a thin spray of flames jetted out. At the same moment, its eyes shot open in startled surprise.

"It's a miracle. Our little miracle," Synty said, squeezing the baby tightly. The dragons and squires began to cry as the two Dwarves rolled their eyes.

The girls followed the two guards back to the antechamber. Sankari was off by herself while the rest of the League huddled around Lontas, who was sitting at a small table across from a Kirvella dragon playing a complex game called Domination.

"Hey, they're back," Kainen yelled. "Congratulations!" he said, running up and hugging her. Bellae felt the rough Elfin skin she had become familiar with as Finn's squire. "I knew you were the One!" he said softly. "Now, on to Patuljak."

The girls made their way over to Lontas, who was smiling. "Did you know the dragons call this Rikja?" Lontas said excitedly. The dragon across from him scoffed.

Domination is an ancient, complex game of skill. The pieces include: a King, General, Knights, Archers, Foot Soldiers, and Stonemasons. The game is played on two parallel boards, checkered black and white, one directly above the other. Two blue squares are used as portals to move up and down between levels. The King and Stonemasons start on second or top level. All other pieces must battle their way up.

Suddenly a stream of twenty Vasama guards flew through the hall on their way into the Council chambers.

"You're going to win," the Kirvella dragon said, standing up. "I underestimated you. Anyway, I must excuse myself."

Lontas stood up excitedly as Arend congratulated him. Turning to Bellae, he instantly saw the sadness floating behind her eyes.

"What's wrong?" he asked, pulling her aside.

"Everything's all right. I'm glad you found someone to play Domination with," Bellae answered.

"Don't change the subject."

"Gimelli has already been after me. I'm fine. Really."

Lontas looked down, "Well, tell me if you want or need to. I'm here."

Bellae smiled as valiantly as she could under the weight of the secrets Stralande burdened her to carry. "I know," she said, giving him a big hug. He blushed as she continued. "This old dragon was just telling me about something that might happen in the future, but it's okay. I can handle it."

"He's dead! Stralande has died!" one of the guards yelled out into the antechamber. His voice echoed off the hall for several moments as the League looked at each other in disbelief.

Chapter Five

Storm Clouds Gather

Scroll 1: An Ending–A Start

"I hope you enjoyed the lecture about the VVI's—the Volcanic Vent Irrigation system—here in the Northern Dwarf Kingdom," a tall Vasama Dwarf said. He was one of a dozen Dwarf warriors escorting them to meet the Eaglians, who would fly the League out of the battle zone and give them a head start to see the Grand Master Elf, Patuljak.

If he hadn't been a Dwarf, Bellae would have sworn he was Lontas' long-lost brother. They both salivated over books, and the two had been inseparable since they discovered their mutual love of learning. While the others fought to stay awake, Lontas seemed to float, riveted by the talk, on the flowing words about how the Dragons and Dwarves controlled, and used, the stream of magma through their "VVI system."

Lontas asked another question, but Bellae blocked it out. The Dwarf began droning about using the "natural tendency of all things, even lava, to flow in the path of least resistance combined with Dwarf and dragon ingenuity…" *Blah, blah, blah…*

She closed her eyes, enjoying the cool rain. So much had happened since they arrived in the Kingdom of the Northern Dwarves that it seemed much longer than several days since she had been by confirmed by Stralande as "the One." The future seemed icily uncertain, her mind using the unknown to throw out frightening potential scenarios.

The rain started to come down harder, making a humming *SHHHHHHH* noise as it fell. To Bellae it felt like the ancient dragon admonishing her to keep his onerous secrets from beyond death.

Looking behind, she saw Kainen, Arend, and Gimelli in animated conversation. There was an excitement in their step reserved only for youth about to plunge into an uncertain, adventurous future.

The words spoken by Stralande in private dampened Bellae's enthusiasm. She understood how traumatically the world was about to be changed and its unimaginable cost.

Gimelli placed her arm around her little sister. Bellae couldn't help thinking she had the best parts of Liberum with her, the warm embrace of her sister and friends. Maybe the castle wasn't her home, but the heart of it was her friends and family.

Bellae looked to Sarskil, their Vasama Warrior guide. He had the faraway look of sadness that occurs with all who have their world blended up by war. The tempest of hostilities uproots the routines previously taken for granted while removing comforts, serenity, and, perhaps worst, certainty of the future.

"Wait!" a huffing blue dragon called out.

"Vlug? What are you doing here?" Sarskil seethed.

"Stralande asked me to give this note to Bellae right before she left."

He sauntered up, waving a small piece of parchment, still breathing heavily from running.

Bellae reluctantly took it.

"Quickly now," Sarskil ordered.

Bellae read, "Dear girl, my last words shall hang upon you. Living long enough to meet you has been my honor.

Try not to get caught up in the trap of taxing stress or pestering pressure of this quest—they are lies and internal fabrications of our own minds. Do your best, and control your perspective. Change this from a horrible responsibility to a chance to help. Rework a daunting quest into an adventurous opportunity. Morph pressure and stress into excitement and enthusiasm.

Even though the stakes are high, don't take whatever happens hence too seriously. Remember that one day, sooner than you like, your coming actions will be but a foggy, tattered memory twirling from abandoned cobwebs deep in the recesses of your mind.

Such is time.

Can't be changed.

Keep moving forward—one step, then another. Enjoy this time— enjoy the odyssey. Regrets have a way of haunting our minds and spoiling our thoughts in the form of sorrow and remorse. Vlug told me he mentioned this—it is worth remembering: If you are to collect regrets, collect regrets of action, not inaction."

The writing became much disordered.

"Everything and all of us eventually turn back into ashes, and my time is done.

Each moment, each day: take one step, then another.

Don't forget to smile.

Yours truly,

The last word was in Dragonese, she assumed it was his name, but it was slurred and written in choppy strokes.

"His last breath was given writing that," Vlug said, smiling at Bellae with kind eyes but reaching for the note.

Bellae handed it to him, and a burp of flame shot from his mouth to set it on fire. His scales allowed him to hold it easily until it was reduced to a small pile of ashes, which, as the wind caught them, whisked them up into the air.

"No one but you and Stralande know what was written, keep it that way and…"

Vlug's words were quickly swallowed by Sarskil yelling, "Down, now! They are leaving." The League was quickly escorted against the side of the mountain as the Vasama warriors surrounded them.

Bellae took several deep breaths, trying to calm her jolted nerves. Her mind alternated between panic at everyone's expectations and dread at failing. *Remember what Stralande said. Just smile.* She closed her eyes and took several more slow deep breaths. *Take the first step. Just take the first step.*

She opened her eyes to see a stream of the green Vioma dragons and their Aer Ridire riders zooming overhead. All the children's jaws dropped at the awe-inspiring sight of thirty dragons and their riders in full battle gear. Even in the fog of rain, you could see the glint of their armor and sense their determination.

"That's our signal to move out," Sarskil said. "They will engage any hostiles in front of us, allowing us to get you to the Eaglians."

Magicians

Scroll 2: I Wonder

"Come in, Prast," Veneficus instructed the Master Magician with whom he had a love-hate relationship. Prast had a deep devotion to Tallcon and had volunteered to give the message to the Knights about changing Friar's name. Veneficus chuckled, thinking about what a failure it had been. "What is it?"

"News from the dungeon, sir. We finished 'interrogating' the Northern Dwarves we captured near Temple Aon Intinn. It seems your plan to mislead the enemy about the Chosen One in the prophecy has failed. No one believes it's Jumeaux. In fact, Bellae has been ordained the Chosen One."

Veneficus felt a surge of rage bubbling up. He was glad he had disintegrated the false prophecy. Better yet, he wished it were in front of him so he could destroy it again. His mind seemed mired on how the Ainmhi Caint had managed to repeatedly trick him. *Some mistakes never stop haunting you.*

"What now?" Prast asked.

"I am going to think carefully about our next move," Veneficus replied, slouching in his chair.

"Yeah, we need to think about it oh mighty cleri-geek!" a Valo seethed. "You want us to rush in, make mistakes?"

"What would you have us do? Go off without a plan?" another chided.

Rolling his eyes, Prast ignored the floating menaces. "General Lidenskap and High Commander Storlax are getting close to attacking the Northern Dwarves with a full-on assault, despite your protests."

"Ah," was all that Veneficus muttered.

"I have to admit, building that Temple Palvoa on the other side of Mount Honoo was a stroke of genius by the Proliate. They have the Northern Dwarves caught in a pincer with Temple Aon Intinn."

"Even if they manage to defeat the dragons and get inside, that place is a death trap. There are a thousand ways they control the flow of magma to broil them. Plus, I feel the Knights will make a decisive first move," Veneficus offered.

"I don't believe the Knights have the power to make a 'decisive' move," Prast spat with contempt.

"Yeah, that's right," a Valo light groused. "The Knights are done for!"

Veneficus ignored the glowing ball's comment. "As I've said, you are underestimating the Knights. My gut tells me they are to play an important role in shaping our future and that of Verngaurd."

"In what way? Do you mean fighting the Dark Warriors? They certainly didn't do so well last time," Prast scoffed.

"What news from our scouts?" Veneficus said, changing the subject. He wanted some time to think on what to do with Jumeaux and the Knights.

"Ah, yes. Good news. There have been an increasing number of attacks against the people of Jaa. The…"

"That's good news?"

"No, of course not. However, the consequences work to our advantage. The warriors of Jaa have officially signed an agreement to fight with our Confederation against the Allied revolutionaries helping the Dark Warriors," Prast said proudly.

"You know, I wonder if in the future we won't find out that the Knights are right?"

"How?"

"It seems that the Dark Warriors are driving certain countries to us and uniting others against us. In the end, we just might discover it has been a ploy to divide us."

"Supreme Master, we've been over this. You yourself have done truth enchantments upon the eyewitnesses and weapons from these attacks. We must deal with the Allies quickly, before the Dark Warriors come en masse. It is time to unleash the Proliate," Prast said, ending with a self-satisfied smile.

"What's our goal here?" Veneficus asked, deep lines of worry hastening across his forehead. "Do we destroy every single Elf of Creber, Northern Dwarf, and Knight?"

"If that's what stops these massacres, then yes."

Veneficus sighed. There were many things he wanted to think on if the future was to turn out the way he hoped, needed.

"What will we do to recover the girl in the prophecy, then?"

Veneficus closed his eyes. After a few moments, he spoke, "Thank you for this conversation, Prast. I need a moment to consider the future of Jumeaux, the girl, and the rest of Verngaurd. We shall talk later."

Prast bowed politely and left. *Tallcon shall prevail in all circumstances. With or without the girl, we shall win,* the pious Magician thought.

Later that day, Veneficus walked leisurely towards Jumeaux, still undecided on how to handle the boy's situation. *I brought Jumeaux to the Citadel only because of the prophecy.* Encouraged by his rage at being tricked, part of him wanted to simply toss Jumeaux out.

However, if there is one thing I have learned over the countless eons it is the truth is in the details. Sometimes the smallest trifle will make the difference in what lies ahead. Just as with the Knights, perhaps Jumeaux will serve some purpose in shaping my future of Verngaurd.

Heading to the green hallway, he found Jumeaux's room. He could hear a heated conversation through the door and, curious, knocked. Jumeaux flung open the door. An expression of panic raced over his face at the sight of the Supreme Master.

"Hhu…hello," he mumbled as the two stood in awkward silence.

"May I come in?"

"Of course, sir."

As Jumeaux rushed around, picking up the scattered array of books and scrolls, he rammed his knee into his chair. Hopping on one leg, he landed on his bed. Looking up sheepishly at Veneficus, his cheeks flushed as the Supreme Master searched for someone else in the room.

"I thought I heard you talking?"

"Um," Jumeaux said nervously. "I was…"

"To whom?"

"Uhh, well, my ah, sister, Gimelli," Jumeaux stuttered. He recoiled at the look in the Magician's eyes. "Honest, we're twins, and I can hear her voice in my head."

Even as the words were coming out of Jumeaux's mouth, his cheeks flushed a brighter scarlet. *That sounds insane.*

"We can talk to each other in our minds," Jumeaux explained. "It doesn't work all the time. We need to concentrate."

Veneficus took a deep breath to control the two battling emotions. He felt rage at not having been told this before. However, there was relief as well. This might be the break he was looking for. Veneficus sat down next to Jumeaux.

"Ow!" Jumeaux yelled as the crosier touched him.

Veneficus abruptly stood up. "What is it, boy?"

"It was the same as when I touched the crystal in class that burned my hand. When your crosier touched me, my sister's voice was really loud in my head. Plus, instead of just hearing her…I could *see* her as well."

Veneficus tried to hide his exhilaration. "Is Bellae there? Is she with your twin?" *The smallest detail is often the most important,* he thought. *Now Jumeaux can be better than any spy or enchantment. All I have to do is keep tabs on the girl while she navigates the prophecy.*

Veneficus' eyes glowed as he spoke out loud, "The Ainmhi Caint had seen to it that only the Chosen One can solve the prophecy." *Once Bellae has the Power Crystals, I can pounce, and take them back!*

Shocker, it's all about Bellae, again, Jumeaux thought.

Veneficus focused on the sulking Jumeaux. "Do you remember when I read you the prophecy, and we talked of the treacherous Ainmhi Caint? The animal talkers?"

"Yes."

"Well, if you are not the One, it must be Bellae. You know how important it is that I reclaim the Macht Crystals. Perhaps the shrewdest course of action is for you to keep tabs on her until she acquires all the crystals. Once they are in her possession, we can swoop in and rightfully reclaim them."

"I'll try to help," Jumeaux said.

"A little revenge on the traitorous Ainmhi Caint!"

Feeling no love for his sister, or any animal talker, Jumeaux nodded enthusiastically as Veneficus continued.

"The One in the prophecy is the key to our survival—so the world will endure. If we don't find the Macht Crystals, our Magician way of life will be lost forever. Bellae, your sister, has to be the one to recover these stolen crystals. She is important in the *short term*. You, Jumeaux, you are the future. Once she recovers them, you will become the great Magician I foresee." Veneficus' expression softened to win him over.

After a moment's pause, Veneficus asked, "Do you understand?"

"I think so."

"Good. How would you like me to tutor you on some advanced magic? In appreciation for your efforts, I will teach you spells not often taught before the Master level."

Jumeaux nodded excitedly.

"Excellent. It shall be done. The world today is filled with war, slaughter, and chaos. To make matters worse, the White Wizard is looking for the crystals as well. Only in my possession can the future be secure. So, I ask again, is Bellae with her?"

Jumeaux nodded decisively. "Yes, she's there. What do you need me to do?"

"Keep tabs on Bellae, where she is, who she is with, how many crystals she has obtained, that sort of thing. Gain her confidence. If they need help, you come directly to me, and we will find a solution. She must succeed in fulfilling the prophecy and finding all the Macht Crystals. Once found, the crystals must come to us or the whole world will fall. Can you help me do that without letting her know I'm involved?"

"I'll try."

"Very good." Veneficus couldn't help smiling.

The smallest detail.

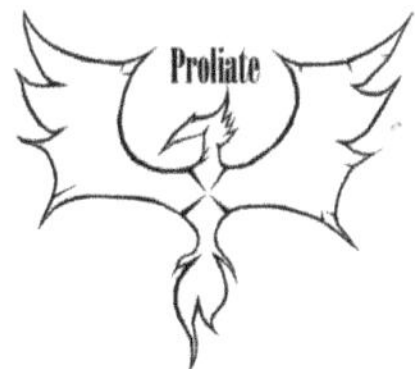

Scroll 3: X's and Ovest

General Lidenskap sighed, his scouts had confirmed the earlier reports of enemy troop movements. Unfurling his map, he made several "X's" where the sightings had taken place. The first was near the Rebelde Plains. *I knew those renegades in the Plains would side with the Knights. Undisciplined and spineless.*

The next "X's" were south of Temple Ovest and the Citadel. *They wouldn't be foolish enough to attack the Citadel, would they?* He had assumed the Allies would attack a Temple closer to their fragile supply lines. Perhaps Temple Palvoa, which had been helping pound the Northern Dwarves. The final sightings had taken place around the Ruins of Murbh and the Cosan Bridge.

A knock on the door startled him.

"Come in!" he yelled more fiercely than he intended. The uncertainty of the coming days had him on edge.

High Commander Storlax entered and approached Lidenskap as he continued to pore over the map.

"What are you thinking?" Storlax asked without a greeting.

"I'm studying the sites that have seen enemy troop movements," Lidenskap said, pointing to the "X's."

"The question remains, what do you think?"

"I worry these movements are a decoy. They must know Proliate forces have been massing for an attack on the Northern Dwarves while the Magicians and their griffins have been harassing their dragons. Clearly, the Northern Dwarves are the strongest of the Allies and the greatest threat to us. If they are aware of this, then why amass around our strongest fortresses, Ovest and the Citadel? They can't be foolish enough to think they could break our defenses? They might as well throw their troops into the sea."

Storlax scoffed. "I honestly don't think they realize how far they have fallen. That said, the few Knights they have left are as good as anyone as the Tournament proved. So part of me believes they will strike at the Citadel as way to divert our troops from the Northern Dwarves. Intelligence I just received from our Southern Dwarf spies confirms their plan to attack the Citadel."

"How pathetic," Lidenskap stated.

"Still, we must be careful. Friar is cunning, and a cornered animal is desperate and dangerous. If they are amassing outside the Citadel, I *do* want to move some of our forces away from the Northern Dwarves and delay our assault there. A sinister alternative would explain the Knights' brazen movements."

"Which is?"

"The Knights are anticipating a large force of Dark Warriors to join them. Your excellent foresight in capturing the message intended for Liberum confirmed their unholy alliance. The seemingly never-ending supply of Dark Warriors combined with Friar's knowledge of this land could be devastating."

"That would make sense. Let's bring half of the troops stationed around the Northern Dwarves at Temples Aon Intinn and Palvoa back to the Citadel to strengthen the defenses here. The half that remains can keep pressure on the Dwarves and provide a defense if the Knights attack there," Lidenskap suggested.

"Agreed. You can't move around here without stepping on a Magician. We can keep the full garrison of Magicians and their griffins where they are to pester the dragons. I will leave you in charge of defenses of the Citadel while I head back to Temple Aon Intinn to shore up supplies and fortification of the temples. If my scouts pick up any troop movements, we will send word and expect the favor to be returned."

"Excellent plan." Lidenskap beamed, hardly able to contain his excitement at being entrusted with the defense of the Citadel. "I appreciate your confidence. The defenses of the Citadel will be ready."

Scroll 4: That's It

Startled awake at his desk by a loud knock, Friar tried to lift his head, but stopped, caught in a drool trap, his face sticking to the damp scroll he had been reading.

"Lovely," he said, carefully removing his saliva-moistened face from the clammy page. Once free, he sat up and began rolling his stiff neck.

I'm too old for all-nighters. "Come!"

Baiulus walked in, pausing at Friar's disheveled look behind a mound of books and scrolls cascaded off his submerged desk all the way to his equally filled couch.

"Still reading? The final battle plan is wonderful."

"You think?" Friar questioned.

"I do."

"It's not perfect."

"Nothing is," Baiulus replied. "Anyway, I can't hold Ritari off any longer. He's not happy you've avoided him after his return from the Citadel. If you were hoping that time would mellow his 'I told you it was a waste to go' attitude, I can tell you it hasn't. He's still hopping mad at his reception by the Magicians and Proliate."

"All right. Send for him."

"No need," Baiulus said with a sheepish grin.

Laughing, Friar motioned for Baiulus to bring him in.

As Ritari ducked his way into the room, Friar could see an edge of humor under his fierce expression. A moment of awkward silence ensued as Ritari and Friar stared at each other.

"No bugs, just…cocky imbeciles," Ritari stated, and they both burst out laughing.

When their laughter settled down, Friar asked, "What are you talking about?"

"Don't you remember your 'sweet honey catches more bugs than a mace' speech?"

"Honey didn't work? Well, time to bring out the mace," Friar said with a rush of adrenaline. "No more doubts, time for all-out war."

"If you didn't remember, why did you laugh?" Ritari questioned.

"You looked so intense I was just relieved to see you laughing."

Ritari chuckled. "Okay." His expression changed, and the smile fell from his face.

"What is it?"

"When I was in the Citadel, they showed me a letter from the White Wizard, to *us*. They swore they intercepted it right outside our gates. Rhyfeler confirmed it coincides with a time we spotted some Proliate troops nearby.

After he described the letter's contents, they sat in silence.

Friar exhaled sharply. "Well, that's it. The Dark Warriors have driven the final wedge between us. While the Proliate possess an obvious numerical advantage, they can't defeat us without suffering incredible losses.

When we are finished grinding ourselves down, the Dark Warriors will come in to mop up what's left of us. A quick and decisive victory over the Proliate and their Confederation could force them, or some of their member countries, back to the bargaining table. We have to come together to have any chance of victory over the Dark Warriors."

"How do we know the Proliate aren't behind this deception?" Ritari asked. "How do we know they aren't trying to get rid of us before dealing with the Dark Warriors?"

Friar raised his eyebrows. "An interesting thought. The Dark Warrior invasion and these fake village massacres have drastically increased their territory. Their piety would speak against such acts of deception. In fact, piety can be a weapon. However, they have a greater weakness, which is also their biggest strength." Friar said with a wry smile.

Baiulus chuckled. "Well, that makes perfect sense. I know you're not sleeping well, but I think you're losing it."

"What I mean is, the Proliate are overconfident and feel unbeatable. They will never turn a blind eye to a perceived injustice. We should know as well as anyone that overconfidence is just as deadly a disease as the plague. We saw its devastating effects on our own ranks during the last Dark War. Look how much it cost us!" Friar roared as he spread his arms out widely in his cramped office. "We will dangle a 'carrot' that their piety can't resist, luring them out of their fortifications. Once out on the battlefield, their overconfidence won't be able to withstand a chance to obliterate us, and they will charge straight ahead. Once they do, we spring our traps."

"That's got to be one big carrot!" Baiulus laughed.

A knock caused Friar's smile to dissolve as a nervous-looking messenger entered without invitation.

"Yes?"

"Sorry to disturb you. We have a-a-a-a…unique guest in…I mean, I've never…it, he, he is…a…and is, at the gatehouse, who—"

Friar interrupted him, "Baiulus, would you see to this? I want to have a word in private with Ritari."

"Ritari, I have something to tell you," Friar said solemnly once Baiulus had left. "If I die, I have officially named you successor to become Friar."

"You're not going to die, and there has to be a better candidate."

"I hate to be the one to tell you this, but death's success rate is one hundred percent. I fear my time will be sooner rather than later. Baiulus is aware of my wishes, and I would expect a smooth transition. Veli Falciss is the only one I see as a potential problem."

Friar held out a hand to silence the protest Ritari was about to throw back at him.

"Listen, my old friend, we have known each other too long. The decision has been made. Complaining will do nothing but drive me closer to the grave. Things are going to start happening fast, so I wanted to let you know, just in case. Also, I want to make sure you understand the precepts that underlie my battle plan. Effort and planning are often erroneously attributed to luck by those who have not endured the sacrifices of forethought and persevering. Ah-ah-ah!" Friar said as Ritari made a move to speak again.

"First, always have the high ground and drive the enemy towards difficult terrain. Second, use counterfeit moves to distract and confuse your enemy. With their attention diverted, slam into them. Third, your strengths attack their weakness. Fourth, understand your enemy and never underestimate them. Finally, always have options. Things on the battlefield change quickly. Battle often pushes plans into the moat.

"Don't forget about a strategic retreat. It is an invaluable option. Allowing your army to be destroyed on principle is ridiculous, and also why Falciss will never be Friar. An army that thinks it has won almost always breaks ranks in pursuit. If you can turn on them in formation, you have them beat.

"The Proliate loathe our innovation because they fear its unpredictability. I will never apologize for a deception that saves the lives of my army, or assures us victory. This is war, not a popularity contest," Friar finished.

Ritari nodded his head but said nothing. Friar detected a hurt look on his face.

Friar sighed, "My apologies. That sounded good in my head, but you are an excellent captain, well schooled in military tactics. It was unnecessary for me to review that which you already know."

"It's fine. I understand. There's so much uncertainty, it just seems as if the floor has dropped out from under our world."

"Perhaps, however, I suggest the floor was never really there to begin with, only the illusion of a floor. Life *is* uncertainty. It sometimes takes a crisis to point out that rather unpleasant reality. That said, we are as prepared as we can be."

A brisk knock came from the door, prompting Friar to yell, "Enter."

"Aquila!" Friar uttered excitedly. Something about the Eaglian's majestic frame brightened Friar's spirits, unleashing optimism.

The normally intrepid Ritari stood up, his mouth agape.

"Ah, my mistake. I forget you have been kept in the dark about our Eaglian friends joining our fight. If you are surprised, imagine how our enemies will feel. This is our friend Aquila. Meet my captain, Ritari."

Arend's father squeezed his large wings through the door. The nervous messenger quickly slithered out as the Eaglian shut the door.

"Aquila escorted Bellae, Gimelli, and Jumeaux to us all those years ago," Friar stated.

A pained look flashed across the Eaglian's fearsome face. His lower lip retracted to reveal his full, terrifying yellow beak.

"Friar, Ritari," he acknowledged with a covering of sadness.

"I'm sorry. You know each other?" Ritari said, still dumbfounded.

"Yes, now that war is a certainty, I will reveal to you our *full* military plan. I had left out the wonderful surprise that for the first time in eons the Eaglians will come out of their Redwoods and fight!"

"We took the task of protecting the last distant relatives of the Ainmhi Caint very seriously, but with Bellae's emergence, we can leave our forests again. The coming war is momentous. It will determine everything," Aquila said, shaking his head to clear the painful memories associated with his journey to bring Bellae to Liberum. Still in awe of his appearance, Friar and Ritari did not catch it.

"Their arrival on the battlefield is sure to be deadly for our enemies. Baiulus and I have been meeting in secret with Aquila to plan their part in the coming battles."

Ritari nodded, staring at the Eaglian's fearsome beak and talons.

"Quite so," Aquila said. "My people are ready for your battle plan and will take the time to pick up your squires and start them on their way to Patuljak. Bellae passed her first test with Stralande."

Friar sat down and sucked in a deep breath, his face echoing the mix of excitement and concern churning in his heart. The prophecy was shrouded in such secrecy that few knew its true meaning and what it would signify for Bellae.

Friar tuned back in at the mention of casualties. "…many good Eaglians. Over the entire mission, twenty of my brothers lost."

"So many?"

"The skies are filled with griffins—Magicians, and wyverns—Watchers. The Watchers have some sort of magical net detecting any significant movement in the skies. We learned this the *hard* way and now try to fly solo, coming together only once near our target."

"Sorry for your loses."

"Thank you. By the way, the Magicians have put out a concocted rumor that the Chosen One is Jumeaux," Aquila stated. "I need to retrieve the rest of the kauhistaa gliders. After we get this batch, we will leave for the Tingij Mountains. Surely, you are aware the Proliate are amassing for an assault on the Northern Dwarves. Believing they pose the greatest risk, they want to knock them out quickly.

"My Eaglians are itching for a fight. They are sick of letting the Vioma dragons have all the fun killing the cursed griffins," Aquila roared.

Friar nodded. "We will all get our chance to kill beyond our fill and propriety. Ritari and I will be leaving for the battlefield shortly, and one of our goals is to draw the Proliate forces away from the Northern Dwarves. Using prestidigitation, we have been purposely misleading the Proliate scouts."

Aquila nodded then rolled his neck while keeping his intense yellow eyes on Friar and Ritari.

"Also, we sincerely appreciate you watching over our squires."

"Of course. Although from here on out, as they journey deeper into the mystery of the prophecy, only they will know where they are headed, and our ability to help them becomes extremely limited," Aquila replied.

"What of my squire, Scelto?"

"He was not with them. Lontas, Bellae, and Gimelli are well. My son, Arend, and his lifelong friend, Kainen, will see them through this quest or die trying."

"Hopefully, it will not come to that," Ritari said, his mind lingering fondly on his squire.

"Will the Northern Dwarves be able to spare the Vioma for the coming battle given the constant griffin and Magician attacks?" Aquila asked.

"The Vioma will come." Friar smiled broadly. "The Saatana will be unleashed."

Scroll 5: Wind in the Sails

Friar, Ritari, and Pumilus watched in silence as the last piece of equipment reluctantly moved into its spot on the deck, wheedled into place on the ship. They bobbed with the hypnotically calm waves at the makeshift port constructed east of the Eluvies Delta, directly south of Liberum.

"That's it, the last supplies of war to be transported are tucked away," Friar said.

"I'm not excited about sailing," Ritari said.

"None of us are. However, it would take too much prestidigitation to move this amount of equipment via land to hide it from the Proliate and Magicians," Friar said, closing his eyes.

He thought of what his father used to tell him, *"Many will never fight. Some follow whoever leads, no matter the cause. A few will rise up to lead. One, every few lifetimes, will lead competently."* Opening his eyes, he focused back on the scene at hand. *Please let me lead well.*

The few Knights remaining on the shore had the grim responsibility of defending Liberum if it were attacked. Cloaked in the damp darkness of night, their grey-black forms seemed to be the ones vacillating up and down as the ship gently bounced on the waves.

Ever since their talk with Aquila, a somber mood had settled upon Friar and Ritari. Esoteric planning had begun to melt, reforming into the reality of all-out war.

"Well, Pumilus, we're honored to have your deft prestidigitation on this voyage," Friar said, trying to be cheerful.

"I was ordered to be here."

"Sounds like you really have your heart in it," Ritari grumbled.

Pumilus glared angrily. "You realize we're here because two of your supply ships making this journey have been destroyed by Magicians?"

Before Ritari could reply, the captain pronounced, "Friar, we are loaded and ready to go, with your permission."

"Of course, captain. I leave everything in your capable hands."

"Very good, sir." The captain began to bark a series of orders, including some to the Dwarves responsible for prestidigitation. Captain Johtaa was originally from Piscium but had moved to the Rebelde Plains after his town had signed on with the Proliate. He was offended at the way they had taken over the traditional Piscium culture, requiring conversion to the austere Proliate life in return for "protection."

"To your places!" Pumilus shouted as the Dwarves from the Rebelde plains skilled at prestidigitation moved to the predetermined spots around the ship. Their flowing white robes began to oscillate in time with the loitsia sticks' rhythmic beat. The Knights on the shore stopped waving as the ship seemingly disappeared, replaced by open ocean.

If you stared hard, you could make out a blurry, unnatural section of water, but it would be concealed at night and protected from detection from all but the deepest scrutiny.

"We are well underway, Friar," Captain Johtaa said, one hand smoothing down his grizzled grey beard, the other resting on his paunchy abdomen. "Easy sailing until we get to the Cliffs of Karst. They are tricky to navigate."

"We are lucky to have someone with your skill."

"I keep thinking that if I could go back to Piscium and tell them you guys have nothing to do with the Dark Warriors, we could avoid war."

"I wish that could work, but these are complicated times," Friar stated. "Sometimes facts are washed away with emotion."

"Complicated times should not mean an entire country has to give up its identity. Trading what defines us as Piscinians for the faint hope of security…makes no sense."

"I agree, but nervously surrounded by all this water, we are grateful for you."

Johtaa laughed. "As long as the water is out there, we are fine," he said, gesturing to the ocean. "Only if water gets *inside* the boat should you be nervous."

"Understood," Friar said, chuckling.

"Anyway, I better get back to the helm. We'll be landing at the narrow area of the Mohado Mire, very near the Ruins of Idor. The Elves of Creber should be there to help you cross over the mire. Try to get a little sleep."

Before the first sun had risen the next morning, a messenger falcon drifted gently down to Friar with news from Veli Falciss. After reading it, as Friar went to find Ritari, he could overhear the captain's shouts of joy as the boat lurched forward and picked up speed, "Now we're moving, boys!"

"We made it past the Cliffs of Karst and have caught the wind—we should have an uneventful journey," Friar informed Ritari. "I just received this message from Falciss. Everything is going according to plan."

Friar unfurled his map. "Once we arrive, we will head up the western spine of the Tingij Mountains to meet up with Sorea and our Knights. We should be joined by the armies of the Elves of Creber and Rebelde Plains just south of the Way of Trepas. The Northern Dwarves will connect with our diversionary force to the east of the pass.

"The bulk of the Knights from Taiheart and Toil Shaor are being led by Veli Pingius and are south of the Citadel. They are traveling under the cloak of prestidigitation and seem to have avoided detection so far. A small diversionary force led by Veli Falciss is weaving its way east of the River Vita. The skill of the Dwarves from the Rebelde Plains is being tested. They are making Veli Falciss' meager army seem like the main invasion force from all three castles, gearing up to attack the Citadel."

"What happens if the Proliate attack the diversionary force?" Ritari asked.

"This must be avoided at all cost. Keep in mind, they are not marching in a straight line. In fact, they are choosing a completely random course. Also, the Dwarves are only occasionally using their prestidigitation and making themselves visible. This weaving around the countryside is going to drive the Proliate scouts crazy and should be unpredictable enough to stay any attacks from the enemy. This will force the Proliate's gaze to their capital, east of the Tingij, while we prepare for the main battle west of the mountain range."

"I hope they don't go after one of the castles," Ritari said with a loud exhalation.

"That would be ruinous. They would easily be overrun by even a meager force."

Scroll 6: Idea

Gimelli shot Bellae a surprised look. She had been trying to overhear what the Vasama Dwarves were saying when her brother's voice came across loud and clear. She looked around for Jumeaux when she heard his roaring voice again.

"What is it?" Bellae mouthed to her sister.

"Jumeaux."

"Gimelli? Are you going to answer me?"

The clarity of his telepathic words startled Gimelli. This time it was crystal clear, as if he was right next to her. If she was honest with herself, the break from his constant, annoying, thoughts had been refreshing. She had spent her entire life trying to keep him out of trouble, while he seemed intent on constantly diving head first into disaster.

"Seriously, Sis. What's going on?" Jumeaux's voice came into her head.

"Um, we're a little busy. Where are you, and what are you doing?"

"I'm in the Citadel, and believe it or not, training with the Magicians," he said, his voice full of pride. *"Are you with Bellae? Is she okay? I'm worried about her."*

Gimelli shot Bellae a quick look. This time she was filled with uncertainty.

"I wasn't sure if you guys had made it. I'm so glad you're safe. This war is just crazy and hard to believe. Is Bellae really okay?" he probed.

"She's here and okay," Gimelli replied. *"How can I hear you so clearly, Jumeaux?"*

"I am training to be a Magician and if I hold a crosier, we can talk clearly even if really far apart. Where are you, by the way?"

Gimelli suddenly had a brief vision of Jumeaux sitting in a room. She saw the crosier and another figure, a man, in the corner. She could not see the details of his face, but he seemed familiar. Something about this did not feel right.

"I'm honestly not sure where we are."

After a moment of silence, he spoke, *"Okay, Gimelli. Listen, I'll stay in contact. Being apart makes me realize how much I miss you. I'm glad you two are safe. Bye."*

Jumeaux let go of the crosier as Veneficus reached for it.

"That was good, Jumeaux. Very good."

"I didn't get the information you wanted…" he said nervously.

"This was our first try, we don't want to push too hard. Keep this up, and they will start to trust you. Did you see anything?" Veneficus asked.

"Well," Jumeaux said, hesitating, "I could have sworn they were flying."

"Really?" Veneficus said. Jumeaux felt emboldened by his sincere interest.

"Yes. It seemed to me they were being carried by a…maybe a griffin." Jumeaux said. Veneficus looked down, processing the information.

"Not a griffin, dear boy. I would know if we had captured—I mean, rescued them. It was likely an Eaglian."

"An Eaglian? They're real?"

A quick knock on the door startled Jumeaux, and Veneficus seemed infuriated.

"Never a moment's peace," he huffed under his breath before shouting, "Enter!"

The door opened, and Magician Fino floated in, his thin form swimming in his blue Master Magician robes. His dark eyes stared out from his ghostly white face.

"Veneficus and my friend, Jumeaux," Fino said excitedly at the sight of the boy.

"Hi, Fino," Jumeaux replied. He thought highly of the Magician that had led him away from the battle outside the Forest of Creber.

"I am sorry to barge in on you, but I would really like to talk with Veneficus, if that is possible."

"Of course. Jumeaux, why don't you head back to your studies? We'll meet again soon for another tutoring session. You did great."

"Thank you, sir," Jumeaux said, unable to hide his smile.

Once Jumeaux left, Fino groveled. "Sorry to interrupt, but I knew you wanted an update before General Lidenskap arrived. As you ordered, we pulled some of the Magicians and griffins away from the Northern Dwarf Kingdom to search for the Knights' army. We will occasionally catch a glimpse of them, and then they simply disappear. I can tell you they are making slow, and sometimes random, but steady progress towards their target, which appears to be the Citadel."

"I see," Veneficus said, turning his back to Fino. He couldn't help but smile. *The Knights have a few tricks left in them yet,* he thought. "We have to tread carefully in the coming battle. We need to diplomatically help even the odds for the Knights."

Fino turned a paler shade of white. "Are you suggesting we are not going to fight with our Proliate brothers?"

"I didn't say that. However, I envision us having a small role, very small."

"To what end?" Fino was having a hard time hiding his outrage despite the fact he did not want to displease the Supreme Master.

"The Knights have an important role to play. The particulars are another matter," Veneficus said with more conviction than he felt.

"But, sir, how do we undertake a small role without seeming suspicious?"

Veneficus laughed. "Leave that to me. Every idea sounds better when you think of it yourself. The key is to plant your notion with such tender subtly into their head that by the time it sprouts they believe it was their idea to begin with. With an unyielding military and religious man like Lidenskap, watch as he boxes himself into a corner."

Just then, General Lidenskap knocked and entered.

Veneficus quickly unfurled his map. "General Lidenskap, excellent. Fino and I were just discussing the upcoming battle. It is hard to believe we have such a large force moving towards us at the Citadel."

"We have skirmished their advance guard, but haven't been able to fully engage the army. The weasels must be using black magic to deceive us. It appears they are foolish enough to attempt a direct assault on the Citadel," Lidenskap hissed.

"I agree. Either the White Wizard is helping them or they are using the appalling false magic, prestidigitation. That said, I think this is another example of the Knights resourcefulness. It would be a mistake to underestimate them. Both Fino and I feel strongly that we, the Magicians, need to play the central role in the battle," Veneficus said, leaning over the map.

Fino tried to hide his look of disbelief, amazed he would take such a huge risk. *What if Lidenskap agreed to let us?*

"The Knights are stronger than you think. Our Magicians would make an intimidating sight in the center of the defense of the Citadel. Imagine our crosiers spreading havoc from below while the griffins shriek from above!" He pretended to be looking at the map while out of the corner of his eye gazing at Lidenskap's twitching right eyebrow.

Veneficus hid a smile. *Now hang yourself, dear general.*

Like a tea kettle about to boil, Lidenskap's twitch progressed to flushing and finally spilled out into an indignant huff. "We do *not* need help! In fact, we, the invincible Proliate, could handle them without you *or* the armies of the Confederation!"

"Dear General, please recall the experience that Friar—"

"You mean H.K.," Lidenskap interjected.

"Of course. He is a master of strategy. In fact, I recollect…"

"Please! The Proliate have advantages in leadership, experience, troops, equipment, and supplies. We need little else to defeat them."

"Well, then," Veneficus stated, satisfied that the general had mentally fenced himself into a tight enough corner. "You don't have a need for my Magicians," he said innocently. Lidenskap hesitated, perceiving the predicament he had managed to crawl into.

"I believe your presence would be appreciated. It would be a morale boost for our troops. Your griffin troops may also be required for air support or defense."

"Ah, I see," Veneficus said, as if he was trying to reconcile how the Magicians would, and would not, be needed at the same time. "Well, it sounds like you want us to act as reserve units, hanging back, but at your disposal?"

Scroll 7: I Didn't Mean to…

"We can't take you any closer to Patuljak. We've suffered too many losses. If we get hit again with a large force, we'll be overrun. Hide here for the night," one of the Eaglians told the League of Truth. His human chest bore several large gashes, and his feathers were stained with the blood of wyverns and griffins. The Eaglians had lost half their original escort fighting over the last several days to get the League west.

Sankari, Gimelli, Lontas, Arend, and Kainen ducked behind some large bushes just west of the Effeus Woods after an exhausting and harried flight. Bellae was trying to calm Crann as the harness used by the Eaglians to carry him was removed.

"Almost there, Crann," she whispered, stroking his neck. The two Eaglians unstrapping him were distracted, their keen eyes constantly scanning the skies. The flight path had become increasingly erratic as they moved between western Jaa and the northern Siochain Pass. They

were desperate to avoid the swarms of Jaa and Proliate troops on the ground, and the magic net above that triggered squadrons of wyverns and Watchers patrolling the skies.

To make matters worse, several squadrons of griffins and Magicians had been closing in on the Eaglians carrying the League. The last two air skirmishes they were unable to avoid had been extremely costly.

"Why don't the Magicians and griffins leave us alone and fight the Watchers and wyverns?" Lontas asked.

"Both groups seem so focused on getting Bellae, they are ignoring each other," an Eaglian replied. "Oh, no. They're closing," he abruptly screeched, as the last strap of Crann's harness was removed. "We need to go. One more big battle, and we all die."

Bellae and Crann joined the others. Several of the Eaglians were trying to convince Arend to hide with the rest of the League. He had tasted griffin blood and was hungry for more.

"No time to argue, Arend. We're following orders from your father, as should you. The League needs you. Lay low for the night and start out for Cappadocia in the morning. You are not far from Leita Falls. You can cross north of the falls and then head to Patuljak. We need to get to the battlefield for Friar's plan. Plus, there are too many looking for Bellae for us to fight, much less you alone.

"Hide when possible and fight only when your wings are against a tree with no alternatives. The skies are too dangerous for large groups."

The battered escort of Eaglians split up before taking to the skies in an attempt to slip through the encircling enemy while drawing them away from the Chosen One.

Later that night, Bellae's eyes fluttered open to see Borb and Grym standing on her chest, pawing frantically.

"What do you need? Oh, sorry, you can't understand that," she said groggily. *What is it?*

"Crann's going nuts. He needs you, now!" Borb squeaked, anxiously. His eyes looked huge in the pale light of the moons. Sitting up to look around, she hit her head on a low branch of the bush they had been sleeping under. It was dark, and, judging by the moons and stars she could see, the first sun's reemergence was still a long ways off. She could see Gimelli, Kainen, and Sankari sleeping around her.

"Move!" Borb pleaded. He spun around in circles several times to let off some nervous energy. Bellae scurried out from under the bush and walked towards Crann. She could see him stomping nervously, his eyes peering south.

"What is it Crann?" she asked, the cool night air shivering her fully awake.

"Arend's on watch but flew off a while ago. Now, something's coming."

"I'll wake…" Bellae stopped after hearing a loud rustling sound directly in front of them. Something was moving towards her at great speed. Straining her groggy eyes, she scoured the bushes while drawing her dagger.

"Wake up the others," Crann advised softly.

With her heart racing, she moved towards her friends. Suddenly, a loud crashing sound rocked the bush right next to her. A dark figure barely missed her as it shot past. It so surprised Bellae and Crann that they stood motionless for a second. The figure was running upright, probably a man. Before they could recover, another thunderous sound of someone smashing into the bush in front of them rang out.

This time she would be ready. Bellae held out her dagger just as a white furry figure slammed into her. The dagger slipped up under the ribs of the attacker as they were both thrown backwards. Gravity and the weight of the body on top her made the dagger pierce deeply, perforating the heart from below. Bellae felt the sickly warmth of blood flood over her hand and arm as the body moaned and twitched on top of her.

Bellae's face tingled under the white fur and trickling blood as she struggled to shove the body off. Gimelli and Kainen began moving slowly under the daze of sleep. Just as the body on top of her went lifeless, a second white furry figure dashed through the bush in front of them. This time Crann took over. The strands of his whip-like tail lashed into the legs of the attacker. The intruder went flying forward, right into Crann's two front hooves which smashed directly into their face. After a brief howl of pain, the figure crumpled to the ground with a splintered skull. Crann added a few stomps on the twitching body.

"What's going on? Where the blazes is Arend?" Kainen called out, the cobwebs of sleep finally clearing.

Bellae was still struggling to push the body off of her when the now-familiar flapping of Arend zoomed overhead. He was moving at blistering speed. Crann used his muzzle to help push the body. As it tumbled off, Bellae let out a weak cry. Gimelli was next to her in a flash.

"Light!" she screamed over her shoulder to Kainen.

"We shouldn't risk it," he replied. "We don't even know what's going on and where…"

"Risk it!" Gimelli commanded back with authority. "Are you hurt?" she asked.

Bellae didn't reply but cried and held onto her sister.

Gimelli fought the urge to scream as she felt the warm blood over the front of Bellae's clothes. She continued to soothe and question her little sister. After what seemed like an eternity, Kainen finally got a fire going.

"Sankari, take over watch. Fly around the perimeter. I don't know where Arend went, or who else is coming," Kainen said nervously.

The Fairy huffed but fluttered up to search the area. Gimelli gasped as light broke out round their camp. Two Jaa warriors lay collapsed in pools of their own blood. One had their head knocked in by Crann. The other had Bellae's dagger sticking out at an angle with blood surging out all over her abdomen. Her white fur cape from the wolf-bear was matted and stained maroon. Her large weapon, the guandao, lay lifelessly next to the dead body of its former owner.

"I didn't mean to kill her," Bellae said between sobs. Gimelli was busy examining her sister and was relieved to find no cuts or injuries.

"It's not your fault," Gimelli soothed as she and pulled Bellae close and rocked her back and forth.

"What did you find?" Kainen questioned frantically as Sankari fluttered back.

"South of here a massive running battle took place. As far as I can see, the ground is littered with a string of dead Warriors of Jaa. I recognize Arend's handiwork for some, but not all. A couple had their heads sliced clean off."

"I guess we have been lucky to avoid their patrols for this long," Kainen said.

The wing beats of Arend prompted them to look up as he drifted down near the fire. A dark and filthy figure was writhing fiercely in his talons. The person was dropped to the ground with an unceremonious thud as Arend shrieked angrily. Kainen drew his kama weapon and stood in front of Gimelli and Bellae.

"Finally caught him," Arend said, bounding onto the ground. "He is one tough dude. I was circling around when I saw this guy fighting off a platoon of Jaa warriors. Their white caps and capes might work great for camouflage in the snow of the north, but out here? Easy targets."

"We should end this guy now!" Sankari said, fluttering closer.

"Just stay back," Arend commanded. "If he had a platoon of Jaa Warriors after him, I figure he must be important one way or the other."

Just then the person groaned and tried to stand up. Whoever he was, he was a dirty mess. Mud and grime covered him literally from head to toe and made his hair stand on end. Even through the grime you could see the look of determination in his eyes. With great effort he drew his sword and motioned a challenge for them to come at him.

"I've had a wicked week, but I am ready for more, so bring it on!"

"Wait!" Gimelli screamed. Gently she lowered Bellae to the ground before slowly moving Kainen to the side.

"What do you think you are doing?" Kainen asked.

She didn't answer but slowly moved towards the muddy figure. He instantly dropped his sword. It clattered to the ground as she proceeded to stand a foot away from him. A tense, awkward silence ensued as the two stared at each other. The girl known for smiles took the definition to new heights as she studied each mud-caked feature, tears of joy streamed down her face.

Several things went through his mind, but all he could come up with was, "Hey."

The two embraced as tears of bliss sprang anew from Gimelli.

Gimelli laughed. "I guess 'hey' is enough," she whispered, a small laugh intermixed with tears. Standing on her toes she softly recited:

> "There is nothing to make it happen hence,
> Against you I have no defense.
> Troubled world I rebuke,
> Save this feeling, no fluke.
> My soul quivers at the sight of you,
> Like hand upon lyre, my heart strummed true."

"That's pretty good. Not as poetic as 'hey,' but I'll let it slide."

She laughed. "Mine's from a poetry lesson. Don't you remember?"

"No, definitely slept through that entire class."

"I wanted to recite it to you forever but was too shy. Now, I seriously don't care."

"I, on the other hand, have always been able to intone to you my ballad of 'hey.' I won't hold it against you."

Gimelli chuckled as the muddy figure paused. "I'm glad I could get dressed up so nicely before you saw me again."

"You look perfect to me," Gimelli said, embracing him with renewed vigor.

"It's Scelto," Bellae whispered through her crying, this time prompted by hope. The fire's light, crackling in anger, softened on the couple, serenely transforming their united forms into shadows merging softly on the ground.

Scelto was glad it was dark, hoping it would hide the tears running down his mud-caked cheeks. He sighed happily, elated to be done trying to be something he was not for the Proliate and Princess Hamaza. He squeezed his old friend a little tighter. Even this far from Liberum, he had found his way home.

Scroll 8: Time is Getting Short

"We are spread too thin as it is!" Pumilus shouted in the Allied camp north of the Mohado Mire.

Friar had to admit the Dwarf looked exhausted. Dark bags hung like sagging quarter moons beneath his eyes. The Dwarves, skilled in prestidigitation from the Rebelde Plains, had been working overtime for months. From covering Sorea and her efforts west of the Tingij, to the troop movements from the three castles, they were spread thin and showing the strain.

Abhac rolled his eyes. The Aer Ridire Dwarf hated being there in the first place, his mind constantly drifting back to the battles raging in the skies above his homeland.

"Do you have any thoughts, Abhac? Ritari?" Friar questioned.

"My dragons and dragon riders are battling all day and night! The griffins by themselves are no problem, but when you add Magicians, and then wyverns, Watchers, we are literally fighting for our lives. When and how are we supposed to cross over here?"

"Time is getting short, and your boys need some rest," Ritari said. "Why don't you mix it up with some Saatana dragons? Let them come out for a few hours a night and then bring out your Vioma and Aer Ridire for the rest of the night. It will ease the Saatana into battle, and it won't be a big tip-off when you leave."

"Are you kidding?" Abhac erupted. "You want us to fly all night over hostile territory, with magical nets to detect us, and then expect us to engage the enemy? All of this while we entrust our home and families to the unpredictable Saatana dragons?"

Friar sighed. "There are no easy answers, my old friend. King Abernan and your ground troops have already taken a huge percentage of the Dwarves skilled in prestidigitation to protect their movements. In terms of the magical net, if you fly up one at a time, and then stay above it, would you avoid detection?"

Abhac nodded, "That might work. We have found the net is not everywhere. Luckily, they don't have that many Watchers."

"The several Vioma dragons serving as scouts around the Way of Trepas and the Rebelde Plains have been amazingly helpful. Your presence in the coming battles will also be essential," Friar said.

"The scout dragons have already gotten into some skirmishes," Abhac said.

"Yes, mostly Proliate, but increasingly some Jaa patrols," Friar said. "Well, good luck."

Abhac raised his tired eyes to the sky before running to his Vioma dragon. He would have a lot of flying to do through enemy-controlled skies to get the message to his troops in time.

Friar turned to Ritari. "You and I will move out to see how Sorea is coming along. The rest of the army will join us when the ship is unladed."

"What have you heard of the Southern Dwarves?" Ritari asked as they moved to their horses. After their protracted boat ride, both were reluctant to get into the saddle for the long ride north along the western edge of the Tingij Mountains.

"We both know they can't be trusted. I have offered to let them to join us but have misled them as to our intentions. They believe we will be attacking the Citadel from the south and east. If, as we suspect, they are feeding this information to the Proliate, it will add credence to our decoy movements."

"What if they agree to join our alliance? Are we going to accept? They could wreak havoc on our lines if…when they turn against us!" Ritari declared.

Friar sighed. His mind raced with their battle plan and the endless chances for it to fall into chaos. He shook his head to clear his mind, but it did not help. "I don't know. I have many ideas, but no answers."

Days later, Friar and Ritari came up to an outcropping of tall bushes and small trees. At first glance, they seemed natural enough, but moving closer, they had the distinct feeling they were being watched.

"Hello, Friar Pallium," a voice cried out, followed by whispering.

After a moment of silence, the trees and shrubs disappeared to reveal a line of white-robed Dwarves from the Rebelde Plains. They stretched their tired arms and necks as their loitsia sticks fell slackly by their sides. Several Knights came up to Friar, who had dismounted, and they embraced warmly.

"Varg," Friar said, relieved. "How are things going?"

"Fine," Varg answered. His squad had been the first to ship out from Liberum to assist Sorea. Varg had a wolf's head, the symbol of their squad, draped over his helmet and part of its pelt down his back. He carried a weapon called a tappaja—a savage axe sat on one side of a four-foot-long pole, while the other side held a hook used for grabbing and dismounting cavalry. A series of old scars ran across the left side of his face, slightly obscured by the large black patch he wore over his eye.

"Sorea is working insanely hard," Varg continued. "I wouldn't want to face a single one of her traps. Her newest invention—the Reka-Sla, or striker—is just brutal. It's not going to kill a lot of troops, but it will absolutely cause terror."

"How's she holding up?"

"Are you kidding? She's having the time of her life."

"This is going to work, Friar," Sorea said later that day. She sorely missed the upbeat attitude of her former squire Gimelli. Her new squire lacked all spontaneity, and it was starting to affect Sorea's sleep-deprived attitude.

"Ritari and I will be heading out with a small force to meet up with the Veli. Keep working hard. We'll be in touch," Friar said. The weight of worry on his shoulders prohibited him from returning her smile. *Can all of the pieces really come together?*

By the light of the moons Ritari, Friar, Lovag, Luchar, and a small force of Liberum Knights slunk through the massive walls of the Way of Trepas. After all of the sedate and tedious preparation, everything seemed to be moving too quickly now.

Scroll 9: North, South, Straight West?

"I know, Scelto," Gimelli said. "But Jumeaux really seems to have changed. He keeps contacting me, genuinely wanting to know how everyone is doing."

"That's what bothers me. He's after something. The Magicians obviously know about the prophecy. They want to get a hold of Bellae and manipulate her to get the Macht Crystals for themselves. How many times have the Magicians and griffins attacked you?"

"He seems sincere," Gimelli said, launching a weak, almost apologetic smile. "I'd rather the Magicians get the crystals than the White Wizard. Hey, what happens to the Macht Crystals when we find them anyway?"

Kainen shook his head. "No one knows. Remember, from here on out it is one step at a time. To protect the crystals, each person involved in the League is only aware of their small part. The end is a complete mystery."

"We all know Jumeaux," Scelto stated hotly, "and people don't change that quickly."

"He's still my brother. I have to believe he can change."

"My advice is talk to him, but don't give him any crucial details," Scelto said.

The two squires had been nearly inseparable since Scelto's return. He had recounted his harrowing ordeal from the time he was swept off the battlefield and taken to the Proliate outpost of Ragorsaf. When he outlined his decision to leave, he thought it best to only briefly mention Princess Hamaza. Even that slight admission was enough to garner a dirty look from Gimelli—that is until he recounted his run-in with torahammas milk and its deliquesce effect on his digestive system and urinary tract.

Next, he described the attack by Vioma dragons that killed the two Proliate guards and his horse. He hid by covering himself in mud and lying still in a small outcropping of trees north of Creber. He somehow wandered up through the Rebelde Plains and ended up running into a patrol from Jaa south of the Effeus Woods.

"I wondered if my bad luck was punishment for drinking so much of the deadly torahammas milk," he said, laughing. He outlined fighting a guerilla-style skirmish with the Jaainians, staying alive until Arend came to decimate the rest.

"Gimelli!" Arend yelled, swooping overhead. "You're next to go over the Leita River."

The League was well north of the Leita Falls, so they wouldn't immediately be swept over the edge of the falls if someone fell in. Crann had already swum across much further north.

"I guess I'm up."

"Hey," Scelto whispered. "I'm glad I found you."

"I'm just glad you cleaned up!" Gimelli said, laughing. "You smelled like torahammas shhh…well, let's just say it was bad!"

"Very funny."

Gimelli stood facing the river with her arms outstretched as Arend dove down and clasped her with his talons, jolting her forward. With the wind whipping by and droplets of water lashing, she flew towards the other side. Gimelli could see the strain of several skirmishes, and carrying the group was starting to get to Arend. He was being asked to shoulder a greater load than anyone else.

"Thank you, Arend," Gimelli said. "Wow, this side of the Leita River is like a different world!"

Arend nodded but paused to take a few deep breaths. "The side we just left is the Effeus Woods."

"The Effeus looked friendly, almost cheerful," Gimelli commented. "This side? Not so much."

"This side of the Leita River is the Arbre Fonce," Arend said.

"The Dark Forest," Kainen added.

"The trees look…sad," Gimelli said, gazing at the ebony conifer trees with needle-like leaves, which mixed with onyx oak trees bearing bark as dark as a starless night. "I see where the forest gets its name."

When they had all made it across, they sat to rest outside the gloomy forest. Bellae brought Arend some water from the river, and he drank a small amount.

"Is there anything else you need?" Gimelli asked.

Arend shook his head and lay back against the dark bark of one of the large conifer trees, one wing on either side.

"All right, we have several ways we can go. I think…" Kainen started.

"Straight through the forest and south of Lake Mali. Then, due west to Cappadocia," Sankari said testily. The smell of mushroom cheese soup, the sounds of the wildflowers swaying in the wind, along the slow-moving gorge rivers flashed through her homesick mind, urging the quickest route.

"The Dark Forest is not to be taken lightly," Kainen stated cautiously. "Everyone knows of the unusual stories that come out of here."

"Don't tell me you believe those tales used to scare children?" Sankari begged.

"They are *not* just stories. We should either travel north along the coast, or follow the Fada River until south of these woods before heading west. We could stay below the wetlands and then travel up the Hada River," Kainen said. Arend, who usually weighed in on such discussions, stayed quiet, exhaustion tugging on his eyelids.

"You mean freeze our arses off up north, or travel over the barren, rocky Hills of Feen? Or wait, even better, traverse the insect-infested Marskimaa Marsh while constantly being wet and miserable? Wow, those sound like really cool options that we should totally and unreservedly consider!" Sankari whined.

"There are too many strange tales about this Forest to—"

"What 'tales' are you talking about?" Gimelli interjected.

"There is a dark curse in this forest, and it will suck out the souls of all who enter," Kainen said with a shiver.

"Oh, how original," Sankari scoffed. "Dark woods mean dark curse. Of course, makes perfect sense."

"I'm *an* Elf, I *love* trees, but these woods give me a bad feeling. The darkness of this forest is deeper than the color of the bark."

"If we head north, my wings will fall off, and if we go south, it will add *weeks* to our travel time—not to mention the nasty bugs infesting the marshlands. If we get side-tracked or delayed on either course, we could starve," Sankari complained. She was hovering about three feet in front of Kainen with crimson streaking her cheeks, and her wings humming angrily.

"What do you think, Arend?" Kainen pleaded. He received no reply as the Eaglian stared off to the south.

"Arend? Arend!" Kainen finally shouted.

"There's going to be a battle, soon. The Knights and their Allies will attack…" Arend started.

Gimelli put her head in her hands. Her Knight, Sorea, would be heading into a major battle without her. She sighed heavily, unable to shake the belief that this so-called prophecy was a waste of time, unnecessarily putting her baby sister in trouble.

"We go back," Scelto said emphatically, Gimelli nodding her agreement. He, too, could only think of Ritari and the other Knights.

"We can't keep having this conversation," Kainen said. "I don't think you really get the importance of this prophecy. Would you leave this quest and throw away the chance to save Verngaurd?"

Rising up, Bellae moved to stand by Kainen. "This ends now. Kainen, Crann, Sankari, and I are going to Cappadocia to see Patuljak. If you want to come along, great. Otherwise, leave. If you stay, that's it, full stop, end of story." Without waiting for them to reply, she turned to Kainen. "Choose a path, and let's go."

Kainen stared at her, his pride bruised. Wasn't he supposed to be in charge? Before he could speak, Sankari flew to Bellae and nodded her encouragement. Crann instinctively went next to Bellae, nuzzling her gently. Lontas immediately got up to stand with his friend. She gave him a look of gratitude and squeezed his hand.

Arend turned, "Sorry, I'm with you all the way. It's just the idea that my dad will be fighting without me…it hurts."

Bellae nodded in understanding.

"Which way, Arend?" Kainen asked his friend.

"Sankari's from Cappadocia. I think she would know the most about the woods."

The Fairy nodded gratefully, a touch of gloating swelling in her scrunched up face.

"Alright," Kainen said reluctantly. "Through the forest."

Bellae hugged her sister and Scelto. "I hope you come, but if you don't, good luck. Love you," she said calmly. Scelto and Gimelli exchanged a look of disbelief.

"Hey, wait a minute. I told you before, I'm coming with you."

"Then, absolutely no more looking back."

"Okay, no more talk of leaving," Gimelli said, marveling at her sister's maturity.

Images of the friends he made while staying at Ragorsaf came flooding back to Scelto, especially his friend Velox. The Proliate were no longer a faceless enemy. He closed his eyes and wished the coming war would not take place. Scelto and Arend silently followed the rest of the League members: Bellae, Lontas, Gimelli, Sankari, Kainen, and Crann. Grym and Borb were blissfully asleep in Bellae's pocket.

Scroll 10: Where Light Goes To Die

"This can't be," Kainen said, panic lacing his words.

The others struggled to keep up as he darted forward, dodging in between branches and over forest debris. Suddenly, the forest became full of thick vines clinging and hanging from branches, and the trunks, normally black, had large sections of brown that gave the appearance they had two trunks, or at least some abnormal growth.

"What do your Elfish eyes see?" Scelto asked as they labored to catch up.

Silently scanning the forest, Kainen stood motionless, save his Elf eyes, which darted with anxiety-fueled swiftness.

The young Elf held up a finger to be quiet before slowly turning and whispering, "We need to get out of here. Slow and steady, back up."

Suddenly a vile moaning sound, at once perverse and seductive, erupted from a nearby tree.

"Oh, no," Kainen lamented as Crann began to buck nervously.

"What's going on?" Bellae asked.

"Fionain," Kainen hissed with contempt and fear entwining around the name. Movement exploded all around them in tune to a harsh cracking racket, which was quickly followed by a fiery slurping sound.

The many vines and part of the trees themselves shook and rumbled, seeming to split in two.

Crann began to shake his head vigorously. *Make it stop!*

"It's alright," Bellae said, even though she was unconvinced.

Scelto drew his sword as the group slowly backed up.

"Stay together and keep moving," Kainen stressed.

Gimelli screamed as several large vines whipped around her neck.

Snarling angrily, Scelto leapt forward, hacking at the creeping tentacles. As his blade sliced through, a hollow, metallic shriek pierced the air.

"Run!" Kainen screamed.

The League turned to run, but several writhing figures separated from the trees in front of them. The grinding sound came from these creatures disengaging from the tree they had been attached to, the moist sucking sound arising from thousands of little mouth-tendrils being withdrawn from deep within the bark of their arboreal victims.

"What the…" Arend squawked.

"Stop!" a rusty voice reverberated, but at that point they were surrounded with no option but to huddle together. Crann shook his head in distress, apparently hearing noises they could not.

As the creatures surrounding them wriggled their way closer, their shape became more distinct.

More tree than human, the arboreal creatures thrashed forward in a vibratory, squirming motion. Larger roots served as their half-dozen legs, while their humanoid top half was covered in moss and small branches. Instead of arms, a horde of thin vines writhed forward longingly where their upper limbs might have been. A vaguely human face seemed to be covered in thin branches and vines, creating a hauntingly eyeless appearance.

"No, no, no, no, no," Kainen seethed. *We can't die before we begin.*

"Invaders!" one of organisms wailed.

After a painful fragment of silence, Scelto looked to Kainen and Arend, who stood staring in horror. Sighing, he finally spoke, "We just need to pass through in peace. We will leave your forest immediately."

His words sent a spasm of activity through the plant-like beasts. Their flailing appendages wriggled and flailed aggressively, and a loud, but almost melodic, grating sound harmonized around them as their tendrils connected in communication.

"These creatures are called Fionain, and I didn't think they still existed. Do you understand what they are saying, Bellae?" Kainen whispered.

Closing her eyes and concentrating, she could hazily pick up a few bits of words out of their melodic chatter. "Sort of. It's not very clear."

"Quick, what are they saying?" Kainen pleaded.

She exhaled, squeezing her eyes even tighter in concentration. "First, they said we are alive—seems obvious, but apparently that's important to them. Then something about getting us to leave…they want us to go…" She opened her eyes and cocked her head to the side in confusion.

"Where?" Kainen asked desperately as their chattering language started to die down.

"It's weird, something about where light goes to die?"

"Light goes to die? What does that mean?" Scelto asked.

Kainen thought a moment. "They want us to go west, where the suns set."

Figure 7: The League has run into the terrifying Fionain. These tree-humanoid creatures walk on six large trunks and have hundreds of lean branches for arms.

Just as their grinding clamor of speech started to die down, two more of their flagellating forms pushed their way towards the League.

"Uh, oh," Bellae said as the original Fionain backed up, creating an impromptu track that led directly to the two approaching vine creatures.

"What?" Kainen implored.

"From what I can get, those two don't want to let us leave, but the others do," Bellae stated. "Most keep saying we're alive and if we intend to leave, should be left unharmed."

"Survive," one of the original Fionain finally seethed, the undulating vines of his arm wriggling together to point towards the two menacing forms standing in their way.

"Survive?" Gimelli repeated. At her word, their loud grinding language exploded in anger. Their creeping projections threshed in agitated jerking movements.

Mixed within their harshly dissonant communication burst a word they could understand, "Survive!"

"I think they are saying if get past those two, we can leave," Bellae said. "Those two disagree about letting us head to where the light dies."

"Why do they want us to head west?" Lontas asked.

"Right now, I would go any direction to get away from these Fionain," Gimelli answered.

Arend drew out his new throwing darts, courtesy of Dwarf blacksmiths. "How do we kill these things?"

"No idea, but let's try for their heads. If myth serves, these parasites don't have a heart or circulatory system like us but instead use their mouth tentacles to tap into a tree's xylem and phloem layers, leeching nutrients out of trees," Kainen said.

"So, no body shots? Got it," Scelto seethed, swinging his sword in hostile arcs.

"Answer?" a Fionain hissed.

"We accept," Kainen said loudly, before whispering, "Not much choice."

A gravelly scratching sound ensued as all the Fionain, save the two standing against them, linked their heaving vines, creating a wall of vine-like appendages and an impromptu fighting arena that meant they had no escape, save through battle.

"Bellae, Sankari, and Lontas, stay back with Crann in support. Arend and Scelto, to the left, Gimelli and I will take the one on the right," Kainen said.

Gimelli and Kainen slowly moved forward as the two Fionain stood in place with their innumerable vine tentacles rippling in agitated gestures.

"Loose!" Kainen yelled as he and Gimelli let several arrows fly in quick succession.

Each one was harmless and knocked down by the swirling, flailing appendages that served as arms.

Arend joined in with his throwing darts, also without success.

After several more failed attempts, Kainen held out his hand to stop.

"Let's not waste the arrows."

Retreating to store their archery equipment with Crann, the squire and Elf drew their swords. Bellae drew her short sword and eyed Lontas, who, shaking his head, went to grab a sword off Crann.

"Oh, I feel so super safe knowing the klutz has a sword," Grym squeaked. *"These vine-guys seem like a super bunch of fun. Let me know if we survive."*

Lontas swallowed hard and held out his sword while tentatively moving his tight legs. Although healing well, he still had some stiffness.

"We've got this, Lontas," Bellae said.

He nodded.

"Let's do waves, one by one," Arend stated.

"Agreed," Kainen said before they regrouped to explain the plan to the squires.

Before they could finish describing the strategy, Crann neighed a warning, and they turned to see the two humanoids heaving forward with a guttural growl.

"Gimelli, let's go!" Kainen yelled.

The two sprinted forward.

"Right!" Kainen yelled, noticing the attacking creature on the right had moved out in front.

Scelto and Arend let them get ahead, only slowly moving forward and to the left.

Gimelli lunged, hacking at the whirling tentacle-like vines swirling around her. Several of her strikes made hits, and the Fionain screeched a grating cry. Focusing on Gimelli, the creature's creeping tendrils exploded out from its body, quickly surrounding the squire.

She screamed as her sword was thumped out of her hands. With her defenses down, vines by the hundreds coiled around her. Several flagellating vines came together to form a stump-like hammer, slamming into her chin. With a whimper she went limp. Sensing her weakness, the creature's vines instantly lashed around her neck while others continued coiling themselves around her whole body. Gimelli came to, her eyes flashing wide in utter panic just before more vine appendages whipped around to cover her face completely.

Enraged, Sankari careened forward while pulling out her peccary tusk sword. Once close to the squirming squire, she began frantically cutting at the vines encircling Gimelli.

Kainen had used this time to sheathe his sword and run towards the wall of Fionain hemming them in. Using the deep grooves of his hands, he quickly scaled the bark-like texture of one of the creatures until he came face to face with its hollow black eye sockets. Shouting, he pushed off and drew his sword while twisting around. Once facing the attacking Fionain, he brought his sword down, crunching, then squishing into the vine-humanoid, sending a gush of thick secretions spraying out, coating the young Elf.

A sickening howl of pain from the creature pierced the air as Scelto came hurtling into the fight. With a crazed look in his eyes, he began viciously hacking at the tentacles encasing Gimelli. Grey sap splattered everywhere with each vine severed.

"Watch it!" Sankari bellowed, nearly cut in two by one of his strikes.

Her distraction was costly, as several vines shot forward, impacting her hard enough to fling her ten feet backwards. Her left wing fluttered weakly, bruised, and the air was knocked out of her lungs. Her head throbbing, she rolled over onto her stomach before blacking out.

Arend was now on the scene but struggling and hesitant due to both the thick forest canopy and Scelto's raging sword strikes.

Bellae let out a low rumble.

"What?" Lontas asked but looked up and saw for himself. "A Nishi? Here?"

Bellae nodded as they watched the ghostly specter float ominously, whispering frantically, behind the Fionain that had been hanging back. "That's why those two stand against us. They're being poisoned by that wraith."

Wordlessly, she moved forward, Lontas and Crann closely following. Crann flicked his head nervously from side to side, keeping a wary eye on the Fionain fencing them in. By this time the Nishi had disappeared, and the second Fionain was quickly making his way forward. This one was larger and let out a horrifying howl of jarring rage. Rushing forward, he instantly attacked Scelto. Several of his vine appendages whipped at the large squire, who roared at the pain.

The first humanoid chattered a grinding howl before thrashing his viney extremities towards the young Elf struggling to remove his sword, still impaled deeply into the neck of the severely injured creature. Kainen's thick bark skin easily absorbed the lashing, which would have severely cut human skin.

Kainen flinched under the shower of sap and gore exploding out as he violently twisted his sword in hopes of threshing out enough space to remove it. With a grating groan, the first Fionain finally started to fall. Using the momentum, Kainen took a few steps along the creature before pushing off with his feet, flying towards the second attacking creature. Stretching out his sword behind his head, he arched his back while flying through the air, preparing for a fearsome blow and hoping to end this battle quickly.

The new Fionain jogged to his right, his thick branch-like legs reminding them of a scurrying spider, before bending, twisting his upper body backwards, parallel to the ground while his legs bolted him forward until he was horizontal under the airborne Kainen. Hundreds of tendrils from either side of his body flagellated upward, completely mummifying Kainen in viney fingers. His sword fell limply as the creature savagely rotated his body upright. The tendrils encasing Kainen's face parted, showing his expression of fear. The Fionain opened his mouth, briefly the inky aperture matched his coal-black eyes, but the gaping ebony was obliterated as hundreds of thrashing tendrils wormed their way out, attaching to the Elf's face. Kainen's eyes widened further in terror as a muffled scream leaked in between the vines spiraling to cover his face.

Arend shot up, flying talons forward, aiming for the creature's head. Two of the Fionain's larger root limbs threshed up, clasping the Eaglian's ankles before using his vine-like fingers to brace Kainen's body. He then somersaulted his entire arboreal form in a three-hundred-sixty-degree flip, whipping the Eaglian around, slamming his head hard into the forest floor.

Arend whimpered briefly before going still, knocked out. Kainen was becoming paler by the second as the Fionain seemed to be sucking blood from his face via his squirming mouth cirri. Bellae shrieked forward, holding her small sword. Flashes of Finn dying, the Nishi, the burden of the prophecy, all melted into searing anger. Twisting her body, she swung her small blade with all her might. The edge of the dagger cut deeply into one of the root appendages that served as a leg.

She howled as a limb from her left swept her feet out. At the same time, one from the right slammed into her side. Bellae was flipped over before falling hard. Lontas exploded forward, slashing at one of the roots that was about to come down on his friend's head. Several smaller vines and larger legs squirmed towards Lontas.

"Scelto, help!" Lontas cried as he was quickly overwhelmed, inhumed within the tightening limbs.

Scelto dutifully checked Gimelli, whom he had recently freed from her own arboreal tomb, courtesy of the now-dead Fionain. Secure in the knowledge Gimelli was breathing, the large squire bolted towards the second humanoid. He arrived at the same time as Crann, the large horse had rushed forward before turning around to use his whip-like tail, part weapon, part defense.

Scelto, with sword, and Crann, with lashing tail, began fending off a blistering series of flailing attacks by the Fionain's vine arms. Bellae was up now, adding her dagger to their weapons to fend off the dizzying, squirming vine attacks. Crann slowly backed towards the creature, the braided weapons that made up his tail repulsing the repeated assaults from the Fionain. The horse neighed a request to Bellae, and she complied by howling wildly and charging directly at the chaparral trunk of the beast.

The Fionain shifted its focus to the charging squire. With a stream of strikes, Bellae was quickly knocked down. Before she hit the floor, multiple vine tentacles were already wrapping her up. Crann, taking advantage of the distraction, stormed in, hurtling a double back kick. One hoof hit low, shattering a root-leg, while the other thudded against its trunk. Howling in pain, the creature released Kainen, who fell flaccidly to the ground. Several close octopus-like root legs heaved towards the horse, while dozens of lashing vines roared forward. Several hits landed on the horse's already sore shoulders. Crann whinnied in pain as he was flipped onto his side. The roots repeatedly slammed down onto the horse's ribs.

Bellae was able to fight back up and together with Scelto they charged forward. After fending off a few attacks, Bellae was sent to the floor again. Reaching in her pocket, she pulled out Grym and Borb. After whispering to them, she tossed them high onto the Fionain's trunk. The two mice quickly scurried upwards, once reaching its head, they began clawing and chewing on the guard-like twigs in front of the Fionain's cavernous eyes, causing it to shriek in agony. Sankari, who had finally recovered, quickly joined in, fluttering around his head, desperately avoiding the jiggling attacks directed at her.

As Crann and Bellae struggled to get up, Scelto bolted forward. Ignoring the dozens of thrashing attacks, he viciously stabbed his dagger hilt deep into the bark-hide of the creature with his left hand. Once it stopped penetrating, he used the dagger as a handle, surging his body upwards and searing his sword up into the head of the Fionain—narrowly missing the mice. A surge of milky secretions flooded down Scelto's sword, splattering onto his face and swamping off the two mice.

The creature's body tensed in jerking spasms before crashing towards the ground. Scelto withdrew his sword. Falling and riding on the creature's arborescent trunk, he repeatedly slammed his sword deep into the face of the Fionain. Each thrust sent a torrent of milky fluid surging out.

After the tree-creature's body battered down, the only noise was heavy breathing and few slithering death thrashes of the Fionain's wiry body.

After a few moments, the row of Fionain fencing them in untangled their appendages and began to chant in their grinding howl. Scelto retrieved his dagger and sheathed his sword before running to Gimelli as Bellae gathered her chittering mice.

"Scelto tried to kill us, while we were trying to help!"

"I know, I know," Bellae said.

"We're fighting for our lives, and by the way, we were turning the tide when he tried to cut us in two!" Grym squeaked angrily.

"I owe you guys."

Kainen tried to stand up but instantly fell back down. Bellae froze, his pale complexion reminding her of Finn as he lay dying. Before she could move to help him, the surrounding Fionain all stomped forward. Using their hundreds of tentacles, they all pointed towards the west and chanted even louder.

"Bellae?" Scelto asked, helping the groggy Gimelli up.

"They are angry—"

"Obviously, what do they want?" Scelto interrupted.

"They say we must go to where the light dies. West. We need to go now."

Bellae moved to prop up Kainen as best as she could. Once close to his face, Bellae could see thousands of small punctures through his thick bark-like skin. Lontas rushed over to Arend, where Sankari was busy trying to rouse him.

"Let me help," Lontas pleaded as the incensed Fairy stopped fruitlessly pulling on a feathery ear. Crann joined Lontas, and together they managed to get him to his talons. Slowly, the League limped westward, the undulating Fionain agitatedly writhing behind them, relentlessly herding them forward.

"I don't know how much further Kainen can go before he collapses," Bellae said, although the sweat trickling down her own brow and quake within her muscles belied she wasn't far from exhaustion.

"No choice," Scelto replied. "Fighting two of those things nearly killed us—no way can we stand against hundreds."

"Bellae!" a sordid voice called out from the forest.

"What the?" Sankari asked.

"Just ignore it," Bellae huffed as Kainen moaned.

"Bellae!" the voice called out again.

"Seriously, what is that?" Sankari asked.

"Give it up, you hag!" Bellae screamed, ignoring the Fairy's question.

"Oh, look at you! Getting a little spicy as you move through this pointless and doomed odyssey. You do know that once you get the crystals, my master is just going to gut you and take them?" a Nishi uttered, suddenly appearing before the weary league.

"You could just lay down, give up, and let those viney tree freaks kill you! All your troubles would be over in a quick moment. Doesn't that sound much better than months of torture? Hmm?"

Bellae softly laid Kainen down. As the Fionain behind them began wailing for them to keep moving, Bellae lurched forward, slamming her forearm talismans into the specter.

With a piercing howl, the Nishi evaporated.

"Those things keep getting more annoying," Lontas declared as Bellae picked up Kainen and started forward again.

"Are you going to tell us what that thing was?" Sankari asked.

"That's a story for another day," Lontas replied.

After slogging forward for what seemed like hours, they came upon a string of wooden masks hanging down by the hundreds. As they approached, it became clear the figures were hung in a long straight line as far as they could see in either direction running north to south. Carved wood, branches, and twigs had been molded and shaped to look like horned monsters. Although not identical, they all had two horns with twigs roughly wrapped around them to look like thorns. Ghastly teeth were roughly carved above sharp, triangular chins and below cavernous eyes.

"Well, those are creepy," Bellae said.

"What do they mean?" Gimelli asked. "Kainen?"

His eyes fluttered with exhaustion. His desiccated mouth was so dry it felt almost numb. "Not sure," he finally announced.

A deep howling noise came from behind them.

"I don't think…the Fionain…like those things either," Lontas huffed, fatigue weighing him, and his words, down.

As Lontas finished speaking, Arend collapsed. Sankari rushed over to try to help heave the Eaglian up. However, Lontas could barely stand himself. His legs were burning, and his sides ached. Bellae's shaking legs gave way, and she too buckled, with Kainen toppling weakly on her.

"The vine monsters are hanging back," Grym said, peeking out of Bellae's pocket.

"Is it safe to rest here?" Scelto asked Bellae.

"I'm not sure, but don't think we have much choice."

The Fionain had stopped moving forward, forming a line just before the frightening masks, but their tendril arms fluttered in wild agitation as a low, rumbling growl seethed from deep within their bodies.

Bellae and Gimelli saw to Arend, Crann, and Kainen while the others kept watch. When they finished, fatigue overcame hunger, and the group fell deep into sleep, with Crann, who needed little slumber, keeping watch.

"We have to move," Scelto said. "We are out of food and water."

"I agree," Kainen stated. His face was looking better after a couple of days of rest, but he still looked pale. "Arend?"

"Yes. But why does my ear still hurt?" the Eaglian wondered.

Sankari blushed, abashed at having pulled on it quite severely to wake him.

Scroll 11: Cool Embrace

"Now this is cool," Lontas said later that evening as a deluge swirled around them in a relentless effort to soak everything. They had walked slowly all day, their lack of nutrition hampering their recovery from battling the Fionain.

Sankari scoffed but said nothing.

Lontas was sitting with his back leaning against Bellae, Scelto, and Gimelli. He was speaking about the raised water barrier Kainen had constructed. After piling up a mound of dirt, he laid sticks in a criss-cross pattern, topping it all with leaves and a cloak so the League could huddle under it. As long as they didn't get up, their backsides stayed dry even though it was pouring. The sky thundered angrily as if upset at the idea they would dare to try to stay even a little dry.

"At least we have our water skins refilled," Gimelli said, trying her hardest to be cheerful.

The next morning arrived without a thought or consideration for how tired, hungry, stiff, and soaked they were.

"This is one barren forest," Crann neighed to Bellae. *"I scouted around, and there is literally nothing to eat. No grass for me, and no berries or mushrooms for you."*

All of them were famished. The food from the Dwarves was finished, and as they moved further west, the forest became eerily quiet and increasingly sterile. Kainen had taken the last watch and was regretting the decision to enter the Dark Forest. *I just hope we don't pay for my mistake with our lives.*

"You don't even hear birds anymore," Arend commented.

"We've got a long journey ahead and need some food. Let's spread out and look. We'll meet back here," Kainen stated.

"Is splitting up a good idea?" Arend cautioned.

Kainen shrugged his shoulders. "We haven't seen anyone since the Fionain, and we are getting weak from hunger. Not sure we have a choice."

I seriously hope there are no lihumari, Lontas thought. *No sitting on logs!*

Kainen and Sankari headed south. Bellae, Lontas, and Arend went north, while Gimelli and Scelto headed due west. Crann stayed at the camp.

After walking for over an hour, the sweet smell of something cooking drifted up to Gimelli and Scelto's noses. Saliva began unconsciously welling up as they became cautiously optimistic, reminded of their hunger by their angrily grumbling stomachs.

Gimelli readied her bow and Scelto drew his sword as they carefully continued. Following the aroma, they came to a clearing lined with unusual structures. There were six huts around a large central cooking pit. They had flat roofs with various shrubs and plants growing on top of the structures. If Arend had flown overhead, he wouldn't have noticed them.

What are they hiding from? Scelto wondered.

Just then, an elderly woman emerged from the closest dwelling to their left. Walking towards the flaming pit in the center of the group of huts, she began stirring a large cooking cauldron suspended over the fire.

"Time for your famous smile," Scelto said encouragingly. He sheathed his sword, and she removed the arrow from her bow.

"Hello there," Gimelli said, smiling.

The woman froze. She wore a black snood to cover the top of her head and grey hair. Her shawl was black, as was the dress underneath. Around her neck hung a large red scarf. She had pale blue eyes peering out from the wrinkled and sagging skin of her face. Her lips were a dark red, glazed with a hint of black. A couple small sores dotted her left cheek. The two squires continued towards her, but she remained silent and unmoving.

"Hello! I'm Gimelli, and this is Scelto. We're making our way to Cappadocia. Could you tell us how far we have left?"

When they were a few feet away from her, they stopped, still salivating at the smell wafting up from the pot. They could hear a rolling boil but couldn't see into it.

"Do you understand us?" Scelto ventured.

The woman turned her head slightly, her eyes darting from Gimelli to Scelto as if she was finally noticing them. Without a word, she rushed back into her house, leaving the squires confused and uncertain.

"Maybe she doesn't understand the common tongue?" Gimelli guessed.

"Probably. This place is crazy remote."

Before they could formulate a plan, a man walked out of the same house.

"Welcome, welcome, welcome!" the muscular man said cheerfully. "You will have to excuse my mother Zlota here. She's terribly shy, and we don't get many visitors."

Gimelli nodded before introducing herself and Scelto again.

"My name is Ichor," the man said with a smile as big as Gimelli's. His garb appeared inappropriate and incredibly clean for life this deep in the woods. Cracking his neck, he gently straightened his black, thick-collared undershirt, which sat dutifully under an ornate black surcoat. He wore elaborate armored shoulder pauldrons. Using black leather gloves, he brushed off his coat. His boots were spotless and polished but seemed a little long and comically wide for his height.

Scelto leaned in, "He's dressed for royalty as opposed to a day of scavenging for food. Something's off, should we get out of here?"

Gimelli shook her head but couldn't help staring. His black hair was long on top and combed over to his right while the sides of his head were shaved—a small stubble popping through. His smile showed blindingly pristine teeth. His ebony eyes sat in cavernous shadows among chiseled, handsome features. His immaculate beard was tightly trimmed, its neatness standing in stark contrast to the unruly facial hair of the Dwarves.

"You're just in time for breakfast, if that is of interest to you?"

"We would be very grateful," Gimelli said, her stomach lurching and rolling expectantly. "We are traveling with some friends as well…"

"Wonderful. Why don't we take care of you two first and then we can go deal with them?"

"That sounds good," Scelto said, hunger overruling caution.

"Scelto, would you mind gathering some more firewood? You can go with my…um, cousin, Liha. Cousin Liha!" he yelled sharply.

A frail-looking girl with hazel-red eyes came out from one of the houses to the right. She wore a black cloak with red inside lining. She, too, wore a thick red scarf around her neck. Her jet-black hair was straight and long.

"Cousin, you have some jelly on your face," Ichor said. "Freshly made!" he added enthusiastically.

Liha quickly wiped her mouth and chin before pulling her veil up around her pale face, then motioned for Scelto to follow.

Scelto hesitated, looking at Gimelli.

"Please, Scelto. You could repay the kindness of a meal and help Liha," Ichor encouraged calmly. "Gimelli, could help my elderly mother, Zlota? We'll be eating in no time."

Gimelli, not wanting to be rude, nodded, and Scelto reluctantly went off with Liha.

Figure: 8: Liha, cousin to the mysterious Ichor, agrees to help Scelto collect some firewood.

"We have a few minutes, as they have a bit of a walk. There is a grove of oak trees not too far from here. We try not to burn these pine trees, as the creosote, that's an oily tar, builds up on the fire pit walls and can even start on fire itself. Why don't you go in? My mother will see you are taken care of," Ichor said.

Gimelli hesitated.

"Why are you dressed so nicely?" she questioned.

"Ah, this is a family heirloom, and I like wearing it on occasion—it reminds me my family of warriors was once large and powerful. Please, she's getting older by the minute, you know," he added with a blindingly white smile. Suddenly, his demeanor seemed forged and something in the way he looked at her gave her an unwelcome chill.

How could I not have seen this before? she wondered as her stomach surged and rumbled. *Could hunger and not wanting to be impolite have blinded me?*

Her eyes searched desperately for Scelto, but he was already swallowed by the darkness of the forest. *Should I call out? Am I imagining things?*

"Please, go in. I will leave you ladies to it while I enjoy the cool air out here for a while, if that makes you more comfortable."

She's just an old lady, Gimelli tried to reassure herself upon entering, the idea of being disrespectful overcoming her judgment. It was sparsely decorated with only a table, two chairs, and one comfortable-looking divan.

"Siiit there," Ichor's mother instructed, her voice sputtering from sparse use.

Gimelli moved to the divan that the elderly women had pointed to. She sat as the woman began to quickly light several excessively large incense burners. Smoke rapidly began fill the hut. Gimelli blinked, as time seemed to slow.

As the physical smoke began to wrap her head in murkiness, Gimelli's brain seemed cloaked in a dull haze, preventing her from thinking clearly. She tried to take a deep breath to sharpen her mind but only ended up inhaling more of the thick mist capped with a heavy smell of incense.

She gasped as the smoke in front of her seemed to coil into the form of a winged serpent. The vapor creature moved to stare directly at her, its tongue flickering in and out rapidly as its eyes widened.

What's happening? Am I dreaming?

Before she could think more about it, the smoky form darted into her nostrils. She shook her head and jumped up onto the back of the couch. Looking around in a panic, she saw only a thick fog of smoke encircling her as the old woman cackled.

"Scared of a little vapor, are you?" the woman said, laughing again.

After another thick breath, Gimelli felt dazed, sliding down on the divan, she struggled to remember what had scared her.

Glancing up, Gimelli did a double take. The old woman's form moved so fast it blurred into a rapidly moving apparition lighting a large number of incense burners that she hadn't seen before. Gimelli closed her eyes and shook her head before turning back to Ichor's mother. She could not make the weird scene go back to normal. As soon as the woman lit one of the incense burners her silhouette zoomed to the next. When she finished, the elderly woman turned back to Gimelli and released a decadent smile.

Gimelli focused on the woman's teeth. Her yellow nubs were all filled to a point. Seeing Gimelli stare at her horrid teeth, the old woman's smile broadened. Gimelli's head recoiled in horror as she saw two black, slithering, fang-like appendages sticking out from her gums and writhing hungrily, struggling towards the squire like insect antennae.

"Oops!" Zlota said, quickly covering her mouth. "Just sit back, relax, and *ENJOY!*" On the word "enjoy" her voice became gravelly and husky while her head shook violently from side to side. A deep chill shivered through Gimelli's body.

"Soak up the ambience. I'll be back," Ichor's mother added.

A warning, deep in her brain, screamed for her to get out. Before she could act, the thick incense, as if sensing her rising determination, swarmed aggressively on all sides of her, before congealing angrily into a thick cloud at the idea that she would leave. In a tempest it whorled around and around her, two large streams pouring up into her nostrils, making her feel incredibly sleepy. The signal to get up faded as her head began to whirl.

Her nose tickled, giving her the urge to sneeze and cough at the same time. After a small hack, she couldn't help but take in another deep breath. Her eyelids grew heavy, and the scream in her head descended into a vague notion.

Interesting, no beds, she thought. Settling deeper into the divan, she began to consider the room. *Where do they sleep?*

The idea of keeping her eyelids open suddenly seemed arduous, and they closed halfway as the aromatic smoke entrenched itself in every nook and cranny of her mind.

She abruptly noticed a large, rectangular pit dug in the corner of the dirt floor, curiosity prompting her eyes to open fully. It looked large enough for someone to crawl into. She instantly remembered the back of the women's clothes and how dirty they had seemed. Another distant warning flashed deep in her brain.

Does she sleep down there? Gimelli wanted to stand up, but the fog of incense hovered thickly, and the idea seemed arduous, so she settled into glancing around the room. Looking up, she saw a peculiar, four-foot wooden beam suspended from the ceiling. Wrapped around it was a thick red rope with innumerable scratches and claw marks on it. She focused on the many loose fibers hanging down in shreds. Her murky thought processes were just trying to figure out what that bar could be used for when Ichor entered.

"Ah, I see my mother is up to her old tricks again. She loves incense. Anyway, I'm ready for a hearty breakfast," he said in a cheerful tone.

"Me…too…wait. Where is…" Gimelli started. Her brain felt muddled and tired. "I mean…I means…? What was I talking about?"

"I love a good breakfast, don't you?" he asked, moving closer. "There are no more people in these woods you know. Now, if you can believe it, we have also almost completely cleared our section of the forest of animals and birds.

"So imagine the lovely surprise when you turned up," he said, flashing a devious smile, framed by perfectly white teeth. We have an uneasy truce with the Fionain. They stay to the east and we to the west, but increasingly hunger drives us into their lands and the Rebelde Plains.

"Oh dear, I think I see a little tick on your head. Those little buggers are just all over the place, one of many hazards of venturing into these dark woods. If it's okay, I will just remove it for you," he said, taking off his gloves.

"You…can you…see it from there?" Gimelli asked, her eyes fluttering wearily as the thick incense sat like a viscid fog in the room.

Ichor's form blurred, instantly moving to sit next to her. Gimelli's tethered mind stared incredulously.

"You—you, and your mother are quick…" she drawled. Even her words seemed to be getting fatigued in the hazy room. "Why you no slow with smoke fog?" she said with great effort, feeling more exhausted with each passing second.

His left arm went up and landed softly on her neck. Gently, but firmly, he began to massage her back. A stinging fear shivered down her entire body at his touch.

I should get up. The thought briefly rose to touch her consciousness, but its strength failed, sinking back down again under the weight of the intoxicating fumes.

The area he was touching became cold and tingly. She was about to protest when it suddenly became warm and pleasant. A relaxed feeling colonized her mind. She could not see it, but small worm-like tentacles were extending out from Ichor's palm, each cord-like appendage slithering as it grew. Every one of them was lined with hundreds of smaller black tendrils splaying out and excreting an oily anesthetic, numbing her skin.

His forearm was bulging and contracting as it propelled additional tentacles forward through his hand, each one foraging for virgin skin on which to ravage. He let out a little gasp of pleasure as thousands of tiny needles emerged from the tendrils and began piercing into her skin, each one hungrily siphoning her blood. His eyes closed, and he sat back to enjoy his feast as more and more of the tentacles spun wildly out from his hand, diving under her cloak, searching for fresh fleshy territory to numb and mine for blood. Soon they would move around and into her carotid artery and the real feast would begin.

Figure: 9: Flawlessly dressed and groomed, Ichor seems out of place in such a remote village. His blindingly white teeth send notification he feeds through tentacles and fangs from his hand.

Ichor smiled energetically.

"Teeth…so…white," Gimelli whispered before her eyes snapped shut.

"Oh, thanks! They have never been stained by food or drink."

He slipped off his large shoes. Gimelli, hearing the thud, briefly opened her eyes. With a little gasp, she realized his feet were deformed claws. His ankles were small but had four large claws jutting out, each one ending in a sharp talon. There was a fifth, larger one sticking out from the back.

"After I feast, if you turn into a vampire like me, dearie," Ichor said in a muculent voice, "I will build you a perch." He pointed up, and an evil, guttural laugh belched out of him. Even in her weakened state, Gimelli startled at its harsh and raspy sound.

"If you don't turn, well…we have too many zombies to feed already, so my undead friends will be happy to feast on your flesh. They'll complain about me draining too much blood, but I have needs."

A small commotion arose from outside the hut. Ichor ignored the noise. *It's probably Liha coming back from getting rid of that wretched and annoying boy.* His minions would feast on his decaying body. "With such good edibles, my henchmen will have no need to hunt for a long time. Thank you for that."

In actuality, it wasn't Liha, but two of the undead villagers scuffling around the cooking cauldron. Scelto, in fact, was the one returning from the trip into the forest.

His bloodied sword drawn, he stood sheltered just inside the forest. The streaks of crimson coating his blade were fresh and plentiful enough to still be dripping. Staying at the fringe of the clearing, he could see the old woman stirring the pot. The villagers were standing with large platters around the cauldron, half feasting greedily, half scuffling.

"More, now!" one of them yelled hungrily. "We had to travel all the way to the Rebelde Plains to get this one, and I'm famished."

The dirt and grime coating the coarse villagers who were now crudely gulping and loudly chomping on their meal made Ichor's pristine appearance even more striking. *We should have known something was wrong.*

He carefully began making his way around the back of the closest hut, gently running his hand along the wall for balance.

Boom!

Something slammed against the cabin's wall, startling him, the vibration tingling through his hand sent him jumping backwards. A loud rattling of chains being jerked and heaved angrily was followed by a horrifying, inhuman howl. A series of chittering shrieks and screams erupted from inside the hut, sending a fiery tingle of fear down his spine.

Once the racket petered out, he quietly moved forward again. Carefully peering around the corner, Scelto was astonished that Ichor's mother and the other villagers did not seem concerned about the tumultuous clamor from the hut. Tilting his head in confusion, he watched the woman grab tongs instead of a ladle as she dished large chunks of food onto plates instead of bowls—odd for a cauldron of soup.

Feeling lightheaded, he realized he was breathing fast, and his heart twittered rapidly against his chest. *Calm down,* he repeated to himself, forcing his lungs into slow, inhaling deep breaths as quietly as he could. He was still shaking from the unprovoked attack in the woods. Absently, he rubbed the spot on his arm where Liha had bitten him.

A din of howls and screams again erupted from the hut. Scelto froze at the barely recognizable word swirling amongst the shrieking, "Flesh!"

The idea it could be humans, and not some creatures tied up, made his knees wobble. A small hole, not big enough to be a window, was just in front of him. *I have to look,* he told himself. His breath quickened, his heart raced again, but he could only stand frozen in place as the rattling of chains and wailing unnervingly continued.

Finally, he moved forward, the smell hit him before he could see anything. He retched as a putrid mix of rotting flesh and excrement forced its way into his nostrils. Slowly, he leaned forward, first one eye and then the other squinting through the small opening. *So many,* he thought, struggling to understand the sights and smells violating his senses.

Dozens of men and women were chained to thick metal poles pounded deep into the ground. As he looked closer, he saw many had large sores scattered about their faces and a sickly, yellow-green hue to their skin, making him wonder if they really were human. While their ragged, bilious appearance made him feel sick, it was the sight and smell of human waste flung about the hut that made him retch again.

Stepping back, he tried to calm his ragged nerves. Looking to those around the cauldron, he now noticed a few small lesions on their skin, which were not quite a normal hue but also not as yellowish-green as those chained in the hut.

His mind whipped back to when, out of nowhere, Liha hit him on the head with a log before clawing and biting at him. After trying to throw her aside several times, he had been forced to draw his sword and slash her across her lower chest and abdomen. Maimed and bleeding, she continued lunging after him. A terrifying image of two black fangs whipping hungrily from her gums as she bared her teeth came flashing back.

Stepping forward, he peered into the hut. He jumped back as one of the chained prisoners stared hungrily at him, his eyes wide with fury and cavernous with hunger. Several deep gashes and oozing sores littered his face. His hair was sparse and thin, and grimy, filed teeth flashed below the two thrashing black fangs sticking out of his gums as he chomped hysterically, ravenously. *I wish I had been hallucinating those black things.*

"Flesh!" he howled. The word sent a storm of screeches and screams burgeoning from the hut.

As rattling chains, inhuman growls, and raging screams continued to explode from the hut, an image of Gimelli flashed in his head. An immense ache soared within him at the thought of her being injured, or worse. Panic surged through his brain.

His eyes frantically scanned for his friend when a deep cackle and loud slopping drew his attention back to the cauldron. The woman sloshed something dripping in green sauce onto one of the men's platters. Scelto gasped at the sight of a human arm and hand, wet and wrinkled. The man hungrily bit into it, ripping and tearing the flesh from it as juice splattered over his face and clothes. The writhing black fangs were hungrily shoveling food into the brute's mouth.

Cannibals! He tried to calm his mind and come up with a plan. *Should I attack? That would attract too much attention, and I don't know how many more are in the other huts, or if they are also chained up. Just get to where that immaculate freak had invited Gimelli to help his loony mother. She has to be there.*

He moved around the outside of the village, cautiously staying just inside the trees while avoiding any of the small openings into the other huts, afraid of what he might see.

Finally reaching Ichor's hut, he noticed smoke pouring out the door. A horrible thought exploded in his mind. *They're cooking her!*

Just as the thought entered his head, one of the villagers feasting on the body parts let out an ear-piercing howl. There was something cold in his voice that sent another chill down Scelto's spine. Revolted, he slipped quietly into the hut.

He paused a moment to let his eyes adjust in the murky darkness of the hovel. As he waited, an uneasy feeling arose in his throat. He began to inhale the smoke and could feel his mind starting to spin. He jumped as a hand grabbed his elbow. Terrified, he spun to see Liha.

"What the…" he breathed in terror. His eyes swept from his bloody sword to her cleaved and lacerated body. A small lake of red blood was already pooling at her feet.

"I was just like your friend once. He sucked my blood and took part of my soul. He's a glutton and always takes too much blood, which turns his victims into something not really dead, yet not fully alive. It makes us into this." She pointed to her bloody body. "The partial-dead instead of vampires like him. His appetite is insatiable, hence the dead forest around us." She sighed deeply and calmly despite her shredded body. A lurching cough sent blood flowing over her mouth and down her chin.

"We lure people here for tentacle-boy over there to drain their blood. Some we let stay the almost dead, like us, and others we get to feast on." She wiped the blood from her chin and licked it hungrily, the two black fangs under her lip ravenously stretched forward, gluttonously slurping up the blood.

"Flesh never tastes as good with the blood drained from it," she said in a hiss, smiling to further reveal the two disgusting and wriggling black fangs.

Stunned by her appearance and starting to be affected by the incense, Scelto was having a hard time focusing. "You're a vampire?"

"I told you…only Ichor and a few of his favorites are. The rest of us he calls his undead, even though we are somewhat alive. That makes it tough to kill us," she said, tranquilly waving her arm to showcase her protruding intestines. "That's why a lot of the men have sores all over their face. While we are hard to kill, we don't heal well," she answered serenely.

"That means injuries add up. Once a partial-dead gets too broken down, their minds fail and they go insane!" Liha said. Her eyes snapped open with crazed zeal. "Then Ichor chains them into one of the waste huts. The Wasted Undead, he calls them."

Figure 10: What Ichor calls the Wasted Undead are broken-down creatures doomed to a demented, shackled existence. All technically still alive, they don't age, but heal extremely slowly. They are most notable for black tentacles wriggling from their gums.

Her two black fangs slithered hungrily towards Scelto. Indifferently, she adjusted the gaping flaps of skin his sword has slashed open, carelessly slurping the escaping intestines back into her abdomen before limping toward him. "Soon your friend will be drained. Listen, Scelto, I like you. You're kinda cute, so…why don't you go next? I promise we won't eat you but will make you one of us. If you join us, you can live forever with me, without growing old."

Scelto shook his head, trying to clear the smoky cobwebs. "Wow, get my blood drained, become undead…"

"Partially dead," Liha corrected.

"Okay. Become *partially dead* then grow disgusting black fangs on my gums? Not die or grow old *but* eventually end up totally nuts with sores all over and chained up in a hut full of my own feces? Tempting."

"Ooooh," Liha moaned. "His tentacles are almost to her big neck vessels! It's all over then."

Scelto turned to truly see Gimelli for the first time. Cord-like appendages were whipping and flying around her head and neck as others were pumping her blood into Ichor. He could see that the ones furthest back on her neck were engorged and crimson from her blood. Others were slinking around, searching for pristine skin to invade. Rage and fear welled up in Scelto, focusing his mind. He pushed away from Liha and raised his sword against Ichor.

"Wait!" Liha said loudly. "Once all the tentacles are released, he has fangs which unfurl from his hand. If he has already sunk them into a major vessel and you kill him, she will die."

Scelto looked at Liha. She was a freakish sight with the major wounds streaking across her abdomen and chest. Blood and entrails had once again slipped out, lopping over her opened abdomen. Unfettered, she grabbed a loop of her intestine and coolly stuffed it back into her gaping gut.

"Sorry, I guess I just can't keep it together today," she joked, but her eyes widened again with psychotic passion.

Gathering the last of his wits, Scelto moved over to Ichor. With all his might, he jumped up, and, using his weight and power, thrust the sword down into Ichor's neck. With a sickening crunch and then a fleshy squish, Scelto's blade severed his spine and plunged deep into his chest cavity. Ichor's eyes shot open in terror as blood gushed everywhere. With his neck cut apart and spine severed, he could not move, and his arms and hands went slack. Some of the countless appendages fell off Gimelli and began thrashing around violently, some whipping aggressively towards Scelto.

Yelling, Liha rushed towards him. He quickly yanked his sword free and slashed horizontally with all his might across her neck. Her head flew up and to the side as her body continued forward for a few steps. Both disconnected pieces were pumping blood randomly about the room. Her hands grasped out desperately for Scelto and momentarily held on to his shirt before her body crumpled to the ground.

Turning back to Gimelli, Scelto's initial adrenaline rush was wearing down and the drugged incense was starting to take hold. With a massive stroke, he severed Ichor's hand and wrenched the remaining tentacles off Gimelli's neck. It reminded him of pulling vines off Liberum's wall. Hundreds of wounds began to ooze blood as Ichor's hand fell lifelessly to the ground. The thin rope-like projections were still writhing angrily on the floor. Fangs within his palm chomped angrily. Scelto kicked and stomped at the tentacles closest to him as they shot forward, still mindlessly rummaging for blood.

Moving quickly, Scelto sheathed his bloody sword and hoisted Gimelli onto his shoulder. He had to get out of the hut and away from the intoxicating smoke. As he left the doorway, the fresh air felt invigorating.

Just as his head began to clear, Gimelli moaned loudly, drawing the attention of one of the feasting undead. Scelto quickly ran between two huts into the forest. The heavy footsteps of the undead could be heard plodding after them. Carrying Gimelli slowed him down, and he could tell they were gaining.

"Unchain the wasted undead!" Ichor's mother howled. "Let them loose!" she cackled. "Let the wasted ones loose!" she repeated before howling into a maniacal laugh.

How in the world am I going to get out of this? Scelto wondered.

Their bloodthirsty calls began echoing around the trees as more undead joined the chorus. Their cry was cut off by a blood-curdling scream fracturing out of the village.

Ichor's mother, Zlota, had discovered her son's body. Her shriek was quickly followed by series of depraved howls, as all the undead of the village were now awake and enraged.

Verngaurd plummets out of Book Three on a trajectory for total war, a casualty of primal power and frail pride. The world topples onto the brutal battlefield that is a world at war in Book Four. We end our journey under rune Uruz as it began: "The world has the unwelcome habit of dishing out abominable challenges—some insignificant, others life and death that require us to fight, or be washed away in the gelid, pitiless sands of eternity."

The external struggle is but a wisp of any war. Raging under muscle and metal, mental battles bristle, nourished by anxiously fast heartbeats and bated breath. On every battlefield those internal conflicts, broiling beneath the armor, often rise in importance above the physical, determining victory or defeat. Each warrior combats their own demons, wrestles their own special brand of fear, fighting with dread, tangling with nerves. On and off the battleground we must attempt to balance mind, body, and spirit. Despite their power, our minds, our wills, are still but lowly prisoners of our bodies and are destined to gasp their last breath if the body falls.

Named after the Norse god, Tyr, who volunteered to lose his hand in order to bind the savage wolf Fenrir. Teiwaz is the rune of sacrifice and courage. It represents the power of sacrifice given freely. It epitomizes the warrior spirit offered up by soldiers in a time of battle. War, with its insatiable appetite for the blood and spirit of the combatants, is always happy to oblige the leaders sending orders to march and die. It speaks perfectly to the upcoming battlefields about to be drenched in the lifeblood of its combatants. The required sacrifice will be on an individual and societal level. Reverse Teiwaz (from the underside of chest four in the Far Forest of England) speaks to the questionable causes of this war as deceit weaves its disruption through the leaders of Verngaurd.

(Aside on Norse mythology: wolf Fenrir was the 3rd child of god Loki. The other gods, considering Fenrir dangerous, wanted to bind him. Fenrir, suspecting a trick, refused to be bound in the chain forged by the dwarves {out of the sound of a cat's footsteps, the beard of a woman, the breath of a fish, the roots of mountains, the sinews of a bear, and bird spittle}. Fenrir agreed to be bound only if a god would place their hand in his mouth. Tyr freely did so, and when the dwarf chain called Gleipnir bound the wolf, he chomped Tyr's hand off).

The convoluted tale of friendship and betrayal reaches its boiling point as Verngaurd tips, irrevocably, into the unspeakable clutches of war. The world finds itself struggling to stay above the surface of destruction, desperately fighting to avoid drowning in the agony of bloodshed sprouting from barbarous conflict. The prophecy quest is finally set, but before they can discover their first task, the fragile League is already on shaky ground. Can they survive maneuvering between an earth on fire and oceans of blood as tectonic battles thunder across the land?

www.ingramcontent.com/pod-product-compliance
Lightning Source LLC
Chambersburg PA
CBHW051123300726
48981CB00022B/532/J